Juniper Lane

Kady Morrison

BIG
BANG
PRESS

First published 2016

Original illustrations by Alexandra Telecky

Big Bang Press
Brooklyn, NY
bigbangpress.com
facebook.com/bigbangpublishing • bigbangpress.tumblr.com
Twitter @BB_Press

Formatting by BookCoverCafe.com

ISBN:
978-0-9904844-3-1 (pbk)
978-0-9904844-4-8 (ebk)
978-0-9904844-5-5 (Kindle ISBN)

1. Fiction. 2. Gay and Lesbian–Fiction. 3. Ohio–Fiction. 4. Family–Fiction.

2015946172

For my mother, whose first language is kindness;
for my father, who looks for light in the strangest of places;
and for Natalie, with whom the feeling was friendship.

June

Mim's fingers are growing cold against the window. It's chilly, she thinks, for spring, although of course she can't be sure. Most of what she recalls of Ohio is sketched over with the extremities of childhood: August afternoons scorched pleasantly in her memory, the lingering sensation of a popsicle freezer-burning her tongue. For years she's held every experience to the standard of her summer weeks spent here, weighed them up and found them wanting. No swimming water was ever so cool or clear as that of the pool in her aunt's backyard. No glass of lemonade was ever so bright or refreshing as that which she made in her aunt's kitchen. No street was ever so placid or picturesque as Juniper Lane, where her aunt's house sat old and proud on the corner of the road.

Still, her fingers grow cold against the window, and she's sure that it's chilly for spring. It can't be expecting too much of the place to think that any Memorial Day party, belated or no, should happen beneath a sky less gray, less drab, less *ordinary*.

"Looks like they're having a good time out there," Mim says.

It's an understatement. What's going on outside, in the center of the grassy island that rests inside Juniper Lane's tight little cul-de-sac, is scenic enough to make up for the weather. It's almost *too* scenic, in fact, somewhere between appealing and genuinely uncanny. Between the decorations being raised, the drinks tables being laid, and the neighbors starting to drift out of their houses in casual clothes that quietly communicate jaw-dropping wealth, Mim almost wonders if this is a movie set, if she's unwittingly become involved in some kind of elaborate punking.

It's the boy, maybe six years old, who's running around in a newspaper hat that really sells it. It's just so over the top nobody would think of making it up. Nobody in their right mind would try to make the average citizen believe in a town where that kid existed; the world is just too cynical.

"I mean it," says Mim, spreading her hand so her palm is flat against the glass. "It looks—um. Like it might be fun, maybe. That's all."

Ruth, from her armchair in the corner, laughs. "Fun. Right. That's a good one, kiddo."

Mim's not sure yet how or who to be around her aunt, with her long gray ponytail and her embarrassment of laugh lines, who is so different from the bleached-blonde woman Mim remembers. She guesses a nasty divorce and twenty years would change anyone, but the Ruth who'd stood poised and stoic to Uncle Jasper's right at Mim's grandfather's funeral, the Ruth who'd offered Mim pool time in the summers and sticky matzo candy at Passover, seems more like a figment of Mim's imagination each day. That woman had been… severe. Aggressively thin and violently opinionated. Even her kisses had been belligerent, these smacking, stinging cheek-pecks that always left Mim rubbing their echo away, after.

That's who Mim had been expecting when she called: the fabled Aunt Ruth of family legend, ice queen extraordinaire, whom even her mother had practically stopped speaking to years before. Mim had been looking forward, in a sickly apprehensive sort of way, to being put through her paces. After the mess she'd made of her life, she thought it a happy coincidence, a lucky break, that the only family member she was willing to speak to was also the one most likely whip her uncompromisingly into shape.

This woman, with her weed-scented armchair, her yellowed teeth, her face that looks nothing like it used to—that looks, honestly, not unlike a peach left to wilt and spoil in the sun—doesn't seem likely to whip anyone into shape. If it were a skill she still possessed, she probably would have applied it to herself years ago; or, at the very least, to her surroundings. Mim almost can't bring herself to look at what's become of the house. Between the paint peeling away from the sideboard and the overgrown yard, the small flecks of brightly colored dye disfiguring various walls, she wonders that Ruth can bear to live here at all.

"For god's sake, Mimosa, go if you want to go." For the last six days, Mim's made a point to cringe every time Ruth's used her full first name, but Ruth either hasn't noticed or doesn't care. She sounds carefree and distantly amused. "Don't let me stop you."

"I'm not sure I even want to." Her thumb squeaks across the glass at the lie. "I mean, I don't—it's not like—I've never met these people, or most of them, anyway. I guess I maybe met some of them, you know, when I was here before, if any of them still live here."

"Oh, they still live here, all right," Ruth says, and cackles. "Old Mary Craddock's been in that house a whole century, and she'll be here another one, you wait and see. That kind of evil needs more than a single human lifetime to develop."

"She was…" Mim pauses, trying to decide how to phrase it delicately, and then whether delicate phrasing is something that Ruth would even appreciate. "Mary Craddock, I mean. She was the woman who—uh—that last summer we all came, and she was—the pool—"

"Kiddo, the last time you were here I was on everything a person could take," Ruth says, waving a hand. "Uppers, downers, whatever; you name it, I was on it." She stops, then, and grins. "Oh, wait. Do you mean that night she got wasted at one of Jasper's damn cocktail parties and fell in?"

Mim winces at the memory, and Ruth laughs. It's an abrasive laugh, almost barking, from the belly and too loud, too honest. She tilts her head back with it, eyes getting almost gleefully wet, and Mim wishes she could leave the room until Ruth composes herself. It feels like walking in on her naked, watching her do this, even though that seems to be what Ruth is like in general these days: naked. Unabashed. Bare. It makes Mim uncomfortable: nobody ever looks as good stripped down as they do done up.

"Right," Mim says, when Ruth finally stops. "I was just thinking it might be weird if I went alone, is all."

"Kid," Ruth says, in a voice thick with exaggerated patience, "it would be weird if you went *with* me. Those people wouldn't spit on me if I was on fire."

"Oh." It's humiliating, how much disappointment sneaks its way into that single word, how audibly Mim's plans dash against the ground. It's so noticeable that she feels it settle over the room, feels it darkening Ruth's mood too.

When she came—showed up practically in the middle of the night, shaking, barely able to speak, barely aware of anything but the slats of the porch below her feet and the light inside the house when Ruth opened the door—she knew she was imposing. She knows she has to be grateful. But she thought that, if nothing else, Ruth would be able to make some introductions, say a friendly hello to some of the neighbors, something, *anything*. It had never occurred to her that she'd be on the outside looking in once again, like always, with no idea how to make her own way.

9

But she's curious, too, can't help but be curious, so she says, "And you? If they were on fire, I mean. Would you spit on them?"

Ruth laughs again, but it's quieter this time, if no less honest. She says, "Any excuse."

"So I go with him," the man is saying, "because, right? What am I supposed to do *except* go with him? It's not like these offers come up every day—or, not to me, anyway. Is it a prestige thing? Congressman? You'd know better than I would."

He pauses, clearly as much for laughter as for a reply. The crowd thronged around him chuckles obligingly as another man—the Congressman, presumably—lifts one hand in the air in protest.

"Danny, Danny," he says, winking, "I'd never dare to suggest I knew more than a Harvard man."

The man who must be Danny throws his head back and laughs. He's... attractive, Mim thinks, after a moment of watching the way his eyes crinkle when he smiles, even if he's laughing harder than the joke probably warrants. She's pretty sure she thinks he's attractive. For the first time in a very long while, this is, at least theoretically, something she should care about: is that what an attractive man looks like? What about that one? What about him?

It's not that she's unaware of the objective answer to the question. Danny, with his strong jaw and his shock of black hair, his pronounced cheekbones and his puffed up, Disney prince chest, is undoubtedly attractive by any conventional standard. She's simply not sure what that means, exactly, in terms of her real-world experience. Is she into conventionally attractive guys? Dell—she swallows convulsively at the thought of him, but can't help but see him clear as day in her mind's eye, as vividly as she's ever imagined anything—was more striking than appealing, a nice enough body but the sort of face he made up for with charisma. Dell had so much charisma it made you forget the other parts of him, she later discovered. Or maybe it made you not believe them. She reaches into her pocket and starts toying with her phone, before she realizes what she's done and yanks her hand away as though it's been burned.

Anyway: does that mean Danny isn't attractive to her? She doesn't really know whether she has a "type" or not. Do "types" really exist at all? Does she want Danny to take her out to dinner, or back to his place for a few hours of fun, or both? (Or, she wonders, neither?)

It occurs to Mim that if this is a game she's playing with herself, in this crowd she might as well call it "Who Wants to Fuck a Millionaire?" She snorts at her own joke, and then abruptly remembers that she is in public, at an event, attempting to ingratiate herself with a group of total strangers to whom she has not spoken a word.

Nobody seems to have noticed her misstep, which is great, except that it's the result of the fact that nobody seems to have noticed *her*.

She shouldn't have come out here. She realizes that now. It's not just that the understated elegance of these people is leaving her mouth dry; it's not just that she's aware that she's staring at all of them—gaping, frankly. It's not even that she's so nervous that she keeps losing track of the conversation, though admittedly that's also a particularly crippling problem.

It's... there's something she could say here, she's sure. Something that would fix it. But this is exactly the reason Mim avoids going to parties on her own: whatever that something is, she's utterly incapable of figuring it out. She always ends up just like this; drifting at the very edge of someone else's conversation, unseen and unheard; and, worst of all, unknown.

"So, who the hell are you?" says someone directly to Mim's right.

It takes Mim a moment to realize that the question is meant for her, and when she does, her face turns bright red.

The woman staring at her—and she is *staring*—has two streaks of brilliant white cutting through her thick, jet-black curls. She can't be more than a few years older than Mim, twenty-six or twenty-seven at the very most, so the white is confusing, jarring; the way her hair is pulled back makes it even more immediately noticeable, since the streaks run straight back to her ponytail. She looks, at first glance, like the bride of Frankenstein, and Mim gapes for an unattractive moment before collecting herself.

By the time Mim snaps out of it, the woman is smiling at her, a slight, curious quirking to the edges of her mouth. It looks good on her, if a little superior. Everything about her looks a little superior, honestly— the jut of her chin, the height that leaves her looking down her nose a few inches at Mim, the flashing hazel of her wide-set, perfectly made-up eyes.

"I," Mim says. "Um."

The woman's smile deepens a little, but it darkens, too, and she widens her eyes in an expression more sardonic than friendly. In the face of her continued silence, Mim tries thinks of an answer, can't; tries again, can't; and cringes at how difficult she's finding coming up with a response to what amounts to the simplest question on earth.

"Mimosa," Mim hears herself say eventually, and regrets it immediately. "No—I mean, sorry. Mim. Just Mim."

The woman's laughing at her now. She can't actually *see* it, her laughter, but Mim knows when someone's laughing at her. The ugly feeling in the pit of her stomach is a dead giveaway, and she lifts her small chin, squares her shoulders, and tries to pretend her face isn't glowing a darker shade of red than her hair.

"Like the drink," the stranger says. Her voice has a gravelly quality to it—there's the suggestion of musicality there, if only it were an octave higher. "Or not, I guess. 'Mim' isn't like anything, is it?"

"Mim's like, this close to walking away," Mim snaps. Which: great. That's great. Way to alienate the only person she may ever get the chance to speak to on this street in seven convenient seconds. "Oh—jeez. Sorry, I didn't mean to—I was only—the name is kind of—"

"A touchy subject, yeah. I got that." Shrugging, and still wearing that sardonic little twist to the corners of her mouth, the stranger holds out her hand. "Nadia. And I'm not sensitive about it."

Ha fucking ha, Mim thinks. Thankfully, this time she's able to reign herself in before it comes out of her mouth. "That's—nice? You live around here, right? I mean, obviously you live around here, or you probably do, what would you be doing here if you... didn't...?"

Nadia stares at her. Again. Mim's spent most of her life worrying that people were staring at her; but now she thinks that if this is what being stared at feels like, it's never actually happened to her before.

"Was there," Nadia says, after what feels like an eon of silence, "a question in there somewhere?"

"I, sure," Mim says, "yes. No. Is there something to drink, maybe? Somewhere?"

That guy—Danny—is still talking, waving his hands and smiling beatifically over the cleft in his chin. Mim casts one glance back at him after Nadia narrows her eyes, nods, points a thumb over her shoulder, and then beckons Mim to follow her. Attractive, Mim decides. She's almost positive.

"I didn't ask for your name, you know," Nadia says. She walks so fast that Mim has to hurry to keep up. "Before. I asked who the hell you were."

"What are you, security?"

Nadia snorts out a surprised-sounding little laugh, which is a relief, since it saves Mim the trouble of freezing up completely in mortification. "Do I look like security?"

There's a tattoo peaking out from beneath Nadia's left shirtsleeve, the very edges of some sort of winding, black-inked bloom. Mim's pretty sure the honest answer to that question—that Nadia looks like someone security might try to keep out—wouldn't be appreciated. "No?" She winces at how desperate she sounds. "I mean, of course not. That wasn't—I didn't mean—"

"Jesus," Nadia says, all the laughter gone from her voice, "don't hurt yourself."

"Sorry," Mim mutters, embarrassed, as they step up to the drinks table, but Nadia either doesn't hear her or chooses not to respond.

From here, standing at the very center of the grassy island, Mim can see the entire street. It's the first chance she's had to take it all in since she arrived—when the taxi had dropped her off at close to midnight, she hadn't exactly been paying attention to the scenery, just clutching her duffel bag in her lap and trying not to cry.

She took that bag from Dell, years ago—no. He'd given it to her, hadn't he, a gift, at the end of her freshman year of college. That'd been a day like this one, thick and little muggy but better for it, sweat beading on the side of her neck and between her toes, dampening the straps of her sandals. Mim remembers that, about the sandals. She remembers leaning against the back of her father's battered old station wagon, the metal warm through her thin t-shirt, Dell's fingers warm against her wrist. She remembers taking a giddy, hiccoughing breath, remembers thinking, *This is real, what it means to be real, the way he loves you over the sweat in your soles.*

"Here," he said, pressing the bag against her chest. He had such good hands even then, back when he was a half-man with no hair on his knuckles. "To remember me by."

And Mim remembers too that she should have said, *As if I could forget you*, when in fact she had blurted out, earnest and unthinking, "But what will you take your stuff home in?"

Dell laughed, the spring sun streaking through his hair, and took her chin between his thumb and forefinger. "Mimosa," he said, fond, "you always find just the wrong thing to say," and it had seemed romantic at the time—maybe it was just the way he said it. Certainly she twitches to think of it now, the recalled warmth of the words laid over every time he said them after that, colder and colder, until they didn't seem romantic at all.

It's enough, that little twitch, to remind her that the spring sun currently beating against her bare shoulders is years ahead of the memory, that she's standing in the center of a party on Juniper Lane with her fists clenched tight at her sides. Slowly, carefully, she unknots them, smooths her sundress, rolls her shoulders back, and looks around. Nobody seems to have noticed her drifting off, thank god. Even Nadia isn't watching, too busy with digging around in a cooler for something—even the cooler, Mim thinks, looks expensive, like everything else here.

The street, Mim thinks, trying to pull herself away from looming, darker thoughts. She was scoping out the street, which she's only been able to see from the various grime-coated windows in Ruth's house for the last six days. Even from limited angles and through a layer of yellowed filth, Mim's been able to tell that it's lovely, but even promised loveliness hasn't been enough to draw her outside. Doing anything but eating the microwaveable meals in the freezer, watching bad television, and passing out has seemed like nothing but asking for more disappointment.

Here, in the glowing late afternoon light, Mim can see her mistake: Juniper Lane is stunning, far more so now than it ever was when she was a child.

What had seemed, then, to be nothing more than a giant's playground, a bright, novel change from the mundane routine her everyday life, hits her squarely in the chest with its beauty now.

On the right corner is her aunt's house; admittedly, an eyesore. Mim's eyes shy away from it, do their best to pretend they never saw it at all. Still, if she tries (and she does), she can think of it as it was when she first knew it, in the days when a purple clematis climbed up the trellis and all the windows still had their shutters. Back when it was a well-kept Colonial, when most evenings found Jasper on the front porch with a glass of scotch and Ruth in the kitchen, the house had a quiet sort of dignity to it. It wasn't the most ostentatious house on the street, but it hadn't needed to be. That had been part of its appeal, although of course Mim couldn't have explained that at the time.

The rest of the houses on the street are a jumble of styles that somehow come together to form a cohesive whole: an elegant, sprawling Tudor with window boxes at every sill, looking like nothing more than something out of a storybook; an asymmetrical red brick house, yard full of bright flowers (and, Mim notices, a profusion of garden gnomes); a yellow brick—

"Earth to Houston, come in Houston," Nadia says, snapping her fingers in Mim's face. She raises her eyebrows when Mim blinks at her, and Mim can't tell if it's in amusement or annoyance. She accordingly resists the urge to point out that Earth would have no reason to call Houston, as Houston is, itself, an Earth base. It doesn't seem like the time.

"Sorry," she says instead, and then, "Thanks," as Nadia hands over a beer without asking if Mim wants it. It's something bottled and unfamiliar, and has sat so long in the cooler that the label shifts underneath Mim's palm. She takes a long sip. It's good, whatever it is. Refreshing.

Nadia doesn't drink her beer. She just stands there, arms crossed over her chest, and fixes her gaze on the workings of Mim's throat as she swallows.

"So, seriously," Nadia says. "Are you a seat-chaser? Because nothing's for sale, okay, you're wasting your time."

Mim does a split-second perceived stupidity calculation—the risk of asking weighed against the risk of guessing—and says, "Sorry, seat... chaser?"

"Yeah, you know. Whatever you want to call it—house hunter, lookie-loo, it's all the same to me." Nadia shrugs, shifting her sleeve on her left shoulder to reveal another inch or so of tattoo. "Anyway, you're better off. Or whoever you're doing it for is, at least. You don't look, uh, bracket appropriate, no offense."

"*Excuse* me? You don't even know me!"

"Yeah." Nadia's voice is slow and almost pitying, as though it's just occurred to her that she might be speaking to an idiot. "That's my point. I don't know you, and you're here, and I know everyone here, so—"

There's a burning at the back of Mim's neck; she's not sure if it's embarrassment or annoyance. "What did you mean I don't look *bracket appropriate*?"

"Dude, chill." Nadia rolls her eyes. "I just meant, you know. *Bracket appropriate*. Like, age, income level, dress sense, that sort of thing. You're not what they're looking for, but I mean it, don't worry about it. It's no great loss."

"Jesus," Mim says. She can feel herself flushing in humiliation at the way her voice wavers on the word, and hates herself for it.

"You *asked*." Nadia sounds irritated now—unmistakably irritated, not just speaking with the vague hint of annoyance Mim is always spotting in strangers' voices. "God, look, I didn't *mean* anything by it. I take it back, if that makes you fucking feel better. Stick like that up your ass, you'll fit right in."

17

It's one of the longstanding curses of Mim's life, her inability come up with the right thing to say in situations like this. That's what she's thinking as she stares at Nadia hotly, her mouth half-parted in rage and her cheeks vivid with shame: that it'll come to her, later, the way it's not coming to her now. That later, she'll relive this conversation a thousand ways, and she'll be more brilliant in each than she was in the last. That later, she'll have this out for herself the way that it should be going now, soothe herself with could-haves and should-haves until she's less fucking horrified.

But right now Nadia's staring at her with this sort of—disdain, Mim thinks it is, or disappointment, curling her lip. She's looking down her nose at Mim and it's so effective, the elegant, aquiline curve under her intimidating eyes, that Mim feels even smaller than she did standing unnoticed at the edge of Danny's crowd.

"Well, I already moved here," Mim hears herself saying. "So I guess you'll just have to get used to me."

It'd be a lame response, a moronic response, even without the way she jerks her thumb over her shoulder to point at her aunt's sad, crumbling house, but the gesture really puts her over the top. Strangely enough, it's this—not the action itself, but how helplessly she finds herself doing it, as though she's a marionette going through someone else's motions—that makes tears sting at the corners of her eyes. Just—she was supposed to be better than this. It was supposed to *go* better than this. She's spent all these stupid fucking years dreaming about this stupid fucking street and she can't even manage to make one stupid fucking friend—

"You," Nadia says, blinking. "Wait, hold on, *you're* Ruth's niece?"

Before Mim gets the chance to answer, she feels an unfamiliar hand settle on her shoulder, hears someone say, "Oh my goodness, can this really be Mimosa? Mimosa Shalit?"

Mim tenses; she doesn't like being touched by strangers, much less by strangers calling her by the wrong name. Once she turns, though, her muscles relax almost immediately. The woman who slides into her field of vision—tall, black, impeccably dressed—is so beautiful that Mim actually finds herself regretting the loss when she pulls her hand away.

"It's Robinson, actually," Mim says, even though she thinks she'd happily answer to anything this woman deigned to call her. "Or, I mean, you can—if you want—"

"Hi, Mrs. Ashcraft," Nadia says, cutting Mim off. Her voice is flatter than Mim knew a voice could go, and Mim realizes, too late and too offended to really care very much, how animated she had sounded during the conversation they were having before. Woodenly, as if through gritted teeth, Nadia adds, "Nice to see you."

"Yes, yes, of course, Nadia," Gale says, without even looking at her. She's looking at Mim, reaching out to grab again—her hand, this time—and beaming. "Robinson, of course, that's my mistake, I'm so sorry! The divorce, obviously, Ruth must have gone back to her maiden name. It was a little before my time, all of that."

"Yeah," Mim says, a little dazedly. Gale's wearing diamond earrings that look like they could pay off her student loans. "Or—I mean—it's fine. It was before my time too, I guess." She doesn't bother telling her that Ruth changing her name wouldn't make much of a difference anyway, since she's her mother's sister. It doesn't seem important, just now.

Gale throws her head back and laughs. Her laugh, like her voice, is light and airy, almost birdlike. Everything about her is birdlike, from the fluttering of her long, tapered fingers to the sharp jut of her jaw. She's dressed in greens and blues, a turquoise scarf tied as an elegant accent into her hair, and Mim can't help but think of a peacock.

"Mimosa," Gale says, putting an arm around Mim and leading her away, "we're going to get along just *famously*. I can tell. I have a sense

19

for this sort of thing, you know. Tell me, have you met the neighborhood yet? I hope not, I'm just dying to introduce to everyone. Well, except for Nadia—obviously you two have already made your introductions."

"Yeah," Mim says, tensing again. When she looks over her shoulder, Nadia's staring after her, glowering. Mim returns the expression as best she can, for all she's sure she's blushing to the roots of her hair. Unthinkingly, she says, "God, is she always like that?"

"Ah." It's this delicate little exhale that is, impossibly, one of the most weighted syllables Mim's ever heard—somehow judgmental and forgiving and piqued, all at once. The frown that slips onto Gale's face to go with it is slight, the kind of expression that can be seen from the corners of the eye alone, probably involuntary.

Lowering her voice, Gale says, "Between you and me, I'd be little careful with her. The Bahjats, well… they've had a rough couple of years, not that you'd have any way to know that. It wouldn't be my place to say anything more, but I just don't think that poor girl can take anything else right now."

"Oh." Mim flushes again, this time in shame. "I wasn't—I mean, I didn't, I would never—I'm not, that's not what I meant to say. I'm sorry, I'm sure she's very nice, I didn't mean anything by it. We just, I don't know. It was a weird conversation, that's all."

They stop at the end of a table loaded with hors d'oeuvres that are, upon close observation, almost comically out of place at what essentially amounts to a Memorial Day block party. Prosciutto-wrapped melon spears are laid artfully over a bed of mixed greens; little bites of what look to be cucumber and smoked salmon are held together with toothpicks. Mim's hands drift towards and then away from them, because she's aware, suddenly and acutely, of the fact that Gale is watching her. This time—Mim can see it in the tilt of her head, the glint in her eyes—she looks like a hawk. Of course, when

Mim blinks, the expression is gone, wiped clean, as though it had never been there at all.

"You should really try the goat cheese," Gale says, already turning away from Mim, waving and laughing, beckoning people over. They start moving the instant she gestures to them, as though they were simply waiting for her signal. "It's exquisite."

The beer in Mim's hand is still sweating. The water gathered against her palm runs down her arm when she lifts it to take a sip, and the sensation feels, for this one fleeting second, like being jolted awake.

When she looks over her shoulder again, Nadia's gone.

"This is Mimosa," Gale coos, chirps, chimes—every time she says it differently, and every time with more enthusiasm than the last. Enraptured though she is, Mim is exhausted just looking at her: the way she draws people towards her and then just as quickly pushes them away, the way she's always got an answer to questions they haven't asked. Mim has said next to nothing about herself—not what she's doing in town, not how long she's planning to stay—but Gale introduces her like an old friend in spite of this. She says, "Mimosa's Ruth Shalit's niece—you know Ruth, don't you? In 5000?" She says, "Mimosa's just told me how much she adores the neighborhood, which I think speaks to her good taste, don't you?" She says, "Mimosa's such a lovely girl, I can just tell already what a wonderful addition she'll be to the street," and the person she's talking to—whomever she's talking to—nods, shakes Mim's hand, walks away smiling, while Mim is left behind trying not to suffocate from the feeling of fraudulence that seems liable to swallow her at any moment.

"That's Mrs. Neary. It's been nearly three years since she moved into 5500," Gale says, voice pitched so as not to carry, as a woman approaches them. This, Mim will come to realize, is how Gale introduces people—name, rank, house number. "Such a… vibrant family, though of course Fred never quite manages to make it to these events. He's got a psychological practice that I hear is thriving, but I simply can't imagine how she does it, four kids under sixteen—Angel!"

This last is pitched louder, clearly meant for the dumpy white woman approaching them, toddling in heels a little too high to manage, lipstick feathering unattractively outside of its intended lines.

"Gale!" says Mrs. Neary, and even that single syllable sounds overwhelmed. Mrs. Neary's eyes are set just a little too far apart under hair that's just a shade too dark for her complexion; despite her smile, the combination makes her look as though she's just come off a terrible scare. "I'm so glad to see you, I've been meaning to talk to you about— well, about a few things, really. You're really very hard to get hold of for someone who lives just across the street, isn't that funny?"

"Oh, you know how it is," Gale says, waving a hand. She laughs, a brief tinkling of distant bells. "When you've got a life as busy as mine, you've got to make time for the things you find important."

There's this brief pause, this hesitation that hangs in the air like a pendulum—or, at least, Mim imagines there is.

"Oh, yes, of course," Mrs. Neary says, smiling nervously, eyes flicking between the two of them, and as Gale swings into yet another round of introductions, Mim finds herself thinking that nobody she knows would believe any of this—her standing here amidst all these hors d'oeuvres and fancy craft beers and well-attired women, listening to this weird gossipy chatter. Dell would tell her she didn't belong, and her brothers would laugh, and her mother—well, who knows what her mother would say? She can hear her voice, suddenly, hesitant: *Don't you*

22

think it's all a bit silly? That's what she had always said to Mim's father driving home after Uncle Jasper's cocktail parties, at which they had been emphatically out of place. *Don't you think it's all a bit silly?*

Mim swallows and looks back at the beautiful street and the people standing in the road in the fading light. *No,* she thinks stubbornly, and puts her mother, and Dell, and all of the rest of them firmly out of her mind.

July

Nadia lets one hand drift over the bulge of her stomach, the curve of her hips, the smooth, rounded surface of her bare ass. She shouldn't be naked in here. It's her mother's, this library with its vaulted ceilings and delicately constructed crown molding, this room she was never allowed in as a child—even fully clothed, Nadia wouldn't fit. Even done to the nines, Nadia would look out of place, rough-edged, against a backdrop as carefully cultivated as this one. There is priceless artwork on the walls. There are rare books on the shelves. There is one photograph on the desk, gold-framed, of two people who look like such a family by themselves that you'd never guess they had a child.

Rashida Bahjat would shit herself to see her daughter standing naked anywhere, let alone to see her standing naked in this, her sanctum sanctorum. Nadia grins and sits down in the desk chair, kicks her feet up onto the escritoire, and closes her eyes.

"He's doing better," Nadia tells Representative Warwick, when he asks about her father, tucking a loose strand of hair behind her ear in the warm summer breeze. It's not, strictly speaking, a lie; Nadia would have to actually know the answer to the question to be deliberately spreading a falsehood. She figures this—the lack of lie, rather than the technicality of it—is what separates her from the rest of her parents' neighborhood. These people would lie if the truth were better. They only don't lie when the truth is *worse*.

Anyway, even if she did know what was going on in Florida—even if Rashida bothered to call her every week, even if Samir were well enough to send more than the occasional postcard—Nadia's not sure what the right answer to Mr. Warwick's question would be. "Still has colon cancer," is her instinct, but in situations like these, her instincts betray her more often than not. She's been told—by lovers and leavers, by unexpected tears and playground gossip, by the disappointment in her parent's eyes—that she's not good at this, that she should bite back her initial response. That saying the wrong thing is far worse than not saying anything at all.

It's not like he's looking for the truth, in any case. Nadia's known the Congressman since she was nine years old, babysat his son all through high school, never mentioned to his wife what (or whom) she saw him doing through the thin blinds on sick days and college breaks. John Warwick's the sort of man who goes through the motions, who always says the right thing but never actually *does* it, and Nadia can't remember the last time he asked her a personal question in a way that suggested he actually cared about the answer.

(Lie. Of course she can—she was seventeen and he was forty-seven, and he wanted to know, *really* wanted to know, whether she'd ever been interested in seeing an older man. It had been hilarious at the time, in that way truly unfunny things always are, nervous laughter hitching at the back of her throat; when she'd told her girlfriend about it, Lola grinned, all edge, and said, "Well, are you?" Like most of her teenage years, it's one of those memories Nadia does her best not to hold onto.)

He's sweating now, Warwick, fat beads dripping down at the edges of his graying hair. Everything about him has been disgusting to Nadia since she was old enough to know what the word meant, but she smiles, weathers the patter of small talk he's only maintaining for appearance's sake, and doesn't call him on the way he looks over her shoulder for someone better to talk to. She thinks, not for the first time, that she should have pushed Cory into letting her work tonight—not that Cory would've been swayed, but still.

It's not that Nadia doesn't understand Cory's point: they're an upscale restaurant looking for catering clients, and these are the most upscale, caterer-seeking residents Barn Ridge has to offer. But Nadia is not the right person to send schmoozing, no matter what her address currently is. There are lots of things that location and parentage will make up for in this crowd, but an overwhelming lack of social skills isn't one of them.

She notices a secluded spot behind a nearby tree and abandons Representative Warwick without saying goodbye: just turns on her heel in the middle of some story about D.C. traffic and walks away.

"Nice talking to you too, Ms. Bahjat," he yells after her, sounding both badly put-out and more like a middle school vice principal than a man who's supposed to represent the political interests of every Democrat in the district. Nadia rolls her eyes—how anyone can make it through the day with an ego like that is beyond her—and snatches a bottle of red wine off a nearby table while the bartender isn't looking. If she's going to white-knuckle her way through this to the end of this night, fortification will be required.

The Juniper Lane Fourth of July party is kind of a legend in Barn Ridge, although the name is misleading. There are always a few uninvited stragglers who actually show up on the street itself, having missed the memo that the event takes place at a lake five miles outside of town. Before Samir got sick, it was one of his favorite nights of the year, an event he threw himself into planning for months beforehand, and tonight, his absence shows. The decorations are lackluster at best, not to mention reeking of Gale Ashcraft's particular tastes. Rashida would be horrified. Nadia almost texts her, but thinks better of it the moment her fingers brush the edge of her phone. Better not to reach out. Better to be able to imagine that she would've gotten a reply if she had.

Well, there's a healthy decision, Nadia thinks wryly, and lifts her wine bottle in the air in a mocking little toast before she takes a swallow.

"Toasts are important, Nadia," Samir used to say, when she was young. It was one of the dozens of lessons he made it his goal to impress upon her while she was still malleable and full of potential. "Everything from the way you draw the crowd's attention to the height at which you hold your glass communicates something about who you are as a person. Toasting isn't about what you say; it's about how you say it, and what *that* says. Do you understand what I'm saying?"

"Uh," said Nadia, who didn't. "What if you get it wrong?"

Samir shrugged. "Oh, well. It's just like anything else you get wrong, duckling. It means you missed an opportunity to do a good job, that's all. There's always a chance to get better."

Nadia's sure they had this same conversation dozens of times over the course of her childhood, but somehow she only remembers the once. It was the first summer after they moved into the house on Juniper; the two of them sitting on the floor of the front porch, next to the still-unhung porch swing, leaning against the brick and watching the sunlight fade from the sky. She must have been six or seven, and she itched with the pride of it, of having his complete attention. Her father was a vital man in those days, tall and broad, with looks she once heard one of her teachers describe as "rakishly handsome," and the personality to match—it was hard for anyone to keep his attention long, with the exception of Nadia's mother. He was so in love with her that people whispered and giggled when they walked by, stopped to congratulate them on their beautiful family, even featured the two of them a few times in the local homeowners magazine, cheeks pressed together, smiling for the camera.

Nadia was never in those photos. She didn't spend that much time with Samir, really, especially not one-on-one. It was, Nadia knows—knew even then—more her fault than his. God knows he'd tried with her. God knows he'd be trying still, if life hadn't gotten in the way.

It was sunset that evening on the front porch, and Nadia rolled her water bottle up and down against her thigh. She liked the soft sloshing noise it made, the way the motion left little bubbles floating behind to tickle her tongue whenever she took a sip. And she was nervous, too, joy and fear warring in the pit of her stomach, because she thought that soon enough, her father was going to ask her a question. She thought that soon enough, she was going to get the answer wrong, and this moment in the glow of his attention would be over.

Sure enough: "You try one," Samir said. "Go on, make a toast! It's bad luck with water, but I'll let it slide this time."

He winked at her, and Nadia grinned—she knew that meant he was joking, even if she didn't get the punch line. "I don't know what to toast to, Daddy."

Samir looked at her thoughtfully, then nodded once and stood. He puffed out his chest and lifted his tumbler of scotch, gesturing with it out towards the street.

"I propose a toast," he said, voice warm and deep, carrying far enough that the birds on the walkway skittered into nervous flight. "To the luck that has brought us here, the perseverance that has kept us here, and the fortitude that will sustain us here for many years to come. These are riches of which many men only dream, and are worth drinking to, on this night and all others."

He took a flourishing little bow and then a long pull from his glass, and even as she giggled and clapped, the cold certainty that she'd never be able to mimic that, or even come close, had already begun to eat its way up h__ throat. She's rarely been as certain of anything as she was in that moment, which, for whatever reason, remains crystalized in her memory. This had been a demonstration of what was expected of her, and she was not capable of delivering. He would ask her, and she would fail him, and he'd leave her out on the porch alone.

Her mother stepped outside a moment later, saving Nadia from having to try her hand at poignancy. Samir swept Rashida into his arms, drawing her in a loose, laughing tango out into the yard, and Nadia was left alone after all.

Nadia takes a long pull from the wine bottle, the bitterness at the back of her throat complimenting the rich Merlot. It figures, she thinks, that it's turned out like this—the two of them clinging to his life in Florida and Nadia here, toasting only herself, dwelling on old memories like he's already gone. There's something so pathetically predictable about it that she snorts, rolling her eyes out at the partygoers steadily filling the park. She was practically born for this, really. She's been training for it for more or less her entire life.

Her phone buzzes in her pocket: Cory, overambitious in both his estimation of her and his idea of acceptable emoticon use, as always. His text says, *Hey :) You land us any big jobs yet? :D Your boss could use a new hot tub cover :P.*

Nadia resists the urge to beat the phone into tiny pieces with the bottom of the wine bottle, but it's a close thing. Cory means well, for all his obnoxious tendencies, and god knows he's not the worst boss Nadia's had in her life.

Couple good leads, she sends in reply, figuring honesty to be less than the best policy in this specific circumstance. Plus, there's some novelty value to it—in person she can't lie for shit. *Will keep you updated.*

Sweet, Cory sends back, along with something that Nadia determines to be a high-five emoji, though only after several seconds of squinting. She takes another gulp of the wine.

Maybe, Nadia tells herself, if she just drinks enough, she'll wake up tomorrow in her bedroom, and all of this will be nothing but a haze of mostly obscured memory.

Probably not. She's rarely that lucky.

"Goddamn it," she says.

It's more a rallying cry than a lament, and it would serve that purpose, too; would send Nadia once more into the fray, if someone directly behind her didn't reply, "You're telling me."

Nadia starts violently, sloshing wine out of the bottle and all over her right sleeve. "The hell?"

"Sorry," says Ruth Shalit, though she doesn't sound it, and steps out from behind the tree Nadia was leaning against. "Didn't mean to scare you, just thought I'd found a sympathetic ear." She eyes Nadia's wine bottle with the speculative look of impending thievery. "You done with that?"

"No," Nadia mutters, but she hands the bottle over anyway. "I thought you never came to these things."

"And I thought *you'd* gotten the hell out of this viper pit we call a town, like anyone else with half a brain," Ruth says. "And yet, here we are."

30

She takes a long swig from the wine bottle—which Nadia finds slightly disgusting, though she'd thought it was cool and cavalier when she was the one doing it—and then grins at Nadia's raised eyebrow. "So, what do you think of it this year? Is it living up to your old man's standards?"

Nadia shouldn't answer honestly. Even if it is Ruth she's talking to, the single least likely person on earth to gossip with (or even talk to) their neighbors, there's a basic decorum to this sort of thing, a graciousness she knows she's meant to adopt. There is a polite lie she is supposed to tell in this situation, just like there is in most others, if her parents are to be believed.

The hell if Nadia knows what it is, though. She snorts, rolls her eyes, and says, "Honestly? If he weren't already in the hospital, this would put him there."

Ruth laughs, loud and long enough that a couple of disapproving heads turn their way. It reminds Nadia that she's always liked Ruth, even if she is a treacherous wine thief. Hers is the only nervous breakdown Nadia's ever witnessed up close—or from across the street, at least, Rashida and Samir whispering about it in hushed tones over the breakfast table—and it's a comfort to her, sort of, for all she feels guilty thinking of it that way. The idea that someone could fall apart that dramatically and come out relatively intact on the other side… well, if nothing else, it's good to know.

"Seriously," Nadia says, "what are you doing here? The last time I saw you at one of these things, you said you'd rather be getting a root canal."

"And I stand by that," Ruth says solemnly. She snags a passing waiter—Nadia has not yet assessed the food options, but if the twee little puff pastry Ruth pops into her mouth is any indicator, they're abysmal. "At least with a root canal, they drug you first."

31

"Whereas you, of course, are stone-cold sober," Nadia deadpans, nodding towards the pilfered wine.

Ruth rolls her eyes. "Please. If a few sips of wine could do it for me, I'd come to all these things." She sighs, and hands the bottle back. "Anyway, I'm only here because my niece bugged me about it for weeks. Not, of course, that she seems to want to have anything to do with me, now that I've gotten her in."

She nods out towards the party, and Nadia looks around until she spots it: the head of red hair, a bright beacon in the sea of dark browns and demure ash-blondes that make up most of the crowd. Mim's talking to Gale Ashcraft, leaning in to catch whatever she's saying, and Nadia feels her upper lip curl in disgust. Their last meeting, however brief, left such a bad taste in Nadia's mouth that she's still thinking of it more than a month later.

Ruth must notice the expression, because she smiles ruefully. "You've met her, huh."

"You could say that," Nadia says. "She's not exactly my kind of girl."

"She grows on you," Ruth says. "Or maybe she doesn't, I don't know—I haven't really spent much time with her. Not since she was little, anyway."

Nadia lifts an eyebrow. "There's a ringing endorsement."

"You know, I remember you being a little less prickly," Ruth says; Nadia's not sure if it's reproach or approval in her voice. "Whatever happened to the little girl who used to bring me brownies? Haven't seen her in years."

Nadia thinks of being ten and leaving a plate of freshly-baked blueberry muffins on the front porch of Ruth's house because her mother had said, that morning, that she'd seen her pulled over and crying on Sycamore Street. She thinks of being fourteen and running little Andy Warwick around and around their block, the two of them shrieking war cries and waving to whomever they passed. She thinks of being seventeen and sitting atop this very hill, listening to her father's annual speech and watching for the fireworks to start, surrounded by friends and family and feeling—for that one, golden moment—that everything was right in her world.

She shrugs. "Guess I lost track of my neighborly spirit."

"Yeah, well," says Ruth. "There's a lot of that going around."

An hour passes before Nadia realizes that she is drunk.

It's not as though she doesn't know how it happened; she's not *stupid*. Everyone here is stupid, with their ugly capri pants and their cardigans in the middle of the summer and their terrible, terrible appetizers, but Nadia knows what's up. She knows she drank most of a bottle of wine, and then most of another bottle of wine, and then a glass filled with dark brown liquid that was presented to her as some sort of important gift.

"An incredibly good bottle—Nadia!" Barry Craddock had said, passing her the glass before she could sneak by undetected. "Your father's not here, but you'll do in a pinch, won't you? Go on, have some. Tell me what you think."

Nadia thought, *Fuck off, you creepy old pervert, don't think I don't see you staring at my tits*, but she figured that wasn't really what Mr. Craddock wanted to hear. Also, the men clustered around him—Fred Neary, Jackson Ashcraft, Representative Warwick— were hardly the sort of people to whom she could speak like that. They'd send her father emails about her shameful behavior and then Rashida would call, hissing furiously over the phone about how Nadia was ruining any chance Samir had at recovery, and the guilt would eat her alive.

Besides, Nadia was a chef, with a trained, refined palate. She could fake pretentious opinions about mysterious alcohol with the best of them.

"Oaky," she said, after taking a deep sip of some truly foul... bourbon, maybe? Scotch? She's never been good with the dark liquors. Nasty, whatever it was—too strong to pick out any individual flavors, and an aftertaste that burned long after she'd forced herself to swallow. "With an interesting smokiness rounding out the more subtle flavors." She swirled the glass in her hand like her father used to do, trying to mimic taking a sniff without actually smelling it at all. "Overall, I'd say it's interesting—not something I'd choose myself, but I certainly wouldn't turn it down."

"Chip off the old block!" Barry said, a little louder than was probably warranted, before slapping Nadia on the back *quite* a bit lower than she would have preferred. The other two men—that is, the two who weren't going slowly and publicly senile—looked less than impressed at her assessment. Probably a trained, refined chef's palate was only an advantage if you also had a trained, refined bullshit instinct, and Nadia's has always been rudimentary at best.

She drank the rest of it, though, throwing it back in one go before setting the glass down on the bar. So it's no mystery, how she got drunk.

What is a mystery is what she's doing: sitting on the top of the set of stairs that leads down to the lake, staring at the back of Mim Robinson's head.

The thing is—the thing *is* that Nadia's been coming to these things for years, this stupid Fourth of July party, her father's favorite party, and she has a tradition. She has a *routine*. She avoids people. She overindulges (in sugar rather than booze when she was a kid, but still).

She grits her teeth and powers through whatever small talk is required. And then, as her sweet, sweet reward, she sneaks away from the revelry, walks down the stairs to the lake, and sits on the little dock to watch the fireworks go off.

The little dock where Mim Robinson is now sitting, shoulders hunched, looking down at her phone.

Which is just, really—if you're going to sit in the best firework-watching spot in the place, Nadia thinks irritably, and not actually *watch* the *fireworks*, then you're just. Wrong. Undeserving. Stupid—*Mimosa*—could sit anywhere, could go find literally any spot in this entire party to text or whatever. Tweet, maybe. She seems like the type.

For some reason, that thought just makes Nadia angrier. The fireworks in the next town are wrapping up now—visible from the lake and gorgeous, but not nearly as close as the ones that'll start here soon—and there sits Mim, tweeting away, utterly blind to the world. She's probably tweeting Gale Ashcraft, all, "@StuckUpNeighborhoodGossip, I love your tacky decorations!" and "@StuckUpNeighborhoodGossip, I think serving little cupcakes with red, white and blue frosting was an inspired choice! Not at all derivative or totally over because nobody in the food community is even into cupcakes anymore."

How dare she, Nadia thinks, aware on some level that this is insane, drunken irrationality and not caring one bit. How dare this girl come here, to Nadia's neighborhood, and act like it's so *amazing*, like she's so *glad* to be here? How dare this kid, who didn't get dragged back here kicking and screaming like Nadia did, who could have gone anywhere and chose this... this... this *backwater*, this over-inflated self-aggrandizing *shit-heap*, how *dare* she turn up and start tweeting in Nadia's personal spot?

"Fuck this," Nadia declares, and stands. She makes her unsteady way down the stairs as noisily as possible, hoping that Mim will turn around and give Nadia the chance to yell at her from on high. Of course, since Mim is the most irritating person *in the world*, she doesn't turn around. She doesn't even look up, just sits there completely, unsettlingly still, and Nadia seriously considers just pushing her into the water.

Mim would scream, though—that's the only thing that curbs the urge. She's that sort of girl if Nadia's ever seen one; she'd scream, and it would become a whole thing, and then her parents would hear about it.

Nadia settles, instead, for snapping the word, *"Hi,"* with as much venom as she can muster when she steps off the bottom stair.

Mim does turn then, but instead of, say, flailing in surprise and falling in the water of her own accord, she blinks twice and then kind of smiles. "Oh, it's just you."

"Just me," says Nadia. "You're really a piece of work, aren't you?"

"What?" says Mim. Then her face flushes, and she says, "I didn't mean—like, I wasn't saying—"

"Oh, save it," Nadia snaps. She drops, gracelessly and too hard, onto the dock next to Mim, grimacing at both the impact and the look of comical horror on Mim's face. "I'm not buying it, you know. The whole *thing* you're selling."

"I'm," says Mim, "excuse me?"

"Don't play dumb," Nadia says, and then nods, emphatically, at her own point. "That's what you do. You play dumb. Or like, innocent. Ingénue! That's the thing. That you play."

Mim opens her mouth and shuts it a few times—like a fish, Nadia thinks. A fish wearing ugly lip liner. Then, flat, she says, "Oh. You're drunk."

"Yeah, and?" Nadia says. "Doesn't mean I'm not honest. *Some* people are, you know. Honest. Instead of sycophantic and like—judging."

"Right," says Mim. "Sure."

And just—god, Nadia thinks. *God.* She's so full of booze and bitterness that it's blurring her mascara, that she has to touch her icy fingers to the corners of her eyes to try and hold herself in, and it's not fair, it's not *fair*, this wasn't supposed to be her life.

"This wasn't supposed to be my life," Nadia announces, not entirely on purpose. Then, when Mim just stares at her: "Oh, what. Is that so like—is that *beyond* you? Do they not have regret wherever you come from?"

"Rochester," says Mim.

"Excuse me?"

"That's where I—you know what, forget it," Mim says, and Nadia glares, for no reason in particular.

The far-off fireworks have stopped, and with them the distant sound of explosions. Now, Nadia can hear frogs in the bulrushes and Mim's sharp intake of breath; it's really pretty generous, now that she thinks of it, to call this place a lake. It's a swamp, is what it is, mosquito-infested and overgrown with cattails, the water a brackish, graying green. Nadia spares a moment to think dark thoughts in its direction.

Mim takes another huffy, offended breath, and it grates on Nadia's nerves to such a degree that she is immediately distracted. She looks to her left, mouth open around something nasty—she's not sure what, but then, she never is. The funny thing about Nadia's temper is that she's almost always surprised by what comes out of her mouth: she means it every time, but sometimes she doesn't know she meant it until it's too late to take it back.

Whatever Nadia was going to say to Mim dies in her throat, because Mim's pointed little inhale wasn't even about Nadia—she's scowling down at her phone, and it's this that makes Nadia say, conversationally, "You know, you're what's wrong with America."

"I," Mim repeats, slow with incredulity, "am what's wrong with America."

"Yep."

"Me," says Mim. "Not, I don't know, student loans, or Congress, or like. Murderers. Not people who kidnap children—hey, are they relieved? Child kidnappers? That they're off the hook because I exist?"

"Well, you don't have to be so," Nadia says, waving a hand. "Dramatic about it."

"I'm what's wrong with America but I shouldn't be *dramatic* about it?"

"I just mean, you know," Nadia says, narrowing her eyes at the half-hysterical crack in Mim's voice, "the phone. The tweeting. That's what's wrong with America, and you're like, I mean, you might as well be—that. As a person."

"I swear to god—"

"No, but look." Nadia is annoyed, now, about how much she's had to drink, because she can't tell if she's explaining herself badly or if Mim's just dimwitted. She is, embarrassingly enough, beginning to think it might be more the former than the latter. "Because we're here, and there are—fireworks, but are you *appreciating* the fireworks? No. You are not."

Mim stares at Nadia like she is insane. "There aren't fireworks."

"Oh, fine!" Shouting this is probably not necessary, but it makes Mim flinch, which is satisfying, so whatever. "Fine, not *right at this moment*, but I mean—Jesus! There could be!"

"Oh my god, you're actually crazy," says Mim. "I thought you were just drunk but honestly, what's wrong with you?"

"Well it's not like it's just fireworks," Nadia mutters, mulishly. "There are things happening, all the time, *experiences*—"

"So I guess you never look at your phone." There is a smugness to Mim's tone that Nadia does not appreciate. "Because you're too busy *experiencing* the world. Right?"

Nadia suspects that this is a dangerously good point. Also, that she is maybe going to vomit. Figuring a tactical retreat to be her best play on both fronts, she burps, hearing her mother's voice chiding her about manners in her head even as she does it. *Would it be more dignified to puke in the swamp, Mother?* she thinks, and then promptly feels like an insane person.

"Gross," says Mim. "Maybe *you're* what's wrong with America, did you consider that? I mean, I could certainly make a case that what plagues our country is — well, rudeness and alcoholism and —"

"I'm not a fucking alcoholic," Nadia snaps, riled. "God, you're so judgmental, listen to yourself. Does it like, rot? At your insides? Looking at people and just, I don't know, *deciding*?"

"Why don't you tell me," Mim shoots back, prissy. "You're the one who came down here on her high horse just to —"

"I bet there's nothing in your life with any *substance* in it and —"

"Oh my god, why are you such a *bitch*," Mim exclaims, and Nadia is so surprised that her mouth snaps shut, and she whips her head around to stare.

There are two spots of high color on Mim's cheeks, a deep, blotchy red that, in daylight, would probably look terrible. In the darkness they're almost flattering, highlighting cheekbones already drawn into sharp relief by the shocked "O" of her mouth. Nadia resents both them and her.

A firework going off, startling and too close, breaks the silence between them. Mim's hand flies to her mouth in horror, and Nadia's more surprised by her own startled laugh than she was by the thunderous noise of the blinding explosion above them.

For like ten whole minutes, they sit in silence, watching the fireworks display, and Mim doesn't say anything at all. Then, right in the middle of the ones that change color — Samir's favorites, and so Nadia's by default — Mim yells, "You know what, though, I don't even *have* a Twitter."

Of course, Nadia thinks. Of course.

August

The paint on the ceiling in Ruth's living room is peeling in six spots. Seven, if you count the corner where water damage is just starting to turn the eggshell pigment a sickly shade of brown; Mim doesn't. It doesn't seem right to count something she wouldn't be able to fix herself—which is not to say that she'd be able to fix the six spots that are peeling, really. She would just peel them more. That's her entire skill-set, ripping things open that probably should have stayed closed, and even that is probably beyond her.

"Get up," Mim says, ostensibly to the ceiling, but actually to herself. Nothing happens.

Ruth left six days ago, and when she went, Mim thought: yes. Mim thought: good. Mim thought that, after two months rattling around this house avoiding her, Ruth's absence would allow her a certain amount of freedom. She thought that with her aunt gone, she could really get down to business, to carving out a space for herself, to making this old house all that it could be. There are curtains that need replacing. There are windows that need cleaning. The paint on the ceiling of the living room is peeling, and one of them needs to do something about it.

"Get up," says Mim, and closes her eyes when she begins to feel, nonsensically, like the ceiling is judging her. "This is pathetic. You are pathetic. You can't lie on the floor forever, you'll starve. You smell. You're out of food. You ate crackers for dinner last night, and you have to pee, and this is not how adults handle their problems. Get up. Get up. *Get up.*"

Her pinky finger twitches as the rest of her body utterly fails to move. If Mim could muster the energy, she'd scream in frustration; as it is, she just grits her teeth and sighs.

There was a point in Mim's life—she's certain—when she was more together than this. The problem is that she can't remember how she managed it. Was it just that there were more people around, and thus fewer opportunities to fall apart? Was she simply a better person back then, before she'd realized that reality was a little more than she could take?

There's always Dell's theory, of course. Dell had liked to tell her that she needed him: that she couldn't get by without him, that she couldn't do anything on her own. Well, really Dell liked to say that they needed each other, but Mim knew what he really meant: she wasn't good enough. She wouldn't be able to make it, to survive, without him being there to help her along the way. The problem was, Dell had a funny kind of idea of help.

Mim shudders just thinking about it. She tells herself: *you left*. She's not in Dell's claustrophobic apartment anymore; she isn't looking at his ceiling. She's looking at Ruth's ceiling, and there's nobody here telling her what to do, under the guise of aid, under the guise of compassion— of love. She's here, in this house, staring at this ceiling because she *can*. She's *choosing* to. And that's better, isn't it? At least a little bit better?

Her phone buzzes against the palm of her hand, and Mim sighs. Dell's the only person who ever texts her anymore—her old friends certainly don't, and she can only assume her family listened when she told them to delete her number—so, really, she should do the smart thing and just ignore it. Instead, she braces herself, already wincing as she picks up the phone and sees...

...An email from Gale Ashcraft. What the hell.

From: Gale Ashcraft <gale.ashcraft@juniperactionfund.org>

To: Mimosa Robinson <orangechampagne@gmail.com>

Subject: Brunch?

Hi honey!

I'm so sorry to have waited so long to reach out to you—I really meant to after the party on the 4th, but things have been so busy and I just haven't found the time. But, as it happens, I was supposed to have brunch at the Club this morning with a dear friend of mine, and when she cancelled on me, I thought: serendipity! This will be the perfect opportunity to sit down with Mimosa and really welcome her to Juniper Lane properly.

So: I can pick you up on my way over if you need (the benefit of a close-knit neighborhood like ours!), but I'll plan on meeting you there. I have a table reserved for 11:00, so I'll see you then—though, of course, if you can't do today just let me know.

See you soon!

Best,
Gale

Mim stares at the email. She closes the email. She opens the email. She stares some more. She considers, for a moment long enough to be embarrassing, the possibility that this email was meant for someone else, but there's her name, "Mimosa," right there in the middle of it. She closes the email. She spares a moment to be more mortified of her email address than she has ever been of anything in her entire life. She opens the email.

"Get up," Mim says, and—wonder of wonders—she actually does.

The inside of Ridge Country Club is... well, the word for it would be *opulent* if it weren't making such an obvious effort to avoid that description. Mim's not actually sure she's ever encountered wealth precisely like this, although she's heard about it, and perhaps glimpsed it through her new neighbors' windows. Every visible piece of furniture is made of polished hardwood, gorgeously maintained but not without the occasional imperfection to indicate that it has withstood the test of time. The floor, too, is hardwood, a dark walnut accented with plush rugs that sink under Mim's heels as she walks.

All around her are people so wrapped up in their day-to-days that Mim might as well be invisible. A group of men in golf clothes walk past, all booming laughter and back-slapping, as a group of serious-faced teenage caddies scuttle along behind them. A tall woman with an similarly tall white dog—a whippet, Mim thinks, or maybe an Afghan hound—stands at the picture window of the front hall, hands clasped behind her back. She looks like something out of a very sinister Norman Rockwell painting, as though in different lighting she could be standing in the opening scene of a bleak, new-age noir. Mim stares, and then is promptly ashamed of herself when the dog turns its head and stares back.

"Sorry," Mim mutters, and then realizes the dog probably can't hear her, and *then* realizes she's apologizing to a dog.

The thing is that Mim's not actually sure what she's supposed to *do* here. Presumably the answer isn't "stand awkwardly on this thick carpet in your inappropriate shoes," but, then, it wouldn't be. Mim's curse has always been to know exactly what she's *not* supposed to do, but never to be able to come up with any viable alternatives.

She could ask the woman sitting at the front desk, probably. "Woman" might be the wrong word—she looks like she's about Mim's age, except with bleached blonde hair and better dressed. Given where she's sitting, it's probably her actual job to do things like tell confused girls where to meet their terrifyingly glamorous unexpected brunch companions—but instead of asking for directions, Mim turns and walks down a random hall before the woman behind the desk can spot her. There was a sour-looking twist to her mouth, and, anyway, it's better not to bother anyone.

It becomes apparent, after about five minutes of wandering around, that Mim has made a Mistake.

It's a word that comes with mental capitalization to differentiate it from an average, everyday error—Mim figured out during her years with Dell that she was the kind of person who needed to have both categories. A mistake, lower case, was something small and fixable, something she could take care of quickly and without anyone noticing; a Mistake, on the other hand, was a real disaster, an action with consequences. Forgetting to buy yogurt was a mistake, because she was the only one who would be bothered by it; forgetting to buy toilet paper was also a mistake, so long as she noticed and ran back to the store before it became a problem. Forgetting to buy toilet paper *and* failing to notice before the toilet paper ran out: that was a Mistake. Maybe not the first time, but definitely after it happened more than once—it was the kind of thing she could have averted, avoided, if she'd only thought about it a little harder. If she'd only been a little more considerate while she was out.

Mim knows that everyone makes mistakes. But Mistakes, she is certain, are avoidable—and people smarter than her, stronger than her, better than her, don't make them.

She should have spoken to the woman at the front desk, sour-mouthed or no. She should have stayed by the front door. She should have approached the freaky Norman Rockwell dog lady and asked her where she might find brunch, or followed the golf guys until she found an employee, or taken the damn ride Gale offered her in the first place. She should have done anything except take a wild stab in the dark and venture off on her own, only to end up lost in a labyrinth of identical wood-paneled hallways and doom herself to be embarrassingly late.

Not sure what else to do—it's not like she has Gale's number—Mim finds her phone at the bottom of her old, threadbare purse and pulls up Gale's email address. She types, "I think I'm going to be late," and then deletes it in favor of, "I'm here but I can't find you," which she then… also deletes. After an agonized few minutes of internal debate, she hits send on the following message:

Hi Gale,

I'm so sorry, but I think I'm going to be a bit late—I've gotten a little lost in the hallways. I should have waited up front for you! The club is really beautiful, and I'm so excited to be here, and for brunch; I promise I'll meet you just as soon as I can find my way to the dining room, and again, I'm really sorry about this.

Thanks,

Mimosa

45

She regrets the email the minute she hits send—not apologetic enough? *Too* apologetic?—but there's nothing for it now. She throws her phone back in her bag and resumes her explorations, trying to forget about it.

"Fucking insane... baroque... maze," Mim mutters, even though she is not, in fact, entirely certain what the word "baroque" means. It's one of those terms she knows from context clues alone, the sort of word for which she's cobbled together her own definition, but wouldn't risk saying in company for fear of embarrassing herself.

She turns a corner at random and finds herself in yet another long hallway, but this one offers a slight variation from every single one of the others. The difference is the walls: atop their wood paneling, these are lined with portraits and commemorative plaques, presumably of club members. The portraits are easy enough to ignore—like the hallways, they're all nearly identical, a veritable cornucopia of jowly old white guys—but the plaques tug at Mim's interest as she walks down the hall.

Mim does not have time to stop and look at the plaques; she must push on, go forth, and strike out boldly towards the escape from this place that must exist somewhere. She does not have time to stop and look at the plaques, no matter how curious she is, because she is late for *brunch* with *Gale*, and that is more important than reading about the sort of people who might frequent this kind of place. "You do not have time to look at the plaques," she says, firmly and with purpose, even as she feels her gait slow to a snail's pace.

"What's wrong with you," Mim asks herself aloud, though she already knows the answer to that question. She could put it on a plaque, even, to be preserved for generations to come.

After a few minutes of looking at what the club *has* preserved for generations to come, Mim wonders if she shouldn't go ahead and

46

commission an engraver. Certainly a stark listing of her flaws, or anyone's flaws, or actually practically anything at all would be more interesting than what's been put up instead. So much of it revolves around golf tournaments that Mim's head spins a little; how could this much golf have been played in one place? Didn't people, at some point, simply expire of ennui? Wasn't there some kind of limit on how much golf the human body could endure before it fell over, assuming from the long stretch of unbroken boredom that it was asleep, or even dead?

Apparently not. In fact, if Mim were to go by this showing, man could survive upon golf alone. This is, in many ways, the grimmest thought she's had in a stretch of months that have been very grim indeed, and she hurries ahead, only glancing at the plaques as she walks.

There is one, though—a bronzed newspaper article with a photograph mounted on a piece of wood—that catches her eye. The headline, "JAF Annual Ball Exceeds Expectations Once Again," doesn't feature the word golf anywhere, and it looks like there's a band in the photo. Mim stops, steps closer, and takes a look at the caption beneath.

"Music executive Samir Bahjat, a Barn Ridge native and founding member of the Juniper Action Fund, poses with family and clients Tempo Drive after their surprise performance at Saturday's gala."

The name Bahjat sets off alarm bells in Mim's head, and she wrenches her gaze back up to the photograph. The members of Tempo Drive are easily recognizable, of course; next to them stands a tall, broad-shouldered man with dark skin and a wide smile. He must be Samir, and the thin, severe-looking woman clutching his right hand is undoubtedly his wife. So that makes the little girl on his left...

"Nadia," Mim says out loud, surprised. Mim has thought of Nadia more than once in the last month, mostly in the course of dreaming up things she could have said to her that night on the dock if she'd only thought of them in time. It's not like she hates Nadia or anything. It's just that Mim's never actually dealt with someone so upfront and confrontational about hating *her*.

This version of Nadia can't be more than nine or ten, and she's *tiny*, short and practically bird-boned, almost unrecognizable as the tall, broadly built woman she'll become. Her pleated gray skirt and shimmery cream-colored blouse—Mim's pretty sure she once owned an identical version of that outfit herself—hang off of her, like they were bought aspirationally and she hadn't grown into them yet.

She is, Mim thinks wryly, a lot less intimidating without the height, the leather jacket, and the eyeliner. She's staring up—whether at her father or at Tempo Drive, Mim can't tell—with an absolutely rapturous expression on her face. It's disquieting: Mim isn't used to Nadia meeting the world with a smile. Of course, Mim's presence doesn't seem to bring out the best in her.

A dinging noise sounds from Mim's purse just as her own mouth starts to curl down, and she jumps in surprise before swearing and digging for it. She's hoping, of course, for an email from Gale telling her *how the hell to navigate this stupid building*, but instead sees the first three letters of Dell's email address.

She deletes the email with a shaking finger, without so much as looking at the subject line, and glances back up at the wall. Great. Another photo of her neighbors. That doesn't help her at all.

"Golf—golf—charity golf," Mim says as she starts walking again, shaking her head at the plaques she passes. "Golf tournament—golf course opening—seriously, does anyone who belongs here do anything but golf?"

"Sometimes we watch other people golf," says a voice, rich and baritone, from directly behind her. "But it's not really the same."

Mim jerks so violently in surprise that she manages to knock several golf plaques off the wall with a horrible clatter, and then kind of hit the man behind her. It is not her finest moment.

"Oh my god," Mim says, staring in horror at the oddly familiar man standing before her. He's tall and dark-haired, with a strong jaw and smile; that last she knows because he's directing it at her, against literally all odds. "I'm so sorry, you just—you surprised me and I swear I didn't mean to hit you, I just turned around too fast and I, uh—sorry."

"I have to say, I've never encountered such a violent reaction to the idea of watching golf before," the man says, touching two fingers to his jaw, before his smile twists ruefully. "Ah, no, you know what, I take that back. I forgot about the time I got kneed in the balls for suggesting we turn on the Masters."

"Oh my god, really?"

The guy winks. "No. But it made you feel better, didn't it?"

"I... yeah, it kind of did," Mim admits. "Thanks, I guess."

"Any time," he says, and smiles again, broader and warmer than before. His eyes crinkle at the corners with amusement, and Mim can feel heat gathering on her cheeks. She leans down to gather up the fallen plaques, hoping the blush will fade while she's got the excuse to keep her face hidden; she's not expecting him to say, "Oh, hey, no, let me get that," or to bend down just as she picks her head up.

Which is, of course, how she hits him in the face the second time.

"Jesus fucking Christ," Mim says, horrified into forgetting anything resembling proper manners at the sound of his pained, hissing breath. When she realizes what she's said, she slaps her hands over her mouth; this, of course, causes her to drop the plaques she just gathered up, which land with a loud, clanging noise on the floor.

"Oh my god," she says, hearing how faint it sounds, "I—just—oh my *god*," and that's when the guy bursts out laughing.

49

"Danny Godwin," he says, when he's calmed down a little, and Mim realizes immediately why she recognizes him: the Memorial Day party. He's still attractive, she thinks woefully, looking at him. "I'd shake your hand, but I'm honestly a little afraid of you, at this point."

"Sorry," Mim says, beginning to sound slightly hysterical. "I'm so sorry, I swear I'm not like—like, a *violent person* or anything, just. Um. God. Sorry."

"Hey, easy now," Danny says. His smile shrinks down to an expression that looks almost kind—Mim's not sure if it's really meant that way, or if she's just projecting. "I was only joking. Truthfully, this has been a lot more interesting than the tee time I'm trying to make, so it's worth a bruise or two."

"Oh," Mim says.

"*So*," Danny says, after a long, awkward pause, "did you want to tell me your name? Since you do know mine now—unless you want to be Golf Girl forever?"

"Ugh," Mim says, without thinking, "that's literally the last thing I'd ever want to be called, it sounds like a superhero with the power to bore people to death."

"What'd golf ever do to you?"

"Mim," says Mim, because she's an idiot. "I mean, uh, that's not— what golf—my name. Is Mim. Mimosa. Robinson. From—your street, actually."

Danny's brow creases in thought for a moment, and then his face lights up so entirely that Mim thinks, for a second, that he looks almost childish. It's an odd, niggling thought, because everything about his physicality says adult male. He practically looks like an underwear model—or a catalogue one, maybe, given the khakis and the light blue polo shirt, the honest-to-god sweater tied over his shoulders without a hint of irony. There's nothing remotely childish about him—Mim, actually, is the child in this situation, since he's also clearly at least ten years her senior.

50

But then Danny says, "Oh, shit, right—I knew you looked familiar! You're my new neighbor," and Mim forgets about it.

"Yeah," Mim says, trying not to feel too mortified, "Ruth Shalit's niece—um, speaking of which, I'm actually supposed to be having brunch with Gale—Mrs. Ashcraft—only I'm not sure, um, where the dining room is."

That expression from before—small, maybe kind—comes back to life on Danny's face, and he holds out a hand to her after all.

"Come on," he says, "I'll show you."

In the ten-minute walk from the Hall of Commemoration (horrifically, this is its actual name, which she learned when Danny said, "How'd you find yourself in the Hall of Commemoration anyhow?"), Mim learns the following facts about Danny:

1. He lives in the large Victorian house next to the Ashcrafts.
2. The house was his parents' before it was his.
3. They gave it to him as a wedding present.
4. He is married.
5. He never really thought he'd be the marrying type, you know? But things happen, you find yourself in certain situations, and it's not as though he has any regrets, really.
6. He is the oldest of four children.
7. His sister is a Doctor Without Borders.
8. His brothers jointly manage the operations of the massive jam conglomerate his family started generations ago.
9. He is heir to a jam conglomerate fortune.

51

10. He loves jam.
11. Except raspberry.
12. But not his family's raspberry.
13. Which is wonderful.

Things Mim does *not* learn about Danny include:

1. What he does for a living.
2. *If* he does anything for a living.
3. What his wife's name is.
4. What his wife does—if anything—for a living.
5. If he has kids.
6. What kinds of kids those kids are if he does have kids.
7. What his opinions are about Mim's plans for the future.
8. Whether he even gives a flying fuck about what Mim's plans are for the future.
9. Why he continues to laugh at Mim's poor attempts at jokes.
10. Whether or not he's actually serious about the jam conglomerate fortune thing, which, quite frankly, seems too insane for him not to be fucking with her, even though he doesn't appear to be kidding.

Basically: it's unlike any conversation Mim's ever had with anyone she considered to be an adult before—at least, if you can call a man talking for minutes on end a conversation. Mim's going to choose to, because—well, because Danny's nice, nicer than anyone here has been so far: Ruth mostly speaks in darkly sarcastic riddles, Nadia pops up periodically to spew abuse, and Mim's got no idea why Gale has summoned her to brunch, but she can't imagine she's going to make a good impression by showing up so hideously late.

And, well, he's attractive. He's a very attractive man, but he's married and older and out of her league in every sense of the word, would never look at her the way she finds herself shooting shy glances at him, and that's kind of nice, too. Mim knows all too well how easy it is to fall under someone's thrall — knows what can happen when she does, knows the sick dark trapped feeling of being held in somebody else's fist, and it's the last thing she wants to do again. But, well, there's a certain thrill to it, isn't there? To look at someone and feel temptation stirring against your better judgment? To wonder? To want?

Better to do it with someone like Danny, impossible and untouchable, than with someone a little more realistic. Better — safer — to allow herself to get it out her system this way than on someone attainable, and run the risk, once again, of letting herself get caught.

"The Grand Dining Room, milady," Danny says, adopting a silly, overly formal voice and offering her his arm. "I believe your dining companion is on the patio. Shall I accompany you to your table?"

"Oh, you don't have to," Mim starts, feeling herself blush, but Danny's already sweeping her forward.

"Gale!" he says, jovial and oddly... huh. He's dropped the silly formal voice, of course, but he still sounds a little different, a little off, somehow.

"Danny?" Gale says, and then makes a great show of lowering her oversized sunglasses to peer at him in a pantomime of shock. "My goodness, Danny Godwin? You're alive?"

Danny throws back his head and laughs. "Very funny, Gale. You know I'd get out more if I could." He lets go of Mim's arm and leans down to kiss Gale hello, and just like that, it's like Mim's invisible. "I can't tell you how nice it is to see you. Adriana's been *raving* about that Fourth of July party you threw —"

"She wouldn't have to rave if you're just show your face every once in a while," Gale says primly. "I mean, honestly, how much work can running a charity *be*, really?"

"You're kidding, of course," Danny says, but there's a question in his tone, and for a hanging moment Mim thinks that there's actually some tension between them—

—And then Gale bursts out laughing, an enticing peal of bells just loud enough to turn a few heads, but not to be really disruptive. "*Obviously* I'm kidding—I mean, what on earth else am *I* doing with my time?" She reaches out and smacks him lightly on the arm. "I'm only saying, you're my own next-door neighbor and I've hardly seen in you in months. People are going to start thinking you and Adri have split up!"

Danny's face twitches at the nickname even as Mim adds *14. Wife's name is Adriana*, and *15. Danny doesn't like it when people call her Adri*, to her mental list of Danny facts. It's creepy, she knows, to keep a list, but she figures she's probably fine as long as she doesn't write it down.

"Let's hope not." Maybe Mim's imagining it, but she thinks Danny sounds slightly strained. "Anyway, I believe this belongs to you?"

"Yes, Mimosa, hello," Gale says. Her tone is flat, and she's not actually looking at Mim when she says it. Mim thinks for a sick moment that she's going to be summarily dismissed, a chance blown in a supremely embarrassing fashion.

Then Gale turns in her seat, makes a small, exclamatory noise, and grabs Mim by both hands. "I'm *so* glad you could make it," she gushes, any hint of flatness—maybe that was all in Mim's head?—gone from her tone. "I was so worried. I mean, I know this place can be a bit of a labyrinth, but most people figure it out on their own."

"I'm sorry," Mim says, "I didn't mean to get lost, I just—"

"Oh, nobody means to get lost, honey," Gale says, cutting her off. "It's just one of those things that happens, you know? I'm just glad you got here, I would have so hated to have to reschedule."

Probably, Mim thinks, uncomfortable under Gale's expectant gaze, there's some response she's supposed to give here. Probably when you change tax brackets there's like, an Intervention crew that comes in and teaches you Emily Post or something, and Mim didn't get the memo because she's just a tourist. Probably *My Fair Lady*—a movie Mim has seen so many times that she could, if she only had a better voice, whip out a flawless Eliza at a moment's notice—is based on an actual, factual situation that occurs behind closed doors in real life all the time.

Unfortunately, Mim is pretty certain that an off-key rendition of "Just You Wait" isn't going to win her any points here, so she has to settle for just wincing and saying, "Sorry," again.

"Do stop apologizing and sit *down*," Gale says, and somehow it comes out more like an invitation than a command. "Danny, thank you for rescuing Mim before they switched over to the lunch menu, I would have been heartbroken to miss the fruit parfait."

"Like they wouldn't make it for you if you asked," Danny says, rolling his eyes and then winking, very quickly, at Mim. "Besides, it was my pleasure. Your girl here is good company."

"Not too good, I hope," Gale purrs. She purses her lips in consternation when Danny reddens slightly, adding, "Oh, sweetheart, it's a figure of speech, of course."

"Of course," Danny repeats. "Well, uh, enjoy your brunch. I should— I've got a—bye."

He hurries away, and a waiter appears in the spot he vacated with startling immediacy. Gale, despite her profession of potential parfait heartbreak only moments before, begins to pepper the server with a series of intense questions about the menu. It's sticky-sweet out on the patio, the air heavy with the scent of hydrangeas and freshly cut grass, and Mim tunes her out for a moment to watch the back of Danny's head as it vanishes around a corner.

The last time she was attracted to someone was... god. Mim can't remember, which is tragic—not just on a minor scale, like a bad haircut or teenagers trying to grow beards. No, it's blubbering-confession-on-Dr.-Phil tragic, the kind of tragic that people whisper to each other about when they think you're not listening, because Mim is twenty-three years old—this is supposed to be the prime of her life and she can't remember the last time the thought of kissing someone was exciting. What the fuck is wrong with her? What kind of life is she going to lead, if this is where she is right now?

"Miss?" The waiter's voice, gently nudging, pulls her back into the moment at hand. "Did you want to order anything, miss?"

"Yes, yes, sorry," Mim says hastily. "I was just—you know what, it doesn't matter. I'll have"—she looks down at the menu, casting around wildly for something to order—"the French toast sounds good, I'll have that."

"And mimosas for both of us," Gale says, winking at Mim before she adds, "and you! White flour before noon! Who knew you were such a rebel?"

What, thinks Mim, along with, *I ate Cheerios, bologna, and frosting for dinner yesterday, white flour is far from the worst I could be doing here.* Out loud, she says, "Oh. I wouldn't, um, say that I'm—"

"Oh, don't let me stop you from living dangerously." Gale sighs wistfully. "You're only young once, as I know all too well."

There is an expectant pause, which Mim, hoping it's the right thing, rushes to fill with, "You're young!"

Gale beams at her. "And you're sweet. I'm so relieved, honestly, I was worried you'd be another terror like that aunt of yours." She gasps the moment the words leave her mouth, hand flying up to cover it. "Oh, honey, I'm sorry, I didn't mean—your aunt is a lovely person, of course.

She and I don't get along, but that's no reason to go speaking badly of her to you. It just slipped out, and I apologize, I truly do."

"It's... fine," Mim says slowly. She's far more curious than offended, and, anyway, it's not like Ruth hasn't said much (much) worse. "Why don't you guys get along, if you don't mind my asking?"

"Oh, who can say," Gale says, waving a hand. "Good fences make good neighbors, is I suppose the root of it all. It just—to be honest with you, Mimosa, it grinds my gears a little to see that lovely old house in such a state. As Chair of the Juniper Homeowners Society, I feel as though it's my duty to make sure the entire street is looking its best. It's such a wonderful place to live, and it should look the part, don't you agree?"

Mim, who has spent the better part of the last week attempting to motivate herself into washing at least one window of her aunt's house, nods vigorously, and Gale beams again.

"I thought we'd understand each other," she says, before settling a hand over Mim's. "You seem like the kind of woman who understands this sort of thing, while your aunt... ah. She's just not the same type of woman, do you see what I'm saying? A lovely person, again, but 5000 is a corner lot. It's the first impression—sometimes the only impression—that people get of Juniper, and she just doesn't seem to care about presentation at all!"

"She used to, I think," Mim says. "I mean, when I was a kid, and she and my uncle were still together."

"Ah, yes." Gale picks up her napkin—her nails, Mim notices, are painted a deep sea foam sort of color, chic but still playful, reminding Mim again of a peacock—and folds it into thirds before placing it in her lap. "The ex-husband. I can't say I know much about him."

"Me neither," Mim says, which is, at least, honest. Her family had come out to Juniper Lane some summers, some holidays—Passover,

Rosh Hashanah, mostly used as excuses for the visits—long drives from Rochester in the car with her brothers that the entire family had dreaded but endured nevertheless. Mim remembers leaving Ruth and her mother in the kitchen and careening into the backyard with the boys, larger than any space they ever had at home. Juniper Lane had seemed like some kind of idyll to her then—expansive, green, beautiful—but she can barely remember Jasper, except for his occasional cocktail parties, his silent ominous presence on the porch in the evenings. He and Ruth had barely ever spoken to each other.

Their drinks come, and Gale insists that they toast—"Mimosas for Mimosa," like she hasn't heard that a thousand times before. She pretends it's a new thing, though, laughs easily and doesn't wince at the taste of the orange juice and the bubbling of the champagne against her tongue. Mim was named after the flower, not that it matters; everybody thinks it's the drink, and she's given up arguing. Her mother used to joke that if she'd just waited a few years to get pregnant, she would've known better, and Mim wouldn't have been saddled with something so awful, though Mim had liked her name as a child, liked the way her mother said it, like it was special—like she was special. It was only when she grew up that she realized it wasn't special, just weird, and had wished for something different.

Stupid, thinking of her, when she's been working so hard to avoid thinking about her for so long. Dell hadn't liked her parents, her mother especially; Dell had explained time and time again all the myriad ways they had failed her. Too much pressure, not enough support—always too much of this and not enough of that. Dell was wrong about a lot of things but she can't unknow or unsee any of that—every crack, every seam in what her parents should or shouldn't have done in her life—all the ways they failed her. It's stupid, now, the way tears prick at the corners of Mim's eyes; it's the carbonation hitting her nose, probably. It's not like she doesn't know better than to cry over spilt milk—something else her mother used to say.

"You have kids?" Mim asks, a little too abruptly, but Gale gives her a dazzling smile.

"Oh, how sweet of you to ask!" she says. "Yes, two, a boy and a girl. Kyle's six and he's just such a wonderful child—I just met with his new teacher for this fall, as a matter of fact. Richard—my husband—he thought we should send Kyle to private school, really take advantage of some of the options for more gifted children in the area, but I couldn't justify it to myself. I said, Richard, with all the time and money we've spent promoting the Barn Ridge school system, how could we send our own child somewhere else? Anyway, I think it was really the right call, Mrs. Nutberger seems just delightful, and very committed to making sure Kyle's learning environment is as nurturing and enriching as possible."

"Uh," Mim says, unnerved by the amount of information she's received, but Gale continues blithely on.

"And *Rebecca*, well, she's such a good big sister to Kyle, it's really very sweet. They just adore each other, which we worried about, you know—eleven years is such a large age gap. What if there had been disinterest from Rebecca, or, god forbid, resentment?" She dabs lightly at the corner of her mouth with her napkin, despite the fact that neither one of them has eaten anything yet and there was, as far as Mim could tell, nothing that needed wiping away. "Luckily it worked out the way it did, and of course Rebecca's an excellent student as well, so that should make for a very smooth college application process. Did you know she's interested in attending Princeton?"

"I... didn't," says Mim, who in fact did not know she existed a few moments ago, and could not pick her out of a lineup. "Good for her."

"We think so," Gale says. "Of course, her father's a Harvard man through and through, but we'd be happy with her at any of the Ivies, really. Anything else is really below her intellectual capacity, we think." She smiles. "Oh, but listen to me, prattling on about my children like they're the only people on earth. Where did you go to college?"

Mim, fortuitously, chokes on her drink; the slight coughing fit that follows gives her a moment to consider her answer. "Uh, UNC," she says when she's recovered herself. Normally she doesn't feel discomfited unless someone asks—

"Oh, I hear that's a fantastic school. When did you graduate?"

Mim winces. Goddamn it.

The thing is, Mim could lie. She could totally lie, and give the year she *should* have graduated, and it would be fine. Gale wouldn't go Googling her to confirm it—Mim should be so lucky, to have someone like Gale care enough to bother—and Mim doesn't know anyone else in this town. The only person who could contradict her story would be Ruth, and Ruth a) probably wouldn't strike up a conversation with Gale if her life depended on it, and b) might not know what happened with Mim's college career anyway. Mim certainly hasn't told her any of the gory details, and it's not as though Ruth is in contact with the rest of her family, as far as Mim knows.

She could also, in theory, tell the truth—that she failed, fucked up, dropped out, that she couldn't handle it, that she wasn't good enough, that she was too much of a disappointment to be awarded a diploma. God, she hates this question.

"I left last year," she says, which is what she always ends up going with—it's the happy medium between the truth and the lie, the answer that lets people hear whatever they want to believe. "It definitely is a fantastic place."

"Glad to hear it," Gale says. The waiter appears with their food, and Mim's hopes that this will distract Gale from the topic at hand vanish when she adds, "And what did you major in?"

"Marketing," Mim says. This isn't a happy medium answer so much as an out-and-out falsehood—she answers this question differently every time. Telling people she was still undeclared, too indecisive to stick with anything for more than a few months, would reveal that she'd left without graduating, which was the very thing she hoped to avoid. So she'd majored in a lot of things, over the last year: sociology, philosophy, political science. Biology for a while, until she said it to a scientist who asked her questions she couldn't begin to answer convincingly. English for a while, until she got sick of people cracking jokes about how she'd wasted her time.

She had, of course, wasted her time. Her money, too. It was a waste, investing so much in an education only to flame out dramatically. It had been a failure. She had failed.

"Did you know, I almost majored in marketing." Gale spears a bite of the frighteningly green salad she seems to have ordered; Mim, recalling the comment about the white flour, pushes her fork hesitantly against the edge of her French toast. "But then I met Richard, of course, and with him being so interested in law, it was hard not to pursue that field myself."

"Oh," Mim says, when Gale pauses expectantly. The expectant pauses, actually, are kind of freaking Mim out—she feels like she's being tested, or perhaps auditioned, for some spot she definitely isn't qualified to fill. "Are you a lawyer?"

Gale laughs, waving one hand dismissively at Mim as she stabs at her salad with the other. "Oh, honey, don't be silly—where would I find the time? No, no, I was pre-law in college, and that was quite enough for me. I did think about law school when Richard was applying, but of course then I got pregnant with Rebecca, and it was out of the question." The corner of her mouth twitches down, but smooths out again so quickly Mim wonders if it happened at all.

"And I mean, thank god. Adri—you haven't met Adriana, have you? Danny's wife?"

"No," Mim says. "I hadn't even spoken to Danny until today."

"Well," Gale says. She glances over both of her shoulders, one after the other, a gesture so clearly telegraphing the impending delivery of a secret that it's almost comical, and then leans in close. "This stays between you and me, of course, but Adri and Danny have been trying for kids for the last year or so, and she just found out last month that she's—oh, I shouldn't share the details, but it's not going to happen."

"That's awful," Mim says, unsure why Gale is telling her this. It doesn't seem like something she should know.

"I *know*," Gale says, sounding near tears. "We've been so close for all these years, and here I thought we'd be taking family vacations together soon—but that's neither here nor there. All I'm saying is, thank god my life played out the way it did. Look at Adri! She focused on her career, waited all those years, and now they can't even use a surrogate, her eggs are all dried up. I mean, can you imagine? Letting your husband go at you night after night because you can't bring yourself to tell—oh!"

Gale's hand flies to her mouth, and she waves a hand at Mim so insistently that for a second, Mim thinks maybe she's choking. She's trying to decide how sure you have to be that someone is in mortal peril before you risk the awkwardness of an unnecessary Heimlich when Gale gasps and says, "Oh! Mimosa! Oh, I really should *not* have told you that, please don't say anything to anyone! Adriana is so dear to me, I just couldn't bear the thought of her dirty laundry flying around town because of my big mouth. You won't say anything, will you?"

"Of course not," Mim says. Then, because she can't help herself: "Besides, who would I tell?"

Gale blinks at her for a moment, confusion creasing her brow. It's the first time Mim's seen her look anything but smoothly composed, and it ages her in a way Mim wasn't expecting, draws into sharp relief the very faint lines at the corners of her eyes and mouth. Gale's one of the more beautiful women Mim has ever seen up close, and it's strange, even unsettling, to see her slip like this. It makes her look alive in a way Mim realizes she hadn't, exactly, before—no, alive's not the right word. *Real.* Still beautiful, but like this Mim can admire the shade of her lipstick; a moment ago, though of course she would have known better, some part of her would have been convinced Gale's lips were naturally that shade of faintly iridescent plum.

Then Gale laughs, that tittering birdlike sound, and the moment is broken.

"God, I've been a terrible neighbor, haven't I?" she says, and then holds up a hand when Mim starts to argue. "No, no, don't bother trying to defend me, I know it's true. You've been here for, what, two months? Three? And I haven't introduced you to anyone. It's just rude of me, especially since I know that aunt of yours can't be helping you meet the neighbors at all—she hardly talks to them herself. Why, I'd bet Danny is the first Juniperite you've had a conversation with other than me since that Fourth of July party, am I right?"

"Well," Mim says, thinking of slurred insistences about putting down her phone and *experiencing* life, "uh, the second one, actually. Nadia and I—Nadia Bahjat, I mean, she and I have, like, talked. Sort of."

"Hmm." Gale nods, taps her chin thoughtfully. "Yes, I suppose you two are close in age, though I'm not sure what I think of her as a friend for you."

"Oh, we're not friends," Mim says hastily, not wanting to misrepresent the situation. "I actually think she kind of hates me."

Gale rolls her eyes. "Typical. I shouldn't talk ill of that family"—Mim in fact specifically remembers her saying exactly this two months ago, but she seems to have forgotten whatever qualms she had then—"not with the cancer and everything, but it really is typical. Samir's a darling, of course, but that Rashida is *just* awful. It's so much easier to be sweet than rude, don't you think? But Rashida's always got something snide to say, and it sounds like the apple doesn't fall far from the tree. I mean! The nerve of it! There's certainly nothing to hate about *you*!"

Mim blinks. "Well, no, I mean, I did kind of — wait. What? Cancer?"

"Yes, cancer," Gale says. "Oh, honey, don't you *know*? Poor Samir's down at some treatment center in Florida, it really is the saddest thing. I mean, talk about someone ill-suited to illness, you know what I mean? One minute he's the life of the party — everyone's always just loved him, he's such fun, if you'd moved to town before his diagnosis you'd know what I mean — anyway, the next minute they're vanishing in the middle of the night, and the next thing you know Nadia's shown up to watch the house. His colon, apparently. Stage three."

"Oh my god," Mim says. There's this buzzing noise in her ears, a sort of distant roar of horror, like thunder rolling in from a great distance away. She can feel her cheeks heating, thinking of Nadia's drunken snappishness, how viciously she herself had snapped back. "Oh my god, I'm a horrible person. She — I — it never even *occurred* to me that something like that was going on. I thought she was just a bitc — uh. I mean, I thought she was just… an unfriendly… person. God, I was awful to her."

"Oh, sweetie," Gale says. She reaches across the table and puts a hand on Mim's, even as she places her other hand over her heart. "You couldn't possibly have known, but it just warms me right to my core that you're so distressed about it. That kind of generosity of spirit — well, it's far too rare in this world of ours, don't you think?"

"Yes?" Mim says. She'd say anything to get her hand free — there's no way to pull it loose that wouldn't be rude, but god, she hates being touched by strangers. "I mean, I wasn't — I'm not trying to be self-congratulatory, I don't think that I'm the best example of —"

"And *modest*," Gale says. She squeezes Mim's hand and then, thankfully, releases it, but the appraising stare that follows is nearly as uncomfortable. "You really are a remarkable young lady, Mimosa."

It's not true, of course; Gale just hasn't known Mim long enough to know better. Mim's never been remarkable, at least not in the way that Gale means. Remarkably awkward? Sure. Remarkably unstable? Without a doubt. Remarkably disappointing? Hell, Mim could get witnesses to testify. But simply remarkable in the truest sense of the word—someone worthy of attention, of note, of talking about? The idea is laughable.

But Gale's still looking at her like she's sizing her up, like beneath her poor posture and bad clothes and ill-concealed freckles is someone worth seeing, and Mim thinks: maybe. Maybe she could *learn*. It's what she came here for, isn't it? So maybe Ruth isn't what she was expecting— fine. Whatever. If she can just figure out what it is, what it is it takes to be a woman like the one in front of her, she can figure out how to become remarkable before Gale realizes she's not.

"You know," Gale says, "my charity—well, Danny's charity, I suppose, but I really do think of it like a third child—anyway, we're looking for some help this summer, and I think you might be a wonderful fit. Tell me, have you ever considered charity work? Do you think it's something you might be interested in?"

"Sure," Mim says, "yeah, that sounds—yes," and thinks that maybe she can see her future in Gale's smile.

September

The summer Nadia turned fifteen, breasts took root and sprouted on her chest overnight—that's what it felt like, anyway. The reality of the thing was something different, months of tenderness giving way to changes she didn't notice until it was too late to brace herself: human bodies don't actually transform in the cover of darkness, of course. They do something far more insidious, erode so infinitesimally day by day that you are lured into a false sense of security, that you sit convinced that you alone live untouched by the forces of change until the morning you don't recognize yourself in the mirror. Until the day you wake up someone else.

Rashida took Nadia to the mall to buy new bras: marched them mortifyingly straight into Victoria's Secret, the last place, Nadia thought melodramatically, that she wanted to be in the world. Pink screamed off the wall at her, bright pop burbling out of the speakers—she couldn't imagine belonging somewhere less. But Rashida was relentless, and after a terrible twenty minutes, Nadia was back in the hallway of the mall, shiny pink bag dangling in her hand. That evening, she pushed herself awkwardly into the wire rims, reached around to try to do up the clasp—and when she came downstairs, her mother smiled at her. "Well, don't you look nice," she'd said, and Nadia had stood next to her while she cooked, and chopped up vegetables.

"Yes, Mom," she says now, holding the phone to her ear with her shoulder as she digs in her bag for her cigarettes, "I remember being fifteen. What, do you think I have amnesia? What kind of question is that?"

"A good one, if you've got a daughter who insists upon acting as though she sprung into this world a fully formed adult." Rashida always sounds like this when she's tired, a bite to her voice that reminds Nadia of nail clippers: getting as close as she can to the quick. "And I don't think I like your tone. You know I wouldn't ask if I didn't have a good— was that a lighter? Are you *smoking*?"

"No," Nadia says on nicotine exhale. It's one of the three lies she's bothered to learn to tell well. The other two—passing as straight and pretending she has any real idea of what's going on with her father's treatment—are omissions more than anything else. It's not exactly what you'd call a skill.

Rashida will be Rashida, though. It doesn't matter that Nadia's lying—even if she *were* telling the truth, her mother wouldn't believe her. For years when she was a teenager Nadia tried to work that one out, to figure out why Rashida was always looking for lies on Nadia's honest tongue, but she's given up. Her mother has trust issues, or issues trusting her, or just... issues. Whatever. It's not Nadia's problem.

"I can't believe you'd smoke on the phone with me," Rashida snaps. "You know how I feel about that, and with your father's cancer—"

"Colon."

"Excuse me?"

"Colon," Nadia says, taking another drag of the cigarette, "cancer. Dad has colon cancer. I'll have to check with the Surgeon General, but I'm pretty sure you don't get that from smoking."

Rashida sniffs. "Don't be insensitive. Cancer is cancer."

"Uh, no," Nadia says, incredulous. "It isn't. Jesus, Mom. I can't believe an oncologist didn't like, spring out from behind a pillar and—"

"There aren't any pillars here," Rashida says. "I thought I sent you a photograph—no, I know I did. Oh, Nadia, I knew you weren't reading my emails."

Nadia grinds her teeth, takes another pull from her cigarette, and puts the phone between her shoulder and her ear again. With her free hand, she starts picking a scab on her knuckle, knowing all too well that sometimes a little pain is the only way she can keep focus all the way through these conversations. Anyway, it's better to think of the parmesan she sustained this tiny wound grating and the lemon risotto she topped with it than to try to work out exactly what it is Rashida wants from her right now.

"I read your emails, Mom," she says. "I read your emails, I read Dad's emails, I email *you* asking for more details—look, can we just—I'm on a break at work. What did you need?"

"Who says I need anything?"

Precedence, Nadia thinks but does not say. It wouldn't be worth it. "You wanted to know if I remembered being fifteen...?"

There's a considering pause, and then: "Oh! Right, yes. Do you remember being fifteen *and*"—this word is loaded, as though Nadia cut her off before she could finish her thought before, which *didn't happen* and is *so annoying* and fuck, she's ripped the scab off—"going with me to the Jewels of Juniper meetings?"

"Oh, god," says Nadia. "Oh god, please no."

"I don't believe you," Lucy had said—or maybe it was Aaliyah—shit, Nadia's fucked too many girls with pink hair. Whoever she was, she was hot and she was laughing and she had said, "Nobody's like that"— Nadia remembers that much. She had said, "Come on, you're fucking with me, this is some kind of like, I don't know. From some bourgeoisie joke book or something, right?"

Oh, right; it was Sonia, has to have been Sonia. She was and remains the only woman Nadia's ever slept with who routinely brought up the proletariat in bed. It doesn't really matter, in the grand scheme of things—which girl it was, not the proletariat—but it makes Nadia feel better to know, just the same. For all that she's spent years cultivating the image of being a person who doesn't remember the names of the girls she fucks, she doesn't actually want to *be* the kind of person who doesn't remember the names of the girls she fucks. That feels like a line she can't cross, and anyway, most of them are worthwhile human beings, even if she doesn't have any real interest in spending time with them outside of a bedroom.

Point being: it was Sonia, of course it was Sonia, with her pink hair and uncomplicated cynicism, in Nadia's bedroom that afternoon. Her apartment then was in a part of Chicago her parents always referred to as either gritty or dangerous on the phone to her, but had described as "up-and-coming" to their own neighbors and friends; Nadia had just wanted someone who would *get it*. Nadia had just wanted someone to know her.

In retrospect, Sonia had been a terrible choice for a confidante, but Nadia had only been nineteen at the time, without even the tentative grip on nuance she possesses now. She'd thought, at the time, that maybe they were cut from the same cloth—that Sonia, who was grating and obnoxious and overwhelming, was afflicted with the same disease as Nadia: the inability to be anyone but herself.

(She wasn't. Obviously. Six months after they stopped sleeping together Nadia ran into her at a party, and she was brunette, demure, holding hands with a man who may as well have been a walking J. Crew advertisement. She looked like someone who'd never even heard the word proletariat, and it made Nadia feel stupid in a unique, unsettling way that she never had before—but that's got nothing to do with this, of course.)

That afternoon, Sonia laughed and Nadia laughed and they each took another hit from the bowl, leaning across the bed to blow the smoke out the window, and then Nadia said, "Seriously, though. For real. There were like... *meetings*, and shit. Where they'd all get together and eat little finger sandwiches and, whatever, congratulate themselves on being fantastic, I guess. Miserable. Depressing as hell, too."

"Finger sandwiches!" Sonia cackled, laughing so hard she nearly fell off the bed. "Oh my god, finger sandwiches, I can't breathe."

Nadia scowled. "Bad ones too, you know? Like, you know what, if you want to make a tiny sandwich I get that, I feel you. But a little creativity, that's all I ask, especially if you're fuckshit crazy rich and you can afford to like, you know. Do it right." She twirled the lighter in her fingers, ignoring Sonia's snorting laughter. "Like, bacon and fig finger sandwiches, okay? That'd be great. Or *lardon* and fig finger sandwiches, with a little bit of arugula to cut the sweetness of the fig. Yeah. *Yeah*. And it'd take the same amount of time to put that together as, ugh, the watercress-cucumber-mayonnaise mess that shows up every fucking time. No excuse for bad food if you can afford good food, you know?"

"I think that's the most I've ever heard you talk about anything," Sonia said, laughter still in her voice. "I knew you were a food nerd, but like, damn, girl. Take it down a notch, you know?"

71

This from a woman with hair the color of cotton candy, Samir's voice said in Nadia's head. She didn't say it out loud, naturally; it was enough to take the sting out of Sonia's dig, just knowing it's what he would have thought.

"It was just—stupid," Nadia said. Insisted. It felt weirdly important, to explain this to someone. "My mom would drag me along because— she said it was because I was almost a woman, but what the fuck was that? I was fifteen, I wasn't almost anything. It was her, though. It was like—I was supposed to be part of, of *something*, you know? But I would just sit there and stare at my hands just thinking that I wasn't—just. I wasn't." She swallowed, knotted her hands in the sheets, looking out the window so Sonia wouldn't see the shine of inexplicable tears in her eyes. "I'm not explaining it right, I guess."

"Hey, whatever," Sonia said. She pulled the lighter from Nadia's fingers and sparked the bowl again. "Tell me the part about the finger sandwiches again, that shit was hilarious."

Nadia thought of her hands in her lap, twisting them together, as her mother sat prim and still across from her. She thought of the sidelong glances, almost pitying, between the two of them, of feeling weighed down, of the histrionic edge to that emotion that she was too much a teenager, at the time, to tamp down. She thought of the chilling sameness of all the women ringed around that table, eating those terrible finger sandwiches and twittering on in a code Nadia couldn't seem to pick up, and swallowed.

"It wasn't supposed to be hilarious," she said.

"Yeah, okay," said Sonia, "but it was. Play to your strengths, right?"

"Right," said Nadia. "My strengths. Right."

Now, Nadia stares at the door of the Craddocks' house for a long, bleak moment, and then checks her lipstick in the reflection of her phone's darkened screen, as though that will change anything.

Her lipstick is, as it was two minutes ago, perfect, and she tries to take some small comfort in that. Maybe she is late to this meeting. Maybe she does hate everything it stands for. Maybe she is going to have to take notes on the neighborhood gossip for her insane mother like she cares about any of it. Maybe she is going to have to take those notes in the home of a woman pushing seventy and her octogenarian creep of a husband—but her makeup is on point, so she's cool. She's great. Everything's going to be totally fine.

Nadia stares at the door some more. Being a door, it doesn't stare back, but the little beady-eyed gnome directly to its right has a gaze unsettling enough for both of them. Briefly, Nadia flips the gnome off. Then, heaving a great sigh, she knocks on the door.

It's not that Nadia's *afraid* of old people, exactly. Being *afraid* of them would be crazy, since they're… well, old. Infirm. Nadia could totally take one of them, if push came to shove—although of course she wouldn't, what with them being elderly and everything. It's not a fear. That's not what it is.

It's just a… *dislike*, Nadia thinks, with a desperate sort of emphasis, as she hears footsteps approaching the door. It's an aversion. It's a strong aesthetic displeasure, because the elderly have a certain feel, a certain smell, a certain set of decorating tendencies to which Nadia objects. There's nothing wrong with that. There's nothing wrong with her. She's got this. She's fine.

Mrs. Craddock opens the door, and Nadia changes her mind. She's not afraid of old people: she's afraid of this specific old person. Which is fair, because she's terrifying.

"Well, well, if it isn't little Nadine," says Mrs. Craddock, peering at Nadia through the coke-bottle glasses that have never managed to

73

truly conceal the evil in her eyes. She has never, in the seventeen years since Nadia's parents moved to Juniper Lane, correctly remembered Nadia's name—which is strange, given that her memory in general is as impressive as her gnome collection. "Here to dig up my rhododendron again? Hmm? *Hmm*?"

Nadia thinks: *I am twenty-six fucking years old, Mrs. Craddock, can we let bygones be bygones? Isn't there a statute of limitations on people being pissed off about landscape vandalism?*

Nadia says: "No."

"See that you don't," Mrs. Craddock snaps. Nadia can already smell the mothballs from the inside of the house. "Come in, come in, you're letting the warm air out."

It's seventy-five degrees outside. Nadia winces, braces herself, and still shudders with horror when she steps through the door and feels the temperature shift up ten clammy degrees.

"They're all in the basement," Mrs. Craddock says, waving a hand vaguely to her left as though that's adequate direction. "I've got to get something from upstairs, but make yourself—"

She trails off, as though actually saying the words "at home" is physically beyond her. Probably, Nadia thinks, it is. Probably she's like the Wicked Witch of the West, only she melts at the touch of kindness rather than water.

From what she can remember, the Craddocks' house hasn't changed much in the past decade, but she'd never spent more than a minute or two inside it in any case. Mrs. Craddock was the kind of adult who felt, deep in her soul, that children should sleep in doghouses until they were old enough to be considered people. Most of Nadia's memories of the place revolve around the glass figurines that still adorn every available surface. They have, unfortunately, not become any less pants-shittingly creepy with age.

The one in the corner has the same unnerving stare as the gnome outside. Nadia looks at it appraisingly for a long moment before she pulls out her phone, takes a picture, and sends it to her dad with the words, "Update: crazy old Mrs. C still old and crazy."

Then she waits. And waits. And hates herself, just a little, for the flare of—whatever, sadness, irritation, *something*—at not getting an immediate response from her cancer-riddled father. It's selfish, having that kind of expectation of him. She pockets her phone, scowling, and turns around...

...Only to see Mim Robinson standing at the door to the basement, staring at her with wide eyes.

"Oh, shit," Nadia says. She means, *Oh, shit, the last time I saw you I was really drunk and I think I called you some names, this is awkward.* But she can see—in the twist of Mim's mouth, the twitch under her left eye—that it came off more, *Oh, shit, you, I hate you*—which, she has to admit, does make sense.

Only: "Hi," Mim says, irritation smoothing off of her face. "Nice to see you."

"Really?" says Nadia, shifting uncomfortably when Mim's eye twitches again.

"Yes," she says, sounding determined. Her smile looks forced.

"It's just sort of... weird, that you'd think it was nice to see me," Nadia says slowly. "Since I've kind of been an asshole to you."

Mim makes a humming sound. "Well!" she says, voice pitched too high. "I mean. It's—I mean, it's fine! You were, uh, maybe releasing some tension, which is, you know, totally understandable and probably good. Healthy! It's fine!"

"Oh," Nadia says, flat. "So someone told you."

This is how it is when you've got a parent with a wasting disease: people get weird. People get *pitying*. Everyone she knows is weird about it.

She even runs into people at the grocery store who are weird about it—and who, exactly, wants to talk about their father's cancer in the meat aisle? Can't people tell, when she stands there digging her fingers so deeply into the package of ground beef she's holding that she breaks the plastic and has to go wash her hands, that it's *not a good time*?

Mim makes this uncertain noise, like she's not sure whether she should confirm or deny, and Nadia, regrettably, doesn't have anything in her hands to break. She could start grabbing tchotchkes and throwing them at the wall—that would be a service to humanity, if nothing else—and she's considering which of the creepy dolls most deserves to die when Mim says, very hesitantly, "Are you okay?"

Nadia stares.

"I mean," Mim says. She doesn't actually finish the thought, though, just stands there, rubbing a piece of her hair between her fingers and biting her lip. "I just—sorry. I thought that I'd... ask."

"Nobody asks," says Nadia. She says it because it's true: people ask *around* it, say, "How are you holding up?" or, "I hope you're doing okay," or, "Let me know if you need anything," but it's not like they ever really mean it. It's all just white noise, interpersonal detritus, the kind of thing you say so you can sleep at night, knowing you're the kind of person who took the time to do so. Nobody ever says anything real—nobody ever asks.

"Sorry," Mim says, sounding it. "I really, god, I have no idea what I'm supposed to—I just thought—"

"No," says Nadia.

"No?" Mim rolls her shoulders, shifts her weight from one foot to the other—she moves a lot. Fidgets. Did no one ever teach her to be still? "What do you mean 'no,' like, is that 'No, you shouldn't keep talking,' or 'No, you thought wrong,' or—"

"No," Nadia says, enunciating clearly, "I am not okay."

"...Oh." This, apparently, is how you stop the Mim Robinson perpetual motion machine: by making things so awkward that she just completely freezes, like a deer in the headlights. Even her *blinking* is hesitant. "Do you want to... talk about it?" she says, though she sounds like she would really rather not be asking the question.

Nadia, to her own immense surprise, laughs out loud. The sound is honest and unfamiliar, and it occurs to her to wonder how long it's been since she laughed like that: fully, wholly, without the assistance of smoke or drink. "Fuck no, I don't want to talk about it."

"Thank god," Mim breathes, and then, "Oh shit, sorry, I mean, if you ever *do* want to talk about it—"

"Stop, stop." Nadia's still laughing as she says it, even as she rolls her eyes. "Jesus. Doesn't that get exhausting?"

"What?"

"'I mean, I'm sorry, I just, it wasn't,'" Nadia says, voice pitching up in mockery of Mim's. Mim scowls. "It just seems kind of tiring, tripping over yourself every two seconds."

"I don't trip over myself," Mim says. "I'm—it's—I'm *friendly*."

"You're sycophantic."

"Just because I'm not an asshole," Mim snaps, and then, of course, looks mortified. Nadia's starting to get the hang of this now. "Oh my god, I didn't—"

"For god's sake," Nadia says, resigning herself to what feels like her fate, "just... look. There aren't exactly a lot of people in our age bracket around here, do you know what I'm saying? So—my point is, why don't we just, I don't know, call a truce? I won't get pissed at you for all the shit you say if you just stop saying the annoying shit. Deal?"

Mim looks gobsmacked. A small, vindictive part of Nadia takes some satisfaction in that, but mostly it just seems kind of pathetic.

"I," Mim says, but Nadia never gets the chance to find out if they have a deal. Gale Ashcraft sweeps into the room, a cloud of perfume and jangling bracelets and clacking heels, and what happens to Mim next is freaky, actually, almost like watching someone turn into a Stepford Wife. Her face goes from blank to utterly rapt unsettlingly quickly, her attention focused entirely on Gale. Even her *body* turns toward Gale, a small but meaningful pivot on her heel leaving Nadia somehow more alone than she was a moment ago.

"Mimosa!" Gale says—why does she call her that? Doesn't she notice the way it makes Mim's eye twitch?—without acknowledging Nadia at all. "There you are, I thought I'd lost you. Come back downstairs, the meeting's just about to start up again."

Nadia's not sure why she says, "Hello, Gale," when, under normal circumstances, she would much rather slip under the radar of either Ashcraft parent. Her voice has a sharpness that she must, at some point down the line, have picked up from her mother—she never meant to do it, but she can hear Rashida's tone, her vowels on the word. "So nice to see you."

"Oh, Nadia," Gale says, and then: the worst one, the most self-serving of all the options: "I do hope your father is doing all right, I've just been sick with worry about him."

There is one reason, and one reason only, that Nadia is back in Barn Ridge: to smooth things over. To calm the waters. To present a sane, healthy, and composed front, so that no one on Juniper Lane thinks this small spot of tragedy has brought the Bahjats to their knees. Her parents were very clear about this—she is their daughter, and this is her duty. She must be the picture of composure. She must do her part.

"So sick you couldn't call," says Nadia, and swears she can hear her mother shrieking from Florida. "That's awful, Mrs. Ashcraft. You should really get that checked out."

It isn't worth it, Nadia tells herself. It isn't worth it to see Gale's mouth open and close in shock. It isn't worth it to hear Mim hastily turn her laugh into a cough. It isn't worth it to watch Gale spin on her heel and stalk off towards the basement, or to see Mim turn and give her this *look*, somewhere between admiration and fear before she follows her. It isn't worth it because her father will hear about it, and her mother, and she will get an email about how much it hurts them when she misbehaves that will make her feel like a terrible person for a month.

It isn't worth it. But it feels worth it, just for a second, before she starts wondering when the axe will fall.

In the meetings of the Jewels of Juniper that Nadia attended in her youth, the ladies discussed such riveting topics as: whether to plant annuals or perennials in the Juniper Lane traffic island, the theme of the traditional Halloween party (inevitably: masquerade), and whether or not to put up signs supporting the school district levy, with the argument, "Signs are tacky," eventually beating out the opposing, "Education is important, and costs money, which we all possess." Once, there was a discussion of potential window-washing companies so rousing that Nadia fell asleep in her chair, and then *off* her chair—though that was worth sitting through, if only because the resulting Scene convinced Rashida to swear off bringing her entirely.

The point being: never, in all the meetings she attended, did Nadia witness a single thing as amazing as Angel Neary standing up on too-high heels, pointing her finger at the calico in the corner, and shrieking, "*Murder cat!*" at the top of her ample lungs. If she had, Rashida wouldn't have been able to *drag* her away from the damn Jewels of Juniper.

"Angel!" Gale says, shocked, "Come on now, we can resolve this like—"

"Are you calling my Bitsyboots a killer?" Mrs. Craddock, drawn up to her full height, actually cuts a pretty intimidating figure, a fact Nadia remembers all too well from her youth. "My sweet, precious baby wouldn't hurt a fly, would you? Would you, Bitsyboots?"

Beautifully, Bitsyboots' response to this is to stand up all the hair on her back and hiss. Everybody in claw range—even Mrs. Craddock— moves a few feet back.

"Your monster," Angel says, "*attacks* my cat. All the time! Every week, it seems like, I find new cuts and scrapes on Montgomery!"

Mrs. Craddock snorts. "Stupid name for a cat."

"Well, I think Bitsyboots is a stupid name for a *killer*," Angel says, her voice getting shriller by the moment. "Or *anyone*. But the fact remains that your cat is a—a murderer waiting to happen! A *danger to society*!"

"Ladies, please," Gale says, and both Mrs. Craddock and Angel, simultaneously, snap, "Shut up!"

"This is amazing," Nadia says under her breath to Mim, who, by a happy accident of seating, ended up in the spot next to her. "This is *so* amazing, this is the most amazing thing that has ever happened to me."

"Bitsyboots *has* clawed up my dog," Mrs. Warwick pipes up from a few seats over. "And you all know Rufus, sweetest dog on the planet— he was more confused, I think, than anything else. We said then that Bitsy should be declawed, but—"

"You want me to maim this cat and I won't do it," Mrs. Craddock cries. "I won't do it!"

Mrs. Clausen-Godwin, who normally doesn't even show up to these things, makes an incredulous noise. "So, what, we're supposed to let the cat maim us? Maim our children?"

"Now, Adri, come on," Gale says, and there's something in that that makes Mrs. Clausen-Godwin freeze, though Nadia can't imagine what. Interesting. "We're all adults here, can't we all just calm down?"

"I'll calm down when her cat stops hurting my cat," Angel says. She sounds near tears. "I can't even let her outside—*and* the Craddocks should be paying my vet bill—"

"Like hell we will!"

"I would also like Rufus' vet bill covered," says Mrs. Warwick, a follower to the end. "Retroactively, of course."

Nadia leans over to Mim again. "We should have brought popcorn. Are they always like this now? Have you been to any others? God, I wish we had popcorn."

"I," Mim says, blinking rapidly. Angel is taking off one of her shoes. "What is she—"

"Shhhh," Nadia hisses, "don't introduce rational thought, they pick up on it—oh my god she's gonna throw the shoe."

This Nadia says with a mixture of horror and delight, because while she is, of course, opposed to cruelty to animals, infighting of this magnitude amongst these structured, coiffed women is too incredible to inspire anything but joy. Also, Bitsyboots, like her owner, is a real bitch of a cat: ancient and bitter, she stalks the neighborhood by day and lies in wait under the bushes by night, waiting to claw the ankles of unsuspecting passers-by. If ever there was a cat that deserved to be hit by a shoe—not that any cat ever deserves that—but if any cat *did*, it would without question be this cat.

"It's the Jeffrey Dahmer of cats!" Angel yells, and whips the heel across the room. Chaos descends utterly.

The cat—a survivor through and through—dives underneath a chair at the realization that a projectile is coming for her. She needn't have bothered, however, as Angel Neary is a terrible throw; the shoe, instead of hitting the cat, whacks Mrs. Clausen-Godwin on the back of the head.

This alone would be high on the list of most incredible things Nadia's ever seen, but in a moment of true serendipity, Mrs. Clausen-Godwin is also holding a large glass full of punch.

It all plays out as if in slow motion: the shoe's impact, Mrs. Clausen-Godwin's cry of pain, the way her arm jerks in surprise. The glass empties and punch arcs through the air, leaving Nadia just enough time to think, *please, please, please,* before it happens: the whole cup's worth of it lands on Gale, dripping down through her hair and onto her crisp white blouse. It's a deep, rich, *Carrie* red. Nadia thinks, based on the taste, that it has to have been at least half-cranberry juice.

To say that Nadia howls with laughter would be inaccurate. It's more a shrieking than a howling, really. Since she is the only one laughing—the rest of the room is standing in stunned, horrified silence—it sounds more maniacal than she'd really prefer, but it's not as though she can stop.

She puts a hand over her mouth in the end, a compromise, and then everyone begins to speak at once:

"Oh my god," says Mim.

"I'm so sorry," says Angel.

"Gale, I didn't," says Mrs. Clausen-Godwin, "you must know I didn't mean to."

"Serves you right," says Mrs. Craddock, sniffing. "Antagonizing my cat that way."

"I," Gale says, sputtering—actually sputtering, this is the best day in history—in rage. "*I* did not antagonize your cat. *I* said that we should all settle down and behave like adults, but no! No!" Her eyes, Nadia notes, are taking on a distinctly crazy edge. "You! All of you! Have ruined! My shirt! The evening! Everything!"

"Oh, god," Nadia mutters, tuning her out and looking around. Mim's moved a few people away—probably trying to distance herself from Nadia's hysteria—and Nadia sidles over to her, grabs her elbow. "Come on, we have to go."

"*We* don't have to do anything," Mim hisses back. "You laughed, she's going to think I was laughing too—"

"We have to *go*," Nadia repeats, jerking her head towards Gale's increasingly intense gesticulation, "before this becomes our fault somehow, okay? You go first if you don't want to be seen with me."

"Becomes our," Mim repeats, blinking, "what are you even—"

"Your funeral," Nadia says, and gets the hell out of Dodge.

Nobody is paying any attention to either one of them: Angel is trying to find her shoe, Mrs. Clausen-Godwin is still insisting on her innocence, Mrs. Craddock is trying to coax the cat out from under the chair, and Mrs. Warwick is attempting to apply club soda to the stain on Gale's shirt. Specifically, she's trying to apply club soda exclusively to the part of the stain covering Gale's breasts—it's a move of repressed lesbianism that Nadia recognizes all too well from her own adolescence, which had heavily featured spilling whatever was nearby on the shirts of various girls and then offering to assist in the cleanup. It was as pathetic a move then as it is now, although, Nadia suspects, slightly *less* pathetic for being perpetuated by a teenager, as opposed to a well-known politician's wife nearing the age of sixty-five.

Nadia spares the requisite moment to feel sorry for Mrs. Warwick, who has been telling Nadia to call her Donna with an air of desperate sexual hunger for easily the past seven years. Closet cases are always sad, but Donna Warwick isn't a closet case so much as a Narnia case— she's so deep in there that someone with a lot more patience and investment than Nadia would need to mount a full-scale expedition to drag her out.

In any case, nobody is paying attention to them because that's how these things go. Nadia used to think she wouldn't qualify as a real person to these people until she turned twenty-one, but by now she's accepted that it won't happen unless, at some point, she starts pulling in more than a hundred thousand a year. She's an extension of her parents, a reflection of them cast in clouded glass, the same way she was as a child. Nobody will notice a thing she does unless it'll get them any traction in the local gossip, because that's all she is to them: a potential story. A data point. It's all Mim is, too, even if Gale has decided to make a special project—or, Nadia thinks darkly, an accessory—out of her.

Mim doesn't appear to know that, since she stops on the stairs behind Nadia and, in a voice too uncomfortable and quiet to be heard over the fray in any case, says, "I, um. I just remembered that I'm allergic? To cats? So I have to go, but thanks for—having me? Um. Okay. Bye."

Nadia chokes on her laughter and turns to see Mim glaring up at her, flushing crimson. She's careful not to make too much noise, so Nadia stomps on the last few steps as hard as she can, just to make a point. Not one of the Jewels of Juniper-ites so much as looks around, and Nadia would bet good money that none of them will notice they've gone, excepting maybe Gale, looking for Mim to—hold her purse, or spit-shine her shoes, or whatever the hell it is Mim does for her—at the end of the night.

The last thing Nadia hears, as Mim shuts the basement door behind her, is the distinct sound of porcelain shattering. She winces. Definitely time to go.

"What the hell was that about," Mim says, breath coming quick, as she follows Nadia out of the house.

"Evil cat," says Nadia. "Crazy ladies. You were there, I don't feel like a summary is really required."

Mim scowls. "No, the—you rushed me out, you said we'd be blamed for—"

"Oh," says Nadia. "That." It's weird, to think that Mim doesn't know this; it's weird to think of it as something that would need to be explained. "Don't you, uh—haven't you ever been, I don't know. The fall guy?"

"The... fall guy," Mim says slowly. "For... what?"

"Just," Nadia waves a hand, "you know. Generally. Something shitty happens and afterward everybody wants to pretend like it didn't—except they don't really, because they want to be able to tell everyone about it—fuck, you know what I mean, don't you? Someone has to have started it, you see what I'm saying? Because otherwise it's just a story about grown-ass women losing their shit over some cat."

"But it *is* a story about—"

"Christ," Nadia says, "do you really not—okay. These people, their egos are *so* fragile, you know? They don't want it to be a story about losing their shit over some cat because they don't want to look at themselves that way, so they twist shit to make it fit instead. It becomes a story about how a cat went insane and everyone freaked out trying to help it, or," and here she twists her mouth into a rueful grimace, "how they let a couple of freeloading kids join the Jewels of Juniper and it caused dissent amongst the ranks."

Mim is silent, and it takes Nadia a moment to realize that she's stopped walking. She turns and Mim's got her hands on her hips, head cocked to one side, and this unsettling expression on her face that Nadia can't read at all.

Suddenly, though, Mim rolls her eyes and says, voice ringing with disbelief, "Oh my god, you're an actual real crazy person."

"Think you've said that to me before," says Nadia, rolling her eyes right back.

Mim shrugs, and kicks a rock absentmindedly. As it rolls away towards the nearest gutter, Nadia realizes, abrupt and too late, that she's been leading them to her own house. "I mean, if you think that everything is some kind of, whatever, conspiracy between our neighbors, who definitely have better things to do—"

"They really don't," Nadia says, reflexive, as they walk up the path to her door. Most of her brain is occupied with trying to figure out what the hell she's supposed to do—what's the socially acceptable way to handle one's semi-friendly semi-enemy in this situation? Is she supposed to say goodnight? Invite her inside? Is Mim just *walking her home*, and if so, how does Nadia communicate to her that she is not someone who gets walked home, but, instead, does the walking? For her part, Mim seems not to have noticed they're standing on Nadia's doorstep, just stops walking when Nadia does and continues their conversation undaunted.

"You're seriously nuts," Mim persists, "they're like, what, Gale's dealing with all the events for the Fund, Mrs. Warwick spends half her time in Washington, they all have kids—I mean, Mrs. Craddock, maybe, I grant you—"

"Do you want to come in?" Nadia says. It would probably have been less weird, she thinks in the hanging moment after it comes out of her mouth, if she'd said it slower. Or more quietly. Or after Mim had stopped talking.

"I mean," Nadia tries again, awkwardly, "if you felt like—coming in for a beer or whatever."

"I, um," Mim says. She scratches the side of her neck again, sounds out of breath—which means that Nadia has actually accomplished the feat of being literally breathtakingly awkward. How novel. "I probably shouldn't."

"Right, of course not." Nadia swallows against the taste of bitterness on her tongue, the desire to lash out in the face of this small rejection. "I mean, I probably wouldn't have a beer with me—"

Mim flushes, even redder and blotchier than usual, and interrupts her, holding up a hand, a sheepish expression on her face. "No, it's not—I actually really am allergic to cats."

Nadia stares, somehow only just noticing that she's covered in hives. "You—what? What? Why did you *stay*?"

"I was sneaking out when I ran into you," Mim says. Now that Nadia's listening for it, she can hear that the shortness of breath has that hitching quality that she, herself, has always associated with the combination of shellfish and her father. "But then—uh. I mean. Crazy ladies. Evil cat. I don't feel like a summary is required."

"Nothing worse than having your words turned back on you by an idiot," Nadia sighs, unlocking the door. "Just—god. Come in. We've got allergy pills and shit, and honestly I don't know if I trust you to make it across the block now, I had no idea you were this stupid. Why don't you travel with an escort? Just, I don't know, a little man who follows you around and tugs on your arm to remind you of shit like this?"

"I don't think escort's really the term for what you're describing," Mim wheezes. "And I didn't forget, I just decided it was worth it to stick around. You're the one who kept saying it was the best thing ever."

"Whatever," Nadia snaps. "Just, I don't know, sit down somewhere or something. Jesus," she adds, mostly to herself, as she turns towards the stairs. Over her shoulder, she calls, "Grab anything you want out of the fridge, but maybe pass on anything that'll put you into anaphylactic shock before I get downstairs, what do you think?"

"Oh, damn," Mim calls back, "and I really wanted one of these penicillin popsicles, too!"

"Hilarious," Nadia mutters, but without animus.

She finds herself becoming increasingly annoyed, though, the longer she roots around in her parents' medicine cabinet. It's not like she knows the girl that well and even if she did, this wouldn't be important. An allergy attack is nothing in the grand scheme of things, just a little blip with a known cause—it's not something like weight loss or exhaustion; it's not one of the little signs that don't mean anything until they mean everything, and it's too late to do anything about it.

Nadia notices her hands, which have closed around a package of Claritin, are clenching tightly enough that the cardboard is starting to tear. She lets the tension bleed out of them, but when she tries to pop a couple of pills out of their plastic capsules she realizes that they're still shaking, and she feels more than hears herself make a small, despairing noise, and sits down heavily on top of the toilet.

It's fucking stupid for her to be this upset, for her to be thinking about—it's not like it'll change anything, going back over it in her head. Nadia turns the package of pills over and over in her hands, fingers worrying at the slightly torn foil edge of one of the plastic capsules. She understands that it's not her fault. She understands because of course it's not, because cancer doesn't work that way, because that's what Samir told her about it.

"I want you to know that it's not your fault," Samir said, after spitting out the admission of liver cancer like it physically hurt him to say. Rashida sat on the couch next to him, her hand gripping his tight in a show of solidarity—there was no space between the two of them, or on either side. Nadia had been keeping an arms length between herself and the world for years and still, in that moment, regretted that she could not slide between the two of them as she had when she was a child; her own chair felt like it was shrinking around her, like it would eventually swallow her alive.

"Of course I know that," Nadia said, instead of, *I'm so sorry*, or, *Don't worry about me*, or, *How far along is it? What can I do?* "Why would I think it was my fault?"

Samir sighed heavily. When he passed his hand over his face, Nadia noticed—really noticed—that his fingers were slimmer than she could ever remember them being, that his cheeks had sunken in and hollowed out. "I don't know, Nadia," he said, "sometimes children blame themselves for these things. I was just trying to be helpful."

"But I don't need you to help me," Nadia said, honestly confused. "I'm an adult, I—"

"Don't you dare antagonize your father at a moment like this," Rashida hissed. "My god, are you that selfish?"

It was the most alive she'd looked in the entire conversation. Hell, it was the most alive she'd looked since Nadia had gotten in the night before, when she'd bounded out of the airport looking for Samir's car in the pickup line only to see her mother, grim-faced, behind the wheel. And for a moment, Nadia thought about playing into it; her mother's eyes were narrowed but Nadia could tell they were wet, and her fingers, too, were thinner than Nadia remembered them being before. Maybe Rashida needed this. Maybe the best thing Nadia could do was to be a lightning rod for her despair, her anger, her fear.

But then she caught sight of Samir on the couch, his gaze hurt, almost comically betrayed, and a hot spike of hatred for her mother shot through Nadia's heart—selfish, after all. Rashida was many things, but for better or worse, she was rarely wrong.

"I was going to say that I should be helping *you*," Nadia said. "Jesus Christ, Mom."

"Don't talk to your mother that way," Samir said, but he sounded— wearied. Tired of her. Tired of both of them, maybe. "I'm going to bed."

They'd waited, Nadia's parents, until the third day of the visit to ask her to move home. They'd waited until she knew every detail of their plan, until she'd been briefed on the diagnosis and their options, how they'd found and fought for a coveted spot at an incredible treatment facility in Florida.

They'd gone over every piece of their estate, made her read their living wills in case something happened, forced her through their lives with a fine tooth comb and then, at the end of all that, played it like they'd simply forgotten that someone would need to mind the house while they went away. They played it like an afterthought, as though she wouldn't know them as the meticulous people who raised her, and expected her to simply agree, and forgive them.

Which she did, of course. Of course she did. But it sits heavy in her chest, that wearied tone of her father's voice and the fact that they felt it necessary to manipulate her into coming home, that they didn't trust her enough to ask her outright. They should have known, anyone should have known that she would do whatever was necessary—what kind of daughter was she, to make them think otherwise? To make her father so tired of her, when everything else on his plate was so exhausting?

She knows it's not her fault, that it couldn't possibly be, that nothing works that way and she's being stupid and she should let it go. But she's still here, isn't she, choking back tears over a package of fucking— allergy medication—because maybe if she'd been better, somehow, if she'd come home more or paid more attention on their Skype calls, if she'd become a doctor like Samir wanted instead of a chef, she would have seen the signs. Maybe if she hadn't been so busy sleeping with every bi-curious girl in Chicago and wasting her time on a passion project instead of a real career and—

"Nadia?" Mim calls. She sounds close, like she's out in the hall—how did Nadia miss the sound of her climbing up the stairs?—and Nadia jumps, starts, wipes hastily at her eyes. She's not fast enough, though, or maybe just needs to be more thorough, because when Mim steps into the bathroom with two beers in her hands, her face falls. It's painfully obvious that she can tell Nadia's been crying, which just makes Nadia want to—hit her in the face, maybe. Scream until her voice gives out. Cry some more.

"Sorry," Mim says very quietly, looking as though she wants to sink into the floor. "I just—I'm so sorry, I just was hoping to grab the—I didn't mean to interrupt—"

"I thought we fucking agreed you'd stop doing that." Nadia growls this, hoping it will hide any hitch in her voice; it doesn't. She shoves the pills at Mim and snaps, "I mean, fuck, I'm, what, sitting up here feeling sorry for myself when you're downstairs asphyxiating and you don't think you're justified in coming and looking for me?"

"It's okay," Mim say quickly, "I didn't mind waiting—or, I mean, obviously I did or I wouldn't be here but I didn't, it's fine, you don't have to—"

"Please don't," Nadia says.

"Right," Mim says. "Got it."

Nadia should say something else—should at the very least give Mim permission to take one of the stupid allergy pills before she actually does die—but her mother has her pegged, all right: she's too selfish for something like that. She just takes one of the beers from Mim's hand and climbs out the window, crawls over to the edge of the roof and lets her legs dangle as she lights a cigarette and tries hard to think of nothing at all.

She's... surprised, but not displeased, when she hears Mim clamber out the window a few minutes later. "Kinda thought you'd leave."

"I thought about it," Mim admits after a second. "But—well, I didn't want to be rude." Nadia snorts—of course, *she's* the rude one—and then sighs when Mim hastily adds, "But I can go, if you wanted me to go I can totally—"

"Shut up and drink your beer," Nadia says, and Mim swallows, nods, does.

The street always looks so benign from up here, still and sleepy. That's why it's been Nadia's favorite spot in the whole house since she was a kid, for all that it used to give Rashida a heart attack to see her sitting up here unprotected.

From here, nothing has to be as it truly is—dark windows can mean rest instead of absence, lit ones togetherness instead of heated argument. It's a fool's errand but the only one Nadia truly allows herself, since she's a fool too often by accident and thus doesn't merit any extra allotment. It's nice, though, she thinks. It's nice to have a few moments, every now and again, to let herself pretend she believes the fiction of this place. After all, it paints a better picture of her than she'll ever measure up to, sketches her out as a devoted daughter with passion, drive, a life perfectly in order that she selflessly left behind. The messy reality—that she is selfish and sorry and scared most of the time, that her father still hasn't replied to her text message and it is eating at her insides, that she resents being made to leave Chicago but was only too happy to desert her empty apartment—wouldn't fit, and it's hard, even for her, to deny that it feels good sometimes to cast it off.

"I don't want you to think that I sit around here rending my fucking garments or anything all the time," Nadia says, after a long while. "This is the first time anything like that has happened in a long time. Frankly, I blame you."

Mim looks at her sideways.

"I seriously don't. You infected me."

"Who says I cry?"

"Everything about you," Nadia says, flat. "Literally every last thing. You scream 'crier,' I'm sorry to be the first one to tell you."

Mim sighs. "You're not."

"The first one to tell you?"

"Sorry," Mim clarifies, "although, that too, and I'd have to be pretty stupid not to have noticed myself. I always cry when I'm angry, which just makes me angrier, which just leads to more crying, you know? And then suddenly everyone thinks you're trying to manipulate them when you're not, you're just—I don't know. Impossible to take seriously. Embarrassing." Her mouth twists bitterly. "My mom's the same way. Or used to be, anyway; maybe she's not anymore. It's not like we really talk."

"Huh," Nadia says, because she doesn't know what else to say—her mother, for all her shortcomings, has never been non-communicative. If anything, she's been overly communicative, leaving Nadia wishing she would just *shut up* sometimes, a thought that feels particularly ungrateful in the wake of this little confession. Not that Nadia knows that it is one—maybe it's not. Maybe Mim thinks nothing of the fact that she and her mother don't speak, and Nadia's sense of discomfort about the whole thing is entirely personal.

She doubts it, though. Nadia doesn't often know the right thing to say, or how best to put someone at ease, but she almost always knows what people mean. And misery, of course, loves company. She recognizes it in the hunch of Mim's shoulders, the clip of her voice, the way her fingernails are slowly shredding the label of her beer bottle.

"Are *you* okay?" Nadia says, because why the hell not. She figures she owes it to her.

Mim smiles wanly in the fading light. "Sure."

"Sure," Nadia says, sardonic, and holds her beer in the air. When Mim clinks her bottle against it in an unspoken toast, Nadia releases a breath she didn't know she was holding.

October

In the nine weeks Mim has been working for the Juniper Action Fund, she has learned the following things:

1. The Halloween fundraiser is *the* event of the year, Mimosa, it is just *the* event, so of course it's absolutely paramount that everything happen absolutely perfectly, don't you agree? I knew you would, I'm so glad I hired you, we just work so *well* together, don't you think?
2. The theme selection for the Halloween party is without question the most important decision you will preside over all year and I simply cannot stress enough, Mimosa dear, how important it is that you take it incredibly seriously.
3. What?! No, of course the theme is not masquerade every year, who told you that? It was that Bahjat girl, wasn't it. I mean, of course her family situation is horrible; poor, poor Samir—it's a sweet thing you're trying to do, but *honestly*.
4. After careful deliberation, we've decided this year's theme is: masquerade! Aren't you just thrilled? I think it's going to be a really incredible party.

5. Mimosa darling, I understand that you were raised without some of the luxuries we're currently afforded, and I know that the suggestion comes from a good place, I do, but we simply cannot reuse any of last year's decorations. Why, none of them would fit the theme! What's more, I have no earthly idea where they even are. I think we donated them to the homeless.

6. Well *I* certainly don't know, Mimosa, I don't manage the money, I only raise it! You can ask Danny if you really want but honestly, honey, I really wouldn't worry, the specifics of what their donation is going towards aren't going to matter to most people. The Fund does all kinds of good for the community, everyone knows that.

7. Oh sweetheart, I'm sorry, I should have explained—the *theme* is masquerade, but of course the party itself is a general costume party. That's a lovely dress and I'm sure you'll find another use for it but you just cannot show up dressed for a masquerade when the *theme* is masquerade. It's just... well, I don't want to use the word tacky because of course you don't know any better, but that is what we're dealing with here, unfortunately. You understand.

8. Mimosa, this is much better! Where did you find this, I simply love the design—actually, honey, could I be a horrible pain and ask you to return it? It's just that I wouldn't want us to show up wearing the same thing and this is just exactly what I've been looking for. Actually, now that I think about it, since you'll be helping out behind the scenes you don't have to wear a costume if you don't want to. It's a lot of unnecessary hassle for you, especially with me making you change things around so much. Do what's best for you, sweetheart.

9. Oh, oh, my costume's arrived! I just have to show you, I had it custom made and I absolutely adore it—what? Oh, that costume

I had you return, I completely forgot about that. I ended up preferring this, you know how it is, people change their minds. I think I did you a favor though, really; that color would not have been flattering with your skin tone.

10. What do you mean, you decided not to wear a costume? Mimosa! It's a costume party!

It's more than a little disturbing to Mim that so much of her inner monologue has begun to sound like Gale, but maybe that's how it works. First you start thinking like someone, and then you start talking like them, and before you know it you, too, wear $2,000 shoes and live with your loving husband and children in a beautiful house always filled with fresh flowers. Baby steps, that's how Mim is going to achieve her dreams. Baby. Steps.

"You understand that the woman is insane," Nadia says, the morning of the fundraiser. She's standing in the very picked-over women's section of the local costume shop, helping Mim locate an acceptable last minute outfit. "Like, this is classic crazy-making behavior. She wants you to buy a costume, but she doesn't, but she does—no, Jesus, not that one. You have to ride the line between slutty and classy."

"I don't think this is slutty," Mim says, scowling down at the lady gangster costume. It comes with a hat.

"No," Nadia agrees, "that is neither slutty nor classy, which is why it has to go back in the pile. If you want to go twenties, go with a flapper dress."

"It comes with a hat," Mim says in a small voice.

Nadia sighs, exasperation mitigated by the slight smile curling her lips, and tugs the costume out of Mim's hand. "Here," she says, shoving her own pile of selections at Mim, "try these."

"Strawberry Shortcake?" Mim says, holding up the costume and grimacing. "Really?"

Nadia grins. "Yeah, that one is punishment for looking at the Native American costume. You have to try it on now, though, those are the rules."

"I didn't," Mim splutters, mortified, "I wasn't going to—I didn't try that costume *on*, I know it's—very—offensive! And wrong! I just, I was only *looking*—"

"God, be whiter, I dare you." Nadia rolls her eyes, puts a hand on Mim's shoulder, and shoves her towards the dressing room. "Spare me the wine and just skip to the cheese, yeah?"

"Was that a cheesecake joke?"

"That was a food joke," Nadia says, "if I wanted to make a cheesecake joke I would've grabbed that Playboy costume—you know, the little gold number with the—"

"Changing now!" Mim says hastily, and heads for the dressing rooms to the sound of Nadia's ringing laughter.

It's—weird, this thing with her and Nadia. It's weird, but Mim can't tell if it's weird because it's actually weird or weird because... well. Mim's had *friends* before, it's not as though she's spent her life as some kind of pathetic hermit, but it's kind of been a while. Dell didn't like her old friends, eventually talked her around to seeing that they weren't particularly kind or supportive people, that they would only abandon her in her time of need—which, now that she thinks about it, had been what *his* friends did to her after they broke up, but whatever. The point is that it's been a while, since she had someone to come shopping for costumes with. Or drink beer with. Or... anything.

On the other hand: "You know it makes you pretty spineless to be doing this right now, right?" Nadia calls into her dressing room. "I mean, she is crazy and you're doing what she says so that sort of makes you crazy, I'm just saying."

"She's not crazy," Mim says, tugging the Strawberry Shortcake costume on over her head. Ugh. Awful. "She's, I don't know. Intense. She's got a lot on her plate."

"Oh, yeah." Mim can hear the eye roll. "I'm so sure. Just backbreaking work, this party planning stuff. How *can* she stand it?"

"I just mean—you know. It's a lot of pressure, and I don't mind if she takes some of it out on micromanaging me, okay?"

"Which makes you—what?" At this point, Mim has spent enough time with Nadia to know this is not a question she's supposed to answer, so she busies herself with cocking the costume hat Just So until Nadia finishes, "Survey says: spineless."

"Yeah, yeah," Mim says. "Let's get this over with, okay?"

She opens the door. Nadia laughs so hard a staff member comes to check on them. It's going to be a long morning.

The thing is that they don't really share much personal information. They spend a lot of time together but when Mim drops Nadia off outside a restaurant later that morning, she realizes she doesn't even know if it's where Nadia works. She assumes, since there's no other reason for Nadia to direct her to a closed restaurant at 10:45 in the morning, but she doesn't actually *know*.

Mim knows Nadia's order from the Chinese place, and what she's likely to pick on Netflix, but she has no idea what her plans are for the future, or whether or not she enjoyed high school. Mim knows what times and days of the week Nadia's free to hang out, but hasn't heard a peep about her father's cancer since that night with the cat fight. God, Mim doesn't even know—

98

"What are you wearing to the thing tonight?" she asks, as Nadia starts to climb out of the car. "I mean, you have to have a costume already, or you would've been looking too. So what is it?"

"Who says I'm even going?"

"Are you going?" Mim has learned, recently, that Nadia is a incredibly bad liar—if asked a direct yes or no question, she will invariably give an honest answer whether she wants to or not.

True to form, Nadia scowls at her and mutters, "*Yes*. I have to, my mother would fly across the country and murder me if I skipped out."

Mim grins. "So…"

"*So…*" Nadia parrots back at her, rolling her eyes.

"*So*, what are you wearing?"

Nadia's gaze from the other side of the car goes evaluative, and then considering, and then wicked.

"Tell you what," she says, "I bet you that you can't figure out who I am tonight."

"Oh, you are so on," Mim says. "What do I get when I win?"

"When *I* win," Nadia says, "you get a healthy ego check and a sense of shame to carry around with you for the rest of your life."

"So—bragging rights."

"Throw in a free dinner," Nadia says, grinning and jerking her thumb at the restaurant. "I mean, if you think you can cook anything that won't kill me when you inevitably lose. Obviously in the unlikely event that you somehow beat me I'll make you something here, but I'd hate to die in Ruth's kitchen for my trouble."

"Sometimes I think Ruth is going to die in Ruth's kitchen," Mim says grimly. She's only seen her aunt twice in the last month— it is, apparently, fall festival season, so Ruth is off god knows where with god knows whom doing, presumably, god knows what drugs—and both times she was standing at the refrigerator, eyes glazed, eating leftover takeout straight out of the box. "So at least you won't be alone."

"Comforting," Nadia says, and does, this time, make it all the way out of the car. "Bye."

"See you later," Mim calls after her, and can't help but laugh when Nadia yells back, "No you won't!"

The gala starts at eight, and Mim's supposed to be there no later than 6:15—she finds herself stumbling out of the house at five after six, costume in one hand and makeup bag in the other. It's a nice night, downright balmy for the end of October, and there are already costumed children swarming the street. Some of them are climbing out of cars parked at the end of the cul-de-sac, and Mim realizes after a moment of thought that this must be one of the wealthy neighborhoods frequented by Halloween tourists, families looking for better candy than their own streets can afford.

She herself was one of those kids once, and an obscure sense of guilt throbs at the base of her spine as she climbs into the car, pulls down to the end of the driveway, and stops to stare up at her aunt's darkened house. Some child, probably, will misread the clear signal the lack of lighting is meant to provide and come knock on the door tonight; instead of getting a treat, or even a trick, they'll just get that cold moment of disappointment, trickling down the back of their neck like rainwater until they shake it off at the next house. It's stupid that Mim feels responsible, but she does. She can't help but think of her own childhood Halloweens, her mother waiting impatiently in the car and her friends chattering excitedly beside her, and how she promised herself she'd never be the person she is right now, leaving a house abandoned at the beginning of the night.

Someone taps on her window. Mim accidentally puts her fist down on the horn in surprise and the window-tapper, unsurprisingly, falls back a few steps and starts hurrying away. The windows of Mim's car (Ruth's old car, but who's asking) are slow to come down—broken after years of being opened for a smoke, according to Ruth—and so Mim finds herself waving two fingers out of the miniscule crack that appears, yelling, "Wait, sorry, accident!" at the retreating figure.

Who turns, and—oh. Wow. It's Gale's daughter Rebecca, Mim's almost sure of it, but she's... Mim's met Rebecca before, but she's been surly, taciturn, and never once looked like this. In all their previous interactions, Rebecca has been wearing an outfit so ever-present Mim's kind of started to think of it as her uniform: scuffed Chucks, black skinny jeans, a baggy gray sweatshirt that hangs down to her knees, with her hair braided into cornrows or, after summer ended, pulled back into a tight bun.

Tonight, Rebecca is still wearing the Chucks, but everything else is startlingly different: a pink A-line dress underneath a white cardigan, a pair of strappy summer heels in her hand, hair down and relaxed into a style that closely resembles Mim's own go-to look. In fact, the entire ensemble is unsettlingly reminiscent of something Mim would wear, and something about it sets her teeth on edge with nerves.

Still, she is, if by technicality only, the adult in this situation, so she braces herself and calls, "Sorry! You need a ride to the thing?" through the crack in the window. Rebecca stares at her for a moment and then nods, jerkily, and walks back over to the car.

"Thanks," she says, sliding into the passenger seat, and then, grudgingly, mutters, "Sorry if I scared you before." Mim almost doesn't hear it, she says it so far under her breath, but still: it's something.

"No problem," Mim says.

"Great," Rebecca snaps.

Silence.

"Excited for the party?" Mim says eventually.

"I'd rather be mauled by wild dogs," says Rebecca.

Shutting up, Mim decides, is the better part of valor, and she resolves firmly not to say anything else unless Rebecca speaks first. Teenagers, after all, are unpredictable creatures at best — god knows Mim had been, for all she sometimes feels like she never really stopped being a teenager, just got stuck with adult problems and heartburn if she eats tomatoes after eight. A quiet drive to the Club is the way to play this, and Mim can handle silence, even if it is weighted and awkward. She absolutely can. She is not hardwired in any way to cut tension of this variety by opening her stupid trap and —

"It's been really nice getting to know your mom over the last few months," Mim says. Goddamn it.

Rebecca scoffs. "Wow. I'm, like, *so* happy for you."

"Right," Mim says. She casts around frantically for a subject change — they're only a few minutes away from the Club, but maybe she can salvage this somehow — and comes up with nothing but a comment on Rebecca's costume.

The problem is, Mim's not strictly sure what Rebecca's wearing *is* a costume; Gale's told her more than once that the way Mim normally sees Rebecca dressed isn't her typical attire. "Such a sweet girl, but you know how it is with teenagers," Gale will murmur, winking, when Rebecca's out of earshot. "She's so determined everyone see her as a serious artist, that's the only reason she dresses that way — left to her own devices she just loves makeup and heels, like the all other girls. What you see is only an affectation. You know what I'm saying, don't you?"

In truth, Mim hasn't known once, but she's always nodded along; it tends to be the best course when Gale asks that particular question. Seeing Rebecca now, though, Mim's even more confused—what she's wearing looks like a costume on her, from the way it fits to the way she moves in it, stilted and uncomfortable, awkward. Teenagers in general are awkward creatures but Mim sees none of the soft happiness in Rebecca's posture that a pretty dress always gave her at that age. She sees only misery out of the corner of her eye—in the hunch of Rebecca's shoulders and the tightness in her jaw—and it makes Mim uncomfortable, distantly sick to her stomach for reasons she can't identify.

Still, it's something to say and she's almost certain, so Mim says, "Hey, I really like your costume," as they pull into the parking lot.

Rebecca stiffens and then relaxes so fast Mim wouldn't catch it if she weren't paying attention; when she smiles, it's more of a grimace, and Mim has to bite the inside of her cheek to keep from wincing at the expression.

"Thanks," Rebecca says as she opens her car door. Mim can't be sure, but she's pretty sure it's an imitation of herself, high-pitched and unflattering. "I just thought it would be funny to come dressed as the daughter my mom always wanted, you know?"

"Um," says Mim.

Rebecca's expression drops, just for a second, into something sad, too old for her years; then she rolls her eyes and slams the car door shut. The windows are closed again, but Mim doesn't need to hear to see what Rebecca's saying: "Enjoy your fucking party."

103

Mim's had a dream like this party, she thinks. Maybe that accounts for the strange sense of déjà vu that sets in as she watches all the impeccably dressed couples rotate together across the dance floor. They look unnatural, almost animatronic, as though Mim has found herself inside a glass-cased construction of what one of these elegant evenings might look like. There's lively orchestral music from the band in the corner, and the costumes are all billowing and elaborate. Of course, they're only play-acting: this isn't a court ball, just a pale imitation of one, a bunch of suburban housewives making their own sad attempt at sophistication.

And then Mim remembers, and has to stifle a laugh:. Zoe Rosenfeld's Bat Mitzvah. Seventh grade. *That's* what this this evening makes her think of, and the realization leaves her practically choking on her champagne. Gale would be horrified, of course—Mim feels a little guilty for even thinking of it—but after all, there *is* something slightly childish about the whole affair. Or, no, maybe not childish—structured? Overdone? It feels like a room full of people playing dress up—which is, obviously, exactly what it is.

Of course, she thinks wryly, Zoe Rosenfeld's Bat Mitzvah had hardly been a banner evening for her. Mim had been odd at thirteen, her shape as awkward as her non-existent social skills; she'd spent most of that night in the corner of the room, chewing on her thumbnail and worrying at the taffeta hem of her party dress. She'd thought, with the wide-eyed, idiotic hope of children who don't know better, that that was how things worked—that if she simply stood around, waited flush with enough wanting, that some boy would come along and sweep her off her feet.

No boy had, obviously, not then and not later. Not in high school, when she stood in the corner at dances chewing on her thumbnail and worrying at the spaghetti straps of her dress; not in college, when she stood in the corner at house parties chewing on her thumbnail and worrying at the ends of her dip-dyed hair. Until Dell sauntered into her life, too good to be true—literally, it turned out—and after Dell... well. Better to stand here now, chewing on her thumbnail behind the nametag table, than to risk another situation like that.

"Jesus," comes a voice just behind her, laughter in the tone. When Mim turns her head Nadia is leaning against a nearby pillar, arms crossed, looking amused. "A little on-point, isn't it?"

Mim scowls and looks back to the table she's supposed to be manning, putting on a fixed smile for the party guests. "You picked it; don't be an asshole."

"I picked it at the store," Nadia says. "You were wearing UNC sweats underneath and had Cheeto gunk on the side of your face; I didn't really get the full picture."

"Hey!" Mim says. She wipes self-consciously at her face, never mind that it's hours after the fact, and feels herself go scarlet. "What do you mean, Cheeto gunk? I don't even eat Cheetos, it's the polite thing to tell someone when—oh, damn, hold on—"

"That is some mouth on you, young lady!" snaps Mrs. Craddock, approaching the table with the air of someone who will not require, but still demand, assistance in the art of locating their nametag. Behind Mim, Nadia snorts. "I knew I didn't like the look of you—just like Ruth, you know! It's all perfectly fine, and then bam! Burning down buildings! Swearing at party guests!"

"Ruth burned down a building?" Mim says, and ignores it when Nadia snorts again and whispers, low enough that only she can hear it, "I think the term is 'smoked out.'"

"Well of course Ruth didn't burn down a building," Mrs. Craddock snaps, snatching her nametag off the table. "It was a *figure* of *speech.*"

"Of course," Mim says, and Mrs. Craddock gives her a look and sniffs haughtily as she walks away. "Crazy old bat," Mim mutters under her breath.

Nadia starts to laugh, the kind of loud, unrestrained guffaw that has people turning to stare. Embarrassed, Mim turns to glare at her, which, she is surprised to find, only makes Nadia laugh harder.

"Be *quiet*," she hisses, but Nadia just keeps laughing.

"The ponytail," Nadia gasps, doubling over, "the *pearls*," and, well, yes, Mim thinks, patting her hair nervously in a way that somehow—who knows why—sets Nadia off on another laughing jag; fine. Maybe this *is* a little overboard. But it was Nadia who suggested the poodle skirt in the first place, muttering in dark amusement to herself about Stepford wives and matching the profile, and Mim didn't want the costume to come off the way she was sure Nadia intended it: as a joke, or worse, a mockery. She likes being Nadia's friend—it's better, certainly, than being her enemy—but she knows a saboteur when she sees one. Nadia wouldn't even mean it, Mim's almost sure, but she can just see it: one of Nadia's little jokes blowing up in Mim's face and Gale giving her that *look*, the one she reserves for disappointments and panhandlers.

She figured, though, that the best defense to perceived sarcasm was a good offense, so she committed to the costume whole-heartedly: she has the pearls—fake, of course—and the shoes, the knee-socks, the whole thing. There's even a scarf in her hair, although it is, admittedly, not pink so much as pink tie-dye—it was the only one she could find in Ruth's closet.

Angel Neary and her triplets approach the table, and Mim tunes out Nadia's slowing laughter in favor of avoiding the stare of what she's come to think of as The Creepy One. She doesn't know his name—she can never remember any of their names, because they are always presented, by everyone including their parents, as "The Boys"—but he is easily distinguishable from his brothers due to his ever-present, preternaturally unsettling stare. Since moving to Barn Ridge, Mim has observed The Creepy One:

- Lighting small pieces of paper on fire in the parking lot behind the Episcopalian church;
- Lighting small pieces of paper on fire in the parking lot behind the elementary school;
- Lighting small pieces of paper on fire in the parking lot behind the Arby's;
- Speedwalking menacingly after at least four pigeons and—and!— one red-breasted robin that Mim is fairly sure was injured;
- Throwing rocks off his roof;
- Throwing rocks off his bicycle;
- Throwing rocks off his roof *at his own bicycle*, an act so senseless that Mim lies awake at night some nights and marvels at it; and
- Rooting through her trashcans.

This last—and, indeed, the leering way he'd crowed, "Your bras!" when Mim had asked what he was looking for—led her, slightly guiltily, to mention him to Gale over lunch one afternoon. Gale had shuddered expressively. "Foul boy," she agreed, "Matthew or Paul or whoever he is, isn't it just impossible to remember their names? Of course there's no way to tell them apart in any case, but it's as though every time I see them they're introduced—"

"As 'The Boys,'" Mim finished for her, thrilling when Gale looked delighted.

"Why, that's it *exactly*," she said, "you always do know just what I mean. Anyway, just do your best to ignore him; it's a pity for his poor mother that he's so disturbed, but the worst thing one can do for a child is to feed their negative behavior with attention."

Mim tries to take this advice to heart now, as the horrible little creep leans across the table while his mother is distracted and says, in a low voice, "Hello, Mimosa."

"Ew," says Nadia, stepping up to the table and—to Mim's deep surprise—cuffing The Creepy One lightly on the side of the head. "Luke, what the hell? Haven't you guys outgrown this yet?"

"No," says The Creepy One, who is… somehow standing next to the triplet Nadia just smacked, who now appears perfectly normal. Even so, it takes until he drops the affect and third triplet picks it up for Mim to really understand what's happening.

"You take turns," Mim says wearily. "Being creepy. To freak me out."

"Well, not just you, you're not special or anything," says the one Nadia identified as Luke. Except then he turns to Nadia and says, "I can't believe you think I'm Luke," so, maybe not.

"I know you're Luke, kid," Nadia says easily, nodding to the other two. "And you're Peter, and you're Silas, and you're going to take Mim off your list of rubes, okay?"

"Whatever," says Silas, "you're not our *mom*."

"Yeah, but I know where you hide the shit you don't want your mom to find," Nadia says, "*and* I know who broke Mrs. Ashcraft's clematis trellis that summer, Peter Neary, so if I were you I'd convince your brothers to back off."

There is a whispered conference between The Boys—Mim lost track of which one went with which name the minute they broke their line to huddle—and then, as one, they scuttle slouchily away. It's left to poor Angel to gather all of their nametags, which she does with an air of bad, rushed graced that matches her poorly chosen shade of eye shadow.

"That was terrifying on so many levels," Mim says, turning to Nadia, whose eye shadow is, of course, impeccable. "But also: amazing. Thanks. You should have come dressed as a wizard."

"Nah," Nadia says, shrugging. "I used to babysit for them, is all. They're not bad kids, just bored, and, you know." She waves a broad, encompassing hand. "Teenager-y."

"Still," Mim says, "the wizard costume would've been fitting—which, hey. That reminds me—you gave me this whole big song and dance about trying to spot you in the crowd, what was that about? You're not exactly in disguise."

Nadia grins. "Oh. I've got a buddy who has one of those full gorilla suits, you know? He bought it off a guy in college, so there's like puke stains and shit all over it, it's disgusting. Reeks of weed and B.O. in there, but I thought it would be worth it for the looks on people's faces."

"You have a sickness," Mim says. "So what happened? Emergency Planet of the Apes party?"

There's a long beat as Nadia's smile falters. "Oh," she says, her voice unusually small, "uh, no. I just decided to go with a different costume."

Mim looks Nadia up and down, confirming her initial assessment: black motorcycle boots, black jeans. A white t-shirt and the ubiquitous leather jacket, black sunglasses hooked in an eyelet on the collar. The only variant from the usual is her hair, slicked back into a French braid with a little pompadour at the top in what Mim assumes is her "formal party" style, the white streaks tucked into the style in such a way as to be all but invisible.

"The costume of yourself?" Mim chides jokingly. "Lazy. Some of us went to an effort here."

And it's weird, just for a second: the way Nadia's whole face falls. The way she turns, just slightly, as though trying to hide herself while she shutters it. It's not like Nadia to take offense at something like

109

that—practically their entire relationship is built on trading insults, and anyway she couldn't care less about this party, about any of the others like it. This is just another command performance for Nadia so it doesn't make sense that she'd care about Mim calling her out.

"Look, I'm sorry, I was only joking around, I didn't mean to—"

"Oh my god, stop," Nadia says. She smiles, but Mim, startled, thinks it looks false. "I finally found a way to turn off that feature, don't start again. I want a drink, how about you? Drink? Great, I'll be back."

She vanishes into the crowd, and Mim, beset by arriving guests, has no way to follow.

It's an hour before Rebecca, sulky and sour-mouthed, stops by the nametag table to relieve Mim of her duties. "My mom says you're supposed to socialize or whatever," she mutters, knocking Mim with her shoulder to push her out of the way. "So, you know. Get lost."

"Do you need me to explain—"

"How to pass out name tags?" Rebecca sneers. "Yeah, I'd be lost without you. I'm a helpless baby just looking for someone to hold my hand."

"S-sorry," Mim says, and hates herself for stammering, for being so freaked by this obviously unhappy teenager. "I was just trying to—you know what, I'll just go."

Rebecca doesn't even reply to that, just uncaps the black Sharpie sitting on the table and starts drawing on her arm. Sighing, Mim picks up her empty wineglass and starts looking around for Nadia. She's got to be around, but Mim hasn't seen her since she brought her drink over; she made some shitty excuse about having to talk to people, like Mim doesn't know she'd rather do anything but. There was something strange about her tone of voice, the set of her shoulders, and if Mim could just find her and figure out what—

"Mimosa! There you are!"

Well, so much for that.

Mim turns, unsurprised to see Gale beaming at her. She's bedecked in a costume Mim's never seen before, a gorgeous, shimmering green dress and a feathered mask—a peacock, she realizes. Of course. It's a fitting outfit for her, but seeing it leaves Mim flush with an unfamiliar bitterness. After all the trouble with the costumes, all the work she put in, it's a little annoying to see Gale wearing something that clearly took weeks to create.

But that's stupid of Mim, probably, not to mention—well—it's not as though someone like Gale is under any obligation to listen to someone like her. Mim is lucky, really, that she's been given the opportunity to be as involved as she has been, and she pastes a smile on her face, determined not to let her momentary bad attitude ruin this moment.

"Hi, Gale," Mim says. It's crazy, but part of her expects to be corrected, to be told to back off to the less familiar Mrs. Ashcraft every time she says Gale's name. "I love your costume."

"Oh, sweetie, I'm *so* sorry you were stuck at that table for so long," Gale says, ignoring the compliment with the air of someone who has received too many to bother. She drapes an arm across Mim's shoulders and draws her towards a knot of people, talking all the while. "I told Rebecca to relieve you after fifteen minutes but of course, you know teenagers, they just don't understand the passage of time the way the rest of us do—oh, Bunny! Have you met Mimosa?"

The next hour passes in a blur of names and faces, of hearing herself presented to frighteningly impressive people; so, like most of the time

Mim spends with Gale. There is, she has discovered, a discernable pattern to the way Gale does this, a basic script:

GALE: Oh, [WHOMEVER]! Have you met Mimosa?
WHOMEVER: I can't say that I have.
GALE: Well, she's our new neighbor on Juniper, and of course she's been helping me at the JAF, we really couldn't do without her. Mimosa, this is [WHOMEVER], they're [some hideously important person who would never, ever speak to you if you weren't standing here with me, and could probably help you figure out, say, a paying job if you knew them better]!
MIM: Oh my god, hi, it's so nice to—
GALE: Oh, goodness, there's [SOMEONE ELSE]! [WHOMEVER], it was so lovely to see you. Do give me a call in the next few weeks, will you? Richard and I would just love to have dinner with you sometime.
WHOMEVER: Always a pleasure, Gale.
GALE [WHISPERING]: Oh, Mimosa, I shouldn't say anything, but [bloodcurdlingly horrible personal information about WHOMEVER].
MIM: Oh my god!
GALE: Hush, hush! Oh, forget I told you that.

Mim has never been particularly good with names, but she excels at both faces and remembering bloodcurdlingly horrible personal information. By the time Gale releases her, drawn away by Adriana Clausen-Godwin's insistence that Gale really *must* join her on the patio, Mim is identifying passing people in her head with such monikers as Ugly Birthmark Who Cheats On His Wife and Tall, Dark, and Embezzling.

Once she has once again found a safe corner in which to chew on her thumbnail, Mim finds herself wondering if perhaps the other children at Zoe Rosenfeld's Bat Mitzvah, lo those many years ago, were each and every one of them carrying some sort of dark secret. It would be in keeping with the theme, and certainly Mim had a number of terrible secrets of her own at age thirteen. Granted, they had largely been about personal hygiene, boys upon whom she had crushes, or wanting desperately for the popular girls to notice her, but they had without doubt been terrible.

Someone taps her on the shoulder, and Mim jumps, terrified that she's going to find Bad Hairpiece Who Should Never Be Left Alone With Young Women breathing down her neck. But it's just Danny, looking windblown and relaxed, wearing a pirate costume. Mim breaths a sigh of relief, and Danny's smile grows beneath his eye patch.

"What," he says, "am I a sight for sore eyes?"

"Oh, um," Mim says, and blushes. "No—or, I mean, that wasn't what I—just, you know. This is… a lot. It's just a lot."

Danny tilts his head, looks her over, and hands her his glass of champagne. "I think you need this more than I do. Didn't you ever learn the cardinal rule of these things?"

"Is it 'get drunk'?" Mim asks skeptically, looking at the champagne glass askance. "Because if it is, I haven't actually heard it, but I could have guessed."

"Sorry, Charlie," Danny says, grinning. "Close but no cigar. It's, 'Get drunk and avoid everyone.'"

"Don't think Gale would like that," Mim mutters, but it doesn't stop her from taking a long sip of champagne. "And anyway, I should probably find—"

"What," Danny says, "your costume buddy? She cut out of here ages ago; I saw her leave. Smart kid."

Mim blinks. "Costume buddy?"

"Yeah, come on," Danny says. "You're in a poodle skirt, she's a greaser, it's all very matchy-match. Cutesy. The Younger Generation sort of thing.

113

Did Gale put you up to it? Because you, no offense, I can see you going along with that, but that Bahjat girl doesn't seem like much of a joiner."

"Oh, no," Mim says, "she's not—I mean, she wasn't—"

"Although, I mean, I guess I don't know," Danny says. "I never really knew her very well. Anyway, she left. No point looking for her, is there?"

"I... guess not," Mim says slowly. Had Nadia really dressed to match her? That... Nadia had been wearing what she always wore; she would never dress to match anyone, unless it was for reasons of mockery, and she'd actually kept that to a minimum tonight before pulling her disappearing act. Which, Mim thinks with some irritation, was really kind of a dick move—she'd promised to stick around and keep Mim company.

"There's the spirit," Danny says, and winks his visible eye. "Now, I remember you hate golf and everything it stands for, but does that extend to actual golf courses? Because I've got to tell you, a golf course at night is a pretty cool place to be, but I'm not taking you out there if there's an arson risk to worry about."

"I'm too afraid of fire to be an arsonist," Mim says, which is a statement of alcohol-influenced honesty if ever there was one.

It doesn't seem to faze Danny, though, who jauntily offers her his arm and then, when she hesitates to take it, drops his lip into a dramatic pout. "Come on, kid," he says, "you can't tell me you'd rather hang out at this party then come exploring with me." Seeming to remember his costume, he strikes a Captain Morgan-esque pose. "Yo ho ho and a bottle of Veuve! We've sand traps to discover!"

"I, um," Mim says, and shifts on her feet, looking nervously over her shoulder. There's no question that she's tempted but she can see, through the French doors leading to the patio, Adriana Clausen-Godwin's head bent in conference with Gale's. "I just—I mean. What about your wife?"

114

Danny's face falls, and he sighs, rubs a hand against the back of his neck. When he speaks, it's rueful. "My wife isn't much for adventure these days. Plus, I mean, the golf course is old news to her, she's played through enough times."

"But won't she—mind?" Mim feels her comfort with him begin to fray at the edges—this reminds her too much of Dell, who was always coming up with excuses to spend time with other women, talking around direct questions; Dell, who got furious with her when she *did* ask—whose rages she eventually learned to avoid at all costs, until her whole life was spent tiptoeing around him and his anger.

"I just—I don't mean to overstep," she says, shaking herself out of her reverie, "I just wouldn't want to—um."

Danny smiles, but there's no humor in the expression—just a creasing sort of weariness that looks out of place on his boyish face. "Believe me, Mim—there's not much I could do that she'd mind anymore. Come on."

It's not a good idea. Mim tells herself that it's not a good idea over and over again as she follows Danny down the hallway, through a winding maze of silent corridors and out into the cool night air. It's not a good idea and she knows it, she's as sure of it as she's ever been of anything—but. But. She's never exactly been in a position to make this mistake before and there's something almost intoxicating about it, to be walking the golf course alone with a funny, gorgeous, married man—an act innocent enough on the face of it, except that of course it isn't at all.

And doesn't Mim deserve that? Hasn't she earned it? She's never thought of herself as sort of woman who would do anything like this, but it occurs to her as Danny laughs and takes off his shoes, runs ahead in barefooted abandon, that she's never actually been in a position to know. She's never been that woman. She's never, really, been a woman at all—she was a girl and then a girlfriend and now, these last few months, a failure. She has never been old enough to see herself as fully-grown—

115

not until right now, and the knowledge settles in at the base of her throat, a sweet and effervescent burning like good champagne.

"You know what's weird?" Mim says, before she can think better of it.

"Gale's kid?" Danny guesses, easy. "Those crab puffs? They were pretty weird, I stopped eating after the first one."

"No," Mim says; when Danny raises his eyebrows, she laughs. "Or, okay, I mean, yes, the crab puffs were weird and Rebecca is—look, that's not what I meant. I was just going to—you know what, it's better if I don't, probably. It's stupid."

"Well, now you've got me curious."

"I just," Mim says, "I was just thinking about... age, I guess. Something about this place makes me feel like—like—oh, I don't know how to explain it, I told you it was stupid. Like I'm letting myself grow up, I guess that's kind of what I mean. Not really, but kind of."

Danny cocks his head; in the darkness, Mim can't make out his eye color or see the fine lines at the corners of his mouth, but she can see one black eyebrow arching into a question. "You trying to make me feel old, Mimosa?"

"Not *trying*," Mim says, and it's flirtatious—womanly. Unlike her. "Anyway, it was just a thought."

"Well," Danny says. He sits down on the grass—the green, Mim thinks this part of a hole is called—and gestures expansively at the space next to him, meaning for her to sit. When she does, he lays all the way back, silent and smiling until she follows suit. "Far be it from me to discourage growing up in others. It's not an inclination of mine, you understand, but I'm led to believe there are some who find it enjoyable."

"I didn't say I was enjoying it."

"Sure you did," Danny says. "Sure you did."

He's quiet for a moment, and for once in her life, Mim is content to hold her tongue. She should be nervous, this is the sort of situation that should make her nervous—and some part of her, she thinks, is quite nervous indeed. It's just numbed, that feeling, wrapped in the surreality of this night and the cool grass beneath her fingers and the choice she cannot, *cannot* be thinking of making. She stares up at the sky and thinks about childhood; about Dell's hands underneath her sweater on a night just like this a thousand years ago; about Nadia's shoulder brushing against hers; about nothing at all.

"When I was a kid I didn't want to be anything," Danny says, apropos of nothing. "Not the President, not a firefighter, not anything. What do you think that says about a person?"

She thinks for a minute, chewing on her lower lip, before tentatively offering, "I think it says... whatever you want it to say?"

Danny snorts. "That's not a real answer."

She can't tell him the truth—that she thinks a child who aspires to nothing might be a child taught too young that his family's jam money would open whatever door he liked—and she tries to think of a flattering lie, something that will be what he wants to hear. What comes out, childish and embarrassing: "Do you know what you want now?"

He turns his head just enough to slant her a sidelong glance, and then punches out a hard sigh. "You know, I don't—I don't do the things I want to do, usually. I do what my wife wants, or what my family wants, and sometimes I do the things I think I should want, even if I don't."

"Oh," Mim says. "That sounds—that sounds—"

But she's distracted, her body feeling borrowed as she leans it closer to his, so that their arms are just barely touching, so that their fingers brush. She wasn't supposed to be the kind of person who does this sort of thing but then again, she thinks as he pushes himself up on one arm and leans over to kiss her—illicitly, on the golf course, under the moonlight, the bottle and his eye patch abandoned on the grass next to them—who is? It might as well be her, she figures. It might as well be her.

November

"D id you know," Nadia says, her voice slow with exhaustion, "that my mother's been painting her nails the same color every week for as long as I can remember?"

"I did not know that." Cory is playing the role of dutiful friend/ employer tonight, letting her sit at the bar and whine at him now that tomorrow's prep work is done. She doesn't know why he hasn't gone home yet. Some part of her thinks maybe he never does.

"Every week," Nadia repeats, instead of asking Cory if he has a secret apartment behind the meat locker or something. "Chanel Rouge Noir. I spilled a bottle of it in the living room when I was eleven."

"Oh yeah?"

"Yeah," Nadia says. She stares down at her own fingernails, ragged and unkempt. There's a scar from a cleaver accident on the knuckle of her left middle finger, a blue Band-Aid wrapped around a fresh cut on her right thumb. "Don't know why I told you that—it's not much of a story. I spilled it, she got mad, my dad calmed her down: there. That's it. The whole thing."

Cory shrugs, rubbing a glass clean. "You're right. Not much of a story."

"I just can't," Nadia says. She rubs her chin, cracks her neck, trying to decide what she wants to say. "Can you imagine, is what I'm saying. Doing the same thing every week for twenty years?"

"Sure I can," Cory says. He gestures at the glasses he's cleaning, the darkened window of the closed kitchen, the few lonely stragglers lingering at the still-open bar. "This shit is pretty much the same every night. Don't see me complaining."

"But twenty *years*," Nadia insists. "There's tradition, I get that, but didn't she ever — get sick of it? Want a change? I mean, you live your whole life with one man, in one house, with one kid, and you don't ever feel like at least, I don't know, trying a purple on for size?"

"Look, Bahjat, I know you're not asking me for advice on understanding women," Cory says with a roll of his eyes. "Because I am the least qualified person on earth for that crap. I've never figured out a single one of you. You're all Greek to me."

"My mother is not *women*," Nadia mutters darkly. "She's my *mother*."

"Tomato, tomahto." Cory shrugs. "Point being, I don't know why she paints her nails purple —"

"Red."

"Whatever damn color," Cory agrees. "I don't know why, and I don't care. She's not my mother, and unless you're gonna get to the point here, I'm going to go ahead and close up for the night."

Over the sound of the regulars groaning and protesting, Nadia sighs. "I don't think I even have a point."

"Great," Cory says, "then you can help me wipe the counters down."

It only takes them ten minutes to shoo the last customers out the doors of Blue Horizon and wrap themselves up in their winter clothes to step outside. It's cold, the frigid bite of the Ohio winter announcing itself in the midnight air, and Nadia pulls herself as far as she can into her jacket while Cory locks the door, only the tips of her fingers peeking out from beneath her sleeves. With the unspoken agreement of smokers everywhere, they each fish their respective pack out of their pockets and light one up, leaning back against the building in a companionable mutual slouch.

Nadia watches her breath, visible in the chill, hang in the air for a long moment before it vanishes, leaving only the smoke behind. She thinks: *Just because you've done something the same way a thousand times doesn't mean you have to do it forever.*

Cory finishes his smoke first, tosses the filter in a wide arc towards the parking lot, checks his watch. "Well, that's it for me," he says. "Enjoy your long weekend, but if you come in on Monday looking anything less than springtime fresh it's coming out of your paycheck—I'm not gonna be buying anything about your tryptophan coma or whatever the fuck. And Happy Thanksgiving, okay?"

"Yeah," Nadia says, and hopes that if he hears the crack in her voice, he'll blame the cigarette. "Yeah, man, you too."

The next day—Thanksgiving Day—Nadia layers two t-shirts and a flannel underneath her leather jacket and locks the door behind her. She's still cold fifteen minutes later, twenty, as she meanders her way along the bike paths that cut through the forest. She's not walking anywhere in particular, just wants to *be* someplace, so she can find herself doing something other than sitting grimly inside her parents' house thinking of what once was. She's always railed against that sort of person, who lives in the past rather than the present, and the idea that she's becoming one—that maybe everyone becomes one in the end, once their best days are behind them—rankles.

And god help her, Nadia thinks grimly, if her best days are behind her. God help her if these last twenty-six years are as good as it gets, because while she wouldn't call hers an unhappy life, there certainly hasn't been much in the way of joy. She had a childhood and it was fine; she went to school and it was fine; she left home and it was fine, maybe could have been better than fine, but then she was called back home again. Most of the time she's spent feeling truly alive has been with food in her hands, and maybe that's why this has gotten to her, this Thanksgiving alone: she could have done so much with it. She had so many plans.

When Nadia first moved back to Barn Ridge it was supposed to be temporary, only a couple of months, with Rashida promising they'd be back by Thanksgiving at the latest. Nadia's draft of the holiday menu had been, of course, a victory feast, a celebration of her impending freedom. They would've had a turkey brined in the salt of being stuck here, garlic mashed potatoes browned on top but pulled out of the oven just before they began to burn. She'd planned three different gravies—choice coming back into her life—and four stuffings for no particular symbolic reason; she just liked stuffing. Green beans for her father, stuffed mushrooms for her mother, a chocolate dessert and a tart with the last of the in-season apples—it would have been gorgeous. Perfect. A traditional American meal, laid out across the table, the only slice of the life her parents always wanted for her that she would ever be able to give them.

Then her parents' plans changed. Plans change sometimes; Nadia knows this. She knows. It's not like their absence is really a surprise, and she should be relieved, honestly. It should be a relief, that she got to skip brining the turkey and running the potatoes through the ricer—it's her *job*, she should be glad for the break.

She should be. But she isn't.

A duck waddles up to her, breaking her out of her reverie, and she scowls at it. Ducks, in her opinion, are upsetting, unnatural creatures — they're too indifferent to humans, neither frightened nor aggressive enough to be dismissed as normal members of the animal kingdom. Nadia always feels like they're plotting something.

"I could murder you," Nadia tells the duck, crossing her arms and glaring down at it. "I'd serve you with a mustard glaze, or maybe just fry your fatback into a really sharply spiced confit." The duck blinks at her, beady eyes empty of concern for its own mortality. Creepy little thing. "Either way you'd be dead, you know, and so whatever you're planning would die with you. I'm just saying. The end is nigh and going to be served on a bed of gently sautéed arugula."

"Sorry," says a familiar voice, threaded thick and warm with laughter, "I'm sorry, but are you threatening that duck?"

Nadia glances up and there's Mim, color high on her cheeks over a soft white scarf, the matching hat sliding up off her head in, honestly, a pretty unflattering way.

"He knows what he did," Nadia says. She glares at the duck one last time for good measure and then shrugs, letting one corner of her mouth tilt up. "Are you stalking me?"

Mim grins. "Says the lady threatening the ducks."

"Well, yeah. If I've got a stalker, I need to know — some people like to do their duck-threatening in peace."

"Doesn't seem like a very peaceful activity."

"Well," Nadia says, and shrugs again, as close to conceding the point as she's willing to get. "What are you doing out here, then, if not stalking me? Enjoying the scenery? Stalking somebody else?"

"You know you're the only stalkee for me," Mim says. Then she visibly bites back the urge to apologize, backpedal, or otherwise take the joke away. Nadia snorts.

"So, what, then," Nadia says, "Are you—hey, actually. Aren't you supposed to be doing the Ashcraft Thanksgiving thing? I can't believe Gale let you out. I thought she'd have you polishing the silver or something."

The easy smile slips from Mim's face, replaced by a tighter, more guarded expression. "Oh," she says, "well. I'm not actually doing that, as it turns out."

"She uninvited you?"

"No, nothing like that." Mim's got her hands in the air before Nadia can blink, as though she's trying to physically ward off any negative reaction. "I was always a last minute addition, you know, it wasn't like—it wasn't like I was an invited guest or anything. Someone else had cancelled, that's all, so Gale said I should come, and then they—un-cancelled, I guess, or something, so now there isn't a seat for me, that's all."

"Right," Nadia says, her mouth twisting sourly—she herself wouldn't go to the Ashcraft Family Thanksgiving Special if it were a paid gig, but she knows, can tell, that it was important to Mim. "Because you take up so much space."

Mim's little frown deepens and quietly, unhappily, she says, "I, um—look, *sorry*, I'm sorry, but is it okay if we just leave it? I know you and she don't really—but I just don't, I don't want this to be a thing, okay? Is that okay?"

"Sure," Nadia says, chastened. "Sure it is."

She starts walking again, slow, measured steps that Mim matches after a beat. They wander for a few minutes without speaking, neither one of them acknowledging that they're following the duck from earlier as it waddles in a direction that Nadia suspects is toward the lake. Sure enough, they turn a corner and the line of the trees—not so thick to begin with—breaks, revealing a small, horseshoe-shaped lake. It doesn't have a beach, per se; most of the water comes up against breaking walls, and the place where it does meet the land is more like a riverbank than anything else, all scraggly grass and water-smoothed stones.

"Christ," Nadia says, marveling a little to see it again. "It's like a fucking time machine, this town, I swear to god."

"A lot of good memories here?"

"Memories, anyway." Nadia sits, after a second, on the top of the nearest breaking wall; it's built out of crumbling gray shale, something that would make her nervous, with her feet dangling only a few feet above the water, if it hadn't looked exactly like this for years. "I spent most of my senior year of high school out here."

"Oh yeah?" Mim sits down next to her and looks around appraisingly. "I can see that, I guess. Looks like it might be a decent place to throw a party."

Nadia laughs. "Who said anything about a party? It was just me out here, most of the time. Well, me and a joint."

"Degenerate."

"Yeah, yeah. I'm sure you were Miss Perfect in high school," Nadia says, rolling her eyes. "'Oh, Mrs. Crabapple, I'm so sorry but I finished this assignment two weeks *early*, I hate to bother you but is there any chance I might get some additional homework—'"

"Shut *up*," Mim says, but she's laughing. "Actually, I was kind of a problem student, if you must know."

"Oh, you were not."

"I was," Mim says, sounding sorry—sorrier than a person should sound about something that happened so long ago. "I mean, my grades were—fine—it was just. I had a hard time."

"Not, I assume, because you were smoking joints out by your equivalent of this lake during class," Nadia guesses, and Mim laughs again.

"No," she says, "not because of that. Just—well, it doesn't matter. Mostly I just—I don't know. There were all these things I wanted to do and I didn't. I didn't know how to do them, I guess. I—look, it's stupid. Forget it. I don't want to talk about it."

She hunches in around herself then, knees folding up to her chest, the tassels of her scarf brushing against the ground, and too late Nadia figures out something she should have worked out from day one. It's not as though it's the first time—Nadia can't help but miss things about people sometimes, when so much is tucked away beneath customs and niceties she's never fully been able to parse—but it stings anyway, particularly strongly in this case, to have been wrong.

From the day they met Nadia had Mim pegged as a social climber, the sort of girl who proves the adage, "It's not what you know but who." It's been her least favorite thing about Mim, the piece of her Nadia had to accept the idea of swallowing before they could become friends, but she realizes, looking at the soft curve of her spine, that she was wrong from the start. Mim tries like hell to make her personality something malleable, something she can change to suit the circumstances, and it never really occurred to Nadia to wonder *why* before now. But she can recognize the aftermath of ostracization just as well in someone else as she can in the mirror. What an odd, jumpy child Mim must have been, to become this odd, jumpy adult.

"Do you want to come over?" Nadia asks unthinkingly—no, not quite unthinkingly. But there's nothing to do but press on now, so she says, "Just, you know. No one should be alone on Thanksgiving, and I was just going to, I don't know, pick up some food and watch old movies or something, but—"

"Yes," Mim says, and then seems to realize she's interrupted. "I mean—sorry to—I just, yes. Whatever you're doing sounds great."

"Great," Nadia says.

"Great," Mim says, and smiles.

The grocery store, unsurprisingly, is mobbed.

"Oh my god," Mim says, her knuckles gone white around the cart handle like she can use it to protect her from the hoards. "Is it always like this?"

"On Thanksgiving? Probably." Nadia picks up a lemon from a display, sniffs it, winces, puts it back, and then repeats the process with another lemon. "Never been dumb enough to come in here today before. I'll tell you what, though, somebody beat us to the decent lemons."

"That is... very sad," Mim says. "Could we make do with a less than decent lemon?" When Nadia just glares at her, she grins, releasing one hand from the cart to wave Nadia off as she rolls her eyes. "Sorry I asked. Well, maybe you can just make something else, it's not like I'm picky—hey. Is that Mrs. Warwick?"

Nadia turns to look, hoping that it's someone else, but, of course, it's not. Of course it's Donna Warwick, in all her tragic, closeted glory, wearing a deep purple pantsuit that looks like it fought its shoulder-padded way out of the eighties and staring contemplatively at the melon display. Why would it be anyone else?

"Maybe if we stand very still she won't see us," Nadia mutters out of the corner of her mouth. This, naturally, leads Mim to slap her lightly on the forearm, and the movement—they're like T-rexes, these suburban mothers; that's really the only appropriate comparison—draws Mrs. Warwick's attention.

"Girls!" she calls. "Girls, over here!"

"I will kill you for this," Nadia mutters to Mim, even as Mim grabs her by the arm and starts dragging her across the floor. "When you least expect it, I will come with the shoulder pads from that jacket and I will smother you to death with them."

"Be nice," Mim chides, "where's your Thanksgiving spirit?"

"I'm not sure. Would you like me to tell you where you can stick yours?" Nadia says, very sweetly indeed, and so Mim is too busy smothering laughter to say hello when they reach Mrs. Warwick's cart. Grudgingly, Nadia takes over the duty herself. "Hi, Mrs. Warwick. Happy Thanksgiving."

"Oh, you too, sweetheart, but you really do have to call me Donna." Mrs. Warwick picks up a cantaloupe, seemingly testing its heft, before she puts it back down on the display. "And Mimosa, so nice to see you! I swear I feel like we're hardly neighbors at all, with how little time we spend together."

"I, oh," Mim says. Mrs. Warwick is still looking at her, but she has, seemingly unconsciously, begun running her palms over the surfaces of two of the cantaloupes. The action makes the melons look like—well, *melons*—and though it's lost on Mrs. Warwick, Nadia can see the telltale red flush creeping up the back of Mim's neck. "Well, I, um. I spend a lot of time, you know, working with the JAF—"

"With Gale, you mean!" Mrs. Warwick's laugh, though booming, is not enough to distract Nadia from the way her thumbs seem to have found the stems on her respective cantaloupes. "She does have a way of monopolizing a girl's time. How about you, Nadia? Keeping busy? And how *is* your father, I do hope he's doing better?"

What is happening with the cantaloupes now is borderline pornographic. Nadia's so distracted by trying not to burst out laughing that the question about Samir doesn't even freeze her up; she says, "Oh, yes, he's fine, he's great," as she struggles to keep the mirth from her voice. Next to her, Mim is holding herself completely stiff, as though she can prevent an outburst through stillness alone—a strategy that seems not to be working, because when Mrs. Warwick picks up both cantaloupes a moment later, she releases an obvious giggle that she hastily turns into a cough.

Mrs. Warwick doesn't seem to notice this—which, Nadia thinks, makes sense, given the magnitude of some of the other pertinent facts she seems to have missed over the course of her lifetime. "Any holiday plans?" she says, placing the cantaloupes with a loving sort of tenderness in her cart; Nadia has to grab Mim's arm and *squeeze* to keep herself from shrieking at the fond little pat she gives them.

"Just, uh, you know. Stuff." Mim's voice is trembling with the effort of holding in her laughter. "And you?"

"Oh, just the usual—we always have the family over, a few of John's staffers who don't have anywhere else to go." Mrs. Warwick's hand lands possessively over the left cantaloupe, thumb rubbing small circles over the top of it. "Why, you two should—"

"Oh shit, I left the bags in the car," Nadia says, because if Mrs. Warwick actually invites them to Thanksgiving dinner she will—die, or explode from held-in hysteria, or something. "The—Mim, you know, the bags—"

"Right, yeah, the bags," Mim says quickly. "Very—environmentally important, bringing your own—"

"Plus the discount at the front," Nadia throws in, "I'd better go get—"

"Well, I think *I'm* the one who should—"

"You know what let's both get them," Nadia says, all on one breath, and then plasters a smile that she hopes is winsome but is probably actually mildly deranged on her face. "Bye, Mrs. Warwick."

"Really nice to see you," Mim adds, "and Happy Thanksgiving to you and your family."

"Oh, you too, sweetness," Mrs. Warwick says. She reaches out and pats Mim on the cheek, and then tries to do the same to Nadia, who— rudeness be damned—leans out of range before she can make contact. "See you around?"

"Sure," Mim manages, and then Nadia has to actually physically drag her outside, because Mrs. Warwick is pushing her cart towards the honeydew and Nadia doesn't actually think they'll survive another round.

They make it outside—just barely—before they start laughing, collapsing back against the bumper of the car, knocking shoulders.

Their second foray into the grocery store is not nearly so eventful as their first, and other than a run-in with the Neary triplets ("These are our *friends*," Silas hissed at her, breaking away from his group of wayward-looking teens for just long enough to do so, "go *away*"), things go smoothly enough. They find themselves back on Juniper Lane just shy of three, and end up going Mim's house on the theory that they can smoke inside there, should they want to. Ruth's gone again—Mim says something about a festival and friends that Nadia doesn't catch, though she hears the twist of bitterness in her voice loud and clear—and Nadia spends a jarring few minutes looking around for pots, pans, even *dishes* that might be serviceable.

"Yeah," Mim says, blank, when Nadia asks; "Ruth doesn't cook much."

"And you?"

"I can;" Mim pauses, winces, and finishes, "Make... pasta?"

"Oh my god," Nadia says, staring at her. "Just—oh my god."

It becomes a cooking lesson, in the end, that ends with the two of them on the floor, dishes and plates scattered haphazardly between them, eating whenever food dings or beeps its way out of the oven. Nadia sautés onions while singing Marvin Gaye into the neck of her mother's favorite Malbec and Mim laughs, leaning back against the cabinets, one hand splayed, wide-fingered across the soft swell of her gut. Around six they hear cars start to pull up at the Ashcrafts' next door, and Mim's face sours, shoulders curling in towards each other like she's making herself seem smaller, and Nadia feels a pang of something like sympathy.

Mim's eyes slip towards the window, hands jerking a little in her lap like she's giving up, like it's supplication.

"Forget them, anyway," says Nadia, rough; she hopes it's the kind thing, but honestly, she's not sure. She's aiming for kind, anyway, and she thinks that's probably what matters.

"Sure," Mim says, eyes still fixed on the view outside. Nadia watches as she lifts her fingers to the glass, touches just the tips of her fingers to the surface before she jerks away as if stung. "Right," Mim says, "right. Sorry, I mean, of course you're right. Forget them."

"Forget them," Nadia agrees. She flicks off the burner and folds down onto the floor across from Mim, appraising her. She's a raw wound of a person: Nadia can't think of anyone she's ever known who reacted so violently and painfully to such seemingly insignificant slights.

And then there's Nadia herself: for so long, she's thought of herself of someone born wearing her personality inside-out, on display for everyone to see whether she liked it or not—herself, come hell or high water. Herself to a fault. But now, looking at Mim, whose every feeling flicks across her face without her even *realizing* it, whose heart is pinned, unmistakable, to her sleeve, Nadia realizes that she isn't on display at all. She practically trembles to think of what it would be like to live such a fundamentally unguarded life—to allow herself such vulnerability. She is, she realizes with a little thrill, almost jealous.

"My parents called," she finds herself saying. She doesn't want to, and it comes out that way, unwilling, like she's hoping Mim won't hear it.

But Mim does hear, because she finally looks away from the window to stare, hard, at Nadia, and Nadia opens her mouth to distract her and finds herself saying it again: "My parents called."

"Both of them?" When Nadia nods, Mim whistles, a soft, two-note trill that would be more appropriate in song than as an expression of surprise. "Is everything okay?"

Nadia can't help it—she barks out a laugh, or what's just supposed to be a little laugh and then turns into a mortifying sound that just makes her laugh harder and then, wheezing, insist that she's going outside for a smoke. Mim trails after her with this strange expression on her face, like she can't decide whether or not she wants to be concerned or not; when they get to the door she hands Nadia a scarf wordlessly. Nadia pulls it close to her face without thinking and inhales deeply, coughing again, surprised, when she breathes in the scent of weed, patchouli, and black cherry throat lozenges. Ruth's, then. She should have known.

"Do you mind if I," Mim says when they step onto the porch, and Nadia blinks at her for a second before she realizes her aborted little hand gestures are, in fact, a request for a cigarette. She's never seen Mim smoke before, but she hands the smoke over anyway and lights it for her. She's lighting her own when Mim says, "Can I ask you something?"

"If it's, 'Do you believe in God,' I will run away," Nadia says, mock-solemn. "I refuse to be in a teen movie, or a horror movie, or a teen horror movie."

She expects Mim to grin and quip something back, but instead she just sort of half smiles and shakes her head—it figures, Nadia thinks, hysterical and almost bitter. Nadia gets life-altering bad, or really *good*, news, and Mim's the one all—whatever Mim is. Preparing to get deep over a bummed cigarette in UNC sweatpants and a mustard-colored cable knit sweater that hangs nearly down to her knees.

"What are you thankful for?" Mim says.

Nadia nearly chokes as she inhales, only saving it at the last second; she hopes, in a voice not necessarily her own but wincingly familiar, that Mim didn't notice the hamster-esqe puff of her cheeks. This feels like one of those moments that's supposed to be Significant, and Nadia has plenty of options should she want to look back at a Significant Moment and find herself obliviously constructing raviolis in her head or, one time, removing something green wedged between her teeth. Just the day before yesterday, she took that phone call with her parents while she was painting her *stupid* fingernails—

"I want to get a question too," Nadia says. It's abrupt and probably weird—the way Mim raises her eyebrows makes Nadia think, *weird, bad, that was bad and weird*—but then Mim smiles and looks right at her, maybe for the first time all night. Maybe for the first time in a while, because it would be weird—weird, bad, bad and weird—for Nadia to notice it like this, otherwise.

"You mean," Mim says, slow, like she's weighing it out, "in exchange to the answer for my question—the Thanksgiving question, you know, the same question fourth graders across the country have answered this week in terrible cursive—I have to offer you the answer to *any* question. I have to write you a question blank check. Is that the offer you're putting on the table?"

"That thing about the fourth graders was really specific," Nadia says, blinking.

Mim shrugs, clearly pleased. "I've picked it up from Gale. She has this philosophy—"

"Spare me the philosophy," Nadia says, face twisting. "Anything but that, I beg you."

"I could tell you," Mim says, and then takes a deep breath, screws up her face into the most determined wince Nadia has ever seen, and finishes, "about what she calls her... 'intimates.'"

Nadia stares at her for a long moment, and then starts to laugh. The idea of Mim and Gale shopping for underwear together is simply too much to bear. She can just see it, is the best part: Mim huddled in the corner of a Victoria's Secret, face as red as her hair, saying, "I, you, I mean, oh my god, uh, sorry, but, I, I," while Gale holds up — god. Nadia is laughing just thinking about it — holds up like, fucking *tangerine panties*, probably. Probably holding them very seriously in front of her and saying, "Oh Mim*osa*, every *wo*man really *must* have a pair of *t*an*g*erine *p*anties, my Richard is *so excited* by *pastels*."

"Stop laughing or they'll hear you next door," Mim says, and she's trying for a stern whisper but it falls apart right from the beginning, sweet-sounding little giggles slipping out around the edges. Conspiratorial, she leans forward and says, "She took me to this like. Mature. Uh. Store."

"She took you to a *sex shop*," Nadia says, open mouthed, too flat-out shocked to even have any fun with it.

Mim flames red to the roots of her hair. "*No*," she hisses, so scandalized that Nadia kind of wants to pat her on the head, "no, of course not. It was just — a store. For more mature. Ladies."

"She took you to the old lady bra store," Nadia says, in slowly dawning realization. "Oh my god, the one at that strip mall —"

"The one right by the *prison*, yes," Mim says. "How did you know?"

"God." Nadia shudder. "Mom used to take me when I was in high school, that place is so awful. Gale *shops* there? Bet that's a little piece of information she wouldn't want people to know — oh man, was the creepy old lady still working there?"

Balefully, Mim says, "Which one?"

"The one with the face like a pinched up grape," Nadia says, and then, when Mim just tilts her head quizzically, attempts to make the face herself in example.

Mim laughs so hard she nearly falls over the edge of the porch, crying, "Yes, yes, grape face," and setting them both off again so many times that eventually Nadia claims she has to go check on something in the kitchen just to break the cycle. There's nothing in the kitchen to check on, of course—she'd hardly have gone outside in the first place if anything cooking needed anything more than very periodic attention— but stops at the stove anyway, stirring something absently while she gets her breath back.

A moment passes, and then two; Nadia hears Mim finally go quiet out on the porch. The silence is rich, warm, broken in the distance by the sound of the wildlife night shift waking up from a good day's sleep. It feels rare, valuable, like it should be bottled and sold or, at the very least, bottled and kept—Nadia stretches her arms over her head and presses her aching diaphragm again the handle of the oven, just the bare strip of skin peeking out beneath her t-shirt pressed against the metal. It's grounding, in its way, a real thing, a tangible thing, and she gets her wits about her enough to pour two mugs of mulled cider and go back outside.

For as long as Nadia can remember, there has been a swing on Ruth Shalit's front porch. The look of it changes—it's been three different kinds of wood over the years, gone through countless cushions, been covered up from the first of every November to the following April Fools Day. Ruth has never been around much, and god knows the whole neighborhood would like her to give at least one or two more shits about the house, but when it came to this one thing, she could be relied upon completely.

Nadia has never sat on it, just looked at it when she was walking past, or when she stared out her window on sleepless nights and used it to mark the passing of time. And yet here Mim is, effortless, the cover tossed carelessly to one side of the porch and her stocking feet tucked up underneath her, just her fingertips poking out of her sweater. Wordlessly, Nadia hands her her mug and sits next to her, and tries to convince herself she's imagining something strangely familiar about it, like she's meeting someone who will, someday, be a very old friend for the very first time.

"I can't believe," Mim says, pulling a long sip from her mug a few minutes later, "that I tried to talk you out of making this."

"Never argue with a chef."

"Well, no, not *never*," Mim says. "Maybe not about food—"

"Never," Nadia says, and sighs in satisfaction. "Let's go with never."

Mim hums, a noncommittal sort of noise, and then says, "Deal."

"Deal with what?"

"No, I mean—from before," Mim says, haltingly, as though she's not sure she really wants to commit to the words coming out of her mouth. "The question blank check—you can have it."

Grinning over the rim of her mug, Nadia says, "The burning desire to know what I'm thankful for overcoming your better judgment, huh?"

Mim just meets her eyes, gaze unnervingly steady, and lifts her mug in acknowledgement. She says, "Something like that."

Swallowing, Nadia nods. "You're going to have to give me a minute to think, I kind of assumed we'd left that portion of the evening behind."

"So you asked me to agree to answer a question you hadn't even thought of yet?" Mim shakes her head and tuts, in an unwitting and terrifyingly exact replica of Nadia's own mother. "Rude."

"Sorry," Nadia says, but it's absent—there are so many things she could ask Mim, so many questions she wants answers to, that she's not sure where to begin. "Can we go back to Gale's underwear for a second? That's not my question, I just feel it's our duty to look further into that important topic."

"You're stalling for time," Mim says shrewdly.

135

"Even if I were, the topic of Gale Ashcraft's intimates would be still be a vital and significant issue in these troubled times." Nadia realizes, belatedly and not without horror, that she's employing a verbal tic of her father's—he'd deliver it better, of course, having perfected over the years this particular bit, but still, the grandiose language and accompanying hand gesture is all him.

Probably this is why she adds, "I mean, you can't tell me you haven't thought about it—*I've* thought about it, and I'm not the one with a crush on her." It's a stupid thing to say, but at least it's inarguably her own.

Predictably, Mim blushes, red flooding her cheeks and the tips of her ears; less predictably, the noise that escapes her mouth is not a gasp of horror but a giggle. "Oh my *god*, Nadia, what are we, twelve? I do *not* have a crush on her."

"Don't lie," Nadia says, singsong, leaning in close with an overdone leer. "You want her, you *need* her, you crave her in the night—"

"Ew! God! She's like forty!"

"You have to admit that she's a handsome woman," Nadia says.

Mim screws her face up in a mimicry of disgust, shaking her head. "She so isn't, what are you even talking about? She's all, you know, delicate bird bones and classical features."

"Spoken like a woman with strictly platonic feelings," Nadia says. She's surprised to hear it come out a little bitter—she was joking, she meant it as a joke—but luckily, Mim doesn't seem to notice.

"My feelings *are* strictly platonic," she says. "I'm just saying—that's not what handsome means. Like, okay, Mrs. Warwick? That's a handsome woman."

"*Mimosa*," Nadia gasps, a hand over her heart. "Don't tell me you have all this time craved the supple flesh of *Donna Warwick*—"

Shrieking, Mim shoves at her with one shoulder, repeating the phrase, "The supple flesh," in incredulous tones as Nadia struggles to keep all of her cider in her cup. "Oh my god," Mim says, laughingly, when she's calmed slightly, "you're so terrible."

"You're the one who called her handsome."

"She *is*, that's what that *means*," Mim insists. "A handsome woman is, you know. An attractively mannish lady. Gale is a lot of things, but she's not masculine."

"And that's how you'd describe Donna Warwick?" Nadia pushes, unable to help herself. "As 'attractively mannish'?"

"Well," Mim says, and winces. "'Mannish,' anyway."

Nadia hoots with laughter and Mim, clearly guilt-stricken, waves a hand at her to stop. "Don't, Nadia, god. She's so sad, she can't help it."

"She can help it," Nadia says, a little sour. "I mean, I get what you're saying, and I'm sure it's not—easy, or whatever. But it's not like she couldn't, I don't know, buy herself a ticket on that lesbian cruise, do the late-bloomer thing. She's not without resources."

"Lesbian… cruise?" Mim says, and then shakes her head, seemingly deciding better of the question. "Look, never mind, it's—I don't think that's really fair."

"You know something about her situation that I don't?" Nadia perks up in her seat a little; a neighborhood scandal would actually be really great for her family right now, might let them slip by under the radar. "*Is* she without resources? Are she and the Congressman concealing the fact that they're totally broke?"

"You take too much pleasure in that idea," Mim says, eyes narrowed, "but no. I meant—it's not easy for everyone. That's what I meant. It must be torture, to live like she does. To deny herself in that way."

"I'm sure it is torture," Nadia says. "I can't imagine living my life pretending to be attracted to a guy, but… why should I have sympathy for that?

137

She's chosen to live as a straight woman—a rich, white straight woman—instead of as a lesbian. Like. What part of that is supposed to be a hardship for her?"

"You really think she made a choice?" Mim's shifted in her seat, put her mug down to fold her arms across her chest defensively. Nadia wonders if she knows how obvious the gesture is. "You think she looked at who she is, at the life she could have, and consciously decided to be a repressed closet case?"

Nadia grimaces. "That's not what I mean. I just—god. It's more complicated than that, okay, and no offense, but what makes you think you even really have any idea what you're talking about here?"

Mim goes still, her face turned away from Nadia's, and for a second Nadia thinks that she's pushed too far, that this is going to be a real fight instead of the play-pretend bickering they usually fall into after a little time in each other's company. But then Mim turns back to her, lifts her chin in the air, and squares her shoulders.

She says, "What makes you think I don't?"

It's not the weirdest way someone's ever come out to her. That award, now and forever, belongs to Bradley Johnson from the fifth grade, who swam up to her one summer day at the Barn Ridge City Pool, spat water in her ear, and then yelled "I'M GAY, FARTFACE," before side-stroking away. But it is, idiotically enough, almost exactly as surprising—which is ridiculous. Nadia just... she never thought of Mim as someone who even *could* be queer, which, she realizes now, is bizarre. She usually gives at least a moment of contemplation to the sexuality of everyone she spends time with, out of a curiosity as to whether they are in her specific club more than any kind of judgment. But she hadn't done that with Mim, had almost gone out of her way to avoid thinking about it.

Because you didn't want to find out if she wasn't, pipes up a thought, unbidden, at the back of her mind. *Because at least if you didn't know, you could let some part of yourself believe you had a shot.*

"Sorry," Nadia says, at the exact moment Mim says the same thing; they both laugh, slightly stilted, and then Nadia holds up a hand so she can be the first to speak. "Really, I am. Sorry, I mean. I shouldn't have assumed, I don't normally do that, I just—sorry."

"Oh my god, stop, don't, it's fine." Mim is bright red, and she buries her face briefly in her hands before she lets out a heavy sigh and says, "It's not like it really. I mean. Counts. I've never actually—you're the first person I've told. Or, I mean—you're the first person I've actually *said* it to."

"You know, you didn't, technically. Say it, I mean."

Mim blanches. "Do I have to?"

"Not if you don't want to," Nadia says. "But—I don't know. I felt better, more like myself, after I got to the point where I could say it out loud. But I don't know that I'm really the model for everyone." Mim shifts in her seat, biting at her lip, and, softer, Nadia adds, "It counts, you know. There's not like—you don't have to have met some kind of threshold or anything. It's not like you can't get your gay card if you haven't kissed a girl."

"I've kissed a girl!" Mim says, and closes her mouth, flushing.

Nadia can't help it: she laughs. It's just—she doesn't mean it meanly but it's just *funny*; she hasn't done this in a long time, been in this position for someone else's first hesitant peek out of the closet, and she's forgotten over the years how much humor is in it for the spectator. For the person going through it, of course, it's wrenching—she certainly has not forgotten what it was like for her—but from this position it's more like watching a baby take her first steps than anything else. She half expects Mim to fall on her butt and start wailing.

"Right," Nadia says, "well, to mark this auspicious occasion, let's get you some tequila and you can tell me all about it." Mim drops her head back into her hands and groans.

It doesn't take much tequila to get it out of her in the end, and it's not really that juicy of a story when it does come out: a college party, a couple of beers too many, a female friend who liked to be edgy and push boundaries and stick her tongue down people's throats. Mim doesn't talk about it like it was some great erotic awakening, just winces and says, "She was wearing really sticky lip gloss," when it comes down to describing the kiss itself, so Nadia doesn't push it too hard, doesn't ask whether they went home together, whether she was someone Mim wanted to fuck.

She says, "So what made you realize you were gay, then?" instead, and Mim starts in her chair.

"I'm not gay," she says. "I'm," and there's such a long pause, so much obvious effort that goes into the word, "bisexual," that Nadia bursts into applause she pretends is sarcastic when she finally says it, makes Mim scowl and look away. "Just—I mean. I look at women sometimes and I want to, to… you know."

"I do know," Nadia says, laughing a little. "You're not a virgin, right? I've never met someone so afraid to say the word 'fucking' who wasn't one."

"I'm not a virgin!" Mim snaps it like she's angry, but the heat in her voice is replaced by uncertainty as she adds, "I'm even, I'm kind of. With someone, right now—a guy. A man, not—it's—complicated—"

"God, god, fine, don't hurt yourself, I don't need to know." Nadia takes a shot of tequila, and then a second one, screwing up her face for a second.

"I never asked my question." The burn from the tequila makes this come out raspy, raw; she clears her throat and tries again. "My blank-check question. I want to ask it now."

Mim groans from somewhere deep inside herself, a full-bodied, hell-bent sort of sound. "Oh my god, Nadia, *please* don't ask me a sex question—"

"What was your childhood like?"

There's a beat, and then Mim blinks at her, obviously confused. "Sorry—what?"

"Your childhood," Nadia repeats. "That's what I want to know about."

"No sex questions?"

"No sex questions."

"Could I convince you to ask a sex question instead," Mim mutters, and then holds up her hands when Nadia opens her mouth to reply. "No, no, I'm kidding. It's not—it was a childhood. It was fine. There's not really much to tell."

"That's okay," Nadia says, shrugging. "My answer's not gonna be that great either. It's still what I want to know."

"Why?"

"Who's the one asking the questions here?"

"Fine," Mim says, but she pours a little tequila into her mug as she says it, ignores the face Nadia makes at the idea of tequila in mulled cider, and takes a long sip. "Do you—I mean, is there anything specific you want to know? Anywhere in particular I should start?"

"Nah," Nadia says. She closes her eyes, leans back against her chair. "Just, you know. Whatever comes to mind."

Mim considers this for a moment. Then she sighs, and says, "Well, okay. It was... I'm the middle child, two older brothers, one younger. The only girl. My father is an accountant—yeah, I know," she says in response to raised eyebrows. "My mom..." She shifts uncomfortably. "I don't know. She was the sort of mom who was very involved in PTA events, if you know what I mean." Rashida, Nadia thinks,

141

would not have stepped within a mile of a PTA event if her life had depended on it.

"I don't know," Mim continues, "My family was—or, is, I guess, I doubt this has changed—they're just. They're very controlled, is I guess the right word? Or stoic, maybe, I don't know. They're just, I don't really know how to explain it. Quiet, but not because they're... they're just not like me."

"What do you mean, they're not like you?"

"They're not afraid," Mim says, very softly. "They're—they're quiet people but it's because they say exactly what they mean to say the very first time they say it, you know? I was always kind of—underfoot. Always messing something up, getting in the way. My brothers were all athletes—Hawthorne was all-state football—and I was this nerdy, bookish kid and I think, I mean—I think they just didn't really know what to *do* with me, does that make sense?"

Nadia thinks of her own childhood, of Samir's disappointed eyes and the angry clench of Rashida's hands at her sides. "Sure," she says, "I get that. You have a brother named Hawthorne?"

She opens her eyes just in time to catch Mim rolling hers. "Yeah. My mom's a botany freak—don't ask me why—so we all have plant names. Hawthorne, Reed, Kale, and—"

"Mimosa," Nadia finishes, grinning. She whistles. "Man, Kale got the short end of that stick, huh?"

"He didn't mind it so much when we were kids," Mim says. "Now that more people are eating kale he hates it—or, I mean. He did, last time I talked to him. Maybe he's made his peace with it now."

"Doubt it," Nadia says. She's thinking of recipes she could make with kale—kale salad, kale smoothie, those fried kale chips Rashida used to make her eat as a kid. She's plucking a cigarette out of the pack she tossed on the table hours ago and rolling it between her hands to conceal her shaking fingers, the fact that she feels drunk all of a sudden.

The thing is... the thing is. The thing is that it's cold like coming winter on this porch and in the haze of twilight Nadia can almost see Mim's mouth expand around the bubble of truth, golden and heartbreakingly honest, that she's getting ready to let escape into the night. Nadia's known for as long as they've been friends that Mim has a History, that there's something under the surface Nadia hasn't been told—it's been a comfort, in its way. She's liked that about them. Maybe it makes her a horrible person or a selfish one, the empty shell she's been accused of being by a roster of sad-eyed pink-haired girls, but she's felt safer in this friendship where trust wasn't on the table than she's ever dared to with someone who offered it freely.

But now it's going to come unraveled: Nadia can see the light of near-confession blooming in Mim's eyes and she can't bear it, she can't take it, she feels as though she's going to be crushed right out from beneath her skin. She leans forward to light her cigarette and comes unbalanced in the process, ends up pitching most of the way forward, until her head is hanging between her knees. Her hair has long since come loose from the bun she tied it in hours ago, with that graceful one-handed motion she's practiced a thousand times: she looks at the ends of her curls brush-brush-brushing against the dilapidated wooden floor and wants to laugh, when she realizes that that's what she feels. *Unpracticed.*

Like anybody is practiced in this. Like anybody on the entire fucking *earth* would be able to tell her how to handle this from experience alone.

"Nadia? Hey, are you okay?" Mim's voice is soft and her hand is so warm on Nadia's back and Nadia isn't doing this, can't be doing this right now. She can't be unspooling this way, because this is not the sort of person she is, has forced herself to become: maybe she can't say the right thing at the right time but she can say nothing, damn it, she can keep her shit and her sorrows to her fucking self. And how—how idiotic, how *embarrassing*, to be doing it this way, at this time, with this girl who didn't even make it all the way to trusting her. Just the idea that Mim *could* was enough to draw this to the surface, this maudlin, brimming part of Nadia that is so desperate to tell someone what's happened she's willing to make a display of it, and she hates herself for it.

"My father doesn't have cancer," Nadia says, and for once in her fucking life she can't be bothered to regret the way it comes out of her mouth: bitter, nearly mocking. She is so angry, whens she hears it aloud, that she says it again—"My *father* doesn't have *cancer*"—like she's throwing a punch.

Nadia feels Mim's hand freeze and then, very slowly, flex out against her back. It's a weirdly sobering thing, because it's just so—*Mim*—this tiny telegraphed sign of the panic she must be experiencing at Nadia's impromptu confession. It's enough to make Nadia sit up, at least, to push the hair back out of her eyes and blink away the tears that are threatening to spill over, to say, "Jesus Christ, I'm sorry. I don't know why I—I didn't mean to, I wasn't going to tell you that."

"Is he," Mim says, so carefully. Nadia's a little frightened by it, the care in her voice. "Is he in remission?"

"He never had cancer," Nadia explains, because she might as well, now. Because now that she's put herself here, in this position where she has no real choice but to explain, the actual telling of the thing doesn't seem so terribly difficult. "He has a—habit, I guess. A drug problem."

"Oh my god."

"Yeah, no fucking shit," Nadia says; it comes out flat, affectless. "So this whole time he's been in some rehab center down in Florida. They've even said that, is the funny thing—the rehab center—but since they *told me he had cancer*, I assumed it was. You know. Cancer rehabilitation."

144

"Oh my *god*," Mim says again. "They—you—why? Why? Would they do that?"

Abruptly, Nadia decides she needs to be smoking the cigarette she's been playing with all this time; she lifts one shoulder and drops it again in answer to Mim and then lights the cigarette and takes a long drag. She lets the words drift out of her mouth next to the smoke, unsure which is more acrid: "They didn't want anyone—the *neighborhood*—to find out, and I guess they thought it would be. Easier for me to lie if I didn't know, probably. They said they wanted to 'spare' me but if they'd really wanted that why tell me at all, you know? But it's much more important that I clear the house of anything that could tempt him when they come home—in two weeks, by the way—than that I keep being 'protected' from the truth. So. You know. There's that."

There is a long beat of silence. Then:

"Nadia," Mim says, voice heavy with honesty, "that is, honest to god, the most fucked up thing I've ever even heard."

"You're telling me," Nadia says, and feels weirdly lighter—looser—for it. "Now: pass me that tequila."

December

December 11

Nadia: what's your opinion on matricide?

Mim: Depends on the circumstance

Nadia: the circumstance is I'm going to murder my mother

Mim: Then I'm against. You would not do well in jail.

Nadia: fuck you, i'm tough

Mim: You'd have to eat jail food

You would have no access to real groceries

No chance you're even allowed a hotpot

Nadia: ...might be worth it

Mim: Oh my god. Have you been brainwashed?

Nadia: course i have. it's the neighborhood specialty.

Mim: Huh?

Nadia: nvm

December 15

Mim: Gale just suggested "tangerine" as a theme for the Juniper Bloom thing I'm dying

Oh my god Nadia I think she's actually going to go with it how am I supposed to get through the planning process without laughing myself to death

Thank god she just changed her mind again. Now it's "nautical." Because that's what everybody wants out of an event in March: nautical

Nadia? You okay?

Hello?

December 18

Nadia: hey sorry i've been hard to reach the last couple days. working a lot.

Mim: No problem! Just glad you're okay. How's your dad?

Nadia: still cancer-free

Mim: Ugh. I'm so sorry—it's such a screwed up situation. Can I help at all?

Nadia: nah. thanks tho

December 22

Nadia: they just told me they want me to stay for another couple of months to "help them adjust" mim i swear to god i don't know what the fuck i'm supposed to do

they're acting like everything's fine and nothing happened and i can't just pretend like it didn't and they're acting like that's like on me

Mim: Jesus. Do you want me to come over?

Nadia: god no. no reason for you to meet them before you have to plus if you come it'll just be the Everything Is Fine show

Mim: Sounds like that's what it is already

Nadia: just leave it

please

Mim: Wanna come over here then?

Nadia: yeah see you in 10

Danny: You free tonight? Up for some you-know-what?

Mim: Sure

Danny: Woo hoo ;)

The funny thing about sleeping with Danny is—well. Nothing about it is funny, exactly, or at least not funny-ha-ha; certainly all of it is funny strange. The weird thing, she means, maybe. The surprising thing.

It's just... it's not like Mim's ever thought about having an affair with a married man before, but she's seen *movies*, she's read books. She knows how these sorts of things are supposed to go. It's meant to be all cloak-

and-dagger, kisses stolen in the cover of darkness and whispered late night phone calls, the sensation of a burgeoning secret growing heavier in your chest. It's meant to be passion-fuelled trips to seedy motels and sex that lights you up like a drug until you're addicted, until you can't get enough.

Instead, Mim is under the covers at a mid-range Hyatt a few highway exits away from Barn Ridge, listening to cars go by on the highway outside as Danny runs his hand idly up and down her back. There is nothing addicting about it. There is nothing about it that feels worthwhile.

"Christmas plans?" Danny's voice is husky and sex-charged; Mim has to bury her face in the pillow to keep from laughing at how stupid he sounds. "Me and the wife were thinking about leaving town for a few days, but I'm thinking we're gonna try to blow that off and stick around."

"Sorry, I'm sorry, but aren't you supposed to," Mim swallows against the way her stomach turns with nerves at what she's about say, but presses on: "not talk about your wife? Right now?"

"It's just not a good time of year for me." Danny's voice is so blithely unconcerned with what Mim's just said—with *anything* Mim's said, ever—that Mim finds herself wondering if she even spoke at all. Maybe enough mediocre sex turns you into a mute. Maybe, between this and Dell, she's hit her quota.

It might be nice, never speaking again. Or never having sex again. Or just... not moving from this spot, turning out to be fused permanently to this bed, all thoughts and desires leeching out of her body until she's just an empty husk for the maids to find. Yeah. That sounds all right.

"Why?" Mim says, instead of any of that. It's her role in this little drama—to act interested. To play along. "Family stuff? Bad memories? They say suicides are higher at this time of year than any other; people get depressed, feel alone. Is it something like that?"

Danny says, "No." And then, in the heavy tones of a man brooding on his assorted wrongs, he says, "It's the Christmas jam."

"The Christmas... jam," Mim repeats. "Sorry, am I supposed to... know... what that is...?"

"I gave them rutabaga last year," Danny says darkly. "I mean, do you have any idea how hard it is to make a decent jam out of a rutabaga?"

"I... don't," Mim admits, at sea.

"Well, it's really hard!" Danny snaps. "But of course there's my sister, freshly back from whatever fuck-ass country she's been in—and I mean, seriously, what is so fucking *special* about being a doctor without borders? I mean, is it really so terrible to be a doctor with borders? What is so wrong with borders?"

"You're not a doctor," Mim says, out of confusion more than anything else, and feels a spike of fear when Danny's fingers tense against her back. Sex with Danny is... fine. It's fine—sometimes it's even good, although not as much, she thinks, as it possibly should be. But she hasn't yet quite managed to rid herself of the ghost touches that Dell left covering her body, in the weeks and months and years leading up to her finally, finally leaving. That led to her, ultimately, winding up on Ruth's porch in the middle of the night. Danny isn't Dell but sometimes... sometimes, when all she can feel is his fingers, it's hard to tell.

His hand relaxes again just a moment later, though, and she feels stupid—sick—for where her mind went at such a little touch. For where her mind is always, always going, whether she wants it to or not. She wonders whether she'll be able to escape it, ever—escape Dell, a feat she managed in body but has not yet achieved in mind. Sometimes she's terrified she never will.

"I *could* have been a doctor," Danny says mulishly. "And it wouldn't even have mattered because she would have been—just—god! And she always brings that stupid, whatever the fuck it is, fancy exotic jam from foreign lands. I bet she doesn't even make it herself, but it doesn't matter, because it's so *unique*. How is anyone supposed to compete with that?"

"I mean," Mim says, letting herself be lulled back into Danny's asinine babble, "rutabaga jam sounds pretty unique."

"And then there's my *brother*," Danny says, ignoring this, "which, like, he owns the company, it's not *fair* to make me go up against that. He's got a whole fleet of jam makers! Jam tasters! Experimental new jam theories! I'm just a well-connected amateur doing the best I can, but do I get any points for that? No, I do not."

Mim, suddenly curious as to whether he even requires fully verbalized answers from her at this juncture, makes a non-committal humming noise into her pillow. It seems to do the trick, because he squeezes her hip, rubs the flat of his palm down the side of her thigh as he continues talking. That's nice, at least. Comfortable.

"I just think," Danny says, with all the annoyed petulance of a child, "that if you're going to do a Christmas jam competition, it should be *fair*. I mean, is that so much to ask, really? Basic fairness? It was much better when we were children, we all had the same resources at our disposal. Now, I mean, I'm basically going to have to give up my entire day tomorrow to make something they won't even like. What's the point, Mimosa? Why bother?"

"You could just," Mim stops, yawns hugely, and finishes, "you know. Not do it this year?"

Danny's laugh is a distinctive thing—it's the morning coffee of laughter, this rich, full-bodied sound that gives Mim a little jolt of pleasure to hear, even now. But like a cup of coffee, it leaves a lingering taste in her mouth when it's over: not bad, exactly, but bitter. Dirty. She's more tired when it's over than she was when it started.

"You're a peach, kid, but that's not how it works in the Godwin family." He resumes stroking her back idly; Mim closes her eyes. "You know our slogan, right? 'A Breakfast Saver In Every Flavor'? That's no joke, we take it really seriously. That's the whole point of the Christmas jam: if we're going to really make *every* flavor, we need to be suggesting new ones all the time."

"That's," Mim says, and thinks *stupid*. She can't say *stupid*, though, because that's not what she's here for, that's not what she's agreed to; she sighs, shifts a little deeper under the covers, and says, "fascinating," in the hopes that it will get him to shut up.

When Danny says, "Isn't it?" she can hear the smile in his voice. "Of course, I still haven't come up with anything, and it's Christmas in two days—well, I guess one day, now. Since it's midnight." He drums his fingers against her ribcage in thought. "Peaches and cream, d'you think? Or, hey, isn't squash in season right now? Yeah—squash jam. Beat that, *Ashley*."

Mim figures that's his sister, but she can't bring herself to ask. She can't bring herself to lie awake listening to him any longer, forced to feign interest even with her body curled away from him and her faced pressed into the pillow. It's a mistake to fall asleep here—it'll just make it worse in the morning, guilt gnawing at the pit of her stomach when she wakes up alone—but better that than this, this feeling that she could float away on the sea of emptiness whose waves keep crashing across her chest and Danny wouldn't even notice.

She falls asleep, and dreams of jam. When she wakes up, it's to a sensation of sweet relief, the sound of the door closing behind him.

It's nearing midday when Mim gets home and lets herself in through the back door; weak December sun is filtering through the windows over the kitchen sink, briefly beautifying the pile of dishes heaped inside. Great. She unwinds her scarf from around her neck and tosses it towards the back door, narrowly missing the menorah that's been sitting next to the dish rack since the last time Ruth was home to light candles. Mim has been remiss in her duties—she can't remember the last time she celebrated a holiday or went to a service. It's funny—her family was never actually very religious, for all that they kept up the necessary customs, but when she got involved with Dell, she slowly let all those old traditions fade out of her life. She doesn't think it was intentional—it just happened, somehow, as so many things with Dell seemed to just somehow happen.

There's relatively fresh wax caked into the bottom of six of the slots, and Mim picks at it a little with her pinky nail. Hanukkah's over now, anyway. It doesn't really matter.

When she takes off her coat, she notices a slight ache in her left shoulder. It's an almost pleasant pain, sex-borne and essentially negligible, but she finds herself stretching away from it anyway, as though she's trying to put some distance between herself and the act the caused it. When she tries to think back to the previous night, to Danny's soft laughter and eager (if not particularly gifted) hands, she finds herself recalling Dell's white knuckles instead, his fingerprints that left bruises for weeks to come.

Suddenly, the sink full of dishes looks like an appealing prospect.

She doesn't even take off her coat for the first few plates, only realizing she should have when she looks down and sees that she's got one puffy sleeve submerged in dirty water. When she does remove the coat, she can't be bothered to do more than drop it on the floor where she stands, because this is—it's—important. Right now. Because she's

153

not going to *be* one of those *girls* who can't just *fuck* whoever they want to *fuck*, she's not going to let herself fall into this *stupid* trap, she might not be any particular sort of genius but she knows well enough what sort of *thoughts* will make her *pathetic* and —

"Hey there," Ruth says from the living room doorway.

Mim is so startled that she drops a dish, which — of course — shatters dramatically across the floor.

"Jesus Christ," Mim gasps, a hand going on her chest, as Ruth lets out a hoot of laughter. "Oh my god, I had no idea you were here, you scared the shit out of me!"

Ruth cackles. "Merry Christmas, kid!"

"Not until tomorrow," Mim points out, and bites down on the inside of her lip before she can add, *And it had better be merry, since with the years you just shaved off my fucking life I may not live to see another one.* "And *thanks*, that sure does mean a lot."

"Christmas Eve, then," Ruth says, waving a hand. "Christmas Eve Day, Erev Christmas, it's all Chinese food to me."

Rolling her eyes, Mim bends down to pick up the shards of glass that are all that remain of the plate she dropped. "What are you doing here, anyway? I thought you were gone until the new year."

"My house, isn't it?"

"Of course it is," Mim says, flushing and cursing herself — too often, she forgets that she's a guest here, that Ruth is letting her stay out of the kindness of her heart alone. "I'm sorry, I didn't mean to say — I'm not *unhappy* you're here, of course it's your house — just forget I said it, okay?"

"Forget you said what?" Ruth says easily. She steps over Mim's hands, questing around for the last few glass shards, to get to the fridge. "You want something to drink? Soda or — uh, soda, looks like what we got is soda."

"Yeah, sorry, I didn't get a chance to go to the store yesterday."

"Out and about?" Ruth's voice is—well, the truth is that after six months of sharing space with her, Mim still doesn't know Ruth well enough to identify what the tone of her voice means, just that there *is* a tone, and that it means something. "Partying down? Painting the town red?"

"Just... at work," Mim says, which is true. She *was* at the JAF yesterday, filing papers and answering phone calls and getting Gale pumpkin spice lattes from the Starbucks down the street, until nearly 5:30. The fact that she then left the JAF with Danny to head for the Hyatt, with whose staff she's gotten overly familiar, is just an omission. Not something Ruth needs to know.

"Right," Ruth says, "right."

She pops open one of the sodas from the fridge. Mim doesn't see her do it—she's dropped the glass shards in the garbage, turned back to the sink, and started on the dishes again—but she hears the distinctive pop and hiss, and then a dull, metallic sort of tapping noise, over and over again. She ignores it at first, but after a few minutes the sound begins to grate, the tap-tap-tapping recalling too clearly the sensation of Danny drumming his fingers along her side last night in thought.

Not that Mim can say that, of course. Of all the sentences that could come out of her mouth, she figures, "Sorry, Aunt Ruth, could you quit making that noise, it's reminding me too much of my adulterous affair," is probably the last one she wants to utter.

She turns her head in the end, just enough to see Ruth's thumbnail as the culprit behind the sound—it's pounding out an agitated rhythm against her can of Diet Coke, putting a beat to the low thrum of guilt in the back of Mim's mind. She finds herself saying, "Aunt Ruth, if there's something you want to say to me, you might as well spit it out."

Ruth's eyebrows lift towards her hairline. "The direct approach," she says. "Huh. Didn't know you had it in you."

"Me neither," Mim says honestly. Maybe she's been spending too much time with Nadia.

Silence hangs between them for a moment and then Ruth sighs, a weighted sort of sound. "Kid," she says, and there's an unfamiliar quality to her voice that sets Mim's teeth on edge. "You're an adult and it's not really any of my business what you get up to, but you're here, and I'm here, and you're doing dishes that've probably been sitting in that sink since October, so I sorta feel like I have to ask where you were last night."

I was out being neighborly, Mim wants to say, and has to bite the inside of her cheek to keep herself from laughing, focus her eyes on a bowl crusted over with something that's long since ceased to be recognizable. "What do the dishes have to do with it?"

"It's, uh," Ruth clears her throat, obviously uncomfortable, "textbook, that's all. Compulsive cleaning, I mean, it's—"

"I'm not compulsive," Mim snaps. "This isn't compulsive."

"I'm not saying it is." The unfamiliar quality to Ruth's voice intensifies, and Mim realizes—feeling a little nauseous over it—that it must be what she sounds like when she's being *careful*. "I'm just saying, you're not home all night, I come in and you're washing dishes you've never bothered with before—I just want to know if everything's all right."

And oh, it's awful—Mim knows it's awful—but for a moment she finds herself hating Ruth, with as much searing passion as she's ever hated anyone, for choosing this moment to be nosy and perceptive and *right*. For asking when Mim didn't want her to ask, after all the time she's spent hoping someone, anyone would; it's not fair, that the questions should come now. Not fair that this time Mim can't just be left alone to wash the dishes in peace because she's old enough, now, to keep her unhappiness to herself, because she's learned through a lack of other options to manage them on her own—and who does

Ruth think she is, exactly? She's not Mim's boss. She's not Mim's *mother*.

"You mean you want to know *that* everything's all right." Mim hears the words come out of her mouth but feels strangely disconnected from them—they're not the sort of thing she would say. "Right? You want me to say that it's fine and I'm fine so you can go on with your day and not have to worry about it. And as luck would have it, it's fine. I'm fine. So you can just forget about it." She closes her eyes as a rush of shame engulfs her, feels her cheeks heating as she adds, "Sorry—that was, I mean. I didn't mean to be rude."

"Sure you did." Ruth sounds almost proud, so Mim doesn't argue with her, doesn't turn around to glare. "Anyway, nothing wrong with a little rudeness, sometimes. Good for the constitution."

"You're the only one who thinks so."

"Bet that Bahjat girl agrees with me."

"You know Nadia's name," Mim says—sighs, because Ruth is obviously fishing for information and Mim's so tired of the way her life has filled up with people playing games. "And she's not rude on purpose, she hates being rude. She just—she says what she's thinking, that's all. She doesn't filter well."

Ruth snorts, but then she goes quiet for so long that Mim starts to think maybe she's left the room, somehow managed to creep out so quietly Mim didn't notice her footfalls. She knows that's not what happened—can, if she's truly honest with herself, hear the soft sound of Ruth breathing, the occasional sip of the Diet Coke—but she feels like she's in some kind of horror movie: like she's that woman who stands frozen in terror before slowly turning around to see what's waiting behind her. Mim doesn't want to turn around. She picks up another dish and allows herself to admit that she is, right now, terrified of her aunt, who for all her pretensions of free-spirited middle age could probably take on every single person who lives on this street and win.

"I tried to kill myself once, you know." Ruth's tone is too jovial for what she's saying, almost conversational, like this is a light chat about her latest travels instead of a horrific personal truth Mim doesn't want to know about. "Right after your uncle left me. Threw back a whole bottle of Tylenol and then decided I didn't want to die. Nothing like calling an ambulance on your own suicide attempt, I'll tell you what. I was so mortified I thought the embarrassment would end up killing me before the drugs could, but what was I supposed to say? That a bandit broke into the house, forced a bunch of pills down my throat, and then let himself out the back door?"

"Uh," Mim says. "That—I'm really—"

"Anyway," Ruth says over her, "the thing about trying to kill yourself is that afterwards, nobody really trusts you not to try again. And, I mean, why should they? If somebody else tried to murder me it's not like they'd send us off together and assume everything would be fine. I was in the hospital for a while, and then I had forced therapy for a while after that. Back then I thought mental healthcare was for idiots and saps."

"But—" Mim starts, and stops, consternated.

Ruth just shakes her head and laughs. "I was certifiable, kid. Look, the only reason I'm telling you this is—I get that you don't want to feel crazy, or whatever. I get not wanting to talk about it, and the hell if I'm gonna make you, but I like you. I've liked you since you were just a little kid, and when whatever it is that's eating at you comes out, I don't want it to be to some jackass 911 operator while you wait for a team to show up and pump your stomach, okay?"

Mim doesn't mean to, but she can't help it—inevitable, like the girl in the horror movie, she turns her head and meets Ruth's eyes. They're kind and well-lined, more knowing than Mim's ever given them credit for, and it's so obvious that they *see* her that Mim would run if she didn't feel rooted to the spot.

"Who says something's eating at me?" she says. It's not convincing—it's anything but convincing—but she has to try.

Ruth holds her gaze for a long moment, and then nods, rolls her shoulders back, and finally starts walking towards the door. "Yeah, well. If something ever is, that's all I'm saying. At least you'll have somebody around who's ready to hear about it."

She leaves. Mim washes every dish in the sink; by the time she's finished, all of them feel clean, and she still doesn't.

There are two men in red dinner jackets standing on Nadia's front lawn when Mim finally feels pulled together enough to walk across the street. She stares at them, hoping that as she gets closer they'll start to look familiar, but the closer she gets the more certain she is that she's never laid eyes on either of them in her life.

"Hello, miss," says one of them.

"Good evening, miss," says the other.

"Uh," says Mim, "hi. Nice to meet you." She waits for a moment to see if anything else—their names, for example, or what they're doing standing outside, in thin red dinner jackets, stamping their feet against the cold but otherwise doing nothing to warm themselves, at the tail end of December—presents itself. When nothing is forthcoming, she steels herself and says, "Uh, are you guys—I mean—did you want to... come inside?"

The men laugh. "Oh no, miss," says the first one. "We're not guests."

"We're the valets, miss," says the second one helpfully. "Mr. Bahjat always uses us for things like this."

159

Mim blinks at them for a moment. Then, mostly to reassure herself that she's not going crazy, she slowly turns her head and looks out at the street. As expected, any cars she can see are parked in their respective driveways.

"Um," Mim says, figuring it's probably stupid to ask but utterly unable to help herself, "isn't this, like—a party for the street? Basically an indoor block party?"

"You'd know better than we would," says the first valet cheerfully. "But yes, that's what it sounded like when we talked to Mr. Bahjat."

"So," Mim says slowly, "aren't most people... walking? From... their houses?"

The second valet nods thoughtfully. "Seems that way, doesn't it?"

"Sure does," agrees the first valet. "Sure does."

Mim waits a moment for them to pick up on the problem. When it becomes evident that that's not going to happen, she sighs and says, "So doesn't it seem a little... I don't know... unnecessary? To you? To have a valet service?"

The men stare at her in blank incomprehension.

"Mr. Bahjat always uses us for things like this," repeats the second valet, in a small, confused voice, after a moment.

"Sure does," says the first valet. "Every time!"

"Right," Mim says, "okay then," gives up, and goes inside.

Once inside, Mim finds herself wishing she'd stayed out.

She has at this point grown used to—for a given value of "used to"—the kind of parties Gale throws. They're not really that hard to manage if you know what you're doing; it's all cocktails and fancy appetizers on trays and, yes, Mim standing in in the farthest corner sipping champagne until somebody comes and forces her to engage, but still. It's a routine, at least. She might not particularly enjoy them, but she at least knows how to behave once she's there.

This party... is not like those parties.

The first thing that hits Mim is the noise; she's never noticed before that all of Gale's events have the same specifically maintained volume, but now that it's gone, she misses it. It's so loud in here that Mim finds herself wondering if Gale has someone on her personal payroll who goes around shushing people like a librarian, or if it's just something about the events themselves suggest a more muted, conversational tone. Whatever it is she does, the Bahjats clearly don't—maybe their budget for it went to the valet guys, or maybe Mim is just feeling a little bitchy, vindictive on Nadia's behalf, fighting off a headache from her sleepless night.

The second thing she notices is that the house, which she hasn't been inside since Nadia's parents came home—"Can't we hang out at your place," Nadia has said over and over, "I just don't want to deal with them today"—looks entirely different than it did the last time she was inside. Mim's not sure how that's even possible, since her understanding of the situation is that Nadia was, essentially, housesitting. Why, Mim wonders, taking in the new artwork on the walls, the unfamiliar rug on the floor, and the furniture they've clearly replaced, would you bother to have someone keep an eye on a house you planned to remodel? Did they just want the place occupied? Is there some kind of secret vault underneath it that needs constant guarding? Given the whole fake-cancer thing, Mim... wouldn't actually be that surprised.

The third thing she notices is the singing.

Drawn as if compelled to the source of the music, Mim pushes through the small crowd that's gathered in one corner of the room. Once through, she can see the five men ringed together in song—

Representative Warwick and Fred Neary on one side, Barry Craddock and Richard Ashcraft on the other, and in the center a dark-skinned man with a deep baritone and Nadia's eyes. She knows, of course, who he is, who he must be, but she can't help but stare at him hoping she's wrong, because he's looking awfully hearty and hale for someone who's spent the last six months in rehab pretending to have cancer. He's looking awfully cheerful for a guy whose daughter has spent the last few weeks dodging Mim's questions and saying, "Look, it's fine, it's not worth freaking out about," whenever she pushes the subject too hard.

And, also, because he's holding a drink. That in particular makes her hope he's an uncle or cousin or something.

The song finishes and the gathered crowd bursts into applause, reminding Mim abruptly that there is, in fact, a crowd thronged around her, filled with neighbors she's rudely ignored in favor of staring blankly at Samir Bahjat. She can't bring herself to tear her eyes away, though, as a woman who is Nadia's spitting image—a woman who must be Rashida—slips in between the smiling men and kisses Samir full on the mouth, laughs easily at something he whispers in her ear and offers to top off his drink. It's just so—Nadia said something about this months ago, something Mim can't remember right now because she's found herself too confused to think. Something about performance, and scapegoating, and people wanting everything to line up nicely regardless of cost. Something that makes a hell of a lot more sense to her now than it did at the time.

"Ah," says a low voice at her ear. Nadia sighs. "I see you've found my parents."

Mim observes a number of things about the Bahjats very rapidly:

1. They touch too much. This is, admittedly, probably not a fair thing for Mim to think, since she can't actually tell if she'd find the touching so appalling if they weren't Nadia's parents, but they are, and it is. If they're within six feet of each other, they're touching—holding hands, hugging, pressing their bodies together. It's weird. It's overwhelming. It makes Mim a little afraid that they're going to start tongue kissing in the middle of their conversation.

2. A justified fear, as it turns out.

3. A *really* justified one.

4. Samir is simultaneously the most and least charismatic person Mim's ever met; it's a weird line to walk, but the man does it. When he's looking at you, talking to you, engaging with you, it's like being in the crosshairs of a hurricane of personality; when he looks away, it's like he's got no idea you were ever alive. Mim goes to get herself a drink with which to fortify herself after the first few minutes of conversation and when she returns to the spot where she was standing just moments before, Samir gives her a look so blank that for a second she thinks he's forgotten who she is. And then he smiles at her, and if she didn't know better she'd think he'd never been happier than just now, in this moment, seeing her. It's unsettling. It's creepy, is what it is. She really, really doesn't like it.

5. There's this—mole, or maybe birthmark—at the very corner of Rashida's mouth, which though clearly not fake looks so incredibly fake that Mim finds herself twitching against the incredibly bizarre urge to touch it. She resists, of course, but it's not like it would really matter if she did, because—

6. Rashida is not a subtle woman and—

7. It becomes very apparent very quickly that she does not like Mim at all.

8. At.

9. All.

10. Nadia, Mim recalls, kind of tried to warn her about this a few days ago. Nadia said, "My mother can be kind of... standoffish? I guess? Is the word I'm looking for?" Mim—because she is a fool—said, "Oh, come on. I'm sure it will be fine."

11. It's not fine.

12. Where Samir is all bright laughter and welcoming handshakes and encouragement to, "Have fun! It's Christmas, for Christ's sake!" Rashida is all dark looks and pained sniffing and, "That's a very *interesting* dress, Mimosa. And how bold, to match it with those shoes—I wouldn't even consider leaving the house that way."

13. Combined with the way they're constantly touching, the effect is a supremely confusing one, making Mim feel like she's impressing them and horrifying them at once.

14. This would bother her a lot more—enough to go hide in a bathroom until she could plan an escape, honestly—if she didn't have something else to focus all of her nervous, unhappy energy on, which she does, because:

15. They treat Nadia like shit.

They don't do it obviously, of course. That would violate the unspoken rules of Juniper Lane, and anyway Mim thinks it might be better for Nadia if they were out-and-out awful. It might be easier for her to handle, if everything were out on the table. But it's painfully obvious, even from a few minutes of conversation with the three of them, that either the Bahjats don't know their daughter at all, or they know her incredibly well and are using that knowledge against her.

"So, Mimosa. You went to college, I assume?" Rashida says, with a pointed look at her daughter. "Nadia didn't, you know. Culinary school. We tried to talk her out of it."

"You know that I've had a job since the day I graduated, right?" Nadia says. She sounds weary, in this unfamiliar but clearly well-worn way that Mim can't stand. "Plenty of college graduates can't say that. Plus, I get paid better than I would as—"

"Come on, Nadia, you know it's gauche to discuss money." Samir rolls his eyes at Mim, as if they're both in on the joke of how rude Nadia's being. "Sorry. Some lessons just never seem to stick, you know?"

"Sure...?" Mim says. "But I didn't actually..." Rashida's eyes are daggers but Nadia's shoulders are slumped and Mim's just not going to be part of this, she's not, even if she hates it when people know about this part of her life. "I went to UNC but I didn't, um. Finish. So actually Nadia's—I mean, I don't know the actual semantics of it or anything but she got the piece of paper, right? And I didn't. So actually I think that makes her, you know. More qualified than I am."

"I see," Rashida says stiffly. To Nadia: "What a lovely friend."

"*Mom*," Nadia hisses, even as Samir waves her silent.

"Now, now, you know your mother didn't mean anything by that," he says. "Mim, my wife didn't mean to be rude—she's a lifelong academic, that's all. I think it's hard, when you really believe in a system, to hear someone disparage it, don't you?"

"Yes, of course," Mim finds herself saying, and then, "I'm sorry, Mrs. Bahjat," before she even fully registers that she *didn't* disparage the system, just expressed an honest piece of her own history.

"It's Professor Bahjat," Rashida says icily. And then, after a beat, "And please, call me Rashida."

"All right, Profes—uh—Rashida," Mim says. Nadia's shoulders are still slumped towards the floor, her face—normally so open—showing none of its typical expressiveness. She looks like a distillation of herself. "What do you teach, if you don't mind my asking?"

"Nadia didn't tell you?" Rashida's tone is light, but Mim notices that next to her, Nadia flinches. "I'm a professor of anthropology at The Ohio State University."

Samir puts an arm around Rashida's shoulders. "That's my girl—always so modest! She is, in fact, the *head* of the anthropology department. Best one they've ever had, too; enrollment's basically doubled since she started."

"And here I thought that was the football program," Mim jokes, only to be met with icy silence, which is horrible. Next to her, though, she hears a very soft, nearly inaudible snort, and decides it was worth saying after all.

She's relieved, a few moments later, when Samir seems to catch sight of someone he'd rather be talking to and drags Rashida off, calling, "Great to meet you, kid!" over his shoulder. Mim shudders at little the word "kid"—she's gotten used to Ruth calling her that, even accepted that from her it probably comes from a place of affection, but she's pretty sure Samir just couldn't be bothered to remember her name.

"So," Mim says.

"Yeah." Nadia runs a hand through her hair, something Mim's only seen her do a few times before; it's thick enough that it lands in layered little sections when she pulls her hand loose, the white streaks momentarily broken into smaller, face-framing pieces. The effect makes her look younger, Mim thinks, which is strange, since it's not as though Nadia's ever looked old, exactly. The bright white—which, Nadia confessed shame-facedly when they bleached it together a few weeks ago, is her way of hiding the fact that she's already starting to gray—is striking against Nadia's skin, offsets her jet-black eyeliner and the bruised berry color on her lips.

"Something on my face?" Nadia says, and then, when Mim blinks at her in confusion, "You're staring."

"I—oh," says Mim, blinking, embarrassed, "I—no, nothing. I was just—you and your mom! You guys look a lot alike."

Nadia sighs. "Yeah, well, that's as far as the similarities go. She wouldn't even let me do the food tonight—some of it's mine, obviously, because I wasn't going to let this whole party torture themselves with her yucca root balls or—you know what, whatever. Forget it. It's fine."

Unsure of what to do without the rest of the rant that would normally accompany that sentence, Mim shifts on her feet. "I thought you wouldn't mind if most of the people here were tortured?"

"Ha," Nadia says—actually says it, instead of laughing. "Yeah, guess you're right." She's not looking at Mim, is instead scanning the room for someone; her parents, probably. "Hey, weird question, but did you happen to smell my father's drink?"

"… No," Mim says. "Sorry?"

"Forget it," Nadia says again. "Just—if he comes to talk to you again, could you try to? I think it's apple juice, but I'd like to be sure."

Mim nods. She isn't really certain what good it would do Nadia to find out for sure that it *isn't* apple juice, and normally she'd say as much, but… The Nadia of the last few weeks has been a little brittle around the edges, a little delicate, and the person she's standing with tonight is almost a stranger, when Mim compares her to her memories of her fierce, foul-mouthed friend. She's almost certain that that's a selfish thing to think—that Nadia is going through something terrible and Mim should be a better friend than this, should think nothing of herself—but she can't help it. She can't help the awful swell of anger building in her chest either, not at Nadia but for her.

"I, uh," Mim says, wondering if she should even bother—Nadia's still not looking at her, and Mim thinks maybe she's forgotten she's here. "I'm going to go say hi to some people, if that's okay?"

"Why would it not be okay?"

"Oh," Mim says, startled, and Nadia does turn to her then. She looks blank for a moment, but then her face smooths out into a well-worn expression, amusement and exasperation wrapped up in a familiar smirk. Mim's so relieved she grins back.

"Mim," Nadia says, her smirk mutating into this little half-smile that crinkles the corner of her eyes, "don't start with that shit again. True, you're the only person at this fucking party that I actually want to talk to, but that doesn't mean I need you to staff me all night. Go; I'll be working in the kitchen when you're done schmoozing and boozing and kissing Gale's ass."

"You mean hiding in the kitchen," Mim interprets.

Nadia rolls her eyes. "I mean throwing away my mother's nasty health-food desserts and making canapés in the kitchen."

"Won't she mind?"

"Eh," Nadia says, and her eyes go distant again for a moment. "Probably. My dad'll thank me, though."

"And you can always blame Mrs. Craddock's cat."

"And I can always blame Mrs. Craddock's cat," Nadia agrees, the half-smile flaring back to life. "Go on, Mim. I'll be fine."

So Mim goes. She does the rounds without putting much thought into it—every one of these people is at least a little bit crazy, but she knows all of them well enough now to deftly avoid each one's sticky areas. A quick hello to Fred Neary, who will take any further conversation as an opportunity for an armchair diagnosis and an encouragement to visit his psychiatric practice; a compliment for Angel Neary, who always looks to be one badly-received outfit away from bursting into tears. A wave for Representative Warwick, who gropes if you get too close, and a quick hug for Diane, who *wants* to grope so badly Mim can feel her trembling slightly through her sweater set. A painful but necessary fifteen minutes of small talk about garden gnomes with the Craddocks, since Mrs. Craddock tends to be creatively punitive towards those she feels have ignored her, and a wide berth for Danny and Adriana, who make Mim feel a little sick to even stand near, laughing together in their chinos and cardigans like a J. Crew catalog spread. A few awkward moments of small talk with Richard Ashcraft, who—though Mim has spent countless evenings in his home, with his wife, at his dining room table—is essentially a stranger to her.

And then Gale, whom Mim never has to seek out—she simply descends, a cloud of pressed silk and tasteful perfume, to steer Mim around by the elbow like a marionette. It's all very familiar. It's all, Mim realizes with a start, very boring.

"Oh *Mimosa*, so lovely to see you," Gale trills, and she must say something else—Mim can see her mouth moving—but whatever it is, Mim doesn't catch it. The noise of the room is fading into the background, impossible to hear over the roar of realization in her ears: these parties are boring. Juniper Lane is boring. Everything about this street, these people, this future she's wanted for herself for as long as she can remember: there's no substance to it, no *life*. It's like—hell, it's *just* like—the sex she's shared with Danny, fine enough at the time but nothing to write home about, always leaving her feeling a little empty, a little lacking, after. Everything here is *boring*, except for Nadia, who hates this place and these people—who might, Mim thinks, have been right about it, and them, all along.

She blinks, coming back to herself, and looks at the little group Gale's assembled—the two of them, Adriana, and a few women Mim's never met before. They must have walked over from the slightly less prestigious Sycamore Drive, Juniper Lane's sister street two blocks to the west—Mim is vaguely surprised Gale is deigning to associate with them at all.

They're next to the kitchen, and Mim thinks longingly of slipping away to watch Nadia make canapés. But she forces herself to pay attention to the conversation—the last thing she wants is to be asked some question by Gale that she can't answer. She feels off-balance enough as it is.

Of course, then she actually starts listening.

"As I was *saying*," Gale says, casting a pointed glance at Mim, "I really shouldn't be telling you anything, but—I mean, it's not as though you don't all already know."

"How could we not? He came around after my back surgery last year, you know," says one of the unfamiliar Sycamore women. "At first it was all, 'Hi, nice to see you, I hope you're feeling better, I brought a roast chicken,' but sure enough, after about ten minutes he started asking after my Vicodin. It was sad, really—I mean, I think he thought I believed him when he said he was dealing with 'chronic pain,' but of course I'd heard by then, and was wise to his game."

"You didn't give him anything, did you?" Adriana asks, and then grins, sharp, when the Sycamore lady shifts on her feet. "God, you did, didn't you? That's terrible, Susan."

"I believe the correct word is *enabling*," Gale says with a sniff. "You really shouldn't have, you know."

"Well!" Susan says, looking hunted. "I wasn't—what was I supposed to do! I couldn't very well say, 'Why, I'm sorry, normally I wouldn't think twice about giving away a pill or two, but I've heard that you're an addict, so take your casserole and go!' I mean, how gauche. How *uncivilized*."

The women, as a group, shudder and nod, as though *uncivilized* is the worst thing a person could be. Mim, who is beginning to feel sick with suspicion as to just who they might be talking about, grinds her teeth together to keep from yelling something that would be uncivilized indeed: "Shut up!" or, "Fuck off!" or, "This is his house, you idiots, this is *Nadia's house*, and if she hears you talking about her father like this after she sacrificed so much for the sake of her stupid parents' stupid reputation her heart will break beyond repair."

She wonders, with wry humor that feels more like despair, what civilization worth belonging to thrives on this kind of dysfunction. She doesn't say that, either. She doesn't figure Gale would like it.

"I told him I had opted out of pain medication after I broke my arm," Adriana says, casting another sharp grin Susan's way. "I thought it was more... ethical."

"Sometimes a lie for the greater good is just necessary," Gale agrees, and then leans in, lowers her voice. "Do you know, I heard—oh, it really is so terrible of me to say—but, well. Look at the man. He doesn't look like someone who's recently been nearly dead of cancer, does he? Full head of hair, and yes, perhaps a bit on the thin side, but he could have stood to lose some weight before he left."

"You know," says one of the Sycamore women who isn't Susan, "that is an interesting point."

"Huh," says Susan. "What are you saying, Gale?"

And Mim can't help it—there's this terror growing in her chest, fear for Nadia and what will happen if the secret Gale's about to expose, the secret she cannot possibly know, comes out. It's swelling beneath her ribcage and clawing its way up her throat, and though she tries with everything she has to hold it back, some of it escapes: a small, desperate noise, barely audible over the sound of the party.

Gale hears it, though. Gale must hear it, because she turns to stare at Mim with those sharp, brilliant eyes, and Mim thinks for the hundredth time that for all she comes across like a hummingbird, a chipper, chirping sparrow of a woman, she's nothing if not a bird of prey. She's a *raptor*, and that little noise Mim made was a confirmation in its way, accidentally but a confirmation all the same, and so it is that she's looking right at Mim when she says:

"Well. *Someone*—and I will not be naming names—let it slip that perhaps Samir's 'cancer treatment' was, in point of fact, a rehab stint."

171

She smiles, slight but no less speaking for it, and Mim wants to throw up; Gale is clearly reveling in the moment of stunned silence, in having known something none of the rest of them did. "You didn't hear it from me."

Mim closes her eyes against the wave of revulsion, waits to hear what normally comes after one of Gale's little scoops: promises that it won't be repeated, all of which, Mim is realizing now, are probably so many lies. When the oaths, false or not, don't come, she opens her eyes only to see all the women standing as if frozen, not moving a muscle, staring at someone just behind her.

Let it be Samir, Mim prays, taking up the practice for the first time in years as she turns. *Let it be Samir, let it be Rashida, at least they deserve it after what they did, please don't let it be—*

Nadia.

She's standing just behind Mim, her face utterly expressionlessness. Somehow, for the first time since they met, nothing she's feeling is visible on her face. It's awful.

Or, at least, it's awful until Mim unthinkingly steps towards her, an arm reached out to comfort her, and Nadia jerks away, the blank mask transforming into a look of fury, of disgust. That's worse. That's the worst thing Mim's seen in a long time.

"Nadia." Gale speaks first, and Mim is gratified, at least, to hear her sound badly shaken for the first time in all the months they've known each other. "I'm so sorry, sweetheart, I didn't realize you—"

"Shut the fuck up," Nadia says.

Gale gasps. "*Nadia*. I understand that tempers are—"

"I said," Nadia says, consonants crisp with fury, hands bunching to fists at her sides, "shut the *fuck* up. Haven't you said enough already? Was that not fucking enough for you, spreading my family's business around like—" She chokes on the words, too angry to speak, and turns on her heel before Gale can say anything else. Mim stands, rooted to the spot in horror, and watches Nadia stalk towards, and then through, the kitchen door.

A moment of hanging silence, and then Adriana fucking—fucking *laughs*, this soft, awkward little chuckle, and Mim spares a second to be viciously, hatefully glad that her husband is fucking around on her before she takes off running.

"Nadia!" Mim yells, when she finds the kitchen empty, the back door hanging open out into the backyard. "Nadia, where did you go? I need to talk to you—Nadia!"

She sees her a moment later, sitting on the ground against the fence that runs along the back of her parents' property, head in her hands, elbows balanced on her knees. Mim runs to her, thinking that she looks—broken down, defeated—until she lifts her head. Then Mim falls back a step in shock at the pure fury on her face, so incontrovertible that it changes even the way Mim sees the shape of her body; now she looks more like a rattlesnake, coiled and waiting to strike.

"Nadia," Mim says, and it comes out on an exhalation, like it was punched loose from her chest. "Oh, Nadia, I'm so sorry, I—"

"You're *sorry*?" Nadia laughs, but it's not a friendly sound—it's bitter, scraped loose, vicious. "You're *sorry*, Mim? Well, great, that makes it all fucking better, then, doesn't it? Good for you, you're sorry—how long did it take you, Mim, huh? Two days? Three? What, did you hop the fence between your houses after I went home that night and climb the trellis to tell her?"

Mim stares at her, unable to process what the hell Nadia means. "I—what?"

"I'm so fucking stupid," Nadia says, and now that Mim's eyes have adjusted to the darkness she can see that she's shaking. "I mean, god, it's not like I didn't know you were so far up her ass you could—I *trusted* you. I fucking trusted you! What the fuck is wrong with me, that I'd do something as stupid as that? When it's so obvious now, fuck, you must have been just fucking thrilled to get such a good piece of gossip. Finally, something worthy of bringing back to Queen Gale!"

"You," Mim says, because she understands now but she can't, she just can't bring herself to believe it, "you think I told her."

"I know you fucking told her!" This, Nadia yells; Mim's sure it's all in her head but she could swear the sound's loud enough to blanket the whole town. "Because I *didn't tell anyone but you*! God, Mim. I thought you were my friend, I thought I—"

The average human heart beats between sixty and a hundred times a minute. Mim knows this, learned it in school and committed it to memory, for, apparently, moments like this: moments when she's sure, despite all evidence to the contrary, that her own has stopped. She is staring down at Nadia and trying to think about anything, anything but this—what Nadia's friendship has come to mean to her, and what it would mean to lose it. What it would mean to lose Nadia, who is looking at Mim like she's some kind of monster.

"You thought you what?" Mim says.

"Get off my property." Nadia is almost whispering at first, but her voice gets louder as she speaks, and when she says it again, she's shouting: "Get the *fuck* out of here, Mim, I don't want to see you, I don't want to look at you—"

"But I didn't," Mim says, even though it's useless. She could chip a tooth on Nadia's certainty and she herself is already falling apart in that way she knows makes her worse than useless, makes her pathetic and worthless and unbelievable, most of all. The words are trembling with the effort to hold back tears and sobs and screams of panic when

174

she says, "I didn't, Nadia, I didn't tell her, I wouldn't ever tell her," and she can hear how affected it sounds, how false.

"You're a fucking liar," Nadia spits, "and if you don't get out of here right now, Mim, I swear to god, I swear to *god* I'll drag you out to the street myself. All through that party of all those people who you just want so much to be, isn't that right? Poor sad little Mim with her big eyes and trembling lip and her *apologies*—it would just break you, wouldn't it? To be thrown into the street like a dog? For everyone to see you as the filthy little wannabe you are; god, I can't believe I ever wasted a second of my time on you."

"Nadia," Mim whispers.

"Go *home*," Nadia screams, "I don't want you here, I don't want to breathe the same fucking *air* as you, get *out* of here," and Mim's running before she can think about it, through the party, into the street, across the porch and into the stale air of Ruth's living room, where the television is on.

"Kid," Ruth says, leaning forward in her armchair and sounding surprised, "you're back early, was the party—kid? Hey, Mim, you all right?"

And it's then—when her aunt, with her weathered face and her studied indifference, gets up out of her chair and lets real concern slip into her voice— that Mim starts to cry.

175

January

Nadia and Mim had this conversation once, a while ago—obviously not recently, since they haven't spoken recently, since Mim turned out to be a snake in the grass, a snake Nadia trusted, like a fool—before everything went wrong. They had this conversation, this quick little chat that meant nothing when it happened and which Nadia can't stop thinking about, now.

Nadia said: "God, don't you ever get angry?"

And Mim said: "Well, yeah, sure, but—I don't know, it's—don't you think it's exhausting? I mean, maybe you don't, but I do. I just don't have it in me to sustain it for long, I don't think. I get angry, but I usually don't stay angry. I don't have the energy for it."

At the time, Nadia had made some crack about Mim's energy level, because honestly, it was a ridiculous thing for her to say; Nadia's never met anyone who talks so fast, whose brain whirs through details and possibilities so quickly. That quip was enough, then, to send them down another path of conversation, and Nadia doesn't even remember what got them talking about anger in the first place now. Presumably one of them was annoyed about something—it's not like it matters, anyway. That's not the part that Nadia's can't stop thinking about.

Because Nadia? Nadia *loves* being angry. Nadia thinks she could happily be angry for the rest of her life.

"Well," says Cory, rolling his eyes, "*that* sounds super healthy."

He's doing this thing he does some mornings when they're getting ready for lunch service, where he leans in through the kitchen window and gossips with her instead of—well—instead of doing whatever it is he does when he's not behind the bar. Nadia's never really asked; he doesn't run this place like she'd run it, if it were hers, but he's a good boss and she doesn't have any particular interest in his managerial process.

She kind of wishes his managerial process involved him fucking off right about now, though.

"You know what I mean," Nadia says, driving her knife into the chicken she's butchering with a little more force than is really required. "It's just—clean, you know? Clean living, that's what it is."

"I am so, so sure that's not what that phrase means."

Nadia scowls. "Oh, come on. It's like—you get angry enough that it burns everything else away, you see what I'm saying?"

"If I get a piece of paper, write 'I promise I will never burn down, shoot up, or otherwise damage Cory Perez's restaurant,' on it and make you sign it, do you think that'll be enough to cover my ass when you snap?" Cory wonders aloud. "Or am I better off just firing you? I feel like that might actually position me as a target of your wrath, but on the other hand, I might feel safer if you weren't physically inside every day."

"Smart, to joke around with the woman who's holding the knife."

"Who's joking?" Cory eyes her, and then takes a careful step backward, hands in the air. "I'm just saying, Bahjat, you've gotten kind of scary to be around. Even the rest of the kitchen staff is freaked out."

"You mean Ray-Jay?" Nadia asks, eyebrows up. "Who could bench-press me with one arm? Or maybe you're talking about Matilda; she did sound terrified when she threatened to disembowel me with her dough divider this morning."

Cory opens his mouth as if to respond, then closes it again, looking puzzled. Nadia takes advantage of his distraction to finish butchering the chicken in front of her and start dredging it for frying; this, at least, is simple, unchanging. She's made chicken piccata a thousand times, will probably make it a thousand more—chicken, white wine, lemon, capers. There's nothing unexpected about it, no danger that it will come at her out of the blue and tell her that it doesn't actually have any capers in it, or that it's not even chicken at all, but in fact pork by which she has been expertly fooled.

She drops the next piece of chicken in the flour a bit too viciously, and has to fan her hands to clear little cloud that arises as a result. Glaring at Cory as if daring him to say anything, she grabs the last few pieces and carefully slides them into the bowl.

Luckily, Cory seems to have missed the whole thing, because he says, "You know, I don't think you really could disembowel someone with a dough divider. Do you? I think it's not sharp enough."

"Really not thrilled that your biggest concern about Matilda threatening to remove my organs is her choice of tool, Cory," Nadia says, starting on the next chicken.

"You're the one planning to commit arson and/or murder."

"No," Nadia says, although she does whack her cleaver into the chicken in front of her with a certain... relish. "*You* suggested I was gonna do that stuff. I'm just standing here. Prepping chickens."

"Prepping chickens like they're a stand-in for whoever you really want to be chopping up and breading in flour," Cory says, and then winces. "Ew, okay, too far. I even grossed myself out. But honestly—do you want to, I don't know, talk about it? Tell me what it is that's got you all—"

"Don't you have stuff to do?" Nadia snaps, fed up. "Calls to make? Reservations to confirm? Anything other than lingering here while I finish the prep work?"

"Other than calling my lawyer to have him draft that contract for your signature? Nah, not really." Cory leans his elbows on the counter and grins. "Why? Am I bothering you?"

"Fuck off, Cory."

"Cheer up, Nadia," Cory returns, but he does, at least, fuck off.

"I don't need to cheer up," Nadia tells the chicken in front of her. "There's nothing unhealthy about a little anger—I *deserve* to be angry, and I like being angry, and I don't need to be fucking judged every fucking second of the day, okay?"

The chicken, of course, does not respond. Nadia glowers at it, swears, and gets back to work.

Seven hours later, Nadia stares at her parents across the corner table at Blue Horizon and hates everything about her life.

"I didn't mean anything against it, Nadia," Rashida says, poking gingerly at her chicken piccata with her fork. "Really, it's lovely, it's just—well, it's not exactly to my tastes, that's all. I never thought I'd say it, but I've really grown to prefer healthier food. Anyway, I'm sure it's much better when you make it."

"I did make it," Nadia says through gritted teeth.

Samir raises his eyebrows, amused. "Oh, yes? When you got up to go to the bathroom, I suppose?" He and Rashida both seem to find this hilarious; Rashida's laughter, though muffled behind her napkin, is unmistakable, and Samir's eyes sparkle with mirth. "I thought you were gone a few minutes too long, but I had no idea you'd nipped into the back to prepare our meals! Your speed is very impressive, you know."

Scowling, Nadia cuts into a piece of her own piccata with enough force that her knife scrapes against the plate. Hastily—before her mother can point out this breach of basic manners—she says, "I did the prep work. I didn't mean I'd actually cooked it while I went to the bathroom."

"I know," Samir says, lifting his eyes to the heavens as though Nadia is a trial beyond measure. "It was a joke, sweetheart. Just trying to lighten the mood. For what it's worth, my steak is excellent."

Of course your steak is excellent, Nadia wants to say. *Your steak is excellent for the same reason Mom's piccata is excellent: this is the best restaurant in town and that's why I work here.* But her father would frown if she said that, would drop his eyes to his plate and cut angrily into his baked potato, would say something he probably didn't even mean to be crushing about how impossible she can be to talk to, so. Nadia bites the inside of her cheek and smiles—a genuine smile, even, despite everything—at the compliment she could find in that sentiment if she really went looking for it.

"I'm glad," she says, instead of anything else that comes to mind, and beams when Samir returns her smile.

It's the first moment since they showed up here that Nadia's found herself at anything less than a rolling boil of unhappiness, and she tries to savor it, knowing that it won't last. For one thing, there is no torture so exquisite as being a customer at her own restaurant—she'd tried to explain that to her parents when they asked for this, specifically requested she make a reservation for the three of them here. It would be better if Samir and Rashida were out here and Nadia was back in the kitchen, flipping and sautéing and yelling for Ray-Jay to stop flirting with the wait staff and bring her some fucking pine nuts already. Instead, she's sitting here, flinching at the instinct to respond every time she hears Maria bark an order and weathering dirty looks from Jackson whenever he passes the table, even though it is her *night off* and she's not actually slacking or over-extending a break.

For another thing, there's been this held-breath sensation over the table the whole night, this taut energy lingering beneath the conversation that Nadia knows means an axe is going to fall. She wishes they'd just say it already, whatever it is they're gearing up to say. She wishes they would just get it over with.

As if in response to this thought, Rashida clears her throat. "Samir?" she says, "Do you want to—"

"Ah," Samir says, wiping his mouth with the corner of his napkin and then folding it neatly in his lap. "Yes, I suppose now is as good a time as any."

If Nadia had a dollar for every unpleasant conversation she's had with her parents that started this way, she'd have real money—like, "move to Hawaii and paint terrible watercolors as a profession" money. *Juniper Lane* money. She tries to think back to every instance of this little charade, her mother's soft prompting and her father's feigned consideration, as though any of them at this table sat down not knowing something was coming. It was the same when she was a kid and they told her they were moving away from the rest of their family—Nadia's aunts and uncles and cousins, her grandfather with his thick British accent and caramels forever in his pockets. It was the same when she was a teenager and they'd seen her kissing Amanda Hawkins and would "do what they could to accept what it meant," this controlled little transaction of a conversation in which no one actually said the word "lesbian," and which Nadia wouldn't realize until years later had robbed her of the opportunity to come out. It was even the same when they came to Chicago and asked her to come home, except that that time Samir's hands were shaking and Rashida's eyes were filled with tears.

181

Uncharitably, Nadia thinks that her father is awfully fucking reliable for a drug addict, and then promptly feels like such a horrible person that she knows the blood must drain from her face.

"Oh, honestly, Nadia," Rashida says, noticing this and—naturally—misinterpreting its cause. "Don't be so dramatic, it's nothing as terrible as all that."

If she were sitting across from anyone else, Nadia knows she would snap back: that last time, it *was*; that she didn't even say anything; that it's not like she can control her involuntary physiological reactions, and expecting her to is ridiculous. But it's her parents, Rashida with her hands folded carefully in front of her mostly-uneaten entree and Samir, tie tucked between the third and fourth buttons of his shirt so he doesn't dirty it, and Nadia's tongue is heavy and immobile in her mouth.

"Sorry," she finds it in herself to say, and wants to laugh, just for a second, at the idea that maybe Mim's compulsive apologizing is contagious—before she remembers all over again that she doesn't care about Mim anymore, and thinks she might not want to laugh again for a long time.

Rashida just nods as if satisfied—impossible, Nadia knows, but whatever—and Samir clears his throat again.

"Nadia," he says, "we found the job applications."

Even as an adult, there is this sensation Nadia experiences when her parents catch her out at something that's not unlike a bucket of cold water being dumped over her head, or being whacked from behind with a bat. It's a little worse this time, since they're in Nadia's *place of work* and she just knows Jackson heard that—with his freaky bat ears and his deep thirst for gossip there's no way he missed it—but. But. Nadia's been trying not to even *think* of the applications she's been keeping in a folder labeled "Music," on her laptop, because she didn't want to jinx it, didn't want anyone to know. She knew her best chance of getting out of here was to do it fast and ruthless, like ripping off a Band-Aid, before her parents or her guilt or her fucking stupid feelings could get involved.

"You went snooping around on my computer?" Nadia says, because, well. That seems pressing, and her safest possible response.

"Always so paranoid," Samir says on a sigh. "No, sweetheart, of course not—I was just looking to see what you were listening to lately, that's all. You've been so helpful this year; I thought it might be nice to surprise you, bring in a band for the annual ball. That's all. I certainly wasn't expecting to find anything but music in your music folder; I wouldn't breach your privacy like that."

"I," Nadia says, guilt and regret washing over her—he'd been trying to do a nice thing and she'd jumped, right away, to the worst conclusion. "I—that's really—I didn't even think you were doing the annual ball this year."

"Why wouldn't he?" Rashida's voice is strained, and she reaches out to grab Samir's hand in a grip that looks painful. "We wouldn't be back in town if we didn't feel we could handle our standing commitments, and anyway, your father loves putting on that event."

"Which, actually, brings us to my point," Samir says. "Honey, of course we appreciate these last few months, but we need you to stay in town a little longer."

He reaches the hand that Rashida isn't holding across the table and wraps it around Nadia's wrist; bizarrely, Nadia finds herself imagining the three of them jumping out of a plane, positioned just like this. Her mother would be wearing the parachute, probably, and she and Samir would be holding hands, fingers threaded tightly together—it would be left to Nadia to dangle below them, wind whipping through fingers denied the opportunity of holding on, only her father's warm grip attaching her to the possibility of survival.

Nadia blinks rapidly. "Are you—is everything—I mean, I thought I was here to, you know. To keep an eye on things while you were in treatment—er—while you were away. Are you... leaving again?" She eyes the empty wine glass next to her father's plate, paranoia spiking inside of her even though it would be stupid to think that he'd somehow ordered wine, filled his glass, and then knocked its contents back in the few minutes she was away from the table earlier. "Do you need to go back?"

"I am not going anywhere," Samir says clearly, loud enough that Nadia wonders if it's even for her benefit or if there's someone here, in this restaurant, that Samir hopes can hear him. "But it's important to me—to your mother and I—that we get a couple of months with you to, well. To perhaps put right some things that have been wrong."

Bullshit, thinks the uncharitable part of Nadia, so angry that it doesn't care who it's talking about, or how much it hurts her in the process. *What's the real reason, come on—you don't care about me that much.*

"Not to mention—of course our relationship with you is the most important thing, but you must think of how it would look," Rashida says carefully. *Ah. There it is.* "I mean, your father coming back from—cancer treatment—and you just cutting out right away. People would... talk."

"People are already talking," Nadia says, even though, of course, she knows better. "You heard Gale Ashcraft at that party—"

"Oh for god's sake, you can't tell me you're still taking that seriously," Samir says, frowning at her. "I told you—nobody important is going to believe that garbage. Everyone who's anyone knows she's not a reliable source; she practically salivates for gossip. It's unseemly."

"The woman is compulsive," Rashida agrees. "I heard she was spreading some story around about Mary Craddock killing neighborhood pets—as though that poor lady needs any more to deal with, Barry's practically a vegetable."

"It was Mary Craddock's cat, actually," Nadia says, "and Barry gropes an awful lot for a vegetable."

"That's an awful thing to say," Rashida gasps, at the same time Samir groans and says, "Come on, Nadia, he's harmless."

"It's—he's—fine," Nadia says, "sure, harmless, fine. But Dad, you can't really think that—I mean, the stuff that she's saying is—"

"Patently false and frankly slanderous," Samir says sharply, and then, quietly, "Lower your voice! We're in public!"

"In any case," Rashida says quickly, before Nadia can respond to that, "I think it would be good for you to have a few more months here, don't you? I've been meaning to tell you, a colleague of mine has been studying the... well, I personally hesitate to call the restaurant industry a culture, but that's what she's calling it, and she's certainly done more research than I have. Anyway. She told me that it's essentially a hotbed of drug use and dangerous personalities, especially in the big cities. I just think it would be safer, if you spent a few more months here with us."

"Well, then it's settled!" Samir beams at Nadia, releasing her wrist at last; she drops it to her lap, rubbing at the warmed stripe of skin as though it will bring her some sort of luck. It hasn't escaped her attention that they've just made a decision about her life without her input, but what is she supposed to do, exactly? If she tries to argue, they'll just talk around and over her until she has no choice but to shut up. If she finds a job and leaves anyway, she's a terrible daughter, and she doesn't think that, after the last few months, she could bear to be that, too: after all, she's already learned that she's a gullible sap, a bad judge of character, and a disappointment to herself and others.

"Fine," she says, and keeps saying for the rest of the night: "fine," when her parents ask if they should order a celebratory dessert; "fine," when her mother suggests they consider Blue Horizon to cater the JAF's annual ball; "fine," when Samir asks if she would mind being the one to drive them home, since he'd like to take a little nap in the backseat.

"Why, thank you, my dear," he says, beaming, and her cheeks hurt from the effort it takes to smile back.

That night, she sits in her room, stewing, avoiding the gaze of her treacherous computer, until she can't anymore, until she has to move. To get out of here. She winds her way through the house, practically predatory, hoping at first to run into her mother or father, to pick a fight over something stupid, but then winds up in the doorway of Samir's study and regrets that thought. Regrets every part of it.

Samir is asleep in the chair in the corner with a book open on his chest and he looks — *old*, Nadia thinks, stricken. Old in a way he never really has before. She can see, in sleep, the things he must be using his sheer force of personality to hide when he's awake: the deep circles under his eyes and the fact that every part of him is thinner than she can remember him ever being, even his hands. Nadia finds herself staring at them — at his hands — and for the first time it occurs to her to wonder what could have happened, to scare her parents into putting him into treatment. After all, he'd been drinking heavily without anyone worrying for years, hadn't he? If Gale Ashcraft was to be believed, he'd been wandering the neighborhood, begging virtual strangers for pills.

It's a terrifying thought, a — ha — a *sobering* thought, and so Nadia does what she was, when push comes to shove, raised to do: she elects to ignore it. Gale, though. There's someone who deserves some anger. There's someone who, if Nadia were to walk in on her asleep in a comfortable chair, she wouldn't feel guilty about waking the fuck up.

"Nadia?" Rashida's voice, drifting down from the second floor, is heavy with exhaustion; Nadia bets Rashida would look old too if she took the time to look, and hastily starts pulling on her boots to distract herself from the thought. "Everything okay down there? I thought I heard someone stomping around."

"Just me," Nadia says, biting back the words, *I wasn't stomping.* "Heading out for a little bit."

"Oh. Where are you going?"

"Out."

"Oh," Rashida says again, and then, words thick with some unidentifiable, held-back emotion, "fine. When will you be back?"

Nadia almost laughs—this is a scene straight out of her high school years, except that back then Rashida would've stormed down the stairs and demanded a fuller explanation, taken Nadia's car keys, and thrown herself in front of the door if she had to. Nadia's willing to bet, actually, that that's exactly what Rashida would do now if she could, if Nadia weren't twenty-six and they didn't both know it. But instead it's this, this pointed, "Fine," this acting as if she's got any control over what's happening here when really, when it comes right down to it, she doesn't. Even if she did take leave of her senses, come downstairs and throw herself in front of the door like she might have a decade ago, Nadia's bigger and stronger than she is, and could easily push her aside.

"Not sure," Nadia calls up the stairs, lacing up her boots with finality and standing up. "But I don't think this'll take too long." And then, before she can stop herself, she adds, "Dad's asleep in the study, if you wanted to. I don't know. Take him to bed or whatever."

It isn't the sort of thing she'd normally say, because Rashida is nothing if not a stickler for propriety, and Nadia's always known it wasn't her place to comment on her parents' behavior. But she's tired and furious and scared, a bone-deep emotion that she can't write off as anxiety or paranoia or any of the other pretty words she knows to dress up the concept. She's scared of her mother, of her father, of what suddenly looks like age—she's even scared of Mim, whose specter haunts the house, the street, the neighborhood. She's scared of all the ways everything feels like it's falling apart, and there's fuck-all she can do about it, except get stuck here as witness, forbidden to run.

"I'll do that," Rashida says, "thank you, Nadia," and that scares her too. Hell, that might scare her most of all.

"Don't wait up," Nadia says, and resists—if barely—the urge to slam the door behind her.

All the lights are on at the Ashcrafts' house. This is annoying. Nadia doesn't find herself storming across the street to deliver diatribes of rage very often—is it so much to ask that she get the opportunity to wake the bitch up? Is it so much to ask that Gale stumble down the stairs, in ugly pajamas, with her hair all over the place like a normal person?

Nadia snorts, because: yes. Of course that's too much to ask. Gale probably sleeps in handcrafted pajamas from France that are specifically designed not to wrinkle, with an *Hermès* scarf tied expertly over her hair and a full face of makeup on. It wouldn't actually surprise Nadia if she didn't sleep at all, opted instead to simply plug herself into the wall like the freaky robot Stepford nightmare woman she's secretly been this whole time.

That, Nadia thinks, is a good place to start. She'll knock, and then when Gale opens the door she'll say, "Hey, you freaky robot Stepford nightmare woman," and then she'll... figure out the rest of it as she goes along.

Nadia's never been much of a planner—that was one of the things she always liked about Mim, in fact, her tendency to turn gut-churning anxiety into a long list of options for any time they spent together. Something in her twists at the thought. If she looked to the right, she knows, she could probably see Mim's silhouette in the upstairs window.

She walks up the Ashcrafts' driveway and along the little path to their front door, and then suddenly finds herself stepping aside when said door bursts open and a scrawny teenager, dressed head-to-toe in black, stumbles out of it.

"I'm never coming back, do you hear me?" The high-pitched voice surprises Nadia for a second, before she realizes it's coming from Rebecca. The last time Nadia really paid her any mind, she was wearing a frilly pink dress and a scowl below hair that looked exactly like her mother's; this angry child scowling at her from beneath thick black plastic-rimmed glasses could not look farther from Gale Ashcraft's oldest spawn.

Gale comes to the door, dressed in, actually, pajamas even nicer than Nadia imagined. She's wearing this delicate gray silk slip under a robe in her signature green, an ensemble that, combined with her toned calves and bare feet, would make her look almost unsettlingly alluring if not for the scowl twisted across her face.

"Don't you dare walk out on me!" she shrieks, and Nadia is forcibly reminded of her own mother, of too many fraught teenage nights count. "We are in the middle of a discussion, and I forbid you to take off in the middle of the night like some kind of lunatic!"

"Oh, you *forbid* me," Rebecca says, voice mocking as she walks backwards towards the street. "Woe, alas. Whatever will I do? I can feel... my feet... rooting... to the spot... "

"I don't appreciate your sarcasm, young lady!"

"Well if I made a list of things I don't fucking appreciate about you it'd be a lot longer than that, *Mom*," Rebecca spits. "Lucky for you, you've got plenty of time to get used to living without it."

She turns, then, and takes off running down the street. Gale yells, "Rebecca!" after her, just the once, before she notices Nadia standing awkwardly to the right of the door; her face freezes in a bug-eyed rictus of mortification, which Nadia would have found incredibly gratifying just ten minutes ago. Without much hope, she tries to enjoy it now—it's not like Gale doesn't deserve this, after all. It's not like she hasn't done worse than what's just happened to her.

"Um," Nadia says, after the moment has stretched out too long to do anything else, "hi."

Gale blinks at her a few times, mouth slightly parted, before her expression twists into one of desperate fury and she whips around. Nadia thinks for a second that she's going to get a door slammed in her face, but instead Gale picks up a vase sitting on a nearby decorative pedestal, lifts it over her head, cries, "God *damn* it," and throws it to the ground.

There is a long, hanging pause, in which Nadia can hear nothing but the pounding of her own heart in her ears, the sound of Gale's ragged breaths. It's strange, the two of them standing in the foyer of this otherwise perfect home, door wide open, staring down at the shards of glass at their feet; it feels like a crime scene, the beginning of one of those murder mysteries where everything wraps up neatly. Where, at the end, the audience gets to go home.

It's never really occurred to Nadia before to wonder what goes on behind closed doors after night's fallen, when the world is quiet and people fill the silence by offering up their worsts to one another. It's always seemed so simple, so predictable to her—the Juniper Lane women and their fancy parties, their vicious rumors, their petty concerns and quibbles and lies. She's known them for years and she'd been so sure, all that time, that she understood them; now, seeing Gale Ashcraft lift a shaking hand to her mouth, Nadia wonders if she's been wrong—if maybe they're as complicated and fucked up and terrified as Nadia is herself. Maybe they're just better liars than she is. It wouldn't be hard.

Eventually, not sure what the hell else she's supposed to do, Nadia closes the door.

The motion seems to jolt Gale away from her drawn-out moment of shock; she releases a soft little, "Oh," and then drops to her knees. Nadia sucks in a sharp breath, thinking she's collapsed, but realizes a moment later that she's just—gathering up the shards of glass into a little pile, piece by shattered piece.

"Stupid," Gale says to herself, "stupid, stupid. Of all the things to break, why would I pick Richard's mother's favorite vase?" Her hands are still shaking; Nadia wonders if she's forgotten she's here. "I can just hear her now, 'Oh, honey, is it so much to ask that you manage the house a little better?' Why *yes*, Miranda, *yes it is*."

"Not to interrupt, or anything," Nadia says, kneeling down next to her, "but you're—you're kind of, uh. Bleeding."

Gale looks down at her hand and the thin but clearly deep cut at the tip of her thumb, and swears very softly under her breath. Nadia doesn't even catch the word itself, just its inflection and meaning, and she's digging around in her jacket pocket before she can think better of it, pulling out the small kit she always carries with her on days when she's working.

"Chef," Nadia says, when Gale stares in obvious confusion at the antiseptic wipes, Band-Aids and plastic finger-gloves she pulls out. "Can't bleed on the food, right? So you gotta keep this stuff handy."

Gale sniffs, a haughty, suspicious sort of sound, but she lets Nadia take her hand and wipe the cut clean. "I thought professional chefs were better with a knife than that."

Nadia laughs; she can't help it. "No such thing as a chef who hasn't cut themselves open a few times. Your basic industry hazard."

"I see." Gale is silent for a moment, seemingly content to watch as Nadia rips open a Band-Aid with her teeth and positions the cotton pad over the cut. It doesn't last, of course; the minute the bandage seals itself against her skin, she comes back to herself enough to demand, "Why are you doing this? In fact, what on earth are you doing here at all, let alone at this hour?"

Christ, Nadia wishes Gale hadn't asked — she's never thought of herself as a particularly kind person, but if Gale had just kept her fucking mouth shut she could have looked at tonight that way: as a kindness. As her better nature winning out. But now she finds a part of herself — a large part, even — chomping at the bit to deliver the diatribe she came here to issue, only louder and meaner. She has more ammunition now, a whole host of little barbs she's only just learned enough to deliver and a weakened opponent besides, and it's not kindness that's keeping her from letting slip those dogs of war. It's basic selfishness — it's Nadia not wanting to have to live with being that sort of woman, of person, of neighbor. There's nothing kind about it at all.

"Honestly? I felt like yelling at you," Nadia says. "But someone else beat me to it, and who wants to play second fiddle, right?"

"I," Gale says, staring. Then, throat visibly working: "Right."

They pick up the remaining vase shards together in careful silence, Nadia gritting her teeth against an assortment of insane urges — to walk away, to scream, to demand an apology, to knock everything else valuable in the room down. When the simple need to *do something* becomes overpowering, she wordlessly stands and searches the — gorgeous, spotless — kitchen until she finds a dustpan and broom, sweeps up their little pile of broken glass and takes it to the trashcan. When she comes back into the foyer, Gale is standing up, and Nadia feels like a terrible person at the relief that washes over her; at the knowledge, heavy in the pit of her stomach, that she would not have been able to find it within herself to help her up.

"Well," Nadia says, but before she can make an excuse and go home:

"You know, I see why she likes you," Gale says. She drops her eyes to the floor, and Nadia's not sure if it's embarrassment or shame, or simply a good imitation of either one. "Mimosa, I mean. I confess that I didn't—I wasn't—Rebecca and I have always had such a complicated relationship and of course your mother and I have never quite gotten along, and I suppose that I... saw in you something that reminded me of... all that. I couldn't understand why Mimosa enjoyed spending her time with you, but I, well—I do, now."

Nadia laughs, but it's a low, hollow sound. "Is that supposed to make everything okay? Like, what, you're cool with me now, so I'll just forget everything that's happened? That's not how it works."

"Do you think I don't know that?" Gale snaps. "Do you honestly imagine I need life lessons from some overgrown—I only thought you should know that I have my reasons for... for being the way that I am. I don't know that they're very good reasons, but I do have them."

"I don't care," says Nadia honestly. "It doesn't change anything, and you can tell Mim that when you—god. When you make this whole story into something it's not and spread it around the neighborhood, probably. I don't care that you'll have your *reasons* for it."

An expression comes over Gale's face that Nadia can't translate—there's this look in her eyes that Nadia thinks she's maybe not old enough to understand, as much as she hates that thought.

"I'm not going to tell anyone about this," Gale says softly. "I couldn't tell Mimosa in any case—she hasn't spoken to me since the Christmas party."

Nadia can't help it—the way her eyes widen, how much her expression must give away. "What? How is that—doesn't she work for you?"

193

Gale shrugs, an artful little gesture. "She quit."

"Oh," Nadia says, and when she says, "I don't care," this time, it *is* a lie. "That's—I mean, she and I aren't—weren't—whatever. It doesn't matter. I don't care what she does."

Gale is looking at her with a peculiar expression. "If you think," she says delicately, "that Mimosa… betrayed some kind of… confidence."

She stops, looking uncomfortable, and pained, and like she'd rather be anywhere else. Nadia can sympathize. "Well, I can assure you that you are *quite* mistaken."

Nadia stares.

"What," she says slowly, "do you… mean."

Gale's face scrunches up. It's not flattering. "Oh, please," she huffs. "You must know what I *mean*. If you think Mimosa told me some— *secret*—about your *family*—" She cuts herself off again, and sighs. "I really don't know why I'm bothering," she says, almost to herself. "It's really none of my business."

It's such a baldly hypocritical statement that Nadia almost laughs, and maybe *would* laugh if her mind weren't going in a million different directions at once, working at such a furious speed she feels almost nauseous.

"Well," Gale says after a long moment, when Nadia hasn't said anything at all. She sounds very finite, and Nadia, who's more than relieved to be done with this whole fucking crazy evening, and desperate to get out of this house, has her hand on the doorknob when Gale adds, tentative, "Are you?"

"Am I what?"

"Are you going to tell anyone," Gale says, so quietly Nadia almost doesn't hear it. "What you saw here tonight."

And oh, oh, Nadia should say yes. She should say yes and then she should canvass the neighborhood, knock on every door, tell each one of these overly involved people just who Gale Ashcraft is when her mask is down. It would be easy — it would be fun — it would be what she deserves, no more and no less, to have her life unraveled and dissected by the self-same public she's been feeding strangers to all these years... but Nadia is beginning to think Cory might have been right, about anger not being quite the same thing as clean living. Telling might be what Gale deserves, but that doesn't make it the right thing to do. That doesn't make it something Nadia could live with, no matter how hot the rage is, that's still burning in her veins.

"No," she says, and leaves before she has to see the relief on Gale's face; before she has to weather a thank you, or, worse, an apology.

When she gets home, her parents have gone to bed, and the empty silence of the house is unsettling, so she climbs out the bathroom window on the second floor, scoots out onto her favorite spot on the roof, and lets her feet dangle, loose, above the ground, watching the street settle down for the night, huddling in her jacket.

She smokes cigarette after cigarette, doing everything she can to keep her mind perfectly blank, until she sees the last light in Mim's house go out.

February

M im turns the paper over and over in her hands. It's the same cheap, three-hole-punched, college-ruled crap she and her brothers used all through school. Her dad used to buy it in bulk at a discount store near their house, and Mim is perversely furious that it seems to have held up through the years. Wouldn't it have made more sense for it to crumble inside its envelope, withered by the passage of time? What is the *point* of spending months listening to her rich neighbors drone endlessly about the difference in quality a few dollars can purchase if it's all going to turn out the same in the end?

She glares at the piece of paper, and then, for good measure, pulls both the envelopes it came in out from underneath her thigh and glares at them too. The larger of the two has her mother's handwriting on the front. Mim hasn't seen it in nearly a year, but it's unmistakable even so: the loops and dips of her R's and Y's, the long, slanting lines of her L's.

The second, smaller envelope has handwriting that matches the paper it contained, which is to say, Mim's handwriting. Or, at least, Mim's handwriting as it looked when she was thirteen—so, basically the same, just messier and less practiced, smudged by a careless thumb at the corners.

Dear Mim,

Hi. Are you supposed to say hi to yourself? I don't want to be rude but I think it's pretty dumb to say hello to yourself. Actually I think this whole letter is dumb, which I can say because Mr. Franklin said he's not going to read any of these letters because they're between we, ourselves and us. Mr. Franklin makes a lot of jokes like that, which you probably remember, because he was your teacher too, which is why I think this letter is stupid.

Anyway this is supposed to be about where we see ourselves in ten years and I don't have anything else to say to you really, except that I can see Zoe Rosenfeld's letter and it looks like it's, like, a love letter. Who writes a love letter to herself? I hope you're not the sort of person who would do that. I don't want to grow up to be anything like Zoe, she's so gross.

I'd just leave it there but Mr. Franklin is wandering around and I don't want him to look at this after all because I'm just sitting here glaring at Zoe, so:

Stuff I'll Probably Be Doing In Ten Years
By: Mimosa R., age 13
1. *Be married to somebody really cute. And tall, but not scary tall or anything. Just a good normal sort of tall, and he should have an awesome name, like Logan or Taylor or something*
2. *Have some kids, like maybe two kids*
3. *And a house! Or maybe an apartment because my brother Hawthorne says that real life isn't like TV and nobody really lives in houses or even in big apartments like on Friends when they're in their twenties,*

because they're all too broke. But he's not in his twenties yet either and he lies a lot of the time so what does he know?

4. *Oooh, I bet I'm cooler than my brothers. I am, right? I hope I'm not being mean about it, though—like, it's good to be cooler than everybody but not if you're mean about it.*

5. *I was gonna write some other stuff but Mr. Franklin says we can start wrapping it up if we feel like it and Zoe is STILL WRITING so I'm gonna stop. I hope Chicken is still alive and actually that's my last thing on my list:*

6. *Have an awesome dog that's only mine and I don't have to share with anybody and that nobody lets Kale name because Chicken is a really dumb name for a dog.*

Love,
Mim

"Whose brilliant idea was this?" Mim says, to the attentive and listening ears of no one at all, as she folds the paper into halves, then quarters. It just seems cruel to have thirteen-year-olds write letters like this to their future selves.

Mim doesn't actually remember much about Mr. Franklin other than that he'd been an entertaining, if not particularly brilliant, teacher, but she can see now that her youth blinded her to his obvious, deep-seated streak of absolute sadism. Who but a sadist would live to see adulthood and then ask this of the children in his classroom? Who but a sadist would instruct a room full of thirteen-year-olds to write and send themselves time bombs in the mail?

It's a stupid list, she knows. She wrote it as a stupid kid: she knows. But it doesn't change the fact that she'll be twenty-four in two days and she hasn't done these things, not even one of them.

Not for the first time today—this week, this month—she pulls out her phone to text Nadia and doesn't know what to say. She types, "My mother sent me a letter," and deletes it. She types, "My mother sent me a letter I wrote myself when I was thirteen," and deletes it. She types, "My mother sent me a letter I wrote myself when I was thirteen and all I want to do is talk to you about it, or about anything else, I know you're angry but if you'd just let me explain I think we could fix this," and deletes it. It doesn't matter, anyway. She'll only embarrass herself by trying.

She texts Danny instead, just a, "What are you doing," into the void, grimaces when she gets, "You, I hope," in reply a few minutes later. But it's something, at least, isn't it—maybe she can't trust or talk to him but at least he's *something*, a smile, a warm touch, and Mim needs something right now.

She shoves the letter and both envelopes into her purse and goes. He's happy to see her, she thinks. Maybe. She feels as though she's watching the whole scene play out from the corner of the room, detached and disconnected, an observer. As though she isn't really there at all. After he falls asleep, she lets a few tears leak out against the pillowcase—the saltwater blends with her eyeliner to leave a stain there that he won't notice when he leaves in the morning.

Ruth is in the driveway when Mim gets home, sitting on a lawn chair in a heavy parka and holding a cup of coffee in her hands. A little bitterly, Mim wonders if maybe her aunt has some sort of inborn walk-of-shame sense, and uses it to embarrass her. It would be the most useless superpower of all time, but for Ruth? It feels like it fits.

"Morning." Mim shoves her fists into her jacket pockets as deep as they'll go as she steps out of the car. It's not like she's unused to frigid winters, but lately her blood feels thin. "Sorry—just my opinion—but it seems kind of early in the year for sunbathing."

"I'm not sunbathing," Ruth says, "I'm getting ready to watch the show. Go get yourself a cup of coffee and join me if you want, we've got a couple of minutes before it starts."

Normally, Mim tries not to engage with Ruth's weirder behavior—life is short and Ruth is strange, and Mim's never really felt the need to delve deeper into that reality. But she's tired and wired all at once, knows already that even if she goes inside and tries to go back to sleep, she'll just toss and turn under her covers, wind up staring at the ceiling in despair. Whatever Ruth is doing out here, it can't be any worse than that.

"Okay," Mim says, shrugging. "Back in a sec."

"Extra lawn chairs in the garage," Ruth calls after her. "And bring me something to eat, will you? A satsuma or something, I think there's stuff in the fridge."

There are no satsumas in the fridge, but there is a block of hard cheese and a couple of pears. Mim grabs all of it and a mug of coffee, heads back outside with another lawn chair tucked under her arm. Ruth looks askance at the cheese for a second but then shrugs, takes it and one of the pears, bites into each in turn before letting out a deep, satisfied sigh.

"And now," she says, "we wait."

A minute creeps by, then two, then three. Mim's back-read her entire Facebook feed, scowling at the thought of Nadia railing against Twitter that night under the fireworks, by the time Ruth elbows her in the side and says, "Kid. Look. It's starting."

Mim looks up, but all she can see is a car backing out of the Nearys' driveway. It must be Angel's—the license plate reads LAXMOM, which Mim doesn't think even mild-mannered Fred would consent to—and there's a large lacrosse stick decal across the back window. It's creeping towards the street so slowly that it's a wonder it's moving at all, but otherwise nothing about it seems particularly out of the ordinary.

"Sorry, but..." Mim whispers, not sure even as she's doing it why she's keeping her voice so low. "What am I supposed to be getting out of this?"

"Shhh," Ruth whispers back. "All in good time."

The car backs, backs, backs down the driveway, creeping along in a perfectly straight line—and then, at the very last second, swerves to the left as dramatically as a car going two miles an hour can manage.

At the end of the Craddock's driveway, there is a small, cheerful—looking gnome holding a sign that says, "Welcome to Our Home!" Mrs. Neary's back tire strikes it just hard enough to set it a-wobble, and for one long, tense second it looks as though it might survive the encounter.

Then, as it was always going to, it falls over, its porcelain head separating from its body with an unmistakable crack.

Ruth cackles. "Oh, it's gonna be a good day. That old bag loves that hideous little gnome even more than all her other hideous little gnomes, she's going to flip her lid."

Before Mim can even open her mouth, there is an unholy shriek from the direction of Mrs. Craddock's yard. Sure enough, the woman herself flies out from her backyard a moment later, wearing what look to be pajama bottoms underneath her puffy jacket and gardening gloves. Mrs. Neary's already made her way out of the driveway, but—to Mim's unending amazement—Mrs. Craddock throws herself bodily in front of the car, preventing it from driving off and quitting Juniper Lane for the day.

"You did that on purpose," Mrs. Craddock shrieks, audible even at this distance. "You have no shame, tormenting an old lady like this! You should go to jail! They should put you in jail!"

"If anyone should go to jail it's *you*, you old crone!" From mousey Angel Neary, this is nothing short of astonishing, and Mim finds herself gasping at the tiny drama as Mrs. Neary gets out of her car and jabs her finger in Mrs. Craddock's face. "*Your* cat attacked *my* cat, *your* husband keeps wandering into *my* yard at night. You gave my children capsaicin poisoning!"

"Your children gave themselves capsaicin poisoning," Mrs. Craddock cries in response. Something pings in the back of Mim's mind, painful despite her distraction—she thinks Nadia might have told her this story, or at least part of it, once. "What kind of child doesn't know better than to rub their eyes after handling a hot pepper?"

"What kind of woman gives hot peppers to a bunch of ten year olds?"

"The kind who assumes their own parents haven't been so negligent as to avoid teaching them basic common sense!"

"That's not basic common sense!" Mrs. Neary is out-and-out screaming now, her face visibly red; it's a wonder the whole neighborhood hasn't woken up. "You—you—monster!"

Mrs. Craddock shakes her trowel—which Mim could have sworn she wasn't even holding a minute ago—in the air. "Gnome killer!"

"Poisoner!"

"Ninny!"

"Evil—cat-haver!" This last, Mrs. Neary delivers at a slightly lower volume, seeming to sense that it is not as strong an insult as its predecessors. Weirdly, this seems to be considered a cessation of hostilities; Mrs. Craddock shakes her trowel one last time before retreating back into her own yard, and Mrs. Neary, shaking her head, climbs back into her car and drives away.

Ruth whistles low in satisfaction, and Mim stares at the place where Mrs. Neary's car was a moment ago and tries to process what just happened. "How did you know that was going to happen?" she asks eventually.

"Sixth sense," Ruth says. "Psychic powers, you know—haven't I told you?" She taps the side of her head and fixes Mim with a serious expression that she only manages to hold for a few seconds before breaking out into that familiar cackle. "No, no, 'course that's not it, sorry. I knew it would happen because it happens every morning. Not that specific fight, of course—that was a good one—but the general gist. It's not even over yet, you'll see. These people put on one hell of a show when they think it's too early for anyone to see it."

This is the kind of statement that Mim would patently disbelieve if she hadn't just seen evidence of it with her own eyes. Since she did, she sits and watches with Ruth through a few other, though less intense, neighborhood squabbles. Mr. Ashcraft and Mrs. Clausen-Godwin have a brief but passionate disagreement about some snow on top of a hedge, which is cut abruptly short by the appearance of Gale, who looks nervously towards Mim and Ruth and then away again. Danny pulls onto the street a few minutes before nine, gives Mim and Ruth a jaunty wave that Ruth returns and Mim ducks her head to avoid. She feels more than sees Ruth notice, and tries not to. Mrs. Warwick, glancing around shiftily before she does it, throws several large fallen branches over the fence between her yard and the Bahjat's, and then Samir, with the same cautious look around, appears a few minutes later and does the exact same thing. The Neary Boys and the Warwick kid (Mim know she should know his name, but she never has managed to remember it) loiter, starry-eyed, outside the Ashcrafts' until Rebecca emerges, holding hands with little Kyle.

With every passing minute, every little trespass she bears quiet witness to from the safety of her own home, Mim feels her disgust for this street, for these people, swell dangerously inside of her. At least, that's what she tries to tell herself—that it's them she can't stand. That it's them she's disappointed in. The truth—that for all their flaws these are just people, perhaps greedy and petty people but people just the same—is too damning for her to look in the face. She, after all, is the one who got swept up in their toxic shit, who dove into it headfirst.

"How can you still fucking *live* here," Mim spits, and even she is surprised by the venom in her voice.

Ruth's eyebrows are near her hairline, but when she speaks her voice is calm. "I don't know, really. I think they're kind of funny in small doses, and I like how much they don't like me. I spend a lot of my time away. It's different, I think, when you're not here in the fishbowl all the time."

Snorting, Mim crosses her arms over her chest, even though she knows it makes her look like the stupid sullen teenager she feels like right now. "Must be nice."

"It's got its perks." Ruth gives her a long look over the rim of her cup of coffee, and then, in a voice as near to gentle as Ruth ever really gets, she says, "Wanna come?"

"What?"

"With me," Ruth clarifies. "For the week. I'm leaving in a couple of hours—it's just a little festival, but it's down in Georgia, and I thought it might be nice to get a couple days of sun. How about it? I could use a hand setting up my booth anyway, and it's not like you're working at the JAF anymore."

Mim winces, because—ugh. She hasn't actually officially *quit* at the JAF, just stopped showing up after Christmas when she decided she couldn't bear to look at Gale, and she feels horrible and unprofessional and deeply, profoundly idiotic about it. "God. Uh, how'd you know about that?"

Ruth gives her a look that is a little too knowing for comfort; a little too knowing to just be about the job. "I may not be the most popular person around here, but I have my sources, kiddo."

"Great," Mim mutters, sliding down in her chair. "That's just great."

Ruth hums in response, and, after a moment, hands Mim the block of cheese. She rolls her eyes but takes it, breaking off a chunk from the only area that hasn't been marred with Ruth's pronounced bite-marks. It's a sharp, rich flavor, too much for her currently nervous stomach, but she keeps eating it anyway, more to avoid answering than out of hunger.

Nadia's parents are the last people on the street to leave for the day. Mim tries not to stare, tries not to squirm in her seat. They kiss showily on the stoop and walk down to the garage, one after the other. Mim's still watching them with an expression of distaste on her face when she realizes that Nadia is standing in the doorway, wearing her pajamas, hair a riotous mess. She stares for a moment, and then looks away hurriedly when Nadia looks straight at her.

Ruth clears her throat and gets up, stretching. "Show's over, kid," she says, sounding amused, and then, as if Mim's answer is a foregone conclusion, "You gotta get packing if you're going to be ready to go when I am. C'mon, we're burning daylight here."

And maybe Mim's answer *is* a foregone conclusion—maybe she really is that transparent, that malleable, that ready to get the hell out of here. She gets up. She follows Ruth back inside without looking back across the street.

She doesn't mean to, but Mim falls asleep just past Canton, her eyes falling shut on a sign that says they're forty miles from someplace called Bolivar. She dreams strangely, half-lucid spirals of imagination that bounce up and bottom out whenever the car hit a pothole or crack. When she wakes up it's to different light, at a gas station north of Charlotte with rust wilting the edges of its iron sign. She yawns and rolls her head against the window; there's drool at the corner of her mouth, dripping down towards her chin, which she hastily wipes away.

"Your turn," Ruth says, dropping a bottle of soda and a Slim Jim in her lap when she comes back from the bathroom and the convenience station it's housed inside. "I'm too old to drive any farther."

"You're sixty-one," Mim says.

"Yeah," Ruth agrees, "which is just exactly how old you have to be not to drive any farther."

Naturally, Ruth passes out nearly the second they get out on the road, her comically loud snoring fading to white noise after a while. Mim flips stations on the radio until she finds something coming in clear—country, and with a little too much Jesus for her taste, but music, at least—and drinks her soda, and then the one Ruth left unfinished in the cup holder. It's not enough to quiet her empty stomach, which doesn't want her to eat so much as to have eaten hours before, when they stopped at a burger joint in Akron and Mim only picked at her meal. She'd been too—something—to eat then, nerves making her hands twitch in her lap, leading her to rip her napkin to shreds, but now she wishes she'd sucked it up.

Mim grins, apropos of nothing, at the thought of what Nadia would say about the hamburger, the look of utter disdain that would appear on her face if she were presented with such a meal. *I'd rather starve than feed myself on that—processed shoe leather.* But Mim's grin twists to a grimace before she can enjoy it; her whole mood sours to remember how badly everything's been screwed up. She eats the Slim Jim almost as a penance, wincing at the salty spice of it and the way it sticks going down her throat. Her whole mouth tastes like it, afterwards, this lingering nasty almost-meat flavor that makes her feel a little bit sick, but there's something oddly satisfying about it. It reminds her, somehow, of the first cigarette she ever smoked—the way the flavor of ash lingered on her tongue when she was finished, an inescapable reminder that she'd just chosen to poison herself.

Dell had handed her that cigarette, not that she blames him for it, really. For other things, sure, but she was never addicted to smoking the way she was addicted to him—to the ways he made her feel, and not feel. She knows, of course, that it was a dark story that unwound between them, that he scored huge gashes down the core of who she was, but sometimes, in these quiet moments, she can't help but remember the highs that went with those lows. He'd been something, when he was on, numbed her out to certain parts of herself—no, he'd been a salve to a series of old wounds—no, he—

Mim's mouth goes dry. Out of soda, she dumps all the ice from the bottom of Ruth's cup into her mouth, crunching down on it like the crackling will drown out the thought: she'd liked him because he liked her so much. Because he grew so devoted so quickly, and part of her thought, *I deserve this*. Because all her life she'd wanted one person, just one person, to love her for exactly who she was, and he'd been dangerous and stupid and so obvious, in retrospect, but it hadn't mattered. Mim had felt seen; she'd felt *recognized*, and it was intoxicating until it was cloying, stifling. Until he whispered against the shell of her ear that he'd kill himself if she left him, his palms cold around her wrists like manacles, and she knew that no matter what choice she made she was a horrible person, a failure, a—

"*Mimosa*," Ruth cries, and Mim comes back to herself just in time to see them listing dangerously close to the side of the highway, to feel the *bump bump bump* of shoulder and jerk the wheel back towards the road.

"Jesus Christ, kid," Ruth snaps, "we'd be road kill if you didn't chew ice so damn loud, what the *hell* were you—"

She trails off, probably noticing that Mim's face is streaked with tears, that her grip has gone white-knuckled on the wheel and that the rest of her is shaking, just slightly, as if in time with the motor. It's mortifying, but that does nothing to stem the tide, which is so out of Mim's control that it might as well have been drawn from her by the pull of the moon. She's not even sure what she's crying about—about Dell, which was ages ago; about Nadia, which still feels like it was yesterday; about Danny, just hours ago, and the way his touch is by far the faintest echo of the three.

"Well," Ruth says, as if to herself, as she reaches out for the wheel, "it'd be insane to let you keep driving, wouldn't it? All things considered. I know, I know, my grandmother always said don't wake a sleepwalker, but all the same. There we go. Tap the breaks, there's a good kid."

Mim buries her face in her hands and thinks, dimly, that this must be what having a nervous breakdown is like. It's a weirdly—*freeing* thought, somehow. Like now that she's done this horribly humiliating thing, proven beyond a shadow of a doubt that she's a mess, it doesn't matter what happens next; like all this time, she was a dam waiting to burst, and now that she has she can finally, finally stop thinking about it.

She cries for what feels like a long time.

They go to a McDonald's. Nadia wouldn't approve.

But it seems like the thing to do, after Mim finally stops crying long enough to notice the thick, uncomfortable silence in the car. She and Ruth manage to—silently—switch seats and get back on the road. For a few minutes, Mim sort of thinks that's how the rest of the trip will be, just her and Ruth stewing in the taciturn embarrassment of what just happened; then Ruth pulls off at the next exit, drives them to McDonald's, and pulls the car into a spot.

They both sit, a sort of stunned hush still hanging over them, until, unable to stand it anymore, Mim gets out of the car. Ruth follows her inside, and though the seemingly endless masses in line in front of them are as loud as they are idiotic, somehow even their conversations aren't enough to drown out the silence between the two of them. They just stand beneath the fluorescent lights and sweat it out, occasionally catching one another's eye and then quickly looking away again. When Ruth orders them both Filets-O-Fish, it's the first thing either of them has said in more than half an hour.

"So," Ruth says finally, when they've both sat down with their flimsy, odd-smelling sandwiches, "what was that about."

"Oh god," Mim says, "I don't—we don't have to talk about this."

"Oh yeah, you're right, we should wait until the next crying jag," Ruth says, eyebrows up. When Mim winces, she sighs and takes a sip of her soda. "Sorry—sometimes I can be a little sharper than I mean to be."

"It's okay," Mim says. She gestures at her face, which she knows is still red and puffy from crying, and probably makeup streaked— she'd had to resolutely look away and pretend not to notice when the checkout girl stared at her. "It's not like I don't get, you know. Emotional slippage."

"Ha," Ruth says. "Right."

"Yeah," Mim says.

The uncomfortable silence descends again.

"Oh for god's sake, I'm the adult here," Ruth mutters, and draws herself up in her seat. "Right. Look: I'm not so good at dealing with this kind of thing on my own, I need an herbal supplement to excel in that field, if you see what I'm saying." Mim nods around a bite of her sandwich, and Ruth huffs out a huge breath, rounding her cheeks. *"But* you can stop acting like you took a big shit on my windshield or something. Unclench. Be at one with the universe, if you believe in that crap.

I don't, really, but you'll see a lot of it where we're going, so you might as well get used to it."

"Uh, sure," Mim says, "yeah. I'll try." She can't bring herself to look at her aunt, so she busies herself with plucking the bun off her sandwich instead. It's a mistake—hungry though she was just moments ago, the insides of a Filet-O-Fish could turn anyone's stomach—and she replaces the bun hurriedly, wipes tartar sauce from her fingers on the cardboard container. "I think I'm okay to drive again now, if you want."

There's no reply, and, seeing no viable alternative, Mim forces herself to look up. She expects to meet Ruth's gaze, expects that flinty-eyed glare that always seems like it's seeing more of Mim than Mim really wants on display; instead, Ruth's staring out the window, her sandwich sitting forgotten in its box.

"You know something funny? Your mom would be handling this a lot better than I am."

Mim stares: it's the first time Ruth's brought up Mim's mother ("Eleanor," comes Dell's voice, unbidden, in the back of her mind; "calling her 'Mom,' just gives her authority over you, can't you see that?"). Without really meaning to, Mim finds herself fingering the envelope that's been folded up in her pocket all day. When she moves her index finger just so, she can feel the faint depressions left by one of the Bic ballpoints her mother's undoubtedly still stealing from work, the sloping curves of her R's and M's.

"Um," she says, "no—no offense or anything, but—how would you know? It's not like you guys are..." Mim swallows, whole body tensing, but says it anyway: "Close."

Ruth shrugs. "Yeah, sure, we're not close now. But she's my sister, kid. You think I don't know her?"

Mim feels foolish, ashamed, immediately. She realizes she's never really thought of Ruth—of her mother—as real people, solid people, with real relationships, independent of her. But of course she is. Of course they are.

"What happened?" she asks.

"Oh, you know." Ruth picks up her sandwich and then waves it vaguely in the air, as if she's already forgotten she's holding it. "Life. Time. Same old story. Ellie always wanted kids, a family, the whole thing; I was just pretending to want that shit, I think. Thank god it never happened. Time came she started pumping you kids out, and we stopped having much in common. And then—well, I don't think she ever really forgave me for not making it work with Jasper, to be honest. She and your dad worked so hard to push through the bad times, and I—didn't. Well, I did for a while. And then—" She shrugs.

"They *did*?" Mim says. "I didn't—I didn't even really know they'd had bad times."

Ruth raises her eyebrows. "What couple doesn't?" She's looking at her almost pityingly. "Your parents are just people like everybody else, kid."

"I—" Mim starts, and then realizes she has no idea what she wants to say. No—what she wants to say is, *They haven't talked to me in months, how would I know?* But isn't she the one who told them not to call? She swallows, and looks away.

Ruth sighs. "Look," she says, "I'm not saying they were always great parents, what do I know. I told your mother I'd give you a place to stay, because I like you, and I always mean what I say. But for what it's worth, kid, a relationship with a parent is a complicated thing. You probably don't want to throw that away, whatever you're feeling right now."

Mim can feel her eyes swimming with tears again, and hates herself for it; she doesn't want to cry, but her body doesn't seem to care. Furious, she tries to dash the tears away with the side of her hand before Ruth sees them, but, of course, fails.

Ruth sighs again. "Come on," she said. "Nothing to make you feel better like the open road."

Mim chokes out a weak laugh.

"What?" Ruth asks.

"It's just—*exactly* what you'd say," Mim says, wiping at her face, and Ruth laughs, and claps her on the shoulder as she gets up.

Ruth drives the rest of the way to Georgia.

Mim leans against the window, watching the country go by, and thinks about her childhood, memories backlit by the glow of streetlamps and passing headlights. She's six and Hawthorne is insisting that he can lift her over his head, is saying, "Come on, come on," until she lets him try and they both topple over, winded, laughing; she's nine and hiding with Kale under the table at Thanksgiving, both of them whispering "Shhh!" and kicking each other in between giggles. She's thirteen, eating ice cream on the back porch with her father after her first breakup, trying not to laugh at the way he adjusts his metal-rimmed spectacles and says, "Well, um, Mimosa, honey, it's—it's—um. Relationships are—um. Well. Ahem." She's fifteen and rereading the hundredth draft of Reed's college application essay, insisting that he still can't say he'd be a "dope" addition to the Duke campus. She's eighteen, biting the inside of her cheek to keep from crying as her mother touches two fingers to the back of her hand at her graduation dinner, whispering, "We're so proud of you," in her ear.

It's not all good, of course. It never is—things wouldn't make sense, otherwise. The world wouldn't line up right. There are unfair fights and personal fouls in her history with these people like there would be with anyone else—their being her family doesn't exempt them from that. But as she thinks about it, she can't seem to line up the idea she's had of them these last few years with what she remembers as reality. She can't find the seam, where it would make sense for her youth as she recalls it to lead to the reasons she pulled away from them: that they were negligent and uncaring; that they didn't really love her.

She wonders, as she crosses the last state line between herself and where she's going, where those ideas even came from, if they were even hers to begin with. The sun is just starting to come up as she starts to think: maybe not.

"Ah," Ruth says eight hours later, taking a deep breath of smoke-scented air, "*home.*"

"Home?" Mim repeats, raising a skeptical eyebrow. "I hate to break it to you, but this festival is only a week long."

Instead of responding to this, Ruth flaps a hand in her direction and sucks in another deep breath, seeming to swell with it slightly, like a tie-dyed bullfrog. Mim suppresses a laugh at that thought—Nadia would've appreciated it, but she has this weird feeling Ruth won't. She distracts herself by looking out at the vista before them: they're standing at the top of a giant hill, the gentle slope of which leads down to the row of tented shops Ruth affectionately refers to as the Shakedown Street, apparently in reference to some Grateful Dead song she's appalled Mim's never heard.

Everything—everywhere—is covered with people, festival-goers who started filing in car by car around mid-afternoon. The air shimmers a little with pot and cigarette smoke; Mim herself has partaken of both over the course of the day, in-between setting up the tents and the booth and organizing Ruth's many and varied wares for sale in the morning. It's been oddly satisfying work, sure, and Ruth's greeted at least a dozen people like old friends, but Mim has a hard time looking at so much transience and uncertainty, this whole society built around a constantly shifting infrastructure, as anything resembling a home.

Then again, maybe she wouldn't know.

"C'mon, kiddo," Ruth says, slapping her too hard on the back. "Let's go get some spicy pie."

There really is a place that sells spicy pizza—"Spicy 'za," Ruth says around a mouthful, "worth every moment of revenge it takes on your body"—and Mim gorges herself on the stuff for the next three days, lost in a haze of sweat and sun and steadily thrumming music. It's weird (it's probably all the fucking pot), but Mim can kind of see what Ruth meant. It's easy to… not think here. Or maybe it's more accurate to say that it's easy to avoid dwelling, to lose herself in the reliable bass line of whatever moment she's currently living instead of any after or before.

Which isn't to say—it's a nice place to visit but Mim wouldn't want to *live* here, couldn't ever build herself around it the way Ruth does. But it's not for the reasons she thought it would be; it's not because these people are dirty hippies or social degenerates, although admittedly with every passing day the ambient smell of the place gathers a heavier body odor component. In fact, nearly everyone she meets amongst the other vendors reminds her of Ruth—kindness and experience etched into faces whose creases point overwhelmingly to lives rich with more joy than sorrow.

They're sweet to her, asking her questions about herself but quickly backing off when they notice her discomfort, inviting her into their smoking circles and seeming to accept, without judgment, her tendency to observe rather than contribute.

It's not the life for her. She needs more structure than this, more permanence—she likes to burrow into a place, and feels almost bereft whenever she remembers that a week from now, this whole little bubble of reality will be gone, and it will be as though it never existed at all. But even with all that, even when she knows in her dance-tired bones that this isn't where she belongs, it's a closer fit than Juniper Lane is. It's a closer fit than Juniper Lane has *ever* been, and that knowledge of startles her so badly that she stops dancing abruptly, causing the guy next to her to knock into her and spill his beer down the side of her arm.

"Oh—sorry," Mim yells, straining to make herself heard over the lightning-fast bluegrass band currently filling the night with sound.

The guy shakes his head, his horrible white-boy dreadlocks whipping through the air, and cups his hands around his ears. "What?"

"I said, 'I'm sorry,'" Mim yells.

"No worries!" he yells back, and turns away from her again to resume his joyful, flailing dance.

No worries, Mim thinks wryly, *if only*, and she picks and stumbles away from the press of bodies in front of the stage, makes her way to a tree at the edge of the forest.

Seeking her breath, she presses both of her palms against the bark of a tree; it's rough against her hands, and her lungs expand with her gentle breathing, out and in and out again. She thinks, ruefully, that she may have overdone it.

Someone taps her on the shoulder. She starts, but when she turns there's just a kid standing there, a college kid, maybe, peering at her through a pair of green-tinted novelty lenses. He's wearing a nametag that says "Hello, my name is FARTS," which makes it hard, Mim thinks, to remain particularly unsettled by him, or, at least, to think him of him as anything resembling a threat.

"Hey, man," he says, "you got fire?"

"Sorry," Mim says automatically, and then: "Wait, I mean. Yes. Yeah. Here." She hands over her lighter and the guy grins at her, an easy, practiced sort of smile that nonetheless makes him look stoned. Well. More stoned, anyway.

"I never ask for a light," Farts tells her, conversational, as he flicks the flame to a cigarette and hands the lighter back. "I always as for fire instead. You know why?"

"Um," Mim says. "No?"

Farts leans close, as if sharing a secret. "Because," he says, his voice dripping with sincerity, "we *are* the light, man." He presses his hand to his chest, as if deeply touched by his own sentiment, and whispers it a second time: "We *are* the light."

Mim manages to contain herself until he's toddled a few yards away, but then she can't help but burst out laughing. Farts hears her anyway, turning around, but instead of the anger Mim's anticipating he grins, gives her a cheerful salute before he slips back into the crowd. She returns the smile at his retreating back, and can't help but think that Nadia would fit here better than she does. Nadia would be pushing her way to the front of the crowds, and elbowing out her own space, and making friends with strangers off that bizarre language of good-natured insults and swear words that Mim's never quite learned to speak. The honest truth of it is that Nadia would make *her* fit better here, too — Nadia would take her hand and pull her into conversations even when she was nervous or shy. Nadia would dare her to try a gator burrito and then shout with laughter at Mim's inevitable horrified face. Nadia would trick Mim into feeling safe even surrounded by this writhing mass of strangers, body warm and safe, protective.

A sudden and acute sense of despair rises in Mim's chest. She feels, just for a moment, like she's going to shatter into a thousand pieces right here on this patch of lawn; she can see the image in her mind's eye, even, a web of cracks spidering down her face and chest, tracing themselves out like a tattoo across her hands. When she blinks to clear the thought all she can see is how alone she is, this solitary figure out on the edge of a mass of togetherness, and her sadness is replaced with a roiling, unfamiliar fury, an anger whose source and direction she can't suss out.

Fists clenched, she walks back into the crowd.

A knot of middle-aged men offer her a joint, and Mim takes two long, harsh puffs, walking away before they can hear her coughing. A woman who reminds her of an older Nadia offers her a bowl, and Mim takes a hit from that, too, and then a long swig from the water bottle that's passed to her next, which turns out to be full of vodka. A group of frat guys who might well be Farts' friends open their ranks to let her through, and one of them whistles when she steps up next to him, yells, "Hi," too loud in her ear. Mim finds herself stepping into his space without really knowing why, winding her arms around his neck and kissing him; his friends are hooting and hollering in her ear, but she ignores them. The guy puts his hands on her waist and kisses her back with a sloppy, drunken abandon, but is either too far gone or too decent to try for anything else; when Mim breaks away from him, muttering "bathroom" and slipping away into the crush of bodies, she hear him yell a forlorn, "Well—uh—thanks!" behind her.

Another bowl is passed to her, there's a hand on her back, then her ass, then brushing against her shoulders. Someone lets her bum a cigarette, or must, anyway—she doesn't remember asking for it but finds herself smoking it, drawing in deep poisoned breaths and exhaling the sweet relief of them, of the burning sensation that lances her way down her throat and into her lungs. She kisses another guy, another stranger, this man whose face she doesn't even look at. His skin tone, in this lighting, looks almost like Nadia's. He also either too buzzed or too kind to take advantage, and he grabs her hands when she pulls away, squeezes and releases when he feels her start to fight him. It sends a shock of—something—through Mim's whole body, this gesture that might have been aggressive or gentle; she has no way to tell which, doesn't stop to find out. She just pushes her way further and further into the mob, getting closer to the stage with every couple of steps, and—

"Hey!" someone says, and Mim turns to see the guy she knocked into earlier, with his horrible matted dreadlocks framing his face. "I remember you!"

"Me too," Mim says, and then he's grabbing her and pulling her to his chest, sinking her tongue into her mouth, and she's letting him, and letting him, and letting him.

This guy—this is what she wanted, she tells herself, as he reaches a hand up to squeeze one of her breasts over her shirt, as he groans a little into her mouth. This is what she wants. He's not very good-looking and taking all kinds of liberties, grinding his tented crotch into the front of her thigh, and that's what she needs right now. She doesn't need to feel valued and wanted and safe—she needs someone who doesn't want anything from her except this, that's all she knows how to give. Her skin is buzzing and her mind is swimming and she feels dizzy. This is what she wants, isn't it? Someone like this guy, who's touching her breasts without even knowing her name? Someone like Danny, who plays with her like a favorite toy and then tosses her aside when he's finished? Someone like Dell, who'd worshipped her some days and raged against her on others, who whispered against her ear poisonous truths she'd known for years but been too afraid to look at or say out loud? Isn't it better to be with someone who doesn't expect anything from her, than someone she'll always, in the end, let down?

"Hey, baby," the guy says, pulling back to undo the button on her jeans, "don't cry, I'll make it good for you, I swear," and Mim blinks at him, uncomprehending. She reaches up to touch her face, more to prove to herself that she *isn't*, she *isn't* crying, and her fingers come away wet—she stares at them, eyes wide, as her impromptu partner undoes his own flies.

And suddenly there is this voice in her head—and she think that it sounds, maybe, like the woman she had once dreamed of growing into, when she was still young enough to have the luxury of imagining that her future was entirely under her own control.

It says: *No.*

"No," Mim says, softly at first, a repetition, almost a question, and then, "*No,*" louder this time, meant for her partner's ears as well as her own. He tries to soothe her and she says, "No," and he tries to slide his hand into her pants anyway and she says, "No," and his expression twists into a scowl and she's yelling it, twisting away from him, her hands going to fists again as she strikes at any part of him she can reach: "No, no, no!"

"You fucking *bitch,*" he yells, lunging for her, intent clear in his eyes and his groping hands, and Mim doesn't think; she shrieks, "*No,*" with as much volume as she can muster and drives her knee up into his crotch, hard. He drops with a cry of anguish and she can see people nearby turning to look, the men confused and the women—every one of them—with dark understanding in their eyes. She stumbles to see three of them step forward, put themselves bodily between Mim and the guy's prone form, and though she knows she was already crying she can feel the tears prick at her eyes now as she couldn't before, weirdly touched at this small act of solidarity. She wonders as she turns and flees—out of the crowd, this time, back up the hill, all the way into her sleeping bag—how many of them were doing it because of shared experience, and the thought both chills and sobers her, helps her guide herself back to steady ground.

When Mim wakes up the next day, it's after noon, and she doesn't ask how Ruth knew to let her sleep. Instead she walks down the hill and gets herself a slice of spicy pie, and, riding the tail end of last night's wave of emotion, eats it wandering amongst the trees that ring the valley until she finds an empty hammock. She climbs inside, gut twisting a little at how ridiculous she must look doing so, and pulls her phone out of her pocket, settling back to look at it.

"*No,*" she whispers to herself, a brief and private mantra. She has some business to take care of, before she loses the nerve. She has some things to do that she should have done a long time ago.

Dell is first, and, biting the inside of her cheek to keep from screaming in anxiety, she opens his text message window, closing her eyes to center herself before she looks at it. For a long time—since that night under the fireworks with Nadia, actually—Mim has simply ignored all of his texts, opened them without reading them and left them for a time when she felt ready. It was easy, doing that, certainly easier than reading them; if she didn't look at them, she didn't have to deal with what they said. If she didn't look at them, she didn't have to deal with what they meant—about her, sure, but about him too, about the kind of person she'd chosen to let in, and then, eventually, let take over.

It is a grim, revealing list of messages. There are hundreds of them—despite herself, Mim is almost impressed as his tenacity—and though each is different, Mim is surprised to realize that they all, more or less, say the same thing. Boiled down, stripped of metaphor and superfluous language, each one essentially reads: "You need me. You'll never survive without me. I need you. I'll never survive without you. If you don't come back to me, whatever horrible things happen to me or because of me are your fault. If you don't come back to me, you'll regret it for the rest of your life. No one else is ever going to love you. Come back so I can help you. Come back so I can fix you. Come back so you can fix me. Come back. Come back. Come back."

She's thought—for the better part of a year, she's thought—that he behaved the way he did because he loved her. That even though what lay between them was something toxic, something foul, it was her fault more than his; that if she'd been better, or known better, none of it would have panned out the way that it did. That although his actions were those of an abuser, he wasn't smart enough to have done it on purpose—that he loved her too much to have done it on purpose—that if she were smarter or stronger it wouldn't have affected her the way it did, because he wasn't doing it on purpose. She's thought, all this time, that all of this was her fault—if not his behavior, then certainly the way it affected her.

She's never really believed that he could have known exactly what he was doing, but it's impossible, confronted with this string of half-mad text messages, not to see that he *must* have. Maybe he didn't know how he was doing it, or why, but his hunger to regain control over her is so obvious that Mim finds herself laughing, a dark but undeniable chuckle sneaking its way out of her mouth. It's just so—ridiculous— that she really believed that this man she lost years of her life to, who mistreated her so badly—who threw her into walls and fucked her even when she didn't want him to, who talked her away from every person she considered important, who took advantage of her doubts and failures and fears—truly cared about her. Truly loved her. That's not what loving someone looks like, and Mim can't help but laugh: she feels as though she's finally managed to pull loose a blindfold she didn't even know she was wearing.

Mim thinks, for a long time, about sending him a message, just one last one. It could say, "Fuck you," or, "I finally see you," or, "I hope a bird shits in your mouth," or, "You're the only person I've ever wanted to watch painfully die," and it would be so, so true. It might even feel good—freeing—to do it. But in the end, she realizes that what he wants more than anything is her attention, positive, negative, or otherwise. He wants her to give him something, anything, a sign that he still matters to her, any little reaction that he can twist into meaning whatever the hell he wants it to.

She deletes his messages, every last one of them, and then, with a trembling finger, blocks his number. Even though she's doing it a year too late, it flushes her with a deep, visceral satisfaction, and she lies in the gently swinging hammock, eyes closed, for what feels like a long time after it's done. For once in her life, her mind is mostly quiet, all her focus pooled around the warmth of the sun on her face, the cooling breath of the wind skating up and along her body, and she lets herself have it, this moment of peace, whether she deserves it or not.

Eventually, though, the noise starts up again; her thoughts, never silenced for long, roar back to life and remind her of the other thing she needs to do before her courage once again bottoms out. This action is easier and harder, too—she doesn't care as much about it, but figuring out exactly what she wants to say and how to say it takes her several agonizing minutes of typing and deleting.

The text she finally sends to Danny reads as follows: "Sorry, but last time was the last time. It's just not working for me anymore, and I won't tell anyone if you won't. Good luck with your marriage—I hope you guys figure things out."

She feels like throwing up when she sends it, and lies tensed in wait for—something. Vitriol, fury, something. Instead, Danny texts back ":(" and then "ok neighbor. thanks for all the fun, i'm around if you're ever horny ;)" thirty seconds later, which makes Mim laugh a little again, though for entirely different reasons. Danny, she thinks, isn't such a bad guy—unfaithful, obviously, and a total skeezeball—but so much closer to decent than Dell ever was that she can't help but forgive him those flaws. She never, ever wants to sleep with him again, but she thinks eventually he'll be a fond memory, or, if not quite that, at least a good story; that maybe someday she'll laugh, and tell a friend about the crazy jam heir she used to fuck, and not feel like she's exposing any raw, tender parts of herself.

Mim abandons the hammock a few minutes later, walks back to her tent, throws her phone into the bottom of her sleeping bag and steps out, refreshed, into the bright sunlight. When she sees Ruth a few yards away, waving a jaunty hello over what looks like a massive Bloody Mary, Mim smiles at her and jogs over, feeling with every step as though she's leaving something heavy behind.

The rest of the week passes so quickly that Mim's taken by surprise when she wakes up on Sunday morning to Ruth grinning at her over her empty duffel bag. "Wakey wakey," she says, tossing the bag at Mim and ignoring her deep groan when it hits her in the face, "time to get packing and head back to civilization. The guys two tents over are cooking up everything they've got left, if you want breakfast. Looked like ribs, burgers, and grilled corn when I walked by—I snagged the last hot dog."

She waves the partially eaten hot dog—no bun, ketchup and mustard dripping on Mim's sleeping bag—illustratively, and also ignores Mim's second groan, this time at the idea of eating charred meat before ten in the morning. Ruth, shrugging, seems not to care, and vanishes back out the tent flap a moment later, calling a hello to somebody in the distance.

Mim lets out a small noise of dismay as she tries and fails to go back to sleep: it's over. It's not like she didn't know, going in, that the festival was only going to last for a week, but she seems to have forgotten that fact at some point along the way. She's adjusted to her environment so completely that it's honestly a little shocking to imagine that, this time tomorrow, she'll be back on Juniper Lane, with no funny hippies to talk to, no shows to catch, no spicy pie.

Her stomach growls reflexively at the thought of spicy pie, though whether in hunger or anticipated indigestion, Mim's not sure. Maybe it's a good thing they're going home—while she's sure it's possible for man to live on spicy pie alone, it's probably not the best idea.

She packs quickly, not having brought much in the first place, and slips away to wander Shakedown Street one last time before Ruth can strong-arm her into helping pack up the tie-dye booth. It's in a state of near-comical disassembly, some tents gone, others almost completely packed away, and still others that clearly belong to the procrastinating owners sitting beneath them and doing their last wake-and-bake of the week. Mim waves at the ones she knows—most of them, at this point—and eyes some of their discounted wares, without much intention of actually buying anything. She picked up a few souvenirs for herself over the course of the week, even a couple of things for her family, though she's not sure when (if) she'll get the chance to pass them along. That envelope her mother sent to her is still tucked into the bottom of her purse, paper worn even thinner after a week of regular handling, but she's decided to leave deciding what to do with it for a later date.

The only thing she's looked for and hasn't found is something for Nadia—not, Mim thinks wryly, that she's really let herself admit until right now that she *has* been looking. It's kind of a moot point anyway, because she's pretty sure, after an entire week here, that she's seen all there is to see, but she pops her head into all the remaining shops anyway, chats a little with each owner.

Nadia likes practical things—nothing that Mim can see quite falls into that category, beautiful though some of the leatherwork might be. Nadia likes things that she can use, things that fit in her broad, quick hands. Mim wants to buy her something she can use—something that will show she was thinking of her. That she knows her. That she cares enough about her, to know. That she cares.

Mim swallows, and looks around, hands on her hips. She looks down the street, and has an idea.

March

On the first Tuesday morning in March, Nadia opens her front door to find a tall, thin box sitting on her stoop, gift-wrapped with the comics section of the local paper. She stares at it for a long time before she sees the small, folded piece of white paper stuck to one side and pulls it loose; when she opens it, her heart tightens in her chest, and she briefly forgets how to breathe.

There is nothing written there. Drawn instead is a long brown branch, several deep green, oblong leaves springing out of its sides: an olive branch.

Nadia takes the box upstairs without even unwrapping it, shoves it into the back of her closet, and spends several days telling herself that she doesn't have any idea who might have sent such a thing. It's only when she finds herself awake in the middle of the night, staring daggers at the spot on her closet door behind which she knows the damned thing sits, that she finds it in herself to peel the newspaper wrappings away. Even then, she doesn't open the box, just leaves it sitting on her dresser to deal with later. She glares at it as she gets dressed for work the next morning, and she glares at it as she gets dressed for bed that night; she glares at it from down the hall as she brushes her teeth, and she glares at it until her eyelids grow heavy with sleep and she can't glare anymore. The day after is her day off, and she goes out to run errands and turns around halfway to the mall, drives all the way home and rips the box open in a small but impressive display of fury, because she just can't take *wondering* anymore.

Inside sits the most beautiful piece of blown glass Nadia has ever seen. She stares at it, transfixed, and feels warmed to the tips of her toes when she puts a hand on and realizes what it is—an oil and vinegar decanter, with a fine glass bulb inside the larger bottle with a separate spout for the vinegar. It's odd and gorgeous and, best of all, *functional*. It fits perfectly in her hand and as she holds it, glass cold against her palm, she has to fight the wild urge to throw it out the window, to go outside and smash it against the carefully constructed cobblestone driveway.

It's exactly the sort of gift she'd never expect anyone to think to get for her, and it's not *fair* that Mim can't just leave to her bitterness and her anger and her poorly feigned hatred. It's not fair of Mim to launch an assault like this; Nadia's defenses are already so low, and what makes it worse is that she knows that Mim wouldn't see it that way. Mim probably bought her this because she saw it and she thought of Nadia, or maybe even *went looking for something Nadia would like*. She wouldn't try to trade little kindnesses for larger trespasses, or guilt someone into forgiveness by attaching a string to a peace offering—instead, she's extended an olive branch without expectation, left it sitting on Nadia's front porch in the middle of the night, when she doesn't even have anything to apologize for.

Mim didn't spread her business around, didn't share Nadia's family's secrets with Gale or anyone else. Mim wouldn't have done that to her, she now knows. Nadia has been stewing over the knowledge, or

229

maybe more accurately stewing in her own self-loathing—her loathing of her parents—just stewing, stewing in a morass of fury and misery. Stewing in the knowledge that when she jumped to conclusions and believed the worst of Mim, that Mim didn't hate her for it—for so badly misjudging her, for refusing her the chance to offer any sort of explanation, for being so quick to toss aside their hard-won bond of trust—she instead chose to extend an offer of peace with no expectation attached. Mim, in true Mim fashion, has apologized, even though she didn't do a damn thing wrong.

Nadia doesn't know what to do with that: doesn't know what to do, what to think, how to feel. So she goes to work, leaves the decanter in her bedroom and then in her kitchen at home, where it sits as a glimmering, beautiful reminder of all that she still has to do. Nadia deals with her parents and her kitchen staff and her customers, and in the background she counts each time she touches the stupid, gorgeous thing as a little penance, a drop in a constantly emptying bucket. She lets this bizarre and beautiful little token remind her of Mim whenever she sets eyes on it, and imagines she is filling it with every toxic, wrongheaded thought that's clogged her heart and head since Christmas, not just vinegar and oil. She imagines, too, that into the emptying space within her where that rage and heartbreak used to sit is a slowly growing well of courage, and that someday—maybe even someday soon—she'll have enough saved up to swallow her pride and makes things right between them.

Ray-Jay greets Nadia two weeks before the JAF's annual ball with a gleeful look in his eyes that is nothing short of terrifying. Nadia stops in her tracks.

"You talked to Cory yet today?" he asks.

"No?" Nadia says.

He snickers. "Might want to. Word on the street is that he's gonna be running the kitchen at the JAF ball, instead of you."

Nadia absorbs this, turns it over and around in her head, trying to figure out what about it Ray-Jay would find funny. If Cory wants to play head chef at the annual ball, she hardly minds—she's happy enough to go as her parents' guest and leave after the meal, as is traditional— or, even better, to skip the stupid thing altogether. She hasn't been in several years, but it's not as though they ever fucking change. Hooray, aren't we fantastic. Hooray, haven't we done such a wonderful job. Hooray, we've donated a miniscule portion of our outrageous annual incomes to some charity, let's enjoy the good feeling that gives us with an insanely expensive party! It's enough to make her stomach turn.

"That's fine with me," Nadia says honestly, and risks sidling past Ray-Jay and back into the kitchen. It doesn't hit her until a moment later, when—

"Oh, god," Nadia says, filled with a sudden sense of dread. "Oh, please no."

She hears Ray-Jay, who has always had a taste for schadenfreude, laughing behind her as she storms across the kitchen to Cory's office, slams the door open and demands, "Tell me you're not going to make me play big boss at the JAF ball. At my fucking parents' fucking party—tell me you're not going to do that to me, Cory!"

Cory winces. "Well. I mean. I *could*, but it wouldn't be... very truthful of me."

"Oh my god," Nadia says. She drops heavily into the chair across from Cory, anger temporarily abandoned in favor of sheer horror. "Oh my god—do you hate me? You do, don't you, you hate me, why else would you *ruin my life*."

"Drama, drama," Cory says lightly, and Nadia takes a moment to bare her teeth at him before dropping her head into her hands in abject despair. "Look, Bahjat, you want to run your own place one day, right?"

"If this is what I have to do to get there then I take back that dream," Nadia says without lifting her head. "I'll, I don't know, I'll aspire to owning a hot dog cart. A taco stand. One of those fried dough stations they set up at fairs—"

"All of which require licensing," Cory interrupts, "and financing, and a customer base, and ideally some marketing, or at least good word-of-mouth buzz. In short: networking, also known as something you are *terrible* at, which is why I'm going to work the kitchen and you're going to work the room at this party, no matter how much you bitch about it."

Hands still covering her face, Nadia lifts her head and peers at Cory with one eye through her fingers. "You're telling me you think your average hot dog cart guy is a networking genius?"

"Better at it than you," Cory says, with what seems to be genuine feeling.

Nadia groans and drops her head again. "You are the worst person I know. You are the worst person who has ever been alive. My new life's aspiration is to spread the gospel of how *completely horrible* you are."

"Somehow I think I'll live," Cory says, very dry. When Nadia doesn't reply to this, he sighs. "Come on. It won't be that bad."

Nadia laughs, slightly hysterical. "Are you kidding? Have you ever actually—it's my *parents*. It's my parents, and all of their horrible friends, and none of them are going to take me seriously as a… a chef, or an aspiring restaurateur, or whatever! They're all going to be like"—Nadia affects the snootiest voice she can manage—"'Oh *Nadia*, it's simply *wonderful* to see you, did you know I heard you were a *lesbian*? Very popular thing to be these days, a *lesbian*, in my day it was all much more hush-hush, behind closed doors, you see, but of course good for *you*—"

Three hours before the Blue Horizon crew is supposed to begin setting up at JAF's annual ball, Cory grabs Nadia's elbow and stops her going back in the kitchen.

"Leave," he says.

"Leave?" Nadia repeats, blank; she's been awake for too many hours, and she thinks maybe it's starting to show. "But there are—things. To do. The tapenade—"

"Is already made. And no," Cory adds, giving her a knowing look, "before you try to tell me it needs a little something extra, or another kind of olive, or whatever: it doesn't. It's good. Go home."

"But," Nadia tries, slightly desperate this time, "the gougères—"

"Okay, that's enough," Cory says. "I'm pulling rank. You're out of here, Bahjat. You've been temporarily relieved of commission."

"I thought I was the *boss* today," Nadia mutters under her breath. She knows, on some level, that she's behaving very childishly—Cory is actually giving her an incredible opportunity here, and god knows he's right when he says she needs to learn to network if she ever wants to own a restaurant of her own. He has her best interests at heart, and she should not be repaying him by shooting him a narrowed-eyed glare and adding, "Though who knows what depths a night with these people could drive a person to."

Cory just laughs. "Yes, yes, terrible people, terrible idea, you'd rather be thrown to literal wolves. I know! Now go home and take a shower, unless you want everyone to think you took a bath in that sauce you insisted on for the cannelloni."

"That lemon béchamel is a *triumph*," Nadia snarls, and is surprised—and, honestly, a little bit gratified—when Cory nods an easy agreement.

"Yeah, yeah," Cory says. "Just go, okay? And remember—the first hour is set-up and prep, and I'll relieve you after the meal. So really, you only have to make nice from appetizers 'til the end of service, and that's, what, like four hours, right?"

"Two," Nadia says, stricken. "Did you not read the schedule I wrote up? Oh my fucking god, this is going to be a disaster. I knew this wasn't a good idea, we have to switch it so I'm running the line, you're—" She stops, takes in the look on Cory's face, and sighs. "Oh. You're fucking with me, aren't you."

Cory winks at her. "Admit it," he says, "two hours seem easier after I had you thinking it was four."

Nadia does leave then, but it's only because it's that or hit the man in the face. As fond as Cory is of her, Nadia's pretty sure that would get her fired.

She goes home and slips on her headphones when she sees that both of her parents' cars are in the driveway. It's just safer, to point to the headphones when her mother attempts to start a conversation, when her father tries to beckon her into his study—it's a struggle to talk to her parents at the best of times lately, and just now Nadia doesn't want to risk it. Even on a good day, she's perpetually just a few conversational missteps away from saying something horrible to them, from screaming or ranting or throwing things—and she knows she can't do that. She has to swallow it, because her father's grown frail and her mother fragile; because that's what a good daughter should do. Nadia's never really been a good daughter, but she knows enough to at least know how to try—for her parents, for all of them—if she can just make it through these last few months and get out of this town without letting everything that's been simmering within her boil over.

Her shower is punishingly hot, and she tries to imagine as she washes her hair that it's possible to clean yourself of something preemptively.

It's a crazy idea, but it makes her feel better to pretend—that her loofah is scrubbing away the way the men are going to look at her tonight, the fake smiles the women will toss her way that she'll have to return in kind. The idea of actually going out of her way to talk to these people makes her skin crawl, even though she'll be doing it as a representative of the restaurant, even though she can just stick to talking about the food. It makes her itch with the urge to get in her car and drive in the opposite direction, but she knows she can't do that to Cory or to the kitchen staff.

She stays under the spray until it runs cold, and then for a few minutes after that, too, so that by the time she climbs out she can kid herself into feeling numbed.

Rashida is waiting for her outside the bathroom door, wearing full party makeup and the black slip that will soon be underneath whatever dress she's planning to wear, bearing a garment bag and a determined expression. Nadia's not really sure why she's surprised.

Like a zombie, she goes through the motions of allowing her mother to dress and make her up, even consents to having her hair straightened after putting up a token protest. She's not sure if it's the exhaustion, or the dread, or the certainty that there *was* something not quite right about the tapenade, but all the fight in Nadia seems to have been washed down the shower drain. So what if she looks like someone else by the time Rashida's finished, in a bouncy black cocktail dress she'd never have chosen for herself? So what if her eye makeup isn't dark enough, if her lips aren't the right shade of red, if her heels are too feminine by half? It's not like it matters that the only things about her that still feel like her own are the spirals of her tattoo peeking out from beneath her sleeve and the two white streaks in her hair. This whole thing is an exercise in pretending to be someone else, so why not, right? It's not like it can possibly make her feel any worse about it. It's not like it can possible make it any harder.

"I do wish you'd stop dyeing it this way," Rashida says, for, oh, probably the seven hundred millionth time since Nadia put the first streak in during high school. She wraps a section of white hair around her fingers and tugs at it gently, letting out a soft sigh. "I just don't understand why you think its looks good. Most women spend their lives dreading the sight of white hair, and here you are, doing it on purpose!"

"I know, Mom," Nadia says, toneless. Why argue? God knows she's heard it all before.

"And I'm sure you see now how much better you look without that all that heavy black eyeliner," Rashida continues. "Your face just isn't suited for that kind of heavy makeup—this is much nicer."

"Of course, Mom."

"You know what would look lovely with that dress? That string of pearls we gave you for Christmas a few years back." She starts rummaging around on the dresser, opening and shutting drawers. "When was the last time you wore those pearls, Nadia?"

"I don't remember," Nadia says. It's a lie, because the actual answer is, "To a Halloween party in Chicago two years ago, right before I gave them to this girl and told her she'd look better in them than I would. If it helps, I'm almost sure it's why she slept with me, and the sex was really incredible!" She would so much rather tell the truth that her palms itch with it, but the Nadia in the mirror—the Nadia that Rashida so obviously wishes she were—wouldn't say that to her mother. Actually, the Nadia in the mirror would never have gotten drunk and given a gift like that to a pretty girl in the hopes of winning her body, if not exactly her heart, for a few hours. The Nadia in the mirror probably wouldn't even have known what to do with that girl if she fell in her lap; the Nadia in the mirror probably likes fancy parties. And pretentious literature. And men.

It's been years since Nadia really thought she had any chance of becoming that version of herself, the girl her parents really wanted. It's been years since she could even bring herself to believe that that girl *was* a version of her; it seemed impossible, that there could exist any combination of circumstances which, if properly aligned, might have forged her into that person instead of this one. She's contented herself with a sort of hopeless, meaningless wish, one of those raw little dreams that had shone with possibility when she was still too young to know better, and which has since grown a bit too pathetic to keep on public display. She has handled that part of herself by the very edges like an old photograph, because she's long since known the reproduction was as close as she'd ever get to the real thing.

But now, looking in the mirror, it's suddenly clear to her that she and her mother are seeing two entirely separate people. She thinks, in a dizzying rush of sadness, *Holy shit, maybe I could have pulled it off*. Nadia, in looking at herself, can see the awkwardness in her stance, the discomfort in her eyes, how exposed and incorrect she feels without her clothes and shoes and makeup and hair—but Rashida *can't*. Rashida has never been able to, and never *would* have been able to, and if Nadia had given the act a real shot instead of resigning herself to being a terrible liar, she really might have been able to convince them she was the person they so hoped she could be.

It never occurred to her, in those days when the schism between who she was supposed to be and who she was actually becoming started to make itself clear, that audience might be a factor in deception. She hadn't considered the possibility that if she looked the part—if she gritted her teeth and acted, however badly, every part of it—her parents might have glossed over her little mistakes, and seen what they always made it clear they were looking for.

Her eyes sting, and she wants to snort with derision and disgust at herself. Tears have their time and their place and she wouldn't judge anyone else's right to them, but she's never been the kind of woman who indulges in that sort of thing unless she truly has no choice. The very *idea* of it, of fucking crying over this—over something so small and so stupid as hair or clothes or makeup or shoes, a path she missed the chance to take half a lifetime ago—fills her ears with a humming static, makes her stomach clench in horror. She couldn't work out in time how to grow up into the person her parents wanted; she couldn't learn to speak the language of soft femininity; she had no choice but to be blunt and honest and uncomfortable with most people most of the time. But strength and practicality, an unwillingness to be broken: those were choices. Those traits she selected by hand, like the makeup that doesn't suit her face and the streaks she puts in her hair, and the idea that she could abandon them so easily, over something so idiotic and small, makes her feel even more wrong-footed, as though she doesn't know herself at all.

It's the sleep deprivation, she knows. It's the sleep deprivation, and the stress of having to act a part, and the fact that she genuinely does care about the menu she's spent weeks planning and going over despite everything else—but Nadia is suddenly so confused and tangled up that she feels a little dizzy, that she has to grip the dresser for support. Rashida, still searching through drawers for the string of pearls she definitely won't find, looks up and gives Nadia a narrow-eyed look of concern. Nadia dredges up a smile from... somewhere.

She gets the distinct impression, based on the face her mother makes, that it is not a very convincing smile. This does not bode well for the evening ahead.

"I hope you're not getting sick," Rashida says, closing the last drawer with a sigh. "Maybe you'll have better luck looking for the pearls than me—anyway, it's a bad night to be ill, you must have so much to do! Maybe you should take some Vitamin C, or—"

"I'm not getting sick, Mom," Nadia says, because if she doesn't act quickly she'll be forced to eat or drink something profoundly disgusting. For a moment, she almost wants to laugh, thinking about all the "cures" Rashida must have pushed on her father before he went into remission, and then remembers the lie all over again and scowls, runs a hand through her too-smooth hair. "I'm just tired. I was up all night going over the menus and equipment; Cory's letting me run the show tonight, so I'm not going to fuck it up."

"Oh." Rashida's lips purse a little in disapproval, though whether at Nadia's language or lack of sleep it's hard to be sure. She always has lived in a magical little bubble where "sleeping" and "doing everything that needs to be done" aren't mutually exclusive; Nadia doesn't know why she could have at least inherited that small but miraculous gift, but it's the sort of question that will never get an answer. "Well, you should take one of those twenty-four hour allergy pills, then—I swear, those things could wake the dead. The last time I took one I didn't sleep for two days!"

"Ha," Nadia says, amused despite everything, "I forgot about that. In Jackson Hole that time, right?"

Rashida shudders. "If I told Samir once, I told him a hundred times: nothing good can come of vacationing anywhere that calls itself a hole. But did he listen?"

"Of course not," Nadia says. She grins, shaking her head. "God, what an awful trip. Speaking sleep deprivation—do you remember the owl?"

"What a question," Rashida says, laughter bleeding into the edges of her voice. "Do I remember the owl—how could I forget the owl? There I was, two days awake, frightening the other guests—"

Nadia rolls her eyes. "You were not frightening people."

"That's your memory doing me a kindness," says Rashida, shaking her head. "I was unkempt and wild-eyed and chattering to anyone who

239

would listen about fifth century etchings, everyone on the mountain was perfectly terrified. And then we come home from a long day on the slopes, because of course your father said a little exercise would be what finally exhausted me—"

"And he was right, because you *were* starting to feel like you could fall asleep," Nadia says, the forgotten strands of a once oft-repeated story coming back to her.

"Yes, yes, that's right, and then"—an unladylike snort of laughter escapes Rashida's mouth—"then we open the cabin door and this absolute beast of a creature! This thing that looks as though it came straight out of a nightmare! Just flies right at me, shrieking like a banshee."

Nadia is laughing now, the memory warming her. "It got a chunk of your hair, didn't it?"

"A chunk of my hair and ten years of my life," Rashida says with a sigh. "We couldn't get it out of the house ourselves, you know; we had to get a man in. Horrible man, as I recall. Took far too much joy in netting the poor creature."

"'Poor creature'?" Nadia repeats, still laughing. "That's more forgiving than I remember you being at the time."

"Well," Rashida says, a smile playing at the edges of her mouth, "they do say time heals all wounds, and, after all, the hair did grow back eventually." Her smile slips, and her voice goes distant as she adds, "And that owl—a barn owl, I think the man said—it screamed from the moment he netted it. Screamed all the way out the door and down the road." She shudders, rubs her hands up and down her arms. "Hard to forget a sound like that, I suppose."

"*I* don't remember it," Nadia says, and Rashida's distant expression snaps back into focus.

"Well of course you don't," she says, brusque now, "your father took you back down to the lodge the moment that man showed up.

You were only a child, and we didn't want you anywhere near someone so... distasteful. In any case, it rather ruins what's otherwise a fairly funny story, wouldn't you say?"

Nadia doesn't get a chance to answer, because her father sweeps into the room then, entirely redirecting Rashida's attention. She's not sure if she's relieved or not. On the one hand, she's got no idea what she would have said, disturbed both by the idea of the owl's echoing scream and to realize, now that she really thinks about it, that the story *isn't* very funny, just sad and maybe a little bit horrible. But on the other hand, she feels oddly as though she's lost something, like if she could have just had a few more minutes with this softened, reminiscent version of her mother, the whole landscape of their relationship would've shifted under their feet.

It wouldn't have been that easy, of course. More likely, Nadia would've put her foot in her mouth, and Rashida would've said something cutting, and then Samir would've come in anyway, forcing each of them to turn away from the other as though the whole conversation never happened. But Nadia aches a little anyway, for the kind of love they seem to have lost, and for the kind of love that maybe never existed in the way it should have at all.

"Well, don't you look perfectly lovely," Samir says, noticing Nadia's unusual appearance at last. She grimaces a little, but when he picks up her hand she twirls for him, another nearly forgotten childhood habit that she slips into without a thought. Samir whistles his approval, says, "If I didn't know better, I'd think you were someone else's daughter," and Nadia doesn't let herself flinch to hear it. He's already dressed in his black tie best, bowtie hanging loose around his neck but otherwise flawlessly put together, and Nadia tells herself that it's a compliment and she should take it as one. That's what he would tell her if she did flinch, after all. No point going through the motions.

241

"Well, while I think your mother would be perfectly fine attending the event in what she's wearing—"

"Oh, stop," Rashida says. She bats a hand at him, but sounds quite pleased. "Gale Ashcraft would have us turned away for indecency at the door."

"That *would* be a tragedy," Samir says with a mock sigh. He winks at Nadia, and Nadia rolls her eyes, but smiles back. "In any case, we must go pick up your mother's real dress from the tailor's—a last minute alteration, the excitement of which I regret to inform you that you missed this morning. I'm sure you've got to start heading to the ball anyway, so we'll see you at the party later, all right?"

"Yeah, definitely," Nadia says. She's not sure what it is—the oddly easy conversation with her mother or the comforting familiarity of this moment, her parents saying goodbye on their way to a black-tie party— but she feels more generous to them than she has in what feels like a long time. She waves them out of her room, and even when she takes a few steps and remembers, unhappily, that she is in uncomfortable shoes and a dress that she hates and on her way to a horrible evening and teetering on the knife-edge of exhaustion, she still feels a bit brighter than she did before.

"Allergy pills," she mutters to herself, and can't help but smile as she roots around in the cabinet looking for them, remembering the last time she went on this particular hunt, with Mim taking wheezing breaths downstairs. She still doesn't entirely believe that whole night really happened—well, the part with the neighbors screaming about the cats, anyway. The part where Mim didn't mention a serious allergy because she didn't want to bother anyone is entirely plausible, and Nadia shakes her head in fond exasperation to remember it. She hopes, without much real hope at all, that Mim's found a way to assert herself a little more in these months Nadia's spent absent from her life.

She finds the package of Claritin exactly where she left them that night, and pushes one of the pills up against the foil backing of the packaging, shakes it out into her hand. But when she looks down, there are two pills resting on the calloused surface of her palm—one little white one that looks exactly like every other allergy pill she's ever seen, and one slightly larger blue one which, though not exactly familiar, she's sure she's seen somewhere before.

Nadia can hear her father's car backing down the driveway as she picks up the blue pill between thumb and forefinger, and holds it to the light. It's one of those sounds that she would recognize anywhere—the crunch of small pieces of gravel, the squelch of rubber on cobblestone, is as much a part of her understanding of *home* as the house itself, and just for a moment she thinks that everything she is has narrowed down into this well-worn piece of sense memory, dissolved into this particular, distinctive noise. If she closes her eyes and listens hard enough maybe she can be seven again, laying awake long past her bedtime in hopes of welcoming her parents home from one of their fancy events; maybe she can be seventeen and sitting on the roof with a pack of cigarettes she shouldn't be smoking, waiting for her cue to scramble inside. Maybe she can be any fucking age but this one, doing any fucking thing but this—maybe she can jump between universes, somehow, to a version of her life where this doesn't happen, where she doesn't have to look this thing in the face and find some way to cope.

Because this—this is a fucking Oxycontin pill, a common recreational dosage, that she recognizes from having been offered them once or twice over the years. This is a fucking Oxycontin that's been hidden here inside this innocuous wrapping for who knows how long—since before the night with Mim, definitely, because god, it was here then; she remembers that, now that she thinks about it. Nadia fucking noticed it then, that there were mismatched pills in this box, and didn't think anything of it, because of course her father wasn't a drug addict at the time. At the time he was a cancer patient doing his damnedest to get better and she was fucking lying awake at night, fucking *worried* about him, and she's honestly not sure which part is worse: that the truth was right here, the whole story, if she'd only thought to really look for it, or that this pill's continued presence in this hiding spot means the man whose priorities she has placed above her own for as long as she can remember has hidden so many drugs around their family home that he has *forgotten* about some of them.

Addiction is a disease—Nadia knows this. She should have compassion—she knows this too. Her parents made a mistake and lied to her but people make mistakes and lie to each other. She herself is not without sins, and she owes them so much—it's her obligation, her *duty* to forgive them, to love them, to let this go. She knows that. She knows. She knows it the way you know something forward and backwards after you've repeated it to yourself for months and months and fucking *months*, but it doesn't seem to help anymore, somehow. It's almost as though that little blue pill, which she flushes down the toilet with its little friends in an assortment of other colors, is taking with it on its journey down to the sewers her ability to keep tamping this anger down.

She thought, once, that she liked anger, that she thrived on it. Now Nadia gets behind the wheel of her car, prettied up into the caricature of herself that her parents would prefer her to be, and knows that anger has turned her into a dangerous, frightening thing. There is a wild animal inside of her that will tear her apart if that's what it takes to make its way outside; it's trying already, claws gouging deep wounds into her stomach, teeth closing painfully around the ventricles of her heart. She is bleeding out across the floor of her beat-up old sedan, but she knows that if she were to cry out for help, pull over to the side of the road and flag down the nearest passersby, all they would see is a pretty young woman in high-heeled shoes and a dress that make her look soft.

And despite that, despite how very badly she wants to give in and let her feral fury free, she can't do that right now. She screams wordlessly at the top of her lungs for three solid blocks to realize it, but she can't *do* that right now, she doesn't have time; she has to go be a team player, and Cory and the staff don't need a wild animal in a person suit, or a hand grenade whose pin has been pulled, or a loaded goddamn gun. They need someone competent and calm and capable of conversation, someone who has it together, and so she has to be that person, at least until the end of the dinner service. She has to swallow it one last time, and maybe she's lost the ability to tamp the anger down, but god knows she can choke it back for few more fucking hours. In some ways, she's been training for it all her life.

"Well," says... a man, Nadia thinks. A human male. Beyond that, she's lost, although she knows that she participated in the traditional introductory exchange with this person, and thus was presumably given his name. Craig, maybe. Jason. Liam. She's pretty sure she's just thinking of random names, since none of those ring even the faintest of bells.

"Yes," Nadia returns, "well." That is not the right response. They were talking about something—the restaurant—food—possibly a color. A color of food? God, Nadia's had so many conversations tonight and none of them have meant anything; what are the words she has to say to make this man no longer be standing here. "It was—wonderful. To talk with you. Here. Tonight."

"To you as well," he says, "here, please take my card," and Nadia does as she's told, although she's uncertain why. Is this man—his card says he's Alexis, she wasn't even close—expecting a phone call? An email? He's going to be sorely disappointed, regardless.

"Thank you," says Nadia, "this is—very good. Helpful. I hope that you—enjoy the party."

"Thanks," he says easily, "you too," and Nadia has to bite down on her own tongue, hard, to keep a wild shout of laughter from escaping her. Even so, a strangled sort of snort slips past her defenses, and she scurries away towards the kitchens before the man who is apparently called Alexis can ask her further questions—possibly, based on the sound that she just made, about her upper respiratory health.

It is not going well.

"It is not going well," she tells Jackson, more than a little desperately, as he walks by with a tray of canapés. She grabs for the tray, but he dodges easily out of her reach. "Please," says Nadia, "*please* give me the tray. I will take it, and I will give it to Cory, and I won't have to talk to anyone on the way. Nobody talks to you when you're holding a tray. I need the tray, Jackson. Give me the tray!"

"You know, I never really understood why the rest of them think that you're crazy," Jackson says, his tone frankly considering. "But I see it now. I think it's the eyes."

"I can't be crazy-eyed with a tray," Nadia says fervently, "the tray will help to conceal the crazy eyes, consider it a public service," but Jackson is already rolling his own eyes and walking away from her. "Technically I'm your boss!" Nadia sort of—well, there's no way around it, she yells it—after him, and several nearby people turn around to look at her.

"Ahaha," she says, "so hard—to find—good help?" Upsettingly, this seems to satisfy everyone. Not for the first time tonight, Nadia considers escaping out of a window.

She escapes to a hallway instead, and the plan, right, the *plan* is to follow this hallway to its conclusion at the kitchen doors, but Nadia's never been very good with plans, and plans have never been very good with her. Perhaps this is why Nadia takes three steps down the hallway only to stop dead at the sight of Mim Robinson leaning against the wall, holding a champagne flute in one hand and one of Nadia's deviled quail eggs in the other. She freezes on the spot.

"I spent hours getting the seasoning just right for those stupid eggs and no one else is eating them," Nadia says after a long moment of doing nothing but staring—or really almost chokes, voice coming out strange—instead of something sane, like, "Nice to see you," or, "Hello."

"Oh!" Mim says, and, of course, drops the half-eaten egg. "I—oh god, I'm sorry, it—uh. It was a really—good egg?"

"There are plenty more," says Nadia, staring at the splatter of yolk on the carpet, which, she feels, summarizes her mental state pretty perfectly right at this moment. "Because nobody else is eating them. Which I said already."

"Hi," Mim says, and blushes; Nadia thinks it makes her look like a sunset, the way it pinks her face beneath her apricot hair in the low golden lighting, and feels *crazy*. "It's... it's nice to—I mean—sorry, I'm..." She lifts the champagne flute, waving it slightly, and winces when some of its contents slosh over the side and onto her hand. "I've maybe had a couple of these and it's a little, I mean, seeing you—like this. You look. Um. You—ah."

Nadia stares at her for a second, completely at sea, before she remembers all over again how she looks tonight and scowls, shifting awkwardly in her uncomfortable dress, her heels, which are scraping horribly at the backs of her feet. She does not want compliments from anybody tonight—not on her dress, and especially not from—Mim.

"My mother did it," Nadia says, clipped. "It's not—I won't, you know. Be doing it again. One time only show."

"Oh thank god," Mim says, rushed, and then hurriedly, "I mean! God! I'm sorry! You look—fine, I mean, it's—it's very pretty, on anyone else it would—but it's—you know—"

Nadia finds herself laughing, sounding slightly hysterical. "Stop, stop. I know I look ridiculous. Honestly, I'm glad to know someone else can tell; everyone else keeps telling me how lovely it is to see me in something respectable."

"It's really not ridiculous," Mim says, earnest now. "If I didn't know you—or, I mean—if you were just a person on the street, I'd think you looked—I'd think you were really pretty." She flushes again, puts a hand to the back of her neck, and finishes, "But since it's you... you just. You look kind of, uh, exhausted, and not... not like yourself. Which isn't to say that you're not, I mean—pretty—the rest of the time..."

She trails off, looking mortified, and takes a long pull from her glass of champagne; Nadia's eyes trace the sinews of her neck, the freckles glowing honey-sweet beneath the pale gold sconces lining the hallway, and she forgets briefly everything that's sitting leaden in her stomach. It seems impossible that there could be any moment of happiness amidst the trappings of this hideous night, but it's been so long since she and Mim stood this close to each other. She thinks—hopes—she can see Mim looking back at her from beneath her lashes, her eyes flicking up to Nadia's face briefly and then away again, fingers of her free hand sliding down from the back of her neck to play with the tail of her messy, side-swept braid. She looks even better than Nadia remembers her looking, though it's been long enough that Nadia can't really tell anymore. Her chest, she thinks distantly, feels strange.

"I got your—thing," Nadia says, not sure if she should presume to call the decanter a present or not, at the same moment Mim says, "I really did like the egg."

"Oh!" Mim says, thankfully before Nadia's always glitchy brain-to-mouth filter can fail to block a truly asinine "good egg" joke. She's still toying with the end of her braid, and her eyes meet Nadia's for the briefest of seconds before they flicker away again to stare fixedly at a point on the wall. "I—I wasn't sure, I mean, I didn't. Know if you'd liked it—gotten it! If you'd gotten it, or even knew it was from me. I probably should have signed the card."

"I got it," Nadia says. She takes a deep breath and then, body moving almost of its own accord, a step forward. The hairs on the back of her neck stand up when she hears Mim's little intake of breath at this small advance on her personal space. "I liked it. I knew who it was from."

Another intake of breath—sharper, more audible this time—and then Mim's eyes meet hers again. Nadia feels fuzzy, light-headed, crazy; she wants to take Mim by the hand and pull her out into the night, beg forgiveness for all that she's done wrong, explain herself once and for all. She wants, she thinks with sudden, razor-sharp clarity, to pin Mim against the wall with her hands, with her hips, and lick the taste of champagne out of her mouth. This, she realizes, is what she's wanted to do for quite some time—for ages—but now—now—

"You didn't, um," Mim says, and though her voice shakes on it a little, she's still maintaining determined eye contact. "You didn't—reply."

"Yeah," Nadia says, hoarse, "sorry."

"It's fine," Mim says, voice slightly too high-pitched.

Nadia knows that when she opens her mouth again that it's all going to pour out of her: everything she got wrong not only about Mim but about life, too, about Juniper Lane, Gale, her mother, her father. She can feel the rising tide of it swell in her stomach and she fights to keep her mouth shut, because it will be too much, because Mim deserves—she deserves what Nadia has been working her way up to all these weeks, an apology she won't have to share with everything else that's unspooling within Nadia tonight. If she tries to do this right now, then things will get messy, and Mim deserves something fresh and clean from Nadia. Some small part of her thinks that they both do.

"*There* you are," says Cory, and then, "...oh." Nadia's sure he thinks he's interrupted something, knows how it must look, the two of them standing so close like this when Cory knows—much to her own irritation—how long it's been since they've really spoken. She should turn and reassure him, she knows. She just wants one more moment here, in this little bubble of quiet, where Mim's hair is catching the light.

"I should," Mim says, and she's talking to both of them but she's looking at Nadia, right at Nadia, green eyes wide and full of warmth. "I should let you both get back to work."

"Right," Nadia says, "yes. Work."

"Right," Mim repeats, and then, after a beat: "But you should... we should... talk. At some point. If you, um, if you want to."

"I want to," Nadia says, hopelessly honest, and Mim's answering smile, for the few seconds it graces her face, illuminates even the darkest corners of Nadia's mind.

"See you, then," Mim says quietly. One last long look and she's gone, slipping easily around Cory and back into the party, and Nadia stands there staring at the spot where she was the moment before, blood singing beneath her skin.

"Dinner service, Casanova," Cory says, interrupting Nadia's reverie. She jerks around, embarrassed, and glares when she finds him grinning at her. "And I thought you were trying to hide from the guests, not make time with pretty redheads."

"Nobody says 'make time' anymore," Nadia says. "Nobody's said 'make time' in like a hundred years." She pulls a face at him and adds, "And I *was* trying to hide from the guests, they're awful and I'm bombing.

You should take my seat at dinner; you're supposed to be doing, what, the steaks, right? So, great, you take my spot, and I'll do the steaks."

"In that dress?" Cory says, and rolls his eyes when she flips him the bird. "Go on, you're doing fine. My spies in the crowd have nothing but good things to say."

"I tried to start a conversation with a woman by telling her that her shoes were the same color as our classic rémoulade," Nadia says flatly, and narrows her eyes when Cory laughs. "She did *not* find it as amusing as you do."

"Ah, well, you win some, you lose some." Cory waves a hand towards the party. "And here, as a parting gift, is a pearl of wisdom from my many years on the schmooze: try to actually eat some of the food instead of just watching everyone else eat it, will you? I don't know why, but people tend to find that unsettling."

"But—"

"Unsettling," Cory says sternly, "and you, bless your weird little heart, do not need any help on that front. Off with you; I have things to plate, and you have wealthy suburbanites to charm."

"Oh yeah, that's *really* likely," Nadia says, but goes anyway, and takes her seat at the Juniper Lane table.

The Juniper Lane table, such as it is, is a little bit like the head table at a wedding; it's the only twelve-top in a room full of tens, positioned at the front of the banquet hall where everyone can see it. There are two seats reserved for every house on the street, and though Nadia has a brief moment of hope that Mim will be taking one of the two that traditionally sit empty—they're technically Ruth's, after all—no one comes to fill the extra spot. This means that it's her, Mary and Barry Craddock, Fred and Angel Neary, John and Diane Warwick, Nadia's parents—she finds she can't even *look* at them, but hopefully they're too busy looking at each other to notice—and, of course, Gale and Richard Ashcraft.

So: your basic nightmare.

Nadia busies herself for the first few minutes of dinner service with smoothing her napkin in her lap, positioning her forks and knives just so. She spends the next few minutes craning her neck trying to see what's going on in the kitchen, until she is eventually forced to admit that, a) she cannot in fact see anything, and b) turning to look across the room is very illuminating vis-à-vis just how many people are staring at them, and it makes Nadia feel uncomfortably like she's going to be having dinner inside of a fish bowl. This leaves no choice but to at least appear to engage with her fellow diners, though as they wait for the first course to come out Nadia mostly tunes them out and tries to think about anything that isn't going to make her, say, lunge across the table screaming bloody murder at her father.

"Oh, Nadia should tell us about the dishes," Gale says, voice practically gushing with enthusiasm, as the wait staff appear with their salads. "After all, it's not often we're lucky enough to eat with the chef!"

"Too right," says Samir, voice is raised in the way it only gets when he drinks. Nadia tells herself she doesn't care, and feels something unpleasant and unnamable in her gut when she realizes she almost doesn't. "Go on, then. Impress us all with your culinary wizardry."

Nadia gives Jackson, who is placing a salad on Mary Craddock's plate, a significant look that she hopes he will be able to translate as a request for swift death. He raises his eyebrows and mouths, "Crazy eyes," before moving on to the next table, so: probably not. She summons up something to say about the salad that isn't, "It's a fucking starter salad, what do you want from me?" and they all seem to enjoy it, which Nadia supposes is something. The next courses are at least a little more interesting, and when the salmon comes out Nadia can't help but enjoy the shower of compliments for the lemon béchamel, never mind that Rashida takes one bite and declares it, "A little too heavy for my tastes, sweetheart, but I'm sure it's delicious, of course."

At the cheese course, Nadia starts drinking, because, hell—Cory said she had to make it through dinner service and it's almost done, she *got through it*, so she's well within her rights to have a few glasses of the excellent red wine she knows they're serving tonight. She knocks back her first glass in one go while she thinks no one is looking, grabs Jackson by the elbow for a second pour before he can scamper away. He glares at her for daring to lay a hand upon him, naturally, but he also fills her glass, so that's all right.

The warm buzz of alcohol eases Nadia into the dessert course, and as she pokes at her soufflé, she can't help but feel that this night, like her lemon béchamel, was a triumph. Sure, she might have struck a few people as odd, but that's practically a Juniper Lane tradition. Hell, Mary Craddock has spent the whole evening telling anyone who would listen that Angel Neary is plotting to have her killed, and Nadia has entertained herself all through the meal with watching Representative Warwick sneaking anything not nailed down into Diane's oversized handbag. Nadia didn't yell at or attack anyone; she didn't attempt matri- or patricide; she didn't run out halfway through. Cory and the staff needed her to be calm and professional and, god damn it, she *did* it, even on a night when she felt like being anything but. Maybe, she thinks, she really can run her own place one day, awkwardness and bluntness be damned. She catches Cory looking at her from the kitchen door, arms folded but eyes proud, and wonders if her having that realization wasn't the whole point all along.

She finishes her soufflé. She has another glass of wine. Even in her uncomfortable clothes she is comfortably full as the meal draws to a close, as most of the others at the table push back their chairs and head for the dance floor. She leans back in her chair for a moment, settling her hand over the slight swell of her stomach, and then she removes it at once when she looks up and realizes she is unconsciously mirroring her father.

That's horrifying, of course, but still: the food was good. The wine *is* good. She didn't snap. The worst is over.

As if summoned by this thought, Gale—who was, until this moment, safely several seats away from Nadia—picks her way over to the chair next to her and sits down. She's wearing her signature green, of course, and the platinum and diamond of her wedding bands are bright against her dark skin as she folds her hands over each other primly on the table.

"Well," she says, in her high, enthusiastic trill, "that was a lovely meal, Chef Bahjat."

"I," Nadia says. She can't help but stumble in surprise at this respectful form of address from this woman, of all people. "That's—nice of you to say. Thanks."

"I wanted," Gale starts, and stops. She touches her wedding rings with the thumb and forefinger of her right hand, then says, "I thought you might like to know that Rebecca is doing… that Rebecca and I have, ah. Been talking about things. That night—what you saw… " Gale shakes her head, eyes sad. "You know, I used to think there was nothing so important as family to me, but, well. Then I married Richard, and everyone—there was always—to be a black woman, in that family, in that world—I had to be better, you understand? Not just *as good*, but better. And suppose I… I may have lost sight of some things. Along the way."

Nadia stares fixedly at the table and stays perfectly still, as though this very uncomfortable conversation is a bear and will go away if she doesn't move—she's probably starting to get a little drunk. "You don't really, um, owe me an explanation."

"Oh, I know," Gale says, and lets out a small, sad little laugh. "Wouldn't it just be the most heartbreaking thing if I told you that it's something of a novelty, knowing there's someone I can trust in this rumor mill of a town?"

"You start most of those rumors," says Nadia, who can't help herself, and Gale sighs.

"Yes," she says. "That is true."

They sit in heavy silence for a moment, Nadia and a woman she used to hate, and whom she now... well, it's strange, to be able to see beneath the skin of a person you never particularly wanted to know that way—a singularly unpleasant sort of intimacy. Nadia flags Jackson for another glass of wine, ignoring his sharp look, and sips at it with the hope that it will, somehow, make this all less awkward; she hopes Gale gets to her point soon, whatever that point may be. Nadia is willing to believe that she's working with her daughter, that her priorities are changing, but she's known her neighbors too long to imagine that Gale isn't looking for something.

"I suppose I just, ah," Gale says, finally. "I thought that perhaps this evening might make us... even."

"I... don't really look at the world like that," Nadia says after a long pause, which is maybe something that's true and maybe something she just hopes is true, but is all she wants Gale to know, either way. After a moment's thought, she adds, "And what do you mean, anyway? My seat at the table? Because to be honest with you, Mrs. Ashcraft, I would have preferred to be in the kitchen. Or whatever corner you shoved Mim into, I guess."

"I did no such thing," Gale snaps, indignant, and then, with visible effort, reigns in her emotions. "I mean, I—I didn't think she'd want to sit at a table with me, after... everything."

Nadia snorts. "And you thought that I would?"

"I thought you were the head chef and the daughter of the largest donor and anything else would have been radically inappropriate," Gale says, voice sharpening again, before she sighs. "And as I said, I thought it might have—my intervention on your behalf—"

"Your what?" Nadia says. "My what?"

"With the catering contract," Gale says, and her voice changes again now, the harmonics shifting into a strange, almost giddy tone. "Oh, but didn't you *know*? Your father wanted to give the contract to JuJu's, that place uptown. He said he was worried a job like this would be too much pressure on you."

"Too much... pressure," Nadia repeats, hardly hearing it. "On... me."

"Well, because of what happened in Chicago, of course," Gale continues, either blind to Nadia's blank shock or purposefully ignoring it. Her voice still has that odd timbre to it, like this is the most fun she's had all night—like something about this, the divulging of secrets, thrills her to her very core. "I mean, of course, to be fired from any job is always painful, but when it's a passion—"

"My father told you," Nadia says, over the roaring in her ears, the blood pounding in her head, "that I left Chicago... and came home... because I was... fired?"

"Well, yes," Gale says, cocking her head and looking at Nadia with concern. "Was that—was that supposed to be a secret? Oh, but sweetheart, the whole town's known for months; it all came out right around when we heard the dreadful news about his cancer." She glances at Nadia and looks a little taken aback, adding hastily, "It's nothing to be ashamed of, Nadia. Plenty of us have been fired at one point or another in our lives, and of course city life isn't for everyone."

Nadia's not listening to her. Nadia's not listening to anything; Nadia's thinking about her father calling her on the phone and asking her to quit her job, her great, fascinating job, her job that she was so lucky to get at her age, to come back to town and keep an eye on their house while they were away for his cancer treatment. She's thinking about the strange, careful way everyone handled her when she first showed up in town, that she thought was because her father was dying of a horrible disease. Which was a plausible thing to think, because it's *what her father told her*—her father who was really a drug addict. Her father whose pills are hidden all over their house. Her father who is standing now, across the room, being honored and thanked for his generous donation like he's a great man and a pillar of the community instead of a *liar*.

She has spent so much of her life trying to be the person her parents wanted, that impossibly perfect daughter, that carefully shaped miniature of the woman Samir so loved. She has spent so much of her life regretting the person she couldn't help but become instead. She dropped her whole life to move back here for him, for them, she didn't even question it; she didn't even leave when she uncovered their sick, horrible lie. They asked her to stay and so she stayed, wanting as always to please them, to manage it now as she'd failed to despite her best efforts for years. All that work, all that sacrifice, and for what? To hear nothing but lies, over and over? To, apparently, be lied *about*? To have served, unknowing, as the white rabbit in her father's fucking magic act, the big distraction everyone kept their eyes upon while he pulled off the real trick?

Nadia is drunk, and she is exhausted, and she is so far beyond furious that every one of her nerves is screaming white hot, and the dinner service is over. She scrapes her chair back. She stands up.

Someone says her name, as she crosses the dance floor. She takes a flute of champagne from a passing tray and throws it back, and then takes another, and someone says her name again as she steps up onto the little platform they call a stage for nights like this, as she pulls the microphone from the hands of a surprised-looking little man in a bow tie.

"Hello," Nadia says, looking out at the crowd—at Gale Ashcraft and Mary Craddock and somewhere, probably, Mimosa Robinson, who doesn't deserve to see this, whom Nadia wishes weren't here tonight at all. She looks out at the servers and guests and all of her crazy neighbors, every last person except her parents, and says, "I'm Nadia Bahjat, and I have something to say."

The room is still for a beat, a hanging moment of quiet in which Nadia's nerve wavers, and then Samir lets out a belly laugh and calls, "Well, then say it already, Nadia! Didn't I teach you? Nobody likes to wait on a toast!"

She stares at him—at the drink in his hand, at the grin on his face, at the shadow her mother makes at his side—and wants nothing more than to make him feel as sick and small as she does.

"To my father," she says, lifting her glass, "who has everything a man could want—good friends. Good neighbors. Money and renown. A job that he loves. A beautiful wife and," Nadia pauses, pulls the hurt from her voice so all that's left is the snarl, "a *devoted* daughter. All the riches a man could ask for, that's what my father has. But you know what he doesn't have?"

If the room was quiet before, it's a tomb now; even the sound of clattering dishes has stopped in the kitchen, and Samir isn't grinning anymore. His face is slack, and he's staring at her with a mix of horror and desperation on his face, Rashida gripping his shoulder so tightly that Nadia can see her white knuckles from here. She closes her eyes, and then opens them again, determined.

"*Cancer*," Nadia spits. "He doesn't fucking have *cancer*."

There is a collective gasp from the room and Nadia sways on her feet as her eyes open, as she looks right at them—her mother and father, whom she has ruined, is ruining right now. And it's poison that's coming out of her mouth, she knows it, she can hear the aftermath of this moment hurtling towards her and she should stop—she knows she should stop—but she doesn't.

"Yeah," Nadia says, waving her glass in the air, "that's right. No cancer. Big lie. What he has, actually, is a drug problem, but he didn't want anyone to know that, did you, Pop? So you, ha, you told everyone who would listen that you were *dying*, you told your own daughter you were *dying*—do you know I laid awake at night and cried for you? Do you know that I wrote a fucking eulogy for you, Dad? While you were really in rehab and I was here, thinking I'd be lucky to ever see you again, when really—when really it turns out I'd've been luckier if I never fucking did, doesn't it?"

She's crying now, she can hear the sob in her voice and she feels sick, the kind of sick she thought he was—the kind of sick that kills you. But she can't stop, it keeps coming out of her, she chokes on it and doesn't know where she finds the breath to say, "All I ever wanted to do was be the person I thought you wanted and you don't care about me at all, do you! You can't! You wouldn't have done this to me if you did, how could anyone—god. God! I kept your secret! Even after I found out, I kept it, I didn't tell anyone, I didn't even tell you how much it tore me up because I didn't want to *burden* you— how could you do that to me? You, you both care more about what all these fucking people," she waves her hand, splashing her champagne everywhere and ignoring it, "these fucking stupid, shallow, pointless people, with all their money and status and petty *bullshit*—you care more about what they think of you than you care about me. And what does that make me? Huh? I'm really asking—what does that make me?"

They stare back at her, all of them, her boss who will have to fire her, her neighbors who will talk about her for years, her parents whose faces are matching masks of horrified shock. They stare back at her, even the redhead in the back with her hand over her mouth to whom Nadia hoped never to show this part of herself, and Nadia *is* going to be sick, actually; she's going to heave and heave until there's nothing left inside of her.

"An idiot," Nadia whispers, "it makes me a fucking idiot," and she drops the microphone, and runs.

April

To make it through the long months of winter when they weren't speaking to one another, Mim got into the habit of imagining Nadia. What she'd say, sure, but what she'd do, too, how far she'd be willing to take a joke or what expression her face might twist into. It was a poor substitute, not to mention more than a little pathetic, but Mim needed something to fill the void that Nadia had left behind. She'd never been great at making friends to begin with, even before Dell encouraged her to cut ties with everyone she'd ever been close to, and the loss—the hours spent alone in Ruth's musty, moldy old house, staring at the ceiling, wallowing in her own misery—had left her even lonelier, more hollow and more aching than she could ever have expected. She hadn't, she'd realized, tried to become someone else with Nadia: she had just been herself, as best as she could. Whatever the hell that meant.

The thing is—she's still doing it. Imagining what she'd say to Nadia, what Nadia might do, even when Nadia's in the room, because Nadia herself isn't doing much of anything at all.

It's not that Mim blames her, really. It's not even that Mim resents her for it, because god knows if Mim had been the one to lose her parents and her job and her self-respect over the course of three terrible, drunken minutes—she too would be practically catatonic in horror and grief. Honestly, she'd probably be worse: Nadia's at least getting out of her borrowed bed most mornings, remembering to wash and feed herself, and cooking Mim and Ruth a meal once every few days and offering them a mechanical sounding, "Thank you for letting me stay here," before retreating to the guest room with her own plate. It's just that that's *all* she's doing. There's no warmth in her voice, no light behind her eyes, not even any of the roiling anger Mim told herself to expect when she chased Nadia out of the banquet hall that awful, awful night. There's just—blankness. She's just wandering around empty, a ghost.

That night—even Mim doesn't like to think about it, so she can't imagine how Nadia must feel. It was awful to watch her explode, of course, but even worse was seeing the way she hunched in on herself, when Mim finally tracked her down across town, sitting on the ground outside Blue Horizon. She had obviously been crying, though she wasn't anymore, and it was clear, too, that she'd been violently sick, though Mim sat down next to her without mentioning her sour breath or the ruin she'd made of her party dress. She just passed over a lighter and one of the cigarettes she'd had the foresight to pick up at a gas station, held Nadia's hand steady when it was shaking too hard to control a flame, and smoked with her in heavy silence until Nadia would allow her to pull her up and take her home.

Nadia only said three words that night, and now, nearly two weeks later, they're still the only words Mim's been able to get out of her about it: "I fucked up. Oh, god, Mim—I fucked up."

Mim didn't know what to say. If she's being honest, she still doesn't.

When Cory stops by for the second time since That Night, Nadia doesn't do much more than give him the dead-eyed stare she's been giving everyone lately, but she does, at least, consent to be in the same room with him, which is an improvement upon his first visit, when she'd locked the door of the guest bedroom upon realizing that he was there, and then refused to respond to a full hour his heartfelt apologies. He hadn't exactly had any choice but to fire Nadia after she'd publicly trashed his entire customer base on company time, but it's pretty obvious that he isn't *happy* about it.

Mim meets Cory in the driveway. He sighs, looking haggard, as Ruth comes around from the back. "She's still not talking, huh?" she says, glancing up at the house.

"More or less," he says.

"I don't think we should be talking about her behind her back," Mim says half-heartedly.

"Kid," Ruth says, looking at her almost pityingly, "you gotta understand—sometimes, when someone hits bottom hard like this, it's up to their friends to pick 'em back up."

"When I hit bottom hard, you left me alone," Mim points out. She doesn't mean it unkindly, but Cory winces, looking profoundly uncomfortable, and Mim turns red.

Ruth just rolls her eyes. "You'll remember, Mimosa, that you showed up on my doorstep after you cut ties with every other member of your family, and were so fragile I thought a stiff breeze might send you running out the door. You're damn right I left you alone; I promised your parents I'd do everything I could to keep you where I could see you, and that's exactly what I did. This is nothing like that."

Chastised, Mim whispers, "I—right, sorry."

Cory clears his throat.

"I'm not mad at you, kid," Ruth says, "but you have to admit you take a gentler touch than your girl does. I'm not so good at gentle, so I left you be. Simple as that."

"She's not my—" Mim starts, and feels herself blush hotly when both Ruth and Cory give her a disbelieving look. "She *isn't!*"

"Leaving aside that obvious pile of horseshit for another time," Cory says, "I haven't known Nadia as long as you have, Ruth—or as, uh, let's say as *well* as you have, Mim—"

"Oh my god," says Mim.

"—*But*," Cory continues as if she hadn't spoken, "you learn a different side of someone when you work the line with them. You just do. And Nadia needs something to *do*, even in the best of times. With something like this weighing on her? She's gonna drive herself nuts before long."

"Well, I," Mim starts, speaking slowly. "I don't really want to be... demanding." *An asshole*, she thinks, but doesn't say. *Like her parents.* From the looks on Ruth and Cory's faces, she might as well have.

"You don't ever want to bother anybody, but since when have you ever been *demanding*?" Ruth asks. "I mean, Jesus Christ, if we're gonna call *you* pushy, then I don't think I want to know what I am. I think you've just gotta suck it up and put on your big girl pants for this one, kiddo. You're the closest friend she's got in this town—"

"Or anywhere, I think," Cory says quietly, and for all she knows there's nothing but kindness behind it, Mim can't help but resent him, if only for a moment, for sharing Nadia's business like that.

"Anywhere, then," Ruth says, though she looks a little sad about it. "Point is, we'd do something if we could, but at the end of the day, you're the one she listens to."

"Trust your instincts," Cory adds. "I mean, there's a reason you guys are so close. Just—try to get her doing something. Get her out of the house, maybe."

"What if she won't go?" Mim says.

Ruth's looking at her shrewdly, and then gives Mim a slow smile, as though she can see something Mim can't. "You know what, kid? I think you'll figure it out."

When Mim goes back inside, she finds Nadia in a position she recognizes—laying spread-eagle on the guest room floor, fingers tapping a soft beat on the carpet, eyes fixed on the ceiling. She doesn't notice Mim at the doorway, so Mim stands and looks at her for a minute or two, at her dark curls, spilled out across the pale green rug, look even longer all laid out like this, and the angle highlights her sharp cheekbones, her full mouth, the arch of her eyebrows and nose. She really has, Mim thinks, a startling sort of beauty, the kind that you read about in fairy tales and romance novels: not pretty in the more traditional feminine sense of the word, but striking, unparalleled. Even as Mim watches, her long, dark eyelashes settle against skin that's a richer bronze than usual in the wash of late afternoon sunlight; her chest rises and falls with slow, even breaths, and Mim wants her with a ferocity that she's never experienced before, so intense that it almost frightens her.

But now is not the time for that, and Mim wouldn't want it to be, not when Nadia is a shell of herself like this. If it happens—and for the first time, Mim is allowing herself to harbor the tentative hope that it might— she wants to be able to touch every part of Nadia, even the intangible

265

parts she seems to have lost track of right now. So she swallows it, not just the sharp hunger but the breathless appreciation, too, until Nadia is just a body laid out in front of her in a position she intimately knows. She wonders whether Nadia is thinking, "Get up. Get up. Get up."

Rather than ask—asking seems pointless—she steps carefully across the rug and lies down next to her instead. When she looks to her right, Nadia is staring back at her, her brown eyes a little less blank than usual, a little more curious.

"Hey," Mim says.

"Hey," Nadia says.

"You wanna go do something?" Mim says. She's expecting a fight—expecting a fight has, in fact, prevented her from asking this very question for days—but Nadia just blinks at her, eyes wide.

"Yeah," she says. "All right."

They start small, that first day—a trip to the grocery store, to restock the kitchen with food. Nadia is quiet at first but Mim needles her, puts terrible pre-made pasta sauces in the cart just to make Nadia snarl and remove them, suggests they buy a horrible-looking piece of steak just to provoke a rant about the merits of grass-fed beef. It's not exactly a deep emotional discussion, but it *is* more words than Nadia's spoken since the annual ball. When they get home, Mim confesses that she has no idea how to go about cooking a steak, and Nadia sighs heavily but teaches her, the two of them bumping elbows at the stove.

They go to the movies the next day, pay for matinee tickets but end up sneaking from one theater to another after their first film's credits roll. Mim's the only one giggling at their petty crime, but she catches a half-smile on Nadia's face as they scurry without any subtlety down the theater hallway. It's something, just like Nadia's hesitant conversation in the car afterwards is something. It's better than nothing. It's a foot in the door.

Over the next seven days, they do everything Mim can think of *to* do. They visit an open air market in a city more than an hour away; they check out all the local bookstores, even the horrifying adult one off the side of the freeway; they stop in at a nearby dairy, where Nadia comes the closest she's been to her old self via an intense argument with the owner about cheese production.

They go to an art museum. They go to a play. They spend a day volunteering at the local food bank, though they are asked politely to consider donating money instead of their time in the future, as Nadia can't help but express her opinions on the quality of the various canned goods they're sorting and everyone but Mim seems to find this exhausting. In short, they take advantage of every distracting thing Barn Ridge, Ohio—and, indeed, the surrounding tri-county area—has to offer, and by the time the week draws to a close, Mim is starting to worry that they're going to have to start doing things over again.

"You're totally out of things to distract me with, aren't you," says Nadia on Sunday evening, correctly interpreting Mim's look of barely concealed panic when she asks about the next day's plans. Nadia doesn't seem… okay, exactly, but she's talking again, and her body seems more occupied by a soul than it did a week ago; Mim no longer feels like she's staring into an abyss of despair when she looks into her eyes. "It's okay. You did really good, honestly, for someone who didn't grow up here. I mean, *I* didn't even know about that trampoline place." The trampoline place, Mim thinks sourly, had not been one of her better ideas.

"They should call that place 'Lawsuits R Us,'" Mim mutters, and then freezes, her fork halfway to her plate of leftover meatloaf. "Wait, you—knew? What I was doing?"

Nadia looks at her. "Was I supposed to pretend not to? You weren't exactly subtle about it."

Mim picks up a loose piece of hair and starts twisting it around her finger in agitation. "I wasn't—I mean—I just don't want you to think that I don't think you were fine, or that I was managing you—I mean, that I don't think you could have... handled it."

Nadia snorts and stabs vengefully at a potato. "Yeah, right. Because I was 'handling it' so well before you started with the field trips."

"Nadia," Mim says, a little bit helpless because—because she's been trusting her instincts, but that's all she's been trusting. She's so unpracticed at this that it's embarrassing, and she's sure that Nadia can tell; that right now, Nadia is evaluating her and finding her wanting. This week of distractions, of throwing every damn thing she could think of at the wall and seeing what stuck, was the best Mim could do, but she's known the whole time that it wouldn't be enough—and, what's worse, she knows that this little spiral of self-pity is as selfish as it is unhelpful. Nadia needs better than this. Nadia needs *her* to be better. Nadia needs someone who can help her sort through this, help her carry this weight that's still so obviously yoked across her shoulders, not some timid mouse who barely knows who she is when she's not trying to fit herself into someone else's desires.

But then Nadia sighs, and puts down her potato-laden fork, and says, "Oh, hell, I'm sorry."

Mim stares at her. "What?"

"You've been," Nadia waves an expansive hand, "I mean, you're letting me stay here—I know, I know, it's Ruth's house, but I wouldn't have been able to come here if you weren't here, you have to know that. You're not—I was really," she pauses, swallows, "I was really terrible to you, and you're not even mad at me, and you've spent all week helping me... helping me keep going. You don't need my stupid, self-pitying bullshit."

Mim takes a moment to process this, and then—she can't help it—a tiny but unmistakable giggle slips out of her mouth. "Sorry," she says quickly, "sorry, it's just—I was just thinking the exact same thing. That you didn't need my bullshit, I mean. I was going to apologize to you."

"Oh," Nadia says. Then, wonderfully, she starts to laugh too—a rich, full-throated sound that warms the whole kitchen, that Mim hasn't heard from her in far too long. "God. We're a fucking pair, aren't we? Do you think one day we'll just like—get stuck in a loop."

"I'm sorry, Nadia," Mim says, and she doesn't know why, exactly, but they're both gasping with laughter now, clutching their stomachs.

"I'm sorry, Mim," Nadia says, all but howling.

"I'm sorry, Nadia!"

"I'm sorry, Mim!"

"You kids are really fucking weird," Ruth yells from the living room, where she retreated with her own plate of leftover meatloaf some minutes before.

"We're sorry!" they yell together, grinning at each other, still laughing, and Mim finds herself thinking—for the first time in a long, long time—that maybe, just maybe, everything's going to turn out all right.

Of course, the next morning she answers the door to find Rashida and Samir Bahjat standing on the stoop.

"Um," says Mim, who thought she was going to be greeting the UPS guy, and is as such wearing booty shorts and a too-big t-shirt that says, *The Man, The Legend*, that she thinks used to be Hawthorne's. "You're—here."

"Yes," says Samir, "we are."

He looks—they both look—pretty terrible, which Mim guesses isn't all that surprising. She thinks she would probably look pretty terrible if someone did to her what Nadia did to them, though she can't really find it in her heart to have much sympathy. For one thing, there's no question that Nadia is torturing herself over what she's done; for another, Nadia's wrongdoings really don't hold a candle to her parents', however all three of them might or might not feel about it.

"We," Rashida says quietly, and then looks to Samir and clears her throat. More firmly, she says, "We were wondering if we could speak to Nadia."

"Oh," says Mim. She just stares at them for a second, wondering if maybe they are some kind of unfortunate mirage, before she says, "I will just—be... right back, then."

She has a moment of indecision about whether or not she should close the door—on the one hand, it would be rude to shut it in their faces, but on the other hand, she doesn't exactly want them standing in Ruth's foyer if Nadia says she doesn't want to see them. She settles, awkwardly, on sort of half-closing it and then scampering away; she thinks she hears Samir mutter, "Strange girl," behind her, but doesn't stop to glare at the door, because she has more pressing matters to deal with.

"Nadia!" she says, bursting into the bathroom, where she last saw Nadia spraying some sort of curl-specific product into her hair. She's moved on to brushing her teeth, but when she raises her eyebrows at Mim it occurs to Mim that: "Oh, shit, you could have been peeing."

Nadia laughs, flecks of toothpaste foam escaping her mouth, and spits into the sink. She wipes her mouth with the back of her hand. "Lucky for us I wasn't. What's up?"

"I," Mim says, "you're. They're. Your parents. Are... here. Outside." Nadia's face freezes, and Mim, too quickly, adds, "I can tell them to go away!

270

They're not actually, like, inside the house. I hope. So I can just run back down there and tell them to go—"

"No," Nadia says.

"No?" Mim says.

"No," Nadia repeats, her voice firmer, her shoulders squared. "I'll— I'll talk to them. Just—don't, leave, if that's okay?"

"Where would I go?" Mim asks, honestly wondering, and Nadia shoots her a sliver of a smile.

"I don't know," she admits. "Just—don't go there."

"I won't," Mim promises, and resists the urge—though just barely— to kiss Nadia on the cheek as she slips past Mim and out the bathroom door.

Nadia's gone for nearly an hour. Mim fills the time by puttering anxiously around the house, peering out all the various front-facing windows in the hopes of catching a glimpse of what's happening across the street. She is unsuccessful, but does accidentally bear witness to a passionate embrace between Diane Warwick and a similarly power-suited female colleague, neither of whom seems to realize that they have not drawn the drapes in the sunroom. Mim and Ruth, whose sixth sense for things like this brought her to Mim's shoulder mere seconds after Mim noticed them, stand transfixed by this sight for several minutes, until it becomes clear that their choices are to look away or see some regions of Mrs. Warwick that no good neighbor should lay eyes upon.

"Do you think," Mim says, horrified at the very idea of it but unable to keep from voicing the thought, "that someone should... tell them?"

Ruth throws her head back and cackles. "Oh, *definitely*. I nominate you! Go on, walk across the street and tell good ol' Diane she's giving the street a show. I'll be just behind you with a camera."

"Ugh." Mim pulls a face, glances back out the window, and deeply, deeply regrets it. "God, you know what? They're... they consenting shoulder pads. Adults! Consenting adults!"

"Think you were closer with the shoulder pads," Ruth says, still laughing. She shakes her head. "Good for Diane. It's about time; she never was very good at playing it straight, and god knows you'd have to be more than just straight to want to see the Congressman naked, even back in the day. That kid of theirs is a goddamn medical miracle, I'll tell you that much." Mim winces in agreement even as Ruth looks around, brow furrowed. "Speaking of lesbians, where's yours?"

"Oh my god," Mim says, "you can't just! You have to stop doing that! She'll hear you one day, and—"

"What, glare at me?" Ruth grins at her, wickedness and amusement crinkling at the corners of her eyes. "Get too self-conscious to moon at you? Because that'd be a win for me, honestly, between the two of you it's like living inside a Hallmark card."

"I hate you," Mim says faintly. "I can't believe I ever thought you were my favorite aunt. You're the worst person in the world."

Ruth slaps her companionably on the back. "Ah, now you're a real Juniperite! Good for you, kid, only took you a year." She cranes her neck again, peering up the stairs and back into the kitchen. "Seriously though, where is she? I wanna know if that soup she made the other day is still good."

Mim sighs and jerks her head towards the window, though she carefully does not look outside again. "Her parents came over. She went to go talk to them."

Ruth whistles, long and low, from between her teeth. "You sure that was a good idea?"

"I don't think what I think matters," Mim says, and Ruth makes a sound Mim thinks signifies agreement.

She wanders off—probably, Mim thinks, to pack herself a morning bowl—and Mim decides she might as well do something productive while she waits for Nadia to return.

There aren't any dishes in the sink, because now that Nadia's cooking most nights, it's easier to just get them done after the meal. There aren't any counters to clean or messes to sweep up, either, because it makes sense to Mim to do those things along with the dishes, while she's already in the right mindset. After a moment's thought, she digs a pair of yellow rubber gloves out from under the sink, stomps out into the backyard, and starts pulling up what has to be seventeen years' worth of weeds from a little patch of earth by the back door. Mim would never even consider doing this out front—she knows too well, from all the times Gale talked her into trying to soften Ruth on prettying the place up, that her aunt takes a weird, horrible sort of pride in how awful her house looks—but she thinks it would be nice if there were at least a few square feet of this property that weren't appalling. She could plant flowers, or vegetables, or something; just a little piece of herself to leave behind, when she goes.

That's a startling thought—the definiteness of it, the "when" and that seems to have snuck up and replaced the "if" in her plans to get out of this town while she wasn't paying attention. Mim doesn't have time to dwell on it, though, because she hears the distant sound of the front door slamming shut, the much more immediate clatter and bang of kitchen cabinets and drawers. She tucks the rubber gloves underneath the pile of weeds—already more than a foot high after ten measly minutes of work—and goes back inside.

Nadia is standing in front of the refrigerator, a backpack held open in one hand and a package of salami in the other. As Mim watches, she throws the meat violently into the bag and grabs something else—plums, maybe, though they vanish into the bag too quickly to be sure—before she opens the freezer and starts digging around.

"Uh," says Mim, "so… how did it go…?"

"I don't want to talk about it," Nadia snaps. "I want to—let's just—" She grabs three bags of frozen vegetables and shoves them into the bag, storms over to the counter and snatches up a loaf of bread. "Let's just go, okay? Just, somewhere that isn't—that's not—here." She zips up the backpack and throws it over one-shoulder, wild-eyed. "Well? Are you coming or not?"

"I'm coming," Mim says quickly, "just let me run upstairs and grab some real clothes? And… hiking boots, I'm guessing?"

"Fine," Nadia snaps, "yeah. Great. I'll be in the car."

She is indeed in the car when Mim gets outside a few minutes later—in Mim's car, in fact, and in the driver's seat. Mim is not actually hugely enthused about the idea of riding shotgun when Nadia's in this kind of mood, but she's not about to make a thing of it; she just sends a quick, *Please don't let this be how we die*, out into the universe and climbs into the passenger seat, double-checking that her seatbelt is buckled.

There was no need to worry, as it turns out. Nadia's driving is faster than usual but is also, oddly, even more controlled; she turns corners sharply but precisely, stops exactly the same distance away from every light and right on the line of every stop sign. She's doesn't speak to Mim as she drives, but there's a different quality to the silence than there was to her frightening emptiness of the week before; after a few minutes Mim remembers Cory saying, "Nadia needs something to *do*," and figures that maybe this atypical white-knuckled precision is where she's putting whatever emotion it is she's trying to work through. She decides to wait her out. She's not sure there's much else she can do.

"Do you mind if I put on some music?" she asks after they've been driving about fifteen minutes, and takes Nadia's tight little wave of her hand as permission. She picks out a playlist full of songs she thinks Nadia will like—a playlist she will *not* be admitting to creating with Nadia in mind any time soon—and is rewarded for her choice by the way she can see Nadia's shoulders begin to relax out of the corner of her eye.

"I love this song," Nadia admits after a while, and even though it's the first thing she's said the whole trip—even though she doesn't follow it up with anything else—Mim knows it for the *thank you* it is, and smiles.

They drive without talking for the better part of an hour, until most of the trappings of civilization have fallen away around them and the four-lane highway narrows into a two-lane road. Mim doesn't ask where they're going, just that they stop at a gas station for cigarettes and drinks; she smokes out the window open window and breathes in the crisp spring air, the scent of the forest that lines the road just now beginning to wake from its winter sleep. She's not surprised when she sees signs informing them of a wildlife preservation a few miles ahead, even less so when Nadia follows them, eventually parking the car in a small, dirt-covered lot. Mim stuffs the bottles of water and iced tea they bought, along with the extra packs of cigarettes, into the backpack, and can't quite duck her head in time to hide her dumb, besotted smile when Nadia plucks it out of her hands before she can put it on.

"Rule is, the crazy person who drives you out into the woods has to carry the pack," Nadia says, returning Mim's smile even though it looks like it costs her some effort.

"Oh, right," Mim says easily, "because otherwise everyone would do it."

Nadia huffs out something that just might be a laugh, and Mim grins at her with satisfaction. "Come on. It's a little bit of a walk, but a pretty one. You'll like it, I think."

It *is* a pretty walk. Mim trails a few steps behind Nadia, who obviously knows where she's going, and forgets to worry for a few moments as she takes it all in. She's been hiking before, obviously, but never in this part of Ohio, and never this early in the year—if she'd been asked, she would have thought it would be kind of depressing, wandering around a forest not fully in bloom. She sees, now, how wrong she would have been; she could never have imagined the strange beauty of this world right on the cusp of becoming. The bare trees, their long limbs reaching out to one another, aren't the drab gray she expected, but red and gold and white, green just starting to peek its cautious head out from knots along their branches. The ground, though thick with mud in some places, is a sea of little miracles—fallen tree trunks that have cracked open and filled up with tiny, wriggling lives, footprints lined up along those of hoof and paw buried in the soft earth.

When they've climbed a little way up the soft sloping trail Nadia picked out, Mim notices a sapling, barely as tall as her knee, with shriveled white leaves dangling from its tiny limbs. She crouches down to stare at it, confused for a moment until she realizes—this tree, a baby next to its brothers, is so small that it must have been swallowed entirely by the first heavy snow. These leaves must have frozen in place before they got the chance to fall, their color leeching out of them over a long winter spent in darkness, trapped beneath the snow and the shadows of the taller trees, the gray Ohio skies. And yet there are little spots of green pushing their tentative way out of its barely-there branches: despite everything, it's lived to see a second spring.

"Come on," Nadia calls to her, and Mim jerks back to herself. She breaks into a light jog to catch up, and is a little thrilled by the thought that the two of them could have been moving so quietly through this forest that the animals weren't frightened away. She's always wanted to be able to do that, though for one reason or another—her loveable but loud brothers, her awful ex-boyfriend who could never pass up an opportunity to talk about himself, her own fear of getting lost were she to wander the woods alone—she's never had the chance to experience it before.

"Sorry," she says as she reaches Nadia, their shoulders knocking lightly together. "Distracted."

"It's all right," Nadia tells her, and maybe Mim's imagining it— maybe it's just wishful thinking—but she thinks she sees Nadia's hand flex briefly towards her own, as though she stopped herself reaching for it at the very last moment.

They walk on: through a grove of pines that creak ominously over the carpet of their dropped needles; down a path that's more tree root than trail; across a small, trickling creek whose ice-cold water splashes against their skin as they walk and startles them into laughter. Nadia shows her how to tell which ones are sassafras trees and explains that, in another few months, they'll be able to chew on the ends of the leaves and taste root beer. Mim's not sure she believes that, but offers up some stories from summer camp in return, half-remembered ghost stories and jokes whose punch lines have been lost to the ages. By the time Nadia puts a hand out to stop Mim from taking another step, they're both soft-limbed with relaxation, all of Nadia's coiled tension released back into the wild.

"Here," Nadia says, "right here, this is it," and she does take Mim's hand, this time, to pull her the last few steps up the hill.

What they reach, when the get to the top, is not exactly a cliff—it's more like the lip of a massive bowl of earth, this deeply rounded depression that occupies at least an acre of land. It's covered, from the bottom all the way up the sides, with a thick layer of wispy yellowed grass—probably preserved, like the sapling leaves, by the snow—and by any traditional definition, it's not particularly beautiful. It's more interesting-looking than it is anything else and yet Mim can see immediately why Nadia would value it, why Nadia would bring her here; beautiful or not, there's an unquantifiable calm to this place that Mim's never quite experienced before, as though peace has collected in the center like rainwater and is lapping at their feet.

They settle into a little grove of trees right on the valley's edge, backs slotting into place against the rough bark, and after they've each eaten a plum and a salami sandwich, Nadia takes a deep breath and tosses Mim a pack of cigarettes.

Mim waits a few minutes — for her to speak, as she's so clearly gearing up to do, or at least to offer her a light. When neither thing happens she clears her throat, says, "Um, is this like, an 'only you can prevent forest fires' thing? Because, I mean, I'm cool not to smoke, but giving me the cigarettes and not the lighter seems cruel."

"Oh, right," Nadia says. She shakes herself, digs around in the bag again, and tosses Mim the lighter; then, with a slightly guilty look, she adds, "Although we do kind of need to be sure not to start any forest fires."

Mim rolls her eyes and sets her half finished can of grape soda between them as an ashtray, nodding wordlessly in thanks when she's passed her a replacement. Nadia's taking deep breaths again, and this time Mim just settles back against the tree, lights her cigarette, and closes her eyes to wait. She hears the ratchet of the lighter as Nadia lights a cigarette of her own, and then nothing but distant birdsong for what feels like a long time.

Eventually, Nadia says, "I used to... I used to come out here a lot, as a kid."

Mim cracks an eye open in interest. "Oh yeah?"

"Yeah." Nadia exhales again, a little shakily this time. "With... with my parents. They kind of..." She laughs, but it's a sad, humorless little sound. "They always thought it was kind of weird, I think? That I liked

278

this place so much, when we'd visited so many cool parts of the world. They didn't really get me—it. They didn't get it, but they came anyway, you know? Because we moved away from the rest of the family, I think, even though I wanted to stay, and they felt guilty. And I loved it here, so they brought me because they... they loved me."

She says that last part so softly, so uncertainly, that Mim wants to shake her, or hug her, or burst into tears, or maybe all three; she doesn't. She just sits in silence and listens, instead.

"You know what the awful part is," Nadia says, "is that I—I don't understand, how they could do that. What they did, I don't see how they could do that to me and still believe they love me. But... I don't really understand how I could do what I did either. I remember, when I was a little kid—I just—I *loved* them so much, I thought they were perfect, even when..." She trails off. "Well, they weren't, obviously. They were pretty fucked up. It was all fucked up. But—" She stops.

She's not looking at Mim, when Mim dares to sneak a glance at her; she's staring out into the distance instead, face screwed up in frustration. "This isn't," Nadia says, "I'm not saying it right, I—I want to understand how you do it."

"How I do what?" Mim asks, baffled.

Nadia gives her a horrible, heartbreaking look, and says, "Forgive people."

"I... I don't know that I'm the right person to ask," Mim says, as gently as she can, after a minute of thought. "It's—I mostly just don't let myself get angry in the first place, to be honest. And it's not like *that's* particularly healthy, but it kind of spares me from having to do the whole, uh. Forgiveness part."

Nadia's looking away again, but it's so obvious that this wasn't the answer she was looking for that Mim squirms in her seat and digs deep inside herself for something better, something more. When she speaks again, even she's not sure what's going to come out of her mouth. "I was... with someone," she starts carefully. "I was—I let someone... Someone hurt me, and I should have left, and I didn't. For a long time, I didn't go." She stops, swallows against her suddenly bone-dry throat, and starts again. "I—I know that it's not my fault. But it still feels like that, sometimes. It still... I don't know."

Mim looks down at her hands because she can't bear to see Nadia's face. She doesn't know what would be worse: to see doubt or pity in Nadia's eyes, or anger over something long since over, or, god forbid, kindness. Anything she can imagine would be horrible, and so she looks at her fingernails, picks flaking polish off one thumb with the other, and forces herself to say the last part, the part that's actually important.

"Anyway, the point is, I don't think I'll ever forgive him," she admits, so quietly that she can tell herself the wind is carrying the words away from her, taking them somewhere far and safe where she'll never have to see them again. "But I don't think that's really the point."

"Yeah?" Nadia asks; her voice cracks on it, but Mim doesn't look up to find out with what emotion. She doesn't want to know.

"Yeah," Mim says. She puts her palms against her eyes and scrubs furiously the building tears there, glad she left the house without makeup. "And mostly it's just—distance, I think. And time, as fucking cliché and unhelpful as that sounds. And I think... I think wanting to helps."

Nadia doesn't have an answer to that, and Mim, selfishly, is relieved; they each light another cigarette, avoiding one another's eyes.

It's Nadia who breaks this silence. "They want me to move back in with them. They want to—go see a family therapist, figure out how we all... how to get back to the way things used to be."

Mim takes a long drag from her cigarette, pushes the smoke out into the wind. "What do *you* want?"

280

Nadia snorts. "Does it matter?"

"Yeah," Mim says, fierce, and forces her eyes up to meet Nadia's. "I think it does."

Nadia's eyes are wide and wet, just this side of shocked, for the second they hold Mim's gaze; then she turns them away again, looks down at the ground. "Not that. I don't want—things the way they were. I don't want to spend my whole life trying to earn it, you know? Even though—even if that's what a good daughter would do." She laughs, an edge of hysteria to it, and adds, "And I definitely don't want to fucking move back in with them. Or even..."

The pause stretches out for a beat too long, and when Nadia speaks again, her tone has changed; it's less anguished, almost... embarrassed, somehow. "I don't," she says carefully, "I don't think I really even want to stay in town, except I'm not really sure where I *do* want to go, and..." She coughs, crosses and uncrosses her legs. "And, well. There's... there's some stuff I don't want to... leave behind."

"Oh," Mim whispers. She can hear her own heartbeat, suddenly loud in her ears—can feel it thumping hard against the thin skin of her wrists. She wants Nadia to mean *her* so badly that it hurts a little. The desperation of it lurches and stumbles around inside of her chest, and she has no idea how she keeps her voice even as she says, "You know, I've—I've kind of been thinking the, the same thing. Ruth's already, I mean, she gave me that car, and I think I might like to—take it somewhere. Go, um, go see my family, maybe, or the Grand Canyon, or... something. Except," and Mim can feel herself go red to the roots of her hair, can feel even the tips of her ears burning, "there's kind of something *I* don't want to leave behind, either."

"*Oh*," Nadia breathes, and when Mim looks up Nadia is smiling and smiling at her, a breath-catching, consuming kind of happiness spreading across her face. It's so surprising—Mim's gotten so used to seeing Nadia at least some shade of miserable—that Mim feels herself open up in reply, knows whatever her own expression must be revealing is more than she should probably show. But Nadia just beams at her, bites the edge of her lip as though she's trying to stop smiling and can't, and the euphoria of it whites out, if only briefly, the vicious reel of worry and panic that's always playing in the back of Mim's mind.

"We could go together," Mim says—babbles, because it falls out of her mouth like rainwater, like the faint sound of the creek in the distance. "Sorry, I mean, or not—you don't like, have to, but just—if you wanted. It could be like, you know. Like a road trip! If you—if you like road trips."

"Sure," Nadia says, still biting her lip against a smile that hasn't faltered at all, "sure, I like road trips. Let's do it. Let's go."

"Right now?" Mim says, who has obviously been made stupid by delight, and hastily tries to cover it up as a joke. "I mean, because I feel like—like probably we should, you know. Plan a route. Have more to our names than salami."

"Well," Nadia says, and there's a sly new quality slipping into her voice, one that makes Mim shiver with anticipation in the cooling afternoon air. "It *is* very good salami."

"True," Mim agrees. She jumps up, nervous suddenly at the degree of warmth in Nadia's eyes—excited and thrilled, but nervous all the same "Do you want to, um—go back, maybe?" She catches the dismay in Nadia's eyes and adds, before she can think better of it, "Just because I think, I mean, this is—the woods, and it's starting to—by the time we get back—it would suck to finally have this conversation and then be eaten by a bear, or walk off a cliff in the dark or something."

Nadia's grin flares back to life as she takes Mim's hand, as Mim tugs her to her feet. They clean up their little area quickly, throwing everything but the can with the cigarette butts back into the bag; Mim takes the can, Nadia takes the pack, and when they've made it a few steps down the path their hands find one another's again, somehow. Mim doesn't know who reached for whom first, just that when she looks down their fingers are twined together—just that they don't let go the whole way back to the car.

It's dark by the time they get back to Ruth's. Nadia—a brighter, more exuberant version of herself than Mim has seen since December—grins at her and hops out of the passenger seat. Mim follows, taking the key out of the ignition, and for a moment they stand in the dark driveway, lit only by lights from the neighboring houses, as if on the precipice of something huge and unspeakable, before Nadia lets out a whoop of laughter and sets off at a run towards the backyard.

Mim chases her, her own laughter bubbling up and out of her, because—because Nadia is running, and so Mim is chasing. Because what they've said to each other, without really saying it at all, has shifted the landscape between them so that Mim feels safe to follow her, wherever she might run. Because sitting next to Nadia in the car under the slowly darkening sky, streetlamps casting her face in warm orange light, was an exquisite torture, a magnificent agony, and Mim has waited long enough. They have both waited long enough.

She catches up with Nadia in the middle of the yard, and—whether by accident or design—they crash together a little too hard, overbalance and tip into the soft grass. Nadia lands on her back with a gentle, "Oof," and takes most of the weight of Mim's fall, too, but doesn't look pained by it, just so crazily, stupidly happy that Mim's breath catches in her chest. Nadia smiles up at her for a long moment before she rolls them both over, so it's Mim spread out across the grass and Nadia looking down, her curls brushing gently against Mim's cheeks. Slowly—hardly daring to believe that she can—Mim reaches up and slides a hand into that thick, soft hair, pushing it out of Nadia's eye's.

"I might," Mim says quickly, the fear of it lancing through her all at once, "I might not be very good at this."

Nadia's whole face lights up—with laughter, with joy, with something that Mim, even now, isn't quite ready to let herself believe is love. "You know, Mimosa," Nadia says, the name beautiful in her mouth as it's never been in anyone else's, "I think we'll manage," and then she kisses her like she means it; like solid proof; like, finally, coming home.

Acknowledgements

I think that I could fill another book with the people I owe thanks to for the production of this one. To say I put my blood, sweat and tears into the production of this novel would be an understatement, but I am far, far from the only one — in fact, there are so many people who put backbreaking effort into getting this produced, into helping me get this produced, that I could not possibly list them all. I'm going to try anyway, but please know, if you're reading these pages and you ever offered me a kind word or a moment of encouragement; if you read my other writing or listened to me ramble; hell, even if you're just one of the hundreds of thousands of people who have pushed through anxiety, depression, and other mental health blockades, whose very existence reminded me in moments when I struggled that I was not alone: thank you so much. I appreciate you more than I can say, and I could not have done this without you.

On to some specific people without whom this book would be so much smoke:

My incredible mother and father, who in addition to being unfathomably brilliant and supportive are far better parents than any featured in this book, and my two fantastic brothers, who are my best friends, confidants, and partners in crime: I like to imagine you all know how deeply I love you, but I thought it couldn't hurt to put it in print. I am so grateful, every day, to know you all, let alone to be your daughter, sister, and friend. You believe in me when I don't believe in myself; you teach me and understand me and make me laugh; you are my favorite people on earth, and I don't know what I'd do without you.

The rest of my family — my grandparents, aunts and uncles and cousins, the whole rollicking lot of you who I am so lucky to know — you are by turns hilarious, insightful, thoughtful, strange, brilliant, beautiful, and possessed of more personality then, perhaps, the rest of the world combined. I know I don't say it enough (I'm better with honest emotion in written word than in print, though only, let's be honest, very slightly), but I love you all an absurd amount. Thank you so much for your years of kindness; I will never be able to express my appreciation properly.

My friends, on the internet and off, who talked me off the emotional ledge, let me call them sobbing at three in the morning, sat with me on Skype while I covered my face with my hands, listened to me list each and every one of my increasingly illogical anxieties, and dragged me kicking and screaming to the end of this: I'm not going to name names because of my deep terror of missing one by mistake, but y'all know who you are, and you know that I love you.

The entire team at Big Bang Press, who I put through hell (I'm so sorry) and who relentlessly stood by me, guided me, and helped me, even when I desperately resisted it: I hope you all know how grateful I am, but if you don't, god, I'm so grateful. I doubt there's anything I could do or say that would negate what a frustrating, anxious mess of an author I've been to work with, but please know that I appreciate you and everything you've done for me more than I could possibly say.

Alexandra, whose illustrations bring life I could never even have imagined to these characters: WORDS CANNOT EXPRESS MY SHEER DELIGHT, nor can capslock, but rest assured that I will be showing people these illustrations for the rest of my natural life. I am so grateful for your skill, talent, vision, and creativity, and so glad to have gotten the opportunity to work with you.

EVERY LAST PERSON who promoted our Kickstarter, who donated even one dollar, or, hell, even thought about donating one dollar: words cannot express how stunned and staggered I am by your kindness and generosity. I expect I will be stunned and staggered by it all my life. *Thank you* for believing in me, us, this project enough to get behind it. Thank you, thank you, thank you. I could stand on a hill shouting it forever and it still wouldn't be enough

The baristas at every Starbucks in the greater Cleveland area: I told you guys I'd put you in the acknowledgements of my first novel for the sheer amount of time you've spent with me over the past few years, and that was no joke. Thanks for the good company and free coffee.

And finally, to Jerry Garcia (the dog): buddy, I know you can't read, or really understand the concept of gratitude in any quantifiable way, and that any acknowledgement I give you here will pretty much mean nothing to you. But! You're important to me and I feel you should be recognized, so. I hope that when, inevitably, a copy of this book falls off a shelf and you eat part of it before I realize what you're doing and wrestle it away from you, it tastes like sunshine and rainbows and raw steak, and maybe like whatever flavor the couch in the living room has that makes you lick it so much. You deserve it. You're a very good dog.

About the author

Kady Morrison lives in Cleveland, Ohio, where she strives daily to find new and creative ways to interpret the word "adulthood." When not frenetically writing fiction, she can most often be found telling jokes to diffuse tension, drinking more iced tea than is strictly advisable, and attempting to interpret the innermost thoughts and feelings of her friends, family, and coworkers. They tend not to find this as enjoyable as she does, although she can't imagine why.

@kadymorrison